Say My

(Book 3 of The Claimed Series)

By:

R. K. Knightly

Say My Name Copyright © 2019 by R.K. Knightly

All rights reserved. No part of this publication may be reproduced, distributed, or transmitted in any form or by any means, including photocopying, recording, or other electronic or mechanical methods, without the prior written permission of the publisher, except in the case of brief quotations embodied in critical reviews and certain other noncommercial uses permitted by copyright law. For permission requests, write to the publisher, addressed to email: rkknightlybooks@gmail.com

This is a work of fiction. Names, characters, businesses, places, events, locales, and incidents are either the products of the author's imagination or used in a fictitious manner. Any resemblance to actual persons, living or dead, or actual events is purely coincidental.

Table of Contents

CHAPTER 1 7

CHAPTER 2 13

CHAPTER 3 26

CHAPTER 4 32

CHAPTER 5 45

CHAPTER 6 52

CHAPTER 7 63

CHAPTER 8 75

CHAPTER 9 83

CHAPTER 10 95

CHAPTER 11 102

CHAPTER 12 114

CHAPTER 13 126

CHAPTER 14 139

CHAPTER 15 152

CHAPTER 16 158

CHAPTER 17 170

CHAPTER 18 177

CHAPTER 19 189

CHAPTER 20 195

CHAPTER 21 207

CHAPTER 22 214

CHAPTER 23 225

CHAPTER 24 230

CHAPTER 25 236

CHAPTER 26 248

CHAPTER 27 255

CHAPTER 28 267

CHAPTER 29 280

CHAPTER 30 286

EPILOGUE	292
BONUS CHAPTER 1	298
BONUS CHAPTER 2	305
CONTACT INFO	311
ACKNOWLEDGEMENTS	312
ABOUT THE AUTHOR	313

Dedication

To Rob, my hubby of so many years that we talk alike, think alike, and finish each other's sentences.

Chapter 1

"Hold up! I smell something!"

Blake Patterson closed his eyes, using all his senses but sight to try and track down the mysterious source of the odor.

Blood. Thick, coppery, and strong, it rankled at him, and he had to force the beast inside him to back down. Whatever the source of the scent was, it surely had to be dead by now. The overpowering fragrance emanating from it was that intense.

But there was also another, fainter smell beneath it. A more feminine spice. It didn't smell rogue, but it was definitely a foreign wolf. Maybe someone who had gotten lost from a neighboring pack.

Whoever it was, they were on death's door, if not already gone.

Not bothering to shift since the smell of blood was so potent, Blake moved southwest towards the road. Not a lot of visitors ventured on this particular highway and this far north in New York State unless they were heading to Canada, so the possibilities of them running into anyone they didn't already know were pretty slim.

Blake had to travel much farther than he thought he would, and was almost right on the road when he saw a small movement in the leaves at the edge of the small ravine that was abutted up against the pavement. If he had blinked, he might have missed it completely.

"Trace! Caleb!" Blake called out to the Delta and Gamma who were hovering back several hundred yards. They were his back up. If there was an injured she-wolf, who knew what had caused her affliction? They were being safe and protecting their Beta, their second in command.

"Blake?" It was Caleb. He came out from behind a tree and looked at him. "What did you find?"

"Look." Blake was pointing to the small body of a foreign female. Beaten, battered, her face more purple than healthy pink skin.

Sniffing, Caleb's nose crinkled at the overwhelming metallic smell of her blood.

"Her heartbeat is faint," Trace stated as he came up from behind them. The two other men jumped at his voice, startled. Trace had a basso-profundo tone that went well with his thick body, but it still rattled them to hear him speak when it was relatively quiet like now. It was almost as if the forest was silent in reverence of the dead. Or dying.

"What do we do?" Blake asked, almost to himself.

"She's as good as dead," Trace stated. "Just leave her here."

That didn't sit well with Blake, and he frowned. He was a protector at heart. "I wonder if she was the one that set off the alarm at the border."

"I doubt she got here by herself in this state," Caleb said, looking at the deep gashes on her skin from afar. "Someone must have dropped her off here after beating her bloody."

"I wonder what she did," Blake surmised. "She's so small and incredibly slender." The female looked too young and too frail to have been the cause of much trouble. Who would do this to such a petite woman?

The small woman's bare ribs stuck out through the tattered remnants of her shirt, the tears most certainly made by the claw marks of another wolf. Maybe even a rogue.

The three men were all looking at the girl when her eyes slowly slid open and she gazed up at them. They were a startling clear blue, giving her an innocence that made Blake realize that he couldn't just leave her there. Even if she was near death, something in him made him believe she deserved a chance at life. The chance they could give her.

"We can't just leave her here," Blake stated, his voice low but certain. "I don't believe such a frail creature could have done anything to deserve such a death as this."

"Then you can be the one to deal with Liam," Trace warned him, effectively washing his hands of the stray wolf. He knew Liam hated to deal with foreign wolves, especially females. He thought them sly, silly creatures for the most part.

"I'll handle Liam," Blake told him as he made his way down the small gulley next to the highway. "He's not been as bad as all that lately."

"Says you," Caleb tossed out. He had been punished only a week before for fraternizing with a rogue that had fled a neighboring pack. The rogue had claimed he was seeking refuge from a cruel Alpha to the south of them. The man had once again been tossed away by their own Alpha like a rotting banana peel, just to the east of their land. Let him seek refuge there, proclaimed Liam.

"The Alpha has no female," Blake reminded the Gamma wolf. "He is bound to get...irritable."

"Then he should seek sexual release with one of the many willing females," Caleb spat back at him. "It's not like there aren't any eager, unmated women to be had at Plumbrook."

"It's not his way," Blake reminded him. "If he is to take a female, it is for life. You know Liam, so don't act a fool."

The small female groaned as Blake tried to lift her from the ground. The large man winced, knowing his actions were probably hurting the fragile-looking creature. When Caleb and Trace protested again, Blake cut them both with a look.

"Get the car, you bunch of ingrates," he told them, ignoring their looks of consternation.

Female stray found in the woods, Alpha, he mindlinked to Liam once Caleb and Trace had gone.

Leave it be, Liam instructed, a growl in his tone.

She's near death and...she's so fucking tiny, Blake told him, his voice conciliatory.

Blake could almost hear the man sigh in his head. Blake and Liam had been best friends since they were pups, and if anyone could get through to the irritable Alpha, it was Blake.

Fine, Liam told him, his voice resigned. *Bring her to the infirmary. We will have Evelyn tend to her and then send her along her way.*

Blake, having been satisfied that the young female was going to be taken care of, waited for Caleb to bring the car around so they could get the unknown girl the help she so desperately needed.

***

Evelyn D'Amato frowned at the unconscious female in the white hospital bed. The Alpha was standing next to her and listening to everything the doctor was saying.

"These," the doctor told Liam, gesturing to the deep gashes on the female's stomach. "Are all claw marks."

"That, I could have guessed," Liam told her, arching a brow. "She was obviously attacked by another wolf. This is not news. Why did you bring me here to show me what I already could have guessed?"

Evelyn looked at her Alpha and blinked.

"The marks on her back are not claw marks," the doctor told him. "They are whip marks."

That, however, surprised Liam.

"Whip marks?"

"Yes, Alpha," Evelyn told him, nodding. "She has been severely whipped and beaten. More than once. She also has fading scars under the open gashes on her back. I am surprised that she lives at all. She's lost a goodish amount of blood."

Liam's jaw ticked, his eyes growing dark.

"She does not smell rogue," Liam stated. In fact, after she had been cleaned of all the blood and dirt, she had a pleasant, flowery smell. Like a mixture of jasmine and freesia.

"I don't think she is rogue," Evelyn told him. "We would smell it."

The woman hesitated and looked away from the Alpha. His brows knitted, wondering what she was keeping from him.

"What is it?" Beaten and battered, what else could possibly be wrong with the slight female before him?

"I...well – when I had the nurses bathe her, they told me something disturbing," Evelyn told him in a measured tone. "After doing a more thorough check, I found that she was not only beaten but...abused."

Liam's jaw clenched again, a sure sign his wolf was becoming agitated within him. Liam was quite displeased as well, much to his own chagrin. She was foreign and he shouldn't care.

"You mean...raped?" he asked, looking down at the fluttering of the unconscious female's eyelids. He hoped she was having a good dream, whatever it was.

"Several times over," Evelyn told him, nodding her head. "And quite recently. She had tearing of the anus and vaginal walls, and she is very swollen. I don't think she was raped by a man, but by some other, foreign object. I could tell by the healing lacerations."

Liam felt disgusted. The poor woman before him was as frail as Blake had described, and though he was no fan of strays, he felt bad for the one before him. Horrible, in fact. He wanted to break something, tear into someone's flesh to be rid of the cold, coiling nausea he had rolling through his gut.

Instead of spilling the contents of his stomach into the nearest toilet, he simply nodded at the doctor before heading toward the door of the private room in the ICU wing of the pack hospital.

"Thank you, Doctor," he told her as his hands met with the cold surface of the doorknob. "Call me when she wakes. I have questions for her."

Liam waited until he was out of the hospital to shift into the black beast that was tearing at his insides trying to get out. He may not have been a fan of visitors, but it was not as if this one had come to his land of her own volition. The doctor had been certain. She had been dropped there, possibly even tossed from a vehicle. Left to die next to the road that led to the Plumbrook Pack in northern New York State.

Hours later, Liam's beast was finally sated. He had ripped apart several rabbits, a deer and – surprisingly – a mountain lion. That last was a shock. They were rare, even in the area north of the Adirondacks.

Slipping on some clothes he had hidden in a tree near his home, he walked in through the back door of his house to find Blake sitting at his kitchen table, eating a sandwich.

"That better not be the last of the roast beef," Liam warned him as he opened the fridge to grab a bottle of water.

"I'll get you more," Blake told him, his face blank.

"What's up your ass?" Liam asked him, uncapping the bottle.

"The female," Blake told him.

"You have a mate, Blake," Liam reminded him, arching a brow.

"It's not that," Blake said, shaking his head. "I went by the infirmary before to check in on her. She was being sedated."

Liam froze and looked over at his Beta. Water from the open bottle spilled over, and a few drops splashed onto his shoe as his brows furrowed above his eyes.

"Why?"

"Nightmare. Night terror. Whatever you want to call it. She was thrashing around like she was being viciously attacked."

"Did she...did she say anything?"

"She could only scream," Blake told him. "If there were any words in there, they were unintelligible. I made Dr. D'Amato tell me everything."

Liam nodded. He understood now why Blake was acting so odd. Rape was an offense in the Plumbrook Pack that was punishable by death. Torture and *then* death, if the female was already mated and taken against her will. It was one of the gravest offenses one could commit.

"At least she's not pregnant," Blake stated. "Evelyn got the blood tests back before I came over. But then again, she's pretty sure the rape was with a foreign object, not someone's dick. Blunt force trauma."

"Shit," Liam muttered and resumed draining the bottle.

"I'm glad she's not pregnant. No one needs a daily reminder of their repeated rape," Blake agreed, nodding at him.

"When will she be awake?"

"Who knows?" Blake shrugged. "With the amount of sedatives they had to give her, it could be hours, maybe even a day, before she finally opens her eyes."

Liam's eyes widened a trace.

"That bad, huh?"

Blake shuddered a bit. "I can still hear her screams. They were terrifying. Like she was being fucking murdered right there in front of me."

Liam nodded. He had his own demons and nightmares too. But that was *then*. Years ago. Too, too many. And yet the memories, the dreams, they always felt so fresh, like an open sore that refused to heal.

And the guilt. It ate away at him every day. If only he had known what would happen, had been able to see the trouble brewing. Maybe…just, maybe…

"I'm heading to bed," Liam told his friend and Beta. "I'll keep you posted if I hear anything from Dr. D'Amato."

Blake merely nodded and finished up the last few bites of his sandwich as he stared blankly out the window.

Wondering. He wondered where the female had come from, and thought back to Caleb's rogue wolf. Had that wolf come from the same pack this female had? It would only make sense if that were the case. Not all packs were as peaceful as Plumbrook.

After washing his lone dish and a couple of utensils he had used to make his food, he placed them in the dish drainer and left out the front of door the Alpha's home, locking it behind him.

Instead of heading off toward his own home to see his mate, Colleen, he headed off toward the trees in search of solitude.

Chapter 2

"And why would I want to mate with a weak fucking bitch like you?" Jeremiah seethed, his breath scaldingly hot against the skin of her cheek.

"We...we're mates," Giselle whimpered out, tears sliding down her face faster than she could swipe them away.

"Stop crying!" he yelled back at her, the irises of his eyes being taken over by full-on black. He was pissed. He always seemed to be when it came to his weak mate. "You look ugly when you cry!"

His words only made Giselle cry harder. What had she done to have such a cruel man as Alpha and mate?

"I-I'm s-sor-ry," she stuttered out, flinching away from him. He would hit her for stuttering. Or for talking. Or for...whatever else he wanted to hit her for that he deemed necessary to punish her.

"Do I have to ram my cock down your throat to keep you from speaking?" he asked, his voice both lower and deadlier. "Because if that's what it takes, I'll have you gagging all night on it."

It had been six months since she had turned 18 and found her mate. She thought she had been lucky, at first. Many she-wolves waited for months, years even, to find their other half. Her parents had hoped that when she did find her mate, that he would be kind and caring. Now, besides Alpha Jeremiah and his Beta, her parents were the only ones that knew she was mated to the cruel Alpha of Blackriver Pack.

Her belongings had been immediately moved into the Alpha's home when he had found her, but it was not the gesture of a loving and caring mate that made him make the transition so quickly. It was his jealousy, his desire to possess, that fueled him. He would have his mate with him at all times, to please him when he so desired, though no one but a few would ever know of the weak Luna he had been gifted with.

Though Jeremiah Bluth made it abundantly clear he didn't want Giselle Kincaid as his mate, he wouldn't reject her, and intended to keep her by his side. She was more or less a form of sexual release and a female to beat on when his temper got the best of him.

Instead of beating his omegas or taking out his anger in training with his warriors, he went back to his home at the end of the day where he would punish Giselle for crimes she had no idea she had even committed.

Talk back to the Alpha? Ten lashes with the whip. Do poorly in training? Twenty lashes. Speak without first being spoken to? Sing or hum? Thirty.

If there was some sort of formula or algorithm for these trespasses, it was beyond Giselle, and she stopped trying to figure it all out. It was pointless anyway. No matter what, he would beat her bloody every day.

It only irritated him when he came back home and found she was partially healed from the beating the day before. He felt the need to brand her again with his own marks of injustice.

"Please," she whimpered out. She hated to give him any sort of pleasure. At first, she thought relinquishing control to him would have helped with his obvious anger management issues, but he continued to beat her even after he had dominated her body sexually, and to his own pleasure. More so, in fact. It was like he was angry with himself that he took pleasure in his mate's weaker body, and it brought out his inner rage. At her. At himself. At everyone.

"Suck it, bitch," he told her as he unfastened his belt and pulled out his dick. It was semi-hard and still painful for her to even look at. He was a well-endowed man, and he beat her even harder if she couldn't take him all the way down. Which she never was able to do. At least not fully.

Clearing her throat of excess phlegm that had accrued due to her sobs, she took him into her mouth slowly before his hands locked around her head and his cock was shoved into her mouth, stabbing the back of her throat. She gagged.

"Shit, I love when your throat locks up around me, my little bitch," he said, tossing his head back while forcing himself further down her throat.

Almost vomiting, Giselle did what she always tried to do. She relaxed her throat and thought of something else. Anything else. Baking with her mom when she was little. Fishing with her father out on the lake. Hiking with her siblings. Many of them were older and gone from the pack now after having found their mates, but her older brother was still around, working in the pack clinic.

Chase was 26 now, with a mate of his own, and she rarely ever saw him. Though she was abused daily to the point of passing out from the pain, she was never taken to the clinic and was attended to by the Beta's female, Kate. Kate was a nurse and completely caring – unlike Jeremiah – but she couldn't do anything to help her other than bandage her lacerations and bring her medicine when needed. Usually strong pain medications.

A few times, Giselle thought to hoard the pain meds so she could escape the world completely one day. An overdose would be a welcome relief after the constant pain that was inflicted upon her daily. But she also knew that since she was a werewolf, it would take more pain medication than the clinic's pharmacy probably had stocked to effectively do enough damage to kill her. Fucking werewolf genetics didn't allow for them to be as affected by maladies, alcohol, or medications as a human would be. Sometimes Giselle wished she were human. She probably would have been beaten to death by now. Painful, but final. This slow death of her body and soul was too much for her to bear.

After Jeremiah fucked her throat until he came, it felt raw and ached. He was not gentle, and it hurt when she had been forced to swallow down his seed.

Throwing her back on the bed, he then continued to fuck her anally until she bled from her ass, the usual lacerations replacing the old ones.

"Fucking pathetic," he hissed out at her as he finished on her face.

Jeremiah left her there to clean herself up, his come still slowly dribbling down her face as he walked off to take a shower. Probably washing away the evidence that he had been with her.

Why not just come inside her ass? It was not like he could get her pregnant that way and have another reason to keep her around. He was merely biding his time until he totally lost control one day and killed her. Then he could take one of his other whores to mate and become his Luna. Though he didn't want her, he couldn't seem to bring himself to kill her purposely either.

Giselle eventually limped over to the bathroom and used a wet towel to wash his seed from her face and then turned on the bathtub. She couldn't put any bath salts or bubble bath in it. Even if he had kindly provided her with some, it would have stung her privates too much to use. Instead, she would have to hope that the scalding hot water would be enough to help soothe her aching and bruised muscles. Either that, or burn her flesh off her and ultimately kill her.

Giselle had once been a part of a loving family at Blackriver Pack. Two caring parents, a protective older brother, and two more sisters. She was the youngest, the baby of the family. Coddled and spoiled, she had thought that having her mate would be all sunshine and rainbows. Her experiences in life had never prepared her for this grim reality.

She sat in the tub, the water gradually cooling to a normal temperature while her red skin turned a light pink. The water was discolored as well with the blood seeping from between her thighs.

She didn't even realize that someone had come to visit until a soft hand came down upon her shoulder.

Giselle flinched before looking up at the visitor.

Kate. Thank God. Or the Moon Goddess. Or...whomever.

"We need to get you cleaned up," Kate told her softly. "Carter's in the other room with one of the pack doctors. Don't worry. It's not your brother."

Carter was Kate's mate and Jeremiah's Beta. Giselle had begged for none of them to tell Chase what was happening. She was afraid he would try to challenge the Alpha and be killed in the process. He had a mate and two children that needed him, so it must have been Dr. Dandridge that Kate or Carter had summoned.

The blood continued to seep from between her thighs after she was washed, and she didn't bother to put on any panties with the overlarge t-shirt of Jeremiah's that she wore. They would be ruined by the blood and would probably have to be taken off anyway so Dandridge could sew her up. It wouldn't be the first time. Or the last, most likely.

Sighing as he placed stitches around her vulva, the doctor looked disheartened.

"I...If this type of abuse continues, she'll be dead before the year is out," he told Kate and Carter softly as he walked over with his soiled gloves to toss them into his red hazmat container. "There is only so much a wolf can take, and she is getting more fragile by the day."

Giselle was used to them talking about her like she wasn't there. For all intents and purposes, she wasn't. She was merely a placeholder until the Alpha would eventually kill her and take another to mate. The man had never believed in rules and bucked all traditions when he could.

Carter and the doctor spoke a bit more before the Beta thanked the man and allowed him to leave.

Walking over to Giselle who was seated on the bed next to Kate, he spoke lowly but clearly.

"Luna," he said. "This can't continue. You heard Dr. Dandridge. We need a plan to get you out of here. For good."

Giselle simply gazed up at him, looking numb and feeling like a heap of trash. If it hadn't been for the fresh trickle of tears falling down her face, Carter would have thought she hadn't heard him.

"Then kill me," Giselle said after a brief moment.

There was a pleading quality to her dead voice, and Kate let out a soft sob. Carter's pained eyes flickered over to his mate before they slid back over to Giselle's.

"You know I can't do that," he told her. "And I know you don't deserve that."

"I don't deserve this," Giselle said quietly, gesturing about the room. "It's like I'm in prison for a crime I didn't commit. I have no life anymore, no friends. I'm forbidden to see my family. I...please – I just want to die."

Carter's jaw ticked with agitation. He had known Giselle – mainly through her brother – since she was young, and this was unlike the vibrant girl she used to be. She had always been a little shy until you cracked her outer shell, but she was kind and warm to everyone. He had never imagined she would become Luna only to be beaten down by his Alpha. An Alpha whose head had grown too big with the power of his title.

Yet, maybe she had something there. If Jeremiah thought she was dead, he would probably request for her body to be taken off his land and then blame a rogue on her disappearance and death.

"I have a better idea, Elle," he said to her, using her childhood nickname to garner her full attention. "Now listen carefully..."

***

Giselle woke with a start. An irritating beeping noise was coming from somewhere, and she looked frantically around the room to figure out where she was, and what the sound meant.

The room was dark, but her heightened wolf senses could still distinguish almost everything in the space.

The last thing Giselle remembered was Jeremiah's eyes. They were black with rage as he pulled back his fist before connecting with her face.

Then...silence. Complete and utter nothingness. It was a relief.

She thought she had dreamed about waking up in a forest and

seeing a few men surrounding her, but it was only a flash and then it was gone.

But...where was she now? It smelled heavily like the antiseptics of a sterile environment. She had only been to a hospital once growing up when she had received a compound fracture to her leg falling out of her treehouse. The leg had to be set quickly before healing kicked in, and she remembered that this is what it had smelled like there as well.

So, she must not be in her own pack lands since she wasn't ever allowed out of the Alpha's home. Carter's plan must have worked, somewhat. But where was she? How far had he traveled in order to get rid of her body? And was Jeremiah unaware that she still lived? God, she hoped so.

Giselle tried to call out.

Nothing. No sound.

Clutching at her throat, she felt bandages there and decided to try and get to her feet to find someone. She needed to know where she was. Though she was certain that this wasn't Blackriver territory, she wouldn't rest until she was completely convinced.

Her legs gave out from beneath her when she stood, and she nearly stumbled before moving away from the bed.

One faltering step. Two steps. Three.

She made her way gingerly over to the door and flicked on the light switch.

The room bathed itself in fluorescent lighting, and she cringed away from the harsh glare of it in her eyes.

The beeping started to escalate, the invasive sound becoming more rapid with each passing moment.

She started to panic, and moved away from the door. She needed to make the beeping stop. Pulling at anything on her body, Giselle found she had something clamped to her finger. It was a foreign object. And there were circular pads on her chest, gleaming white and stuck onto her skin with little wires attached.

Giselle pulled everything off of her body and the beeping stopped. Only then, it was followed by one continuous loud noise. Like the beeping had turned into a high-pitched shriek that threatened to break her down with its insistence.

Giselle clamped her hands over her ears to try to quell the sound, but it was almost useless. She could still hear it, and her hands only dampened the sound the slightest bit.

On her knees now, she crawled over to the corner of the room in her flimsy hospital gown and panties, folded her knees to her chest, and wished she could make a sound. *Any* sound. Just so someone could find the source of the noise and make it go away.

As the tears poured down to her chin, the door to the room opened swiftly, and Giselle looked up to see a female in a white coat.

The woman seemed to be mid to late 20's and was a pretty blonde with sparkling blue eyes. She was of medium height, maybe five foot six or seven, and wearing sensibly low heels under black slacks.

Looking over to the small creature huddled in the corner, Evelyn D'Amato saw her flinch away from her as she moved to come closer.

Giselle gave a high-pitched scream and another nurse came running into the room.

"Call the Alpha," Evelyn told the frightened nurse. "Tell him the patient is awake."

"Is...is she rogue?" the nurse asked, nose crinkling.

"Does she smell rogue to you, you idiot?" Evelyn asked, immediately becoming irritated with the moronic nurse. "She is a patient only. Now, do as I say."

A few minutes later, Evelyn was waiting in the main lobby for Alpha Liam, who had been awakened from a deep sleep for this.

Seeing him in his black leather jacket over a muscle shirt and black jeans, he rushed into the facility and went straight to Dr. D'Amato.

"Where is she?" he asked, voice still thick from sleep.

"She's awake and in her room," Evelyn told him. "But there's a problem, Alpha."

"What is that? Does she refuse treatment? Send her away if she does," Liam spat out, irritated that he was being awoken for a non-compliant, trespassing she-wolf.

"No, Alpha," Evelyn told him. "She doesn't speak."

"She refuses to or cannot?"

"I believe a bit of both," Evelyn told him. "She tries to make sounds, but nothing comes out. For all intents and purposes, she is a mute."

***

Liam took Evelyn's information in with a few rapid blinks. It was difficult for him to fathom that any damage done to such a hearty species would cause this psychological and physical trauma in one so young.

"I will get her to speak," he said firmly. "Where is she?"

"Alpha, the girl is not only traumatized, but her throat was nearly torn from her neck," Evelyn warned him. "It is not just that she is unwilling through some sort of psychiatric cause, but her throat needs time to heal as well. It would be unwise for her to strain it until she is completely recovered. It may also traumatize her further. If you need to question her, at any rate, please be gentle."

Liam slowly closed his eyes and thought for a moment, thinking of a way to get the information he needed without breaking the girl. If anything, at least get her to tell him which pack she hailed from.

"Evelyn," Liam finally said. "Do you have a spare notepad and a pen? I will ask her questions that way."

"Of course, Alpha," she said. "Give me a moment to fetch them."

The doctor went to the reception desk and pulled out a thick yellow pad and a ballpoint pen. Walking back to him, she bowed her head in respect and gave the items to him.

"Now bring me to the girl."

Evelyn took him back to the last room on the right and again warned him of the frailties of the girl, emphasizing her fragile mental state which seemed teetering and unwieldy at best.

Opening the door, Evelyn went in first before Liam followed. The room was blindingly bright and he looked over to the bed, watching as the girl sat up straighter, pulling the thin sheets up farther, as if to hide herself from the unwanted visitors.

"Miss, this man is Liam Stark, Alpha of the Plumbrook Pack," Evelyn told the girl gently. "No harm will come to you in his presence."

The girl gazed over at Liam, looking even more frightened and seeming to tremble slightly in her bed.

Unfazed by her trepidation, he walked over a few steps towards her and watched as she flinched backward, a high-pitched whimper the only sound in the room.

Liam took the girl in. She did not look dangerous, but danger could sometimes come in a pretty, pint-sized packages. He knew that all too well.

Large, blue doe-eyes made even wider by fear looked back at him while her hair tumbled in gentle waves down past her shoulders. It was jet black and looked fine as silk, though it might have been ages since it had been properly cared for.

"Little wolf," Liam said in a calm manner. "Your beaten body was found on the edge of my lands near a highway. I need to know what you were doing there and where you come from. But first, please, tell me your name."

He pushed the pad of paper and pen towards her and watched as she stared blankly back at it before blinking and taking it from him.

He watched as in slow, methodical cursive, she penned her response.

My name is Giselle. No surname. I cannot tell you where I come from and why I'm here.

Reading the words, Liam's bright blue eyes seemed to grow cold as he looked back at her after he finished reading her response.

"Why can you not tell me? Do you not know, or do you refuse to answer an Alpha's question?"

Though he tried not to, the words came out sounding cruel and blunt, and Giselle jerked back at his tone. Her eyes immediately became glassy and a tear spilled down her cheek, though she made no other sound but for a loud sniff.

Fuck.

"Alpha," Evelyn murmured softly so that only he could hear.

Liam closed his eyes again, trying to remember that this was no rogue, no interloper. At least not of her own free will. She could not have made it from the nearest pack in the condition she had been found.

"My apologies," Liam told her, his voice a bit softer, bordering on contrite. "We are mistrustful of strangers here at Plumbrook, and I need to know you are not a threat to us. If you could, please, answer my question."

He gave her the pen and pad back and watched as she reluctantly put pen to paper and wrote her response.

I know where I come from, but I do not belong there anymore. I am afraid that if I tell you, you will send me back and I only just escaped with my life. I did not know where I would be left. I passed out before being dropped at the side of the road.

Liam read again and understood. He nodded at her.

"Is there a reason you had to flee, or were you being punished and escaped from your pack's cells?"

I am no fugitive. I am merely someone who wishes to start fresh. The only way to do that was to flee.

"And what or who do you flee from?"

That – I cannot tell you. You would surely send me back. If you make me tell you, you must promise to kill me before sending me back there, because I am as good as

dead if I return.

Liam read it through twice. Then a third time. He didn't understand fully, but he was certain she did not, and would not, tell him the truth if he pressed her for an answer now.

Liam caught a movement in his peripheral vision and saw that Giselle was motioning to take the notepad back. Perhaps she had more to say after all.

Why can I not speak?

Liam deferred to Dr. D'Amato for this information, and Evelyn explained the physical trauma first.

"You may regain your voice back in time, though it is up to you and your mental state on how quickly you learn to speak again," she told the younger woman. "It will take time and hard work, but I am sure that if you put your mind to it, you will regain the ability to speak eventually."

Evelyn smiled at her and Giselle's face seemed to break into a soft, demure smile as well, her cheeks becoming pink at the kind words. She'd had so very few of them spoken to her in the past six months.

Giselle motioned for the pad with a small, slender hand. Evelyn gave it back, and motioned for her to write what she wished.

Am I still in New York State? When may I leave the hospital?

"Yes, you are still in upstate New York and as you are awake and stable, you may leave any time you like," Evelyn told her, looking back at the Alpha who was watching their exchange with rapt attention. Like he was trying to solve a riddle.

"You should not move around much for a while, but there is no need for you to stay here," Evelyn continued. "Alpha, is there a place in the Packhouse where Giselle may stay?"

At that, Giselle froze and her face paled. She was not good around strange people – or, in this case – wolves.

"The Packhouse is full at the moment," Liam said after blinking.

Evelyn looked back at him and tilted her head. The last time she knew, there were at least four unoccupied rooms in the Packhouse and she hadn't heard of anyone moving in these past several months.

"If you would like, you can stay in my home," Liam said, continuing smoothly. "I have several unoccupied rooms and some spare clothing my sister left before finding her mate. She was about your size but has gained some since having given birth to her son."

Giselle took in the man with her own scrutinizing look before nodding her head in assent. Whether she was too scared to decline his offer or just wanted to leave the hospital was anyone's guess. It was not like she had anywhere to go.

"I will have my Beta get some things from my home for you to wear and we can leave," Liam said before turning to walk out the door.

Before leaving the room, Liam turned back, his eyes downcast, staring at the floor.

"You may take your respite on my lands for the meantime," he told Giselle. "If you wish to join our community, we may talk about that in the future. Just...something for you to think about."

He walked out the door, his heavy boots making a hard, clomping sound on the linoleum as he moved past the other rooms in the hospital.

***

"You *what?*" Blake hissed out, irritated he had been woken from his sound sleep to play fetch-the-foreigner's-clothing. He was not some lady-in-waiting or maid.

"It just came out," Liam said, cutting his eyes at Blake. He didn't regret offering Giselle home and hearth. She seemed like a gentle soul, and he found he couldn't toss her aside after only just recovering from her horrific wounds. The girl had been broken both physically and mentally, and something in him was convinced she was no danger. When he had offered her a place to stay and possibly more, it was on a whim, an instinct. He trusted his instincts implicitly, and knew better than to ignore them.

"You were the one who brought her here," Liam reminded his Beta. "You wouldn't have brought her if you felt she was a threat, so don't turn this around on me now."

"Yeah, I offered her a place to recover, not to stay forever!" Blake frowned at the Alpha's rash, in-the-moment decisions, especially the one where she lived in his home with him. For the longest time, no one had lived with the Alpha. Not since *her*.

"Let me worry about where she sleeps," Liam told him. "You just worry about getting to my house, picking up something for her to wear, and getting back here. You're not the only one that wants to go back to sleep."

Blake cut a glance at his friend and Alpha, and loped off toward the clinic door before turning back.

"Hey, Liam?"

"Yes?"

"Uhm...underwear?"

Liam thought about that. He didn't know if she would be averse to wearing another female's panties, but he realized that that may be too intimate of apparel to share with someone else. Even if they were clean.

"No bra. Just grab a pair of my boxers, some sweatpants, and a t-shirt. She's not going to be modeling in Milan any time soon," Liam finally told him and watched as Blake's wide body left the building.

***

Once Giselle was dressed in clothing that was even larger on her small frame than he had originally thought, Liam walked her toward his house, which was the largest and most extravagant building in the community. It was also the brightest, as he had left the lights on before heading to the hospital.

"I know you cannot speak back to me, but for what I have to say, I don't need an answer right away," Liam told her, watching as she nodded gently back at him.

"I understand your trepidation about telling us which pack you come from, but at some point, I will need to know," Liam told her and watched as her form faltered slightly on the asphalt of the small backroad. "If you are to become one of us, we will need to know if there is a danger posed to us from whoever is pursuing you. Once you break the bond with that pack, their Alpha may feel it as well."

Giselle slowed her pace, thinking. She hadn't thought about the bond that the Alphas had with their pack wolves. They could feel when someone was out of their territory or if they pledged to another pack, and that last part frightened her the most. Surely Jeremiah would feel when – or *if* – his true mate pledged to another pack.

Liam coaxed her along and led her into his home before watching her look around the foyer of the house. It was large and bright, unlike the darker, more foreboding looking home of Jeremiah.

"I will give you a tour of my house tomorrow," Liam told her before walking toward the curvature of the stairs. "Your room will be next to mine in case you need anything, though I doubt you will do much but sleep tonight."

She nodded her head again at him, this time tilting it at him afterward, as if trying to figure the man out. Liam truly wished he could tell what she was thinking. If she wasn't so fragile, he may have forced her to speak.

"I will have some paper and pens brought to you in the morning so you can communicate," he told her and stopped in front of a large oak door before opening it up for her.

The room was large, but not ostentatious. It was simple in design, with a queen-sized bed and oak dressers bookending it. There was an overstuffed chair and a few bookshelves that Giselle immediately wanted to inspect. They were her favorite part of the room by far.

"This is my sister's old room," Liam told her. "She had left some clothing when she found her mate, and you are welcome to anything in here as she will not be needing any of it anytime soon."

He watched as Giselle immediately went to one bookshelf and started to run her hands over the spines of the many books that lined it. Liam's sister was a book fanatic and devoured any genre that could be read, so there was a good mix of them to choose from.

Liam couldn't help but smile a bit at the apparent bookworm. He had never been one to read anything more complicated than the sports page, and his sister had been the voracious reader among the two of them. Just like their mother before her.

Giselle started to slide out a book and seemed to stop herself. Her head snapped to Liam's and she looked frightened, as though he might be mad if even one book was out of place.

"You may use anything in here as well," he assured her. "My sister has mated halfway across the country and is living in the Rockies at this time. Even if she were to see you in here touching her things, she would not fault you and insist you read as much as you like. She is a very generous woman."

Giselle seemed to study him again, as if to test to see if he was telling the truth. Slowly though, she picked up the book. It had been one of his sister's favorites when she had still been living in the Alpha's home. *Thirteen Reasons Why*. They had made the book into some TV show so it was no wonder that Giselle had gravitated toward it. It had been quite popular at the time it aired.

"Did you watch the show on Netflix?" Liam asked, gesturing toward the book.

Looking confused, Giselle looked down on the book as if it was in some foreign language. Shaking her head, she walked over to the bed and set the book down on it, looking at it before opening the front page and caressing the dustjacket.

"I will let you rest," Liam told her, heading toward the door. He had been standing in the corner by the closet. "There is a bathroom through that door for you to wash in the morning. I usually get up early and my housekeeper comes to cook for me as I do not know how. If she is not around, please help yourself to cereal, or eggs and bacon. Just don't burn the house down. I've come quite attached to living here."

She looked over at him again as if terrified. When she saw his small, teasing smile, she returned it shakily and nodded at him in affirmation.

"Goodnight, Giselle," he told her before closing the door behind him and moving toward his bedroom. He felt like he could sleep for another eight hours, but he doubted he would be able to rest for that long. He was never one for too much sleep these days.

Chapter 3

Giselle woke up the next morning wondering where she was. Her heart raced for a few moments until she sniffed the air and realized she was not in her own bed at Jeremiah's house and was far, far away from the brutish man.

As her heart slowly calmed, she thought of the Alpha whose house she was in. He seemed nice enough, but so had Jeremiah at first. Then again, most of Jeremiah's issues were borne of his jealousy and anger. Jealousy that anyone should touch what was his, and anger that his future Luna was a lowly Omega. He felt he had deserved far better, and used to tell her so often.

Looking over at the clock on the wall, she saw it was just past 7:30 AM. She wondered if the Alpha was gone or still in the house. She needed to find out some things and talk – well, *write* – them out for him.

Clothing. She needed clothing, so that meant she needed money to purchase it. She had left with none and if she used any credit cards or debit cards she had been given, it would give away the fact that she was not as dead as she *hoped* Jeremiah believed.

In order to get money to buy clothing, she would need a job. A job in the nearest town would only draw attention to her as the newcomer, and she didn't have any skills with which to offer this new pack. If she decided to stay that is. She wasn't so sure about that. She would be both a liability and a weight on the community. *Useless*, like Jeremiah had told her so many times.

Walking into the bathroom, she decided to take a shower and hurried her way through it. Scrubbing herself and then brushing her teeth, she found a comb in one of the drawers and she meticulously picked her way through her hair, irritated with the multitude of knots.

When her hair was smooth and straight, she figured she would let it dry naturally and then took the stairs to the bottom floor, making almost zero sound on the hardwood flooring.

Using her heightened sense of smell, she made her way into the kitchen and looked into the fridge. She had only eaten oatmeal and some dry cereal while living with Jeremiah, so she opted for the first hearty meal she'd had in months.

Bacon. Sausages. She found a dozen fresh eggs, and decided to make herself some of those as well. She could use it for putting on some weight. Giselle knew she couldn't really rock the whole skeleton-esque look for very long, and it was beyond unhealthy.

As she was pulling out some pans and a bowl to whisk eggs in, she sniffed the air, sensing another presence with it.

The Alpha. So, he *was* still at home.

Looking toward the door, she saw him come through the entranceway, doing up the last few buttons on his shirt.

When Liam looked over at the tiny female, he noticed she was wearing tiny shorts and a long-sleeved shirt. The sleeves were far too long on her and drooped over her hands unless she rolled them up.

"You should roll up the sleeves so you don't catch fire cooking," he told her and watched as she put down the utensils and pushed her sleeves up her skinny arms.

"No...like this." Liam walked over to her and folded her sleeves up meticulously, roll after roll. After he finished, he stepped back.

"There. Much better," he said and walked over to the fridge. He didn't like the strange, wide-eyed look she gave him. It was unnerving, piercing. She looked at him as if she could see inside him and witness the mess he was.

She made a sound – an ugly, strangled one, and he looked over at her. Gesturing to the food, she pointed at the bowls, food, and then pointed at him.

"You want to know if I would like some food?" he asked.

Nodding, she smiled softly at him.

"Sure, though the housekeeper should have been here by now."

Liam looked off into the distance, presumably trying to reach out to someone through the pack's mindlink. He eventually hummed in understanding.

"She is still at home. Her littlest one is ill," he told her, though she didn't understand why he felt the need to explain. "Go ahead and cook if you have the mind to cook for a ravenously hungry wolf."

While Giselle whisked eggs, Liam left the room for a moment and came back into the kitchen with a pad of paper and a pen.

"You should always bring this with you, whether you think you will need them or not," he told her. "Not everyone is as good as I at reading your hand signals and gestures."

She nodded at him and turned to place strips of bacon on one skillet and the freshly beaten eggs in the other. She let them simmer as she walked over to the pad of paper and wrote.

How do you like your eggs? was the simple question.

Looking up at her after reading it, he blinked and breathed out.

"I'm not picky," he told her. "Scrambled, omelet, whatever you make is fine."

Cheese?

Nodding and smiling, the Alpha said, "Sure."

Breakfast was quieter than Liam was used to, and he found that he didn't mind it one bit. His housekeeper was always chattering on about her children. Which was okay the first 57 times she told the same story. New teeth, colic when they were little, vomit, and diapers; they weren't topics he really wished to discuss over breakfast, nor at any other meal.

Giselle picked up the pad of paper and wrote for a long time.

Why aren't you at work already? I thought you would be gone long before this. I hope I didn't throw off your routine. Also, I need to get clothing. Underwear mostly, and would like to know how I can earn my keep so that I may be able to afford them.

Liam took a while to read it, and answered her questions as he went along.

"I was supposed to go in earlier, but I slept too long," he said. "I guess the middle-of-the-night call to the clinic woke me up and kept me awake far longer than I anticipated. You didn't wake me. I got up around 7:15. As for clothing, I will have someone come around to get your size. Do not worry about earning your keep for now. We have a rainy-day fund for such instances as this and we hardly ever use it. As for your occupation here at this pack – what are your skills, or what is it you like to do?"

Giselle thought for a moment and then wrote.

I'm sorry to have kept you up last night with the visit to the hospital. As for clothing, I would like to earn my keep, just like everyone else. I can still do some things, but my skills are limited to pretty much anything I can do around the house. Cooking, cleaning, things like that. I haven't had a job before. The only other thing I like to do is sing.

Liam smiled sadly. It was ironic that what this girl would love most was something she was unable to do at the moment.

"Well, we have no jobs open for *Resident Songbird*, so cooking and cleaning would suit nicely," he told her. "In fact, since you are staying with me, I think it's best you become my housekeeper instead of Sofia. She can be loud and obnoxious, and as much as I love kids, I feel like I'm living with hers without the benefit of having them around."

Giselle looked like she was almost about to giggle. *Almost*. No sound came out though, and she looked down at her empty plate, saddened by the fact she couldn't make even the simplest of sounds.

Liam put his hand on her shoulder and then tipped her chin up to him with a callused hand.

"You'll get your voice back, little wolf," he told her softly. "Then you can sing me lullabies every night so I can finally rest."

Grabbing the pen and paper, she wrote quickly.

You have problems sleeping? Have you tried warm milk with honey?

Laughing, the usually stern Alpha shook his head.

"I've tried everything except medicines," he told her. "And I don't wish to become addicted to a substance due to the amount that it would take to put me down for the night. I get by just fine with a few hours a night."

May I ask why you don't sleep well?

Liam's face fell for a moment, but he schooled his features and gave her a lazy half-smile.

"Tell you what," he spoke, using a napkin to wipe around his mouth. "When you tell me where you come from and why you're running, I'll tell you why sleep evades me. Deal?"

Giselle nodded, but still looked uncertain.

Standing from his seat, Liam looked down at the forlorn creature and sighed.

"I'll have one of my she-wolves come around and get your sizes," he told her. "Bras, underwear, and some clothing that will actually fit you. You're swimming in my sister's stuff."

Though he had to admit, they looked damn good on her anyway.

***

A knock roused Giselle from the book she was reading. Going to the door, she looked out the side window first before seeing it was a female wolf with red hair, a snub nose, and sparkling blue eyes. She opened the door, not knowing what to expect of the woman outside of it.

"Hi! I'm Colleen, the Beta's mate," the woman told her before coming into the house after Giselle opened the door. "I'm surprised to see Alpha Liam actually has a visitor, though I know you are an unintended one at that."

Giselle nodded and looked for her pen and paper. She had kept it nearby as Liam had advised, but had left it on the coffee table near the couch she had been sitting on.

"Blake told me you can't talk, and Liam said your name is Giselle," Colleen kept prattling on. "It might be better if you *don't* talk around me. I talk enough for three people and it can be overwhelming for some. But let's go ahead and figure out your sizes."

They eventually looked around Giselle's bedroom and found the smallest of clothing that Liam's sister had owned. They still floated around her smaller frame, but it gave them a starting point. Jeremiah hadn't allowed her underwear or bras as he only ripped them off her when he was of a mind to. Not that any of them would have fit her anymore.

"I know Liam said you are somewhat on bedrest and that you shouldn't go now, but we should have a girl's trip to go shopping once you're better," Colleen told her, smiling.

Giselle didn't know what to say to that, so she just nodded and watched as the vocal young woman walked out the front door with her list of things to purchase for her with a hearty "see ya later".

Sitting back down on the couch, Giselle eventually ended up falling asleep while reading her book.

***

Her nose was high in the air, sniffing for the wonderful scent. She had just turned 18 a few days ago and she knew what that smell meant.

It meant that she had found her mate. Following it to the source, she saw the Alpha, Beta, Gamma, and Delta all training with the pack warriors. Dozens of men on the grounds, and one of them was hers. She didn't know how to differentiate which, so she just waited and watched.

Watching the men battle each other in both human and wolf forms was always interesting. A lot of horseplay along with some well-intended smack talk was to be heard, and the Alpha would sometimes break up the fun to get back down to business.

A storm was due this afternoon; she could sense it from the way the breeze suddenly shifted that it would soon be upon them. Dark thunderclouds could be seen to the west and Giselle got up reluctantly to head inside before the rains came.

Standing up from her place beneath the tree she was nestled under, she felt the winds shift again and the sound die out as the warriors moved away from the impending torrents of water they would see from the downfall.

Giselle started to walk towards home until she heard a shuffling noise behind her. Frightened, she turned around and caught a whiff of the scent moments before she saw who it was.

"Alpha," she said, lowering her head in respect. "M-my apologies if my presence disturbed the warriors."

"Look up, little one," the strong voice of Jeremiah Bluth demanded. "What is your name and rank?"

"Giselle Kincaid, Omega rank, sir," she said in a low voice. She was not ashamed of her rank, but it was not often that an Omega was paired with an Alpha. Like was mated to like most often.

"I see, little mate," he told her, voice stiff. "And how old are you?"

"18, sir," she said, not looking directly into the cold eyes of the Alpha. She hadn't known such a rich, chocolatey brown color could be so icy, so dead.

"I need to meet with your parents, Giselle," he told her, forthright. "You will need to come with me to my home. As future Luna, it is yours now as well."

"Yes, sir," she said, cowering beneath his cold, hard glare.

His eyes...they were the first things she saw, and they should have told her all she needed to know.

Jeremiah Bluth was as coldhearted a wolf as anyone had ever known.

Chapter 4

Alpha, there seems to be some sort of commotion at your house, Blake told Liam through mindlink.

What sort? Who's there? I only left Giselle there and Colleen should be at the store picking up some essentials for her, Liam replied.

Liam had been on the training fields and was now meeting with Evelyn on how to help Giselle recover her voice. The news was both uplifting and depressing. She would be able to physically speak as soon as her throat was healed, but the doctor was afraid that the trauma she suffered could keep her mute much longer than that. It only made Liam want to know more about the strange wolf that had been dumped on his land like a sack of unwanted debris.

I don't think anyone is there but...there is screaming. No words. Just screaming.

Giselle. She could only scream. No words.

"I will be back later to speak more about this, Evelyn," Liam told her before moving swiftly toward the door.

"Yes, Alpha," the woman replied and moved behind her desk to catch up on some long overdue paperwork.

Liam started at a brisk walk toward his home, but was soon speeding along and giving Usain Bolt a run for his money once he heard the screaming coming from within his usually silent home.

As soon as his door was open, he saw that Giselle was tossing and turning as she whimpered on the couch. Then...another scream and Liam shut the door quickly behind him before moving toward the couch.

"Giselle! Giselle! Wake up!"

He tried to wake her with his words, but they were drowned out by her own pained screeches. If Liam hadn't been standing there watching her torment, he would have thought someone was torturing her with hot branding irons or slipping bamboo shoots under her fingernails.

Sinking to the ground on one knee, he started to gently shake the girl.

"Wake up, Giselle!" he told her, louder this time.

Nothing except for another resounding, blood-curdling scream.

"Giselle! Giselle! Wake up for me!"

Eyes, blue and bloodshot, popped open before the tears started to run down her face. Giselle then curled into a ball, a sniffling, sobbing mess. The only sounds it seemed she could make were ones of pain and suffering, and it hurt Liam to know that what she wanted more than anything was to sing like a bird, not screech and sob like a banshee.

"Are you alright?" he asked, concern layered in the tones of his voice.

She stopped sniffling for a moment and shakily nodded her head. It was an obvious lie. Deciding to ignore that, he went into the kitchen and got a mug out before filling it with water from the tap.

He put the mug into the microwave, heating the water while he got out a teabag and a jar of honey. Figuring her throat must be sore from her wailing, he tried to ignore her sniffles and found himself fighting to go to her. He wasn't comfortable being so close to strange people, though he might make an exception for Giselle. She seemed to be more of a shell of a person than even he was. And he was a mess, albeit a self-proclaimed one.

The microwave beeped and he set about putting a teabag into the hot water and adding some honey. Bringing it out to her, he placed it on the coffee table next to her head and watched as her shuddering breaths became more even, less frenzied and desperate.

"You should sit up," Liam told her, gesturing to the mug. "Drink that. Hot tea with honey. For your throat. It must be sore from all that screaming."

Nodding her head, Giselle sat up and took the mug in both hands. She blew on it to cool it and finally took a small sip, closing her eyes as she did.

"Better?" he asked, to which she nodded back at him with big, watery blue eyes. There was just a hint of something in them. Trust? Gratitude? He couldn't tell, and he picked up the pen and paper, happy to see it nearby as he had advised.

"Was it a nightmare?" Liam asked, pushing the pen and paper toward her.

Giselle looked on the items and hesitantly picked them up to write.

Nightmare...reality. They're one and the same to me.

Looking at her words, Liam's eyes creased with some unknown

emotion and he looked up, studying her.

"Are you willing to tell me what it's about?" he asked, all the while knowing the answer probably would be "no".

Giselle chewed on her lip, nibbling at it until she eventually let it go. She plucked the pad from Liam's hands and wrote.

I will show you.

Giselle stood and turned, placing her mug back on the coffee table and then lifted up the back of her shirt a few inches.

At first, Liam didn't know what he was looking for. Then, he saw it...a scar. A very *odd* shaped scar.

Moving forward, Liam looked closer and had to stifle a shocked gasp. It wasn't just a scar; it was initials.

No. A brand.

JB

He immediately felt an odd rage stir within him, an anger he hadn't felt in years. Well, at least not this strongly.

Pulling down her shirt for her, he had seen enough.

"Is that the person who did this to you?" he asked, his voice a low, guttural growl. He gestured to her whole body, not just the brand she carried.

Giselle didn't turn to face him, scared. He sounded angry. At her? She didn't know. But she nodded and flinched as he huffed out in disgust.

Liam watched as the girl recoiled, her shoulders bunching up as if readying herself to receive a blow. His gaze softened, and he worked to relax his stance a bit.

"I'm not going to hit you, little wolf," he told her softly. "What has been done to you...it angers me, but only because it is the sorriest type of person who would brand another in such a way. It must have been painful. Silver?"

Giselle nodded and relaxed her shoulders. She had known he wasn't going to hit her, but her response had been a knee-jerk reaction. One that was ingrained in her over the past 6 months. Embedded, you could say. Like the brand. A brand that would never go away for as long as she lived. Yes, a part of her would always belong to her cruel Alpha mate.

Turning around finally, Giselle was surprised at the level of concern she saw in Liam's eyes. He stared at her until she felt the overwhelming need to look down at her feet.

Shaking his head as if clearing it, Liam came out of the anger-fueled daze he was in.

"We should bring you to the doctor, have her check your throat," he told her and walked toward the kitchen. "Go upstairs and change. Colleen should be back in another hour or so with your clothes, so we have enough time for a quick trip to the clinic."

***

"She was screaming when I got there," Liam told Evelyn quietly as the doctor made hasty notes. Giselle was with one of the nurses who was taking her blood pressure and temperature. The nurse was talking to her like she was a deaf-mute, and Giselle had the oddest look on her face. Like the nurse was the one that needed a serious check-up. It made Liam smirk a little bit. She was the same idiotic nurse from the other day, and she was still too moronic to even realize that being unable to speak was not the same as not being able to hear.

"Well, her throat is almost healed up completely, so in a couple of days you can try to get her to speak," Evelyn told him.

"Me?" Liam asked, surprised. "Why me?"

"She trusts you," Evelyn told him, nodding over to Giselle who had stopped scrutinizing the nurse long enough to look over at the two of them talking about her. "If anyone can get her to talk, it would be you. You already have a rapport, even if it is in just hand gestures and writing."

"What about that nurse?" Liam asked, listening as Evelyn scoffed.

"She's completely clueless," Evelyn told him. "I'm surprised she learned to speak herself. How she became a nurse I'll never know. And I don't think their rapport is that great either. Just look."

They watched as the nurse spoke louder, as if Giselle was half-deaf. Giselle, in turn, cocked her head like the girl was touched in the head.

"You have a point," Liam said, sighing. Along with his duties as Alpha, he would have to become a speech therapist to a shell-shocked female who had been a mere stranger to him twenty-four hours ago. "Any suggestions?"

"Start out small," the doctor told him. "Small words, maybe names. Start with yours. It's easy enough and only two syllables. Or Colleen's name since she knows her as well. Blake's is good too."

"Right," Liam said and stood from the desk chair. He called over to Giselle. "Ready to go? Colleen should be back any time and it's nearly time for dinner."

Giselle smiled softly, her eyes wide, thankful that she could finally leave the clinic, and especially the simple-minded nurse, behind.

Once they got back into the Alpha's home, Giselle went immediately to the kitchen and started to root through the cabinets and freezer.

Curious, Liam followed her and went to see what she was doing. He saw that she had taken two steaks from the freezer and was getting ready to thaw them in the microwave. Along with a couple of potatoes and some frozen green beans, he watched, fascinated, as she silently went about cooking them dinner.

***

"Wow," Liam said, collapsing back in his seat. His old housekeeper had been a good cook but she had never been able to stay long enough to make dinner for him. She usually just cooked something earlier in the day and he would heat it up when he was ready.

"That was...you're a damned fine cook," he told her, approvingly.

Giselle smiled, pleased, before blushing. She hadn't had a compliment in what seemed like ages, unless it was to tell her she was a good girl that day for pleasing her Alpha mate with her mouth. Those days at Jeremiah's were few and far between though.

"Dr. D'Amato said that you can start trying to speak in a couple of days. You are almost completely physically healed."

Giselle was whipping out her pen and paper faster than Liam had ever seen. They were never far from her now.

Will I be able to sing again? Ever?

She looked sad when she passed the pad over to Liam, and he looked back up at her.

"Run before you can walk," he told her encouragingly. "If we can get you to speak, I am sure you'll be singing around the house in no time."

Giselle was pleased with that and smiled brightly at him. The intensity of it hit him right in the gut, but then her face froze and she looked reticent, though she took back the pad of paper willingly enough.

Do you think I should go by a different name – like a nickname? I don't want my identity to be known freely. Just in case.

Liam nodded back at her.

"Good idea," he told her. "What about...'Elle'? Would that be good? It *is* part of your name already."

She smiled, nodding her approval at the idea.

"I'll tell Colleen, Blake, and the medical staff to call you Elle from now on," Liam told her. "But you will have to eventually tell me where you came from and how you ended up here."

The reminder didn't seem to worry her as much, and she just nodded her head before writing on the pad of paper.

Soon.

***

The two of them watched TV for a bit after dinner, some show Liam had never seen before. He didn't have much free time for frivolous hobbies and they were really only waiting for Colleen to come back. The girl was taking longer than usual at the mall. Probably robbing the man blind by proxy of his credit card.

When they were halfway through a rerun of *The Deadliest Catch*, there was a knock on the door.

Liam sniffed and shouted out, "Come in, Colleen. The door is open."

She was inside before he could finish his sentence, and had Blake in tow with a myriad of bags filled to the brim with clothing and other essentials.

"Hey there, big guy," Colleen chirped as she sashayed her ass into the room. Blake came in, more subdued, shaking his head at his female. She had no sense of propriety. Luckily, Liam had known Colleen his whole life and allowed her to speak freely with him, so long as they were not within earshot of the pack.

"'Sup, Col?" he asked. "Did you use *all* of the rainy-day fund? Hope you enjoyed it. It's the last time I give you the pack credit card by the looks of it." His eyes wandered to the bags she and Blake held in their collective arms.

Elle looked over at Liam, trying to gauge whether he was upset with the amount that Colleen had purchased for her. It was much, much more than she honestly needed. She scrambled to get her pen and paper, and scribbled hurriedly onto it.

Too much. I don't need half of that stuff!

She gave the note to Liam who read it and tossed the pad of paper back at her.

"It's fine," he told her, waving away her anxiety over the purchases. "Honestly, I have a daily spending limit on that card and no one from the bank called me to approve any overages."

"Lee, your daily spending limit on that account is $3,000," Colleen told him. "I already knew that before I went to the store and picked up this stuff. I have a great knack for finding sales. C'mon,

Giselle. Let's go upstairs and make sure all this stuff fits you."

"Oh yeah, and call her *Elle* from now on," Liam told her. "Incidentally, it's what we should all call her. Please let Evelyn and the staff at the clinic know on your way back."

Blake nodded and brought the rest of the bags to the stairs before heading back out to the truck. He was driving a red Ford F150 that was overflowing with bags in the truck bed.

"Go on, Elle," Liam told her and she trotted past him slowly, looking back as if wanting to say something, a worried expression on her face.

"Honestly, he has more rainy-day money than he knows what to do with," Colleen told her when Elle was in her bedroom and looking at the innumerable bags. Even when living with her parents and siblings she hadn't owned this much clothing and the thought was daunting. Nothing came for free. She knew that all too well.

"Besides, I had oodles of fun picking stuff out for you. Best time ever, save for shopping for myself and some alone time with my man." Colleen's bubbly exuberance was infectious, and it was difficult for Elle to stifle the grin her ebullient new friend brought to her face.

"I thought you might be a size 4, but I think that after you bulk up a bit – you know, have had a few decent meals and such – you'll be a solid size 6. Like me!" Colleen looked at her and flashed a mischievous grin. Elle felt that the girl would come over often to borrow her clothing.

"So...the underthings are there in those bags." Colleen pointed in the general direction of a series of bags that looked to have come from some lingerie store. "You can put those away while we mix and match outfits and make sure they all fit."

Elle placed a bra over her chest and found it was too large. Not by much, but still too large for her small breasts.

Seeing her frown, Colleen laughed at her and assured her they would fit. Eventually.

"Like I said, once you've gotten a few decent meals in ya, you'll fill those puppies out," Colleen said and watched as Elle blushed a pretty pale pink.

"Come on over here after you're done," Colleen told her as Elle started to put away her panties and bras. "I bought you some dresses too that I am sure would go very much appreciated at social gatherings."

Colleen winked. She had a playfully impish sort of smile.

Elle knew that she was going to probably regret having Colleen do her shopping for her.

***

Elle looked at the stranger in the mirror. Her head was quirked, barely recognizable, and she was dressed in something other than the baggiest and most unbecoming of clothing.

"Oh, that's absolutely perfect for the next bonfire," Colleen said, giving herself a mental pat on the back. She then watched as Elle looked at her with a confused stare.

"Oh, once a month the pack has a bonfire," Colleen said. "Food, dancing – it's loads of fun. You should come to it. That is…" Colleen looked at Elle, regarding her as if the vision of her might float away soon.

"Are you going to stay here at Plumbrook?" Colleen asked, the words tumbling out of her mouth like a steaming pile of word vomit. "Tell me you are! I don't know where you came from or where you want to go, but I think that you would like it here."

Damn those puppy dog eyes of Colleen's. Aimed directly at Elle's fragile little heart and squeezing.

Elle thought for a moment. It wasn't as if she had any other place to be. And at least here she wouldn't be mingling amongst the people in the nearby towns and packs. They rarely ventured outside their own territory without good reason.

And it felt…*safe*. Safe here on this land, safe in Liam's home. Even safe with the Alpha himself. And that surprised Elle. She thought after a taste of one evil Alpha male, she would have sworn off them altogether. But something was different about this man. Something that made the two of them similar. Both broken, embittered souls looking for healing, restitution, maybe even something more out of life than just *being*.

Liam had so much as said that he had his own problems that led to his frequent bouts of insomnia. Though Elle wondered what they were, she knew that he wouldn't tell, at least not until she spilled her guts as well. And she was getting close to that as well, surprisingly.

Slowly, Elle made up her mind and she smiled at Colleen, nodding her head.

"That's great!" Colleen said, jumping up from the side of the bed and scurrying toward Elle to grab her hand.

"We have to tell Liam you want to stay!"

With a sharp tug, Colleen pulled Elle toward the stairs by her arm, clutching at her and chattering the whole time as they walked.

"...and we should get you some makeup. When you're feeling better anyway," Collen said. "Something nice and soft. Light, because you totally don't need to overdo it. You're pretty enough without it, and..."

Colleen's words faded in and out, clogging Elle's muddled mind. Something about makeup and soft. Whatever *that* meant. A bonfire and dancing. Elle hadn't danced in forever. She loved music, but she hadn't been able to let it take over her body since before she went to live with Jeremiah. She had loved to sing, but he always commanded her to stop cawing at him like some damned mynah bird. He had told her he hated whatever she was singing, and that it was giving him a headache. So, she only hummed to herself in the middle of the day when she was cooking, cleaning or doing some other domestic chore. And *never* when Jeremiah was supposed to be around. She was almost mute around him, even before the damage had been done to her vocal cords.

"Lee! Guess what!"

Colleen took the last of the steps two by two, forcing Elle to run down after her. She skidded to a stop in front of both men, an out of breath Elle behind her.

Both men's gazes snapped over to the women, Liam's eyes bugging out a bit before schooling his features and averting his eyes.

He honestly didn't know whether to curse or praise Colleen for that dress. Though Elle was still too slender to fill it out properly, he could only imagine what it would look like once she was a normal weight for her size. Hell, even if she was a little over the norm, that dress would have looked fabulous – as it did now.

The dress was a dark navy blue, setting off her crystalline eyes and lily-white complexion. Dipping down between her bosom just a touch, it made Elle look more mature and – paired with her wide blue eyes – sexier.

It also seemed to want to test the fabric of Liam's boxers and the sleep pants that he was wearing. Thank God he was sitting down and his lap could not be seen clearly.

Shifting in his seat, Liam fought hard not to completely ogle the young girl and settled for clearing his throat.

"What?" he was finally able to rasp out at Colleen.

"Elle says she wants to stay at Plumbrook," Colleen announced with a dazzling smile.

"Really?" Blake asked, sounding surprised himself.

"Yes," the girl affirmed, looking for approval from Liam, who simply nodded and forced himself to look over at Elle again. Without giving her the once over. It almost worked.

"You do know what that means, Elle?" he asked. "And remember – you tell, I tell."

Liam watched as Elle gulped loudly and slowly nodded her head. He saw that she had visibly paled a bit, but looked resolute in her decision.

She cleans up good, eh? Colleen shot to Liam through the mindlink.

You did this on purpose, didn't you? Liam asked, voice accusatory.

Maybe, Colleen admitted.

Why?

Liam could hear the sigh in Colleen's voice even before she spoke to him.

She trusts you, and having her around has been eye-opening to say the least, she told him.

How so?

Colleen glanced over at Blake who was saying something out loud to Elle. She was too engrossed in her chat with Liam to give a second thought as to what they were discussing.

You have a soft spot for her, Colleen told him. *I haven't seen you this tender in years. Not since...*

She let that thought peter out, not wanting to finish the sentence. Not when she knew it would hurt Liam. And knowing that he would understand what she meant anyway.

She could have a mate somewhere out there, Liam told her.

Colleen wanted to snort, his voice sounded so stiff. It seemed that Liam didn't like that idea – not one bit.

I'm not saying you have to do anything about this. But that girl needs some confidence, and if a few men flirting and telling her she looks pretty helps with that, my job's been done.

Liam's jaw flexed angrily as his eyes flashed. Colleen's widened in triumph.

I knew it! she practically hooted with delight through the mindlink. *You like her! You want her to-*

Enough, Colleen, Liam snapped, shooting daggers at her with his eyes. *No matter what, Elle is not ready to trust anyone, intimately or otherwise.*

Liam could see the question in her eyes before she spoke it.

Later, he told her. *I'll tell you later what I mean. It's...disturbing to say the least.*

***

As soon as Elle went back up to her room to put away the rest of her clothing, Liam jerked his chin at Blake and Colleen.

Study. He needed them in his study, which was soundproofed for security reasons.

Once the two had followed Liam into the study in the back of the home, Blake closed the door and walked up to the desk, joining Liam and Colleen.

"What is it?" Colleen asked, voice small and unsure.

"Liam, what's going on?" Blake asked, as he hadn't been privy to the conversation between Colleen and his Alpha.

"Blake, I need you to do something for me," Liam told him, voice controlled and cold. "This is to be of the utmost importance and cannot be mentioned to anyone outside of this room." Liam shot Colleen a glance. The girl was a bit of a gossip, but could keep a secret when she had to. And this time she would have to.

"What is it, boss?" Blake asked, going into second-in-command mode immediately.

"I need you to get me a list of all registered male wolves with the initials J.B. from the surrounding areas," Liam told him. "New York, New Jersey, Canada, Vermont, Connecticut, Massachusetts, and Pennsy. All male J.B.'s above the age of say…16."

"What? Why?" Blake asked, confusion etched on his face.

"Before leaving her pack, Elle was…*branded*," Liam said before taking a deep, cleansing breath and closing his eyes. He ran a hand through his hair, sifting the black strands through his fingers.

"Branded…wait – *what?*"

"Someone…someone with the initials of J.B. branded Elle on her lower back," Liam told them both, his mouth a thin, straight line. "With silver."

Colleen gasped at the same time that Blake uttered a string of curses.

"Sh-she told you this?" Blake asked when he had finally calmed down enough to speak.

"She showed me," Liam told him, shaking his head. "After you told me about the ruckus here this afternoon, I came back to the house and found her tossing about and shrieking in her sleep. When I asked her what the dream was about, she answered it by showing me the mark on her back."

"It's silver. It'll never go away," Colleen said, awed and shocked.

"Someone – some *asshole* – branded her like cattle. Like she was a piece of property."

"A mate?" Blake asked, wary.

"Possibly," Liam said, shaking his head. If he had been anyone else but Liam Stark, he would have had a hard time believing a mate could do that, but he knew better. "Or possibly someone else. Someone that wanted her for himself only. He branded her and treated her like shit to keep her in line and afraid. Afraid to run. Afraid to talk back. Just...afraid in general."

"I have a hard time believing a true mate would do that to his woman," Colleen said, voice watery and eyes red-rimmed and glassy.

Liam shook himself. He was starting to get angry, livid again. Looking over at Blake, he locked eyes with him.

"I want you to make me a list of all J.B.'s and bring it to me as soon as possible," Liam told him. "If she won't tell me who he is, I'll confront her with the list and get her to tell me which one is the bastard."

***

It took Elle another hour and a half to sort out all of her clothing. Colleen had started to mix and match some sets, and Elle picked up where she had left off, sorting, then hanging them up together in the closet. After that, she placed the shoes away on the shoe rack and packed up all of Liam's sister's items so as to not get them mixed up with hers.

Finally done, she saw it was nearly 10 PM and wondered if Liam was asleep yet. She wanted to thank him again and let him know a few things about her.

Walking over to the notepad on the desk in the corner of the room, she took a few moments to think and then wrote down a message.

After completing the note, she opened the door to the hallway and walked to Liam's bedroom door. There was a faint shuffling inside, so she knew he was still awake.

Knocking a few times, Liam told her to come in immediately.

Upon opening the door, she saw him sifting through his sock drawer before closing it and looking over at her.

Struggling with her reluctance, Elle walked in and gave the notepad to Liam, who looked at her for a moment before reading the note.

I just wanted to thank you again. It's much too much,

but it is appreciated. I promise to earn my keep.

I know that you want to know who I am and where I come from, but I would like to tell you bits and pieces first. I don't know how much I can share before I fall apart. It's difficult for me to speak about it since I was forbidden to before this, but I would like to try.

Liam looked at her and took a deep, steadying breath. Though he *did* want to hear what had happened to her, he knew that his anger was close to the surface. He didn't know how much of her tale he could handle before wanting to break something in his anger at whomever had broken the girl's spirit and body.

Nodding, Liam walked over to the bed and sat down on it before patting the space next to him and gesturing to it with a hand.

Taking one step forward, Elle understood that not only was she going to be giving, but also receiving.

You tell, I tell.

Chapter 5

Elle gripped the pad of paper so hard that her knuckles turned white before looking over at Liam and nodding her head, resolute.

Smoothing out the creases she made on the yellow notebook, she started to write slowly.

Though she started at a snail's pace, it was like watching a snowball rolling down an increasingly steep hill. An avalanche of words seemed to take up page after page, Elle's slim hand moving faster and faster until she read over what she had written and handed it over to Liam.

I met my mate six months ago. I could smell him on the training grounds of our pack lands, but couldn't tell which one he was. Every male was there practically. I had recently turned 18 and was an Omega. I was not ashamed of my status because I know it takes all kinds of people or...well, wolves in this case, to make up a pack or community. At least I wasn't ashamed at the time I met him.

I was heading home because a storm was coming when I heard a noise behind me. Once I turned around, I saw him. My mate. It was the Alpha of our pack. I was so shocked that I was paired with the Alpha that I just said yes to everything he said at first. It was easier then. Saying no only proved to be a problem when I realized what type of person he truly was.

He took me away from my parents, but that was not the issue. It was to be expected, especially with an Alpha. He swore them, and my siblings, to secrecy, as well as his Beta and the Beta's female. No one but my family, the Beta, and his mate knew about me. He didn't want anyone to know that he was mated to an Omega, but he couldn't seem to be able to reject me outright either. I was housebound in his home, only allowed to do menial, domestic chores, and then please him with my mouth or body when he came home from...doing whatever it was he was doing during the day.

At first, I just went with whatever he said, but when he began to beat me, I started to retaliate. One time he almost killed me because I was not allowed to go to the Pack hospital. The doctor or Beta or his mate would always tend to my wounds. After a while, I just stopped fighting back. I was wounded, bruised in my soul, and barely given enough to eat daily. My mate told me I was too fat, too small, too weak to be his mate, and that he deserved more in his female. I begged him to reject me and he broke my jaw when he punched me in the face. That night he branded me with silver and told me that even if he was stuck with a weak female like me, I belonged to him and to no one else.

The Beta, Carter, and his mate were kind to me and wanted to help. Carter came up with a plan, a plan to save me.

They had me break something in the house just before my mate came home. It was the urn that held his mother's ashes. I felt bad for doing it, but it was the only way that he would get angry enough to think he had killed me when he beat me this time.

You see, he had been trying to be gentler when the one doctor came by a week before the urn incident. I had suffered some serious wounds over a six month period and the doctor warned him I was headed for a brain injury and...well, the doctor didn't outright say that my mate was beating me, but he said that if I had any more serious 'mishaps', it could spell my death. Ironically enough, it kept my mate from beating me too hard for a short while. He would hit, but never too hard. Cut, but never too deep. I tried doing other things to make him beat me, but he was able to keep his temper under control for the most part. I don't know how; I just know that when he got too angry, he would leave the house for a few hours. He could have been fucking someone, I don't know, but I didn't honestly care. I was too broken to honestly give a shit anymore.

So, Carter told me I had to do something unforgivable to get my mate to beat me to the edge of death. He would think that I was dying and Carter would convince him to *have me dropped off outside of pack lands, pretend a rogue or something had gotten to me, or just let the elements do their work on my corpse. Carter said he would be the one to drop my body off since so few people knew I was the Alpha's mate. And my mate wouldn't trust just anyone with the disposal of a corpse.*

In a nutshell, the plan worked. I "dropped" the urn while cleaning, and he went ape shit. Beat me and even shifted – hence the claw marks you saw on me. Carter took me away in a car to 'get rid of me' and dropped me on the edge of your border. I was in and out of consciousness so I didn't actually know where I was until I woke up in the hospital and heard some of the nurses talking about Plumbrook. I had heard of it before, of course, but my pack never strayed far from home. By the Alpha's orders.

The whole point was to get me off pack lands and hope that someone – anyone – would come along to save me.

I think Carter knew what he was doing and I thank God for him. He knew just where to drop me off so that someone would come along and find me when they went looking for the interlopers.

Honestly, I didn't even care at that point whether or not someone found me. I was free of my mate, even if it had killed me. I think I even preferred death over the pain I felt – both the emotional and physical.

Liam read the words again and again. It was clear-cut, concise, but it was still hard to understand that it had been this poor creature's reality. A reality she had borne for six months. Six excruciating fucking months.

Anger welled up, hot and heavy in Liam, and his bright blue eyes blazed with a fury he tried to keep hidden from Elle. He didn't want to frighten her with misplaced fear of him. Liam, at least, would never hurt her.

"Who?"

Elle blinked back at him, the single word being the hardest single question she'd had to answer, ever.

"If you think I cannot find out who this Alpha shit is by myself, just remember that you mentioned the Beta's name," Liam told her, not unkindly. "There aren't too many Betas with the name Carter, I'm sure. If there's more than one in the whole tri-state area, I'll eat nothing but leafy greens for a week."

He was right. Carter was not necessarily an uncommon name, but pair it with his rank, and it would take less time to find out which Alpha had a second-in-command named Carter than it took for Elle to write out her little tale of woe.

Nodding her head, Elle gestured to the notepad so she could tell this Alpha. This time when she wrote, it was methodical and slow, as if writing the name would cause the man to appear out of thin air.

His name is Jeremiah. Jeremiah Bluth. Blackriver Pack.

As soon as Liam read the words, his face darkened, his brows knitting together in the middle as if in concentration or...disbelief.

When he looked back up at her, there was a strange look on his face. It was one of recognition, and Elle wondered if she had spelled her own doom by admitting her origins.

***

"Alpha, we have looked along every border and there is no sign of a body."

The head warrior of Blackriver, Jack, was giving his briefing to Jeremiah, who was sitting behind his desk, fiddling with papers, but not getting much done.

"No scent of her either?" Jeremiah's robust and gravelly voice grunted out.

"None," Jack stated with a firm nod. "We even went as far as foreign pack borders on all sides. Artemis thought he smelled something, but it was days old and very faint."

"In which direction?"

"West of here, but the scent was so fleeting, he said he couldn't be sure," Jack explained.

"Keep looking," Jeremiah told him, lacing his hands through his long, blond hair in irritation. "There has to be something, even if it's just a body. Animals would have left most of the bones, and the elements wouldn't have made them deteriorate this quickly – if there were any."

"Yes, Sir," Jack acknowledged, and left the office in a hurry.

Sitting back in his seat, Jeremiah couldn't think what had happened. When he had beat his little mate nearly to death, he thought that it had been a good idea to get rid of the body on foreign lands so that it would be assumed she had been killed by rogues. But now that certain people were starting to ask questions, he was bound by duty to look for something he had made go missing himself.

His mate. The weak, pathetic creature was not fit to be his Luna. She was beautiful, yes. As all mates are to their other half, she was everything he found physically attractive in a female. Hair as dark as a raven's wing and wide, cornflower-colored eyes, and such a petite little frame. Tiny in fact. She had been the average weight for her stature, but being mated to an Omega had made Jeremiah try to find anything unattractive about her that he could point out and use as a weapon against her. Perhaps if he had pushed her far enough, she would have taken the decision out of his hands and done away with herself, leaving him blameless.

Well, not *entirely* blameless. She had been far stronger than he thought, and had lasted thrice as long as he could have imagined. Who would have thought that an Omega, a subservient little bitch, could be so resilient? That was until he had beaten her until her heart had weakened and her body was almost unrecognizable.

He had shifted in anger and slashed at her body with his claws, pushing back the wolf mentality inside him that wished to shield his mate from harm. Even now, the beast inside him snarled and spat at him, yearning for its mate as completely as Jeremiah tried to block out *his* need for her. A need he never thought he could feel for anyone.

Why couldn't he have been paired with someone with a little clout, of a higher echelon? Why did it have to be her?

While his heart and mind had warred with each other and his inner wolf, he found himself moving closer to her at nights in the bed that they shared in his home. Her unconscious, eyelashes fluttering in the throes of REM sleep...it was the only time he could allow himself to breathe in her intoxicating scent and relish the feel of her small, soft body fitted against his. He couldn't let her see that he *did* care, because he wouldn't allow himself to become attached to her and the weakness she brought out in him, the tenderness he never allowed anyone to see. Not since *she* died when he was still young.

And damn Giselle's family. While he was mauling his small, defenseless mate, he didn't think of what he would tell her parents, her brother. And when they came around looking for her the day before, he had told them – no, *promised* them – he would look for her until she was found. In fact, he had lied outright and told them that he'd had Carter searching everywhere for her. She had gone out one day and hadn't come back, he said to them. And then he lied again and told them he had been searching since she went missing but had been keeping it a secret since he had been planning on announcing her as Luna by the end of the month. He alleged he didn't want his pack to know he had lost his mate.

Lies, lies, and more lies, until they piled up on top of each other and hid the truth. He had no plans for letting anyone know – *ever* – that he was mated to a lowly wolf with the low ranking of Omega, and never would. He needed a strong coupling, one with a female of higher standing, one who would give him strong children through their combined blood. Blood of an Alpha with a Gamma, Delta, or Beta bloodline. He would settle for nothing less.

And then to top everything off, they couldn't even find her body. He was certain that they would at least find her corpse, even if it was only bones. His "search" for his mate, and the Kincaid's youngest daughter, was turning into a real quest to find the dead body of Giselle Kincaid. He could not stop until he found some trace of her.

His mind told him she was gone, and a part of him – most likely that of his wolf – mourned her, but something, some indecipherable thing inside him, knew something wasn't quite right.

Carter thought that perhaps some animal had drug her away and feasted on her body in the privacy of its own den, but even with all the caves and caverns in that part of the state, they should have at least smelled her decaying body. So far they had come up with nothing, not even a trace of her, except for that fleeting scent off to the west that Jack had mentioned.

Perhaps she was far stronger than Jeremiah had thought and she was still alive somewhere, being tended to by humans or by another pack. He knew it was doubtful. He had seen the death in her eyes, but...there had been something else. A light, almost like she was glad to be going, and that made him ill at the thought of it.

And sleep. Sleep. Ever since she hadn't been around to lie in his bed with him, it had been infrequent and fitful. It made his usual bad temper even more pronounced and he found himself snapping at everyone these days. Even Carter, and the man was his best friend.

A knock on the door brought Jeremiah out of his thoughts.

"Come in," he called out, his weary voice sluggish with exhaustion.

"Jere, any word?" Carter asked as soon as the door was closed behind him and they were alone.

"None," the Alpha told his friend. "How can she have just

vanished into thin air? Something should have been found by now. Even a scrap of fabric, unless vultures or mountain lions eat cotton as well meat."

"Well, you know what I think about it all," Carter told him, nodding his head.

"Yes, I know," Jeremiah said quickly, his temper threatening to flare up again. "But I don't buy it. If the men don't smell her, they should at least smell her corpse – but nothing!"

"Well, the only thing we can do is keep looking, and if she's not found within a week or two we can declare her dead and have a memorial or something. Closure for her family and friends," Carter said.

"I suppose," Jeremiah said, his heart sinking fast. Again, his wolf rioted in the back of his mind, wanting to find her – the woman he was destined to be with, but couldn't.

"You never wanted her in the first place," Carter reminded him bluntly.

"Y-yes, you're right." Only it didn't seem true, because it wasn't. She was all he could think if, even more so now that she was gone. Dead(?) and gone. "But...it doesn't feel like she's gone. I would have felt something, wouldn't I?"

"You never marked and mated, so we will never know for sure," Carter said, jaw tightening in agitation at his friend.

"You think I'm a fool," Jeremiah told him, nonplussed.

"I...yes. Yes, I do." Carter wouldn't lie if the man asked him a question as such.

"Do you understand why I can't have her?"

"No, I don't understand, but I am not an Alpha."

"She'll weaken me, weaken the pack," Jeremiah claimed, his voice low.

"She would strengthen you *and* our pack," Carter disagreed.

"She's an Omega."

"And your destined. Mistakes in matings aren't made unless we carve them out for ourselves," Carter said, biting back the harsher words he wished to say.

You fucking fool. Too focused on your power to see that your mate is your better half, that she would temper your rage if you would only have let her in.

But Carter was glad he had helped the little would-be Luna escape from what would certainly have been her death. If not the physical one, then her spiritual demise under the authoritarian

Alpha, Jeremiah Bluth.

Chapter 6

"Jeremiah?" Liam didn't need to repeat the last name. He knew it all too well. Or, at least he thought he had. The man had been a friend of his when they were children.

Elle cocked her head uncertainly and then nodded.

"Blond hair, brown eyes? Beauty mark on his left wrist in the shape of a mushroom?" Liam asked, trying to make it clear they were speaking of the same person.

Elle's eyes widened in fright. Liam knew the man.

She stood up from the bed, looking ready to flee the room at a moment's notice. Hell, she was ready to flee the state at this point.

She knew it had been a bad idea to talk about this with a man she hardly knew. Or in this case, write about it. She was sure Liam was going to send her back to him. Mates weren't meant to be apart, no matter what the circumstances.

The tension in the air made the atmosphere thick and cloying, and Elle's feet moved away from the Alpha on his bed. As she was about to make a break for the door, Liam stood up, one hand held out in a halting gesture.

"Stop, Elle," he said. "I won't tell anyone where you came from, and I won't contact Jeremiah. I promise you this."

She didn't know whether to believe him or not, and she bent her knees slightly, legs spread in a defensive stance. He may be an Alpha, but she would not go quietly if he meant to bring her back to Blackriver Pack.

"Elle, please listen to me," Liam's voice was serene, almost drowsy, and it calmed her somewhat, though her emotional feelers were still out and testing the flavor of the air.

Slowly, Liam made his way over to Elle and placed a gentle hand on her elbow in an attempt to calm her and bring her back toward the bed so he could have his say.

"It's true that I know the man," Liam told her, a cautious Elle following him towards his bed. "Most Alphas have at least heard of the each other, particularly the ones that live close by our territories. Jeremiah, though – he is someone I know personally. Or I should say *knew*, because we used to be friends at some point."

The way Liam said Jeremiah's name with distaste made Elle feel marginally better. There was bad blood between the two – that much she could tell.

"At one point when we were young, I would have considered Jeremiah Bluth one of my closest friends," Liam admitted. "That was until we were in our teens and his mother passed away."

Elle blinked big eyes at him, nodding for him to go on.

Liam relaxed, sure Elle would hear him out and not run from him, at least for the moment.

"There's about one and a half years age difference between Jeremiah and I," Liam began. "When I was 13 and he was going on 12, Jeremiah's father decided that being Beta of Plumbrook wasn't good enough for him and he decided to challenge the old Alpha of Blackriver, Elias Grady. Elias had 5 daughters before his wife bore him a son. It was thought that his mate could only bear him females and many thought him too weak to lead the pack. Word got around that his female was pregnant again and, this time, they got confirmation before the birth. It was going to be a boy and Jeremiah's father, Jonas, decided to strike and take over his pack.

"Jonas timed his attack carefully and some say he had a spy within Blackriver who would tell him when Elias was at his weakest," Liam explained. "When Elias' mate went into labor, Jonas attacked and defeated Elias, who was quite distracted by the birth of his son. He was killed just as his son, Tobias, was being born. The Beta of Blackriver was livid and fiercely loyal to Elias. He went to attack Jonas to keep him from ruling the pack, and instead ended up killing Jeremiah's mother, Lucinda instead."

Elle had heard a version of the hostile takeover before from her father who loved studying the histories of his pack, as well as others. It suited him as a hobby since he was a teacher by profession. Still, everything her father had said almost sounded like a fairytale, some story that happened in some far-off land instead of on the territory she had lived and grown up on. It was almost as if she was hearing this information, for the first time, from Liam.

"Jeremiah loved his mother dearly and was distraught," Liam explained. "After her death, he became cold and distant, not speaking to his friends and swearing he hoped to never find his mate. Once he hit puberty, he changed his tune and he started to say he hoped his mate had strong blood. Gamma or better. You see, his mother had been an Omega before she had been mated with his father and Jeremiah always thought that because she was an Omega, she was too weak. I think his distaste for...mating with you stems from all of that. He thinks that if he has a mate of "low" blood, he will lose her as well. I don't think he hated you; he just hated what you are."

It made sense to Elle. She had been too young to remember much of what had happened. She was only 7 at the time of the exchange of power to the Bluths, and it had been overnight and swift. Too swift for another challenge to come Jonas Bluth's way. Especially after he had killed the Beta who had accidentally killed his mate.

"Elle," Liam said softly. "I'm not saying that what he did is understandable or right. I'm just simply giving my opinion on why he may have rejected you for your status in the pack. Personally, I have no problems with Omegas, were I mated to one or not."

Elle nodded and grabbed the notepad that had been discarded on the bed.

Why did you say he was your friend? What happened that tore you apart?

Liam looked at her and sighed.

"Elle, do you remember when I told you that if you told me your story, I would tell you mine?"

Elle nodded, wondering how this pertained to her mate.

"Well, the reason Jeremiah and I no longer speak has to do with my past," Liam told her, piercing her with his intense cerulean blue eyes. The color of them seemed to change with his mood.

Elle licked her lips, wetting them, and watched as Liam's eyes flickered to the motion and then back up at her irises. She nodded again with her head, gesturing for him to go on.

"Jeremiah...after he pulled away from his friends and became the cold, calculated monster he is today, only remained close with two people in his life," Liam told her. His Adam's apple worked up and down as he swallowed loudly around the threatening lump in his throat.

"He only remained tight with his father and his sister," Liam said, his voice low and husky. "His *twin* sister."

Elle was confused. All the time she had been with Jeremiah, he had never mentioned his sister and she had assumed he was an only child.

"I see that you are confused, little wolf," Liam told her, wishing he didn't find the look on her face so freakin' adorable. It pinched at his heart. "Listen closely. All will make sense soon."

Liam got up from the bed and walked over to his dresser. Opening a drawer, he sifted through his socks and came out with a small photo album. It was brown leather with gold engraved lettering. Liam seemed to weigh it in his hands for a moment before bringing it back toward the bed and setting it down in his lap. He breathed deeply for a few moments before opening it up and quickly flipping through the pages.

Elle could see that many were of Liam and what she assumed was his family. An older gentleman with a woman, the woman being the spitting image of Liam with her dark hair and startling clear blue eyes. They were vibrant against her pale, creamy skin.

Liam flipped the pages until he was a third of the way through the album. Slowly, he flipped another page and turned the book around to show Elle. He pointed to one photo in particular of him with a female with flaming red hair and chocolate brown eyes.

The female appeared to be late teens or early twenties and was being held by a smiling Liam. She was perched on his knee and he had his arm around her waist. They both looked happy, and she wondered how old the photo was.

"That is Cecilia, my mate," Liam told her.

Elle startled, and looked up at him.

Mate? But...what?

"Cecilia came from your old pack, Blackriver," Liam said. "I met her the year I turned 21 a few years ago. At first, I was ecstatic to have finally found my mate. I wouldn't have to attend The Claiming and find myself a female from the other unmated she-wolves. I had wanted my own true mate, not a cheap imitation.

"At first, everything was great. Unicorns shooting glitter out their asses and the like," Liam said, a small, sad smile on his face. "When things started to go south, I knew something was off about Cecilia. She..." Liam blinked and sucked in a steadying breath before continuing. "She started to act strangely around the time we marked and mated. It was like she was a different person, and I would sometimes find her mumbling to herself when no one was around."

Elle looked at Liam, concern in her eyes. This must be why he didn't sleep well. His mate – wherever she was – was obviously unwell. It was a blow to him, to be sure.

"I convinced her to go to the pack clinic and Doctor D'Amato ran some physical and psychiatric tests to find out what was wrong with her," Liam looked down at the photo and then back up at Elle. "She was eventually diagnosed with schizophrenia, meaning she heard voices that weren't there. Sometimes, the voices would tell her to...to do things. To herself, to others. She was prescribed all types of medications for the condition, but once she felt well enough, she would stop taking the medicine, thinking she was miraculously cured. But mental disorders are not like infections. They don't go away with a rigorous course of antibiotics. They're...for life."

Liam pointed to the photo and tapped on it.

"This was the last photo I have of her before she became really ill," Liam said, brows knotting together over his sculpted nose. "I couldn't bear to take photographs of her when she was unwell. She was disheveled and I didn't want any reminders of her illness. This is also the only photograph I have to remember her by."

Liam looked at the photograph one more time and closed his eyes as he shut the small book with a soft clapping sound.

"Elle, Cecilia passed away at the age of 20," Liam told her. "She had stopped taking her medication and the voices...they came back. They always did after she stopped taking her medicines. Satan, the ghost of Hitler, FDR – they were all people she imagined that spoke to her, telling her to do...evil things to herself and others. Once, she tried to suffocate me in my sleep because she believed I was trying to slowly poison her food. She had to be sedated and hospitalized for a full month. When she came out, she was a zombie. Flat affect, no personality. She was like a completely different person. She wasn't *my* Cecilia anymore. She was a medicated shell of a person and I hated it. But, I loved her and would have done anything to see her happy and well."

Liam put the book away and came back to the bed before hunkering down in front of Elle and placing a warm hand on her knee.

"Cecilia killed herself about two weeks after she left the hospital," Liam croaked out, his jaw twitching. "She pocketed her medications in her cheek and then spat them out the window into the snow."

Elle slowly raised her hands out to her sides in a *how* gesture.

"She slit her wrists before hanging herself in our bedroom," Liam said, eyes bright and glassy. "I guess she wanted to be sure she got the job done. But – that's not all.

"Cecilia was Jeremiah's twin sister," Liam rasped out. "She killed herself and Jeremiah... Jeremiah blamed me for it."

Elle's eyes widened, looking doe-like as ever when Liam told her about his previous mate. Her fingers clenched slightly before she reached out for her notepad, taking it from its place on the bed and writing quickly on it.

I'm so sorry, Alpha. I thank you for sharing your story with me. I hope you don't mind if I ask a personal question since we are having this heart to heart.

What will you do without your mate? How will you hand your pack down without a mate to have pups with?

Liam smiled – not his sad, dreary smile, but one that was thinking of this kind and caring female in his midst. One who thought of other people's problems before her own.

"I was thinking of giving power over to the first-born son of my sister," Liam said. "But she lives so far away – halfway across the country – that I don't know if Arden will let her oldest son move 1,500 miles to another pack to take over. She is very much the motherly type figure, one I could see becoming a helicopter parent in the future. If she isn't already."

Arden. Such a pretty name. But if you cannot hand the pack down to your nephew in the future, how will you choose someone worthy of your station?

"You sound like Blake," Liam told her with a smile. "He's always bothering me to choose a mate at The Claiming. I thought he was going to hogtie me and force me to go this year, but the Elders have been generous in giving me some time to get over the death of my true mate. And giving me ample time to find a second chance one, if one exists for me."

It is not likely for that to happen though, is it? I heard of a she-wolf with two mates on the west coast who, under very mysterious circumstances, mated with two males successfully, one her second chance mate. I hardly believed it. I thought they must be smoking their own crops over in California.

Liam barked out a laugh, a hale, hearty sound that made Elle smile at the whimsical look in his eyes. It wasn't an expression he seemed to wear too often. At least not that she had seen.

And now she knew why.

"Yes, it is difficult to find a second chance mate, which is why The Claiming ritual was put in place," Liam explained, though Elle already knew that. "I suppose that since it's been a few years, the Elders will most likely start to hound me to attend. They aren't very lenient, though they have loosened the reins a bit in the past few years."

Will you attend? The Claiming, that is. To be mated to

one the true way is difficult enough at times, but to choose someone at random would be a lot harder I would reckon.

"I may not have to," Liam told her. "There has been talk about giving males with deceased mates the right to choose whether to participate or not, particularly Alphas."

Elle's brows furrowed cutely over her eyes, her lips thinning in unconcealed disapproval.

"I know it's not fair," he told her. "She-wolves don't seem to garner as many rights as the men in Were society, do they? Most unfair, in my opinion. But there's an even greater a gap when it comes to hierarchy. The higher up you go in the pecking order, the more leniency it seems that you accumulate. I assume it was the same at Blackriver. From what I know of Jeremiah and the additional information you have told me, he doesn't seem a man to hold any regard for lower ranking wolves. Pathetic, if you ask me."

It takes all kinds to form a society. Imagine if we were to have a society of only Alphas...they would end up all killing each other. Or Omegas....there would be no security and utter chaos. Omegas were meant to serve, and I am not ashamed to count myself among them.

Liam smiled again, this time even wider.

"Nor should you be," he told her.

***

"Excuse me?"

Blake blinked, thinking he couldn't have understood Liam correctly. Perhaps he hadn't had enough caffeine that morning. Stupid K-cups. He was convinced they were watered down imitations of the really good stuff. The kind of coffee that put hair on your chest and ass and pumped you up with so much hi-octane go-go juice that a man – or wolf – could take on a small army and suffer from nary a scratch or two.

"You heard me, Blake," Liam told him from behind the desk in his office. "Elle is to get full pack protection, before and after she takes her oath as a wolf of Plumbrook."

"The fuck, Liam?"

"I know who **JB** is," Liam said, stopping the next words that wanted to come barreling out of Blake's open mouth.

"Who? Who the fuck is he?" Blake asked. If the anger had been directed at Liam, Blake would have lost his nuts. As it was, Colleen was going to flip her shit when she found out. She was acting half mother hen and half big sister to Elle and was already sharpening her proverbial knives so she could filet the offending man's cock and serve it to him on a platter.

"Jeremiah Bluth," Liam stated, a growl lingering under the man's name.

"The fuck?"

Liam sighed.

"Do you know any other cuss words today, or were you planning on helping me teach Elle to swear first?" Liam asked. "I was going to start with important words like *the*, and *food*, and maybe some people's names, but if you wanted to start her out more colorfully, please let me know."

"I just...*fuck!* Jeremiah? The Alpha?" Blake was slow on the uptake today, banging on only half the cylinders in his engine that morning.

"Yes, Jeremiah, the usurper's fucking son," Liam reiterated. "None other."

"He's going to come looking for her if he doesn't find her body," Blake pointed out.

"Not necessarily," Liam said, sitting back in his chair. "He could decide that she was most likely carried off by scavenger beasts or that she was tossed into one of the lakes or rivers."

"But their bond-"

"Minimal at best," Liam interjected. "He never marked her, and there was no emotional tie beyond the initial mating pull."

"Are...are you sure?" Blake looked dubious, and the creases in his forehead spoke like Braille to the blind of his concern.

"Positive," Liam said. "She could have died and he wouldn't have felt it. Not that he would have cared."

"Right." Blake still looked doubtful, but trusted his friend implicitly.

"Okay, now that we're through with that, you can tell me what Colleen has prepared for the monthly bonfire," Liam told him, already moving on from the business of Jeremiah and his unappreciated – and now protected – mate.

Blake let his eyes do all the talking for him and rolled them exaggeratedly.

"You know Colleen," Blake told him. "Going overboard as usual. Wanted to pay a fucking band because this will be Gi-uhm, Elle's first bonfire and everything. I told her to cool it, but you know what I always say when she gets this way."

"Right," Liam said, shifting uncomfortably.

"If you would just pick a chosen mate or attend The Claiming-"

"We would have a Luna that could do it instead of Colleen," Liam finished, having heard this line for what seemed like decades of his life.

"Or just someone else besides me and you reeling her in when she gets a little too gung-ho," Blake added. "A calming influence. Someone like..." He dramatically snapped his fingers in his little "Ah, Eureka!" moment. "Someone like Elle!"

Liam narrowed his gaze on Blake. He could smell Colleen all over this "suggestion".

"Not you too," Liam told him with a sigh. "Please tell me that this was all Colleen's idea and not something you thought up yourself."

Blake shrugged, winking at his friend.

"I promised her I would bring it up at least once," Blake said on a laugh. "I honestly don't care who you choose to be your mate as long as it's not one of those fucking wretched plastics that wear so much makeup they resemble that creepy clown from *IT*. Shit's nasty."

"I promise to take a mate someday," Liam said, tamping down on rolling his eyes. He had been saying that for the past year to Blake and still couldn't choose. No one appealed to him on that level.

Well, that was until quite recently.

***

Elle had woken up, clearing her throat to test if the minimal pain had gone away. There was a slight twinge, but it had been on the top membrane of her throat, not internally, and that had made her smile. Perhaps she could start practicing talking today.

A couple of days had gone by and, little by little, the pain in her body had eased until it felt no stronger than a slight ache in her muscles – the kind you might have felt after a vigorous workout at the gym. Not that she had ever been one to attend a gym. Music, not muscles, was more her thing, and she wondered if Liam had an iPod or something hanging around. She could do with some tunes while she kept house for him.

As she was mopping the kitchen floor after having dusted, swept, and wiped every surface in the room clean, she heard a sound coming from the front of the house.

"Knock, knock!" a cheery voice sing-songed from just inside the front door.

Elle was going to need to lock the front door to keep Colleen from barging in at any time of the day or night. Liam may have been used to it, but it always startled Elle, making her heart race in her chest and think of all the worst possible scenarios of who it could be. Jeremiah or one of his evil-doing henchmen topped her list of likely suspects, though she hoped the smell of other wolves and the fact that she was on another pack's land would keep him far, far away from her. Not so much for her sake as for the good shifters of Plumbrook. She hadn't met many yet as she was still skittish when it came to strangers, but she could tell that they were a close-knit group, made up of decent wolves who only wished for peace amongst themselves and other neighboring packs. At least that was the vibe she was getting as she watched them move about from the upper windows of the Alpha's home in between cleaning, cooking, and whatever else needed to be done around the home.

Scheduling her time always worked best for Elle. Though she could be flighty and lose herself to her music at times – be it in her head or out of it – if she didn't make herself a schedule, she ended up sidetracked and gazing off into space. Getting lost in her own mind, her mother had called it, shaking her head. Therefore, she allotted different days for different chores.

The thought of her mother made Elle sad, wondering if she would ever be able to see her family again. Colleen had taken to her like a fish to water and Blake pretty much followed along with whatever Colleen did. Liam was far more caring than any Alpha she had ever met, though he didn't often show it in public. His demeanor inside his home differed drastically from the stalwart, reticent one he portrayed in front of his pack. But that was sort of to be expected. Any hint of his love for comic books and the occasional Rom Com, and he was sure to be seen as a little less macho in front of his pack. And they weren't exactly menacing traits to outsiders either. Appearances were everything.

As she let the kitchen floors dry and walked toward the sound of Colleen's voice, she swiped an arm over her forehead, catching the thin sheen of sweat on her brow with her small forearm.

Smiling as a greeting, Elle walked towards Colleen, whose eyes lit up to see Elle coming toward her, seeming completely at ease in the Alpha's home and with her.

"Are you done being domestic for the day?" Colleen asked, watching as Elle eyed the bags she had in one of her hands.

Elle nodded, then gestured toward the bags, a quizzical look on her face. Colleen's grin grew wider in response.

"Have you forgotten? It's the bonfire tonight and we're going to get ready together," Colleen reminded her.

The bonfire. She had completely forgotten and she was absolutely drenched in sweat.

"Don't worry," Colleen, who had gotten very good at reading Elle's facial expressions, said. "We have plenty of time as it's not for a few more hours. They'll start lighting the timber at 8-ish or so, but they'll have the meat started on the spits even before that."

That sounded good to Elle and she nodded, her smile resurfacing.

"Well, first things first, my friend," Colleen said, nose wrinkling a bit. "You're dripping with sweat and that can't be comfortable. Let's get you showered and then we can pick out something to wear. I brought some makeup I think would look good on you. Less is more since your natural complexion is quite lovely. I say some mascara and lip tinting gloss or a peachy color lipstick possibly?"

Colleen continued to talk as she walked with Elle to the stairs. She chatted the whole way up and Elle was sure that she would have followed her into the bathroom to continue her soliloquy if Elle hadn't specifically closed the door behind her to get undressed. Shower time should be peaceful and, while Colleen's constant babbling didn't bother her, she wanted to be alone in the bathroom and test out her own voice.

It was only a rasp so far, but at least it was something. It was both encouraging and disheartening, but she was certain she'd be able to make noise, or even words, soon enough. The doctor had been most sure she could heal, though the progress made would be unknown for a while.

Wrapped in a robe, Elle made her way to her bedroom where she could hear Colleen still talking. To herself or on the phone, she had no clue – not that it mattered.

"...showering, then we'll get ready and come down after they start the spits," Colleen was saying. "I think introductions should be done slowly...no need to overwhelm...hey, let me call you back."

Elle cocked her head, asking a silent question as Colleen looked over at her in the doorway.

"That was Blake," Colleen told her. "He's with Liam and they're just finishing up so they can get home to get ready. Men are so lucky they don't have to put on makeup or high heels to look good."

Elle's eyes widened and she shook her head. She wasn't a fan of heels. Ballet flats or sneakers were more her thing, and she hoped she had something to go with whatever she was sure Colleen would hassle her to wear.

"Read 'ya loud and clear," Colleen said with a smile. "We'll keep the foot apparel on the down low – literally." Then she beamed at Elle and opened her closet door.

"You ready to do this thing?"

Chapter 7

A trickle of wolves – in human form, of course – started to arrive around 8 PM. Many of the first were families with little kids who couldn't stay as long, and the younger, unattached folk who were always quick to get the party started. Since Colleen had overseen the planning of the event, she was there first, along with a shy Elle who watched the comings and goings with bright, anxious eyes.

It wasn't that she was truly frightened of crowds or overwhelmed with the number of people coming, it was more that she was looking out for any faces that seemed familiar to her. Mates were found, moves to another pack were made. You never knew who you would run into in the grand scheme of things.

Colleen, being the social butterfly she was, seemed to know everyone's name, rank, and shoe size. It was amazing that she could keep them all straight. And when introducing Elle, she always prefaced it with a disclaimer about Elle's inability to vocalize.

"Jason, come meet Elle!" Colleen called over to a young man around Elle's age. He sauntered over with a broad smile before taking in Elle's small form.

"Jason, this is Elle. She's new here and still recuperating from an injury to her throat," Colleen said in her rapid-fire manner of speaking. "She can't speak yet, but she understands you and if she has anything to say, she's got that handy little notepad she can use." She gestured to the pad of paper in Elle's hand.

"Hey, Elle," Jason said, his grin widening. "Welcome to Plumbrook. What brings you here?"

Before leaving for the party, Colleen had come up with some answers to the commonest of the questions she would probably receive. The biggest, of course, being where she came from and why.

"In a nutshell, her parents moved to the area for work recently, and since her Dad's a cop and on call much of the time, they're staying in town," Colleen told him, practiced words shooting from her mouth like bullets from a gun. "She's staying in the Alpha's home where she works. It makes more sense that way."

Jason's surprise was only made apparent by the slight widening of his eyes. Then he nodded in understanding. As if it was every day that a new wolf made their home with the Alpha who had never before taken in boarders, much less one so young, pretty, and apparently unattached.

"I see," Jason said, his voice measured before blinking and coming out of whatever thoughts that had been hurtling through his mind for the briefest of moments.

Colleen walked off to greet more guests, her loud voice ricocheting off the sides of the buildings around the spits and bouncing back with rock-solid precision. It was enough to give one a headache.

"So, where are you from originally?" Jason asked, seeming to latch onto a topic he was comfortable with.

California. San Diego to be exact.

Elle had been there once to visit a relative a few years ago, so she at least knew a little bit about the city.

Smiling, Jason responded. "Much different weather in New England. Have you ever seen snow?"

Once when I went on vacation. My parents thought it would be fun to learn how to ski. We came back 2 days later with Dad's foot in a cast. He broke it in two places after he decided to tussle with the wrong tree.

That much was at least true. Her family had headed to a ski resort once in southern New York State and had never gone back after her father's little incident.

Jason laughed, his voice booming out as he tossed his head back. Elle smiled back at him, wishing she could hear her own laugh again. The thought was sobering, but she pushed through it with a smile.

"If you don't mind me asking, what's your rank?" Jason questioned, eyes brightening a bit.

Omega.

"Me too," Jason said, his demeanor brightening. "I just turned 18 a couple of weeks ago. What about you?"

Elle hesitated. If she admitted she was 18, he could ask if she was mated. That would have set off a bunch of uncomfortable questions that Elle didn't know how to answer. Answer the truth and Jeremiah *could* find out about her. Answer with a lie, she would have to live that lie. And that made her uncomfortable.

In the end, she ended up telling him the truth about being 18, and the boy just nodded, face falling for a moment until he replaced it with another hearty smile.

"No mate then I take it," he said a little stiffly.

No. You?

"Not yet," Jason said. "It's still early though. I would like to meet her, but not everyone does find a mate anymore. Or if they do, it doesn't always work out, ya know?"

Elle smiled sadly. She knew that all too well, though she thought Jason was exaggerating. While it was true that not everyone found their perfect match, 99.9% of the time the coupling worked out for the better, and not like Elle and her Alpha mate.

Jason and Elle talked for a while, and Elle started to ask so many questions her hand started to cramp up.

"What's wrong?" Jason asked, watching as Elle flexed her wrist and fingers.

Not used to writing so much. I can't wait until I get my voice back.

Jason laughed and reached out for Elle's hand, starting to massage the wrist and muscles surrounding it. Elle sighed, a little uncomfortable with the familiar gesture, but it felt too good to make the young man stop.

"That's my fault," Jason said with a grin. "I've sort of talked your ear off. This should help."

He continued to talk to her about life in the pack, well-known stories as well as stories of his own youth. He didn't ask questions, to which Elle was grateful for. Her hand was sore, and Jason was able to pick up on some of her hand gestures and facial expressions. It helped a lot since she did have questions, but her hand was practically humming with fatigue.

"What's going on here?" asked a curious, deep voice that was all too familiar to Elle.

Jason and Elle looked toward the sound and found the Alpha, two drinks in his hand and his eyes locked onto where Jason was massaging and kneading.

***

"No big announcement. I was very clear with that," Liam said to Blake and Trace, who were in the Alpha's office and standing across the desk from where he stood. "We'll let her meet people at her own pace. Colleen's sociable and talkative enough to take away most of any awkwardness Elle may feel at meeting the pack as a whole."

It was past 8:30 PM, and they were running late to the function. The warriors had come by with news of another group of wolves searching the edges of their territory, and Liam was afraid that they might be shifters from Blackriver. He had increased patrols immediately and sent out a group of wolves with the head enforcer as a liaison in case they tried to encroach on their land. They had waited as long as they could before the head enforcer had mindlinked him to say that no one could be found.

Perfect. Maybe they had given up. Liam was almost positive that since they did not smell rogue, they were most likely looking for Elle. He didn't want to think that at first, but he could find no other reason why unknown wolves would search the areas just beyond his territory. He hoped they gave up soon.

The three spoke and made up an enhanced patrol schedule for the next few days, Trace eventually running off to meet with the head warrior who would be back at any time now.

"I've got to change and then I'll head to the bonfire," Liam said, placing his leather jacket over his forearm and moving toward the door.

"Colleen says Elle is doing fine," Blake said as the two of them left the office and headed out the front door. "Making friends and such."

"Friends? What friends?" Liam asked, his voice quick and tight.

"I didn't ask specifics," Blake said blandly. "I'm not the party police, Liam. Go see for yourself if you want to know so badly."

He would. His jaw ticked in irritation at his second in command, and his pace increased slightly. He told himself that he needed to make sure that Elle was surrounding herself with the right people and not some of the wolves – like the plastics – that would take advantage of her kind and giving nature.

After a quick shower, Liam dressed, ran a comb quickly through his straight, black hair, and walked out his front door. The noises from the bonfire were getting louder, so he knew that almost everyone was there.

As he made his way through the crowd, many of the wolves nodded at him with respect or greeted him, calling out to their Alpha and wishing him a good evening. Liam nodded back, smiling down on occasion at some of the braver toddlers who came up to him to hug his legs. Those brave little souls were quickly pulled away by embarrassed mothers and apologetic fathers who greeted Liam before pulling their children into their arms to let the Alpha go about his business.

"Colleen's outdone herself this time," Trace mused from behind Liam's left shoulder. "We've got enough food here to last a week."

Liam's lips twitched. The spits were crackling with deer, pig, and other meats, while there were coolers filled with beverages and tables stuffed with side dishes.

"Colleen thought this was a proper way to greet the new wolf," Liam explained.

"Has she taken the oath yet?" Trace asked.

"Not yet," Liam replied. "I was going to wait a little bit until she got more of her voice back."

"Ah."

Trace remained quiet, looking on in amusement as Liam scoured the crowd, searching. He could only surmise who he was looking for, but if he was a betting man, he would have guessed it would be Elle. The man seemed overly protective of the mute wolf, having taken her so easily under his wing and offering her pack protection like she had been born and bred at Plumbrook.

Trace's eyes met with Blake's, and the latter raised a brow, looking at Liam pointedly and then jerking his head over his shoulder to his right. Trace figured Elle was that way, and cleared his throat before speaking.

"I think I see Colleen that way," Trace said. "Elle must be with her." Trace was better at subtle than Blake was.

Liam moved toward where Trace was pointing without saying anything, though his steps were more assured, making Trace think he was right on the money when he thought the man was looking for his newest almost-pack member.

Colleen was talking with a group while tossing out commands to others that were preparing more food. How she held a conversation and ordered people about was something Liam found hard to fathom, but she did it with aplomb and easy grace.

"Oh, there's Elle," Trace said, looking past Colleen and her group mingling.

Liam's eyes flickered over to Colleen's left shoulder and saw that Elle was there, nodding at someone, her face a little strained and shoulders tense. He couldn't see much more than her head, but it was enough to know that she was chatting with someone, and Liam's feet moved forward to the coolers where he grabbed two drinks at random and walked toward Colleen, Elle, and whomever she was speaking with.

Liam looked around, noticing that many people were watching the new wolf as well while she chatted with...well, someone. Liam still couldn't see who it was, but he didn't like the looks that many of the unmated males gave her as they talked and watched the newcomer with interest. A few looked merely curious, but most of the men watched her with a little too much curiosity for Liam's liking.

And no wonder. What the fuck was she wearing? This had to be Colleen's doing. Only Colleen would dress Elle in something that would be more welcome on a dance club floor than a barbecue/bonfire.

Liam could immediately tell that Elle had gained a little weight. Her arms were no longer bone thin, and her breasts had filled out a bit more. He was sure the bras that Colleen had purchased for her would probably fit now, but that didn't matter at the moment. There was no way in hell what she was wearing would need a bra underneath it.

The dark burgundy dress was simple, hugging her soft curves and accentuating her small waist. It was only a few notches above putting her in spandex and calling it a day.

Jeremiah was a fucking fool to have let this one slip away. It appeased Liam somewhat, that Elle had given him the slip and was now looking healthy on his own territory instead of twig-thin and terrified.

Liam also could finally see over the crowd to who Elle was chatting with. It was an Omega named...Johnson? Josh? He couldn't remember off the top of his head, but one thing he did know – he didn't appreciate the familiarity between the two and how close they stood.

And the fact that the young man seemed to be holding her hand in both of his.

Eyes narrowing minutely, he walked over to the two, nodding to a smirking Colleen who had caught sight of him, and went up to Elle and her friend.

"What's going on here?" Liam asked, his eyes fixed pointedly at their connected hands.

"Alpha, I was just rubbing some of the soreness from her wrist," the young man said, dropping Elle's hand like it was a hot potato. "We were talking quite a bit and she nearly filled the entire notepad with her writing."

Liam saw that Elle had a pen and paper in her left hand, clutching it like a security blanket.

Hmm...

"Are you hurt?" Liam asked, ignoring the fact that Jason stepped another foot away from Elle and was watching the Alpha with interested eyes.

Elle shook her head and mimicked writing before holding her sore wrist and feigning a pained expression.

"Here, I got you a drink," Liam told her, handing it to her and taking the pad of paper and pen from her. He placed them into his back pocket where they stuck out a bit. "Let me see your wrist."

Maybe he should get her an iPad or something if her thin little wrist was going to be a problem. She could type on it and – let's face it, now – it was probably a bit more environmentally friendly. Save the trees and all that.

"This okay?" he asked, catching Elle's eyes as she looked up and nodded. He was massaging her wrist, his warm hands pressing and manipulating the joint to get to all the sore spots.

They stood there in companionable silence, Liam tending to her wrist as Jason got up the nerve to tell them he was taking his leave.

"Well, it was good meeting you, Elle." Liam could tell just how good it was for him to meet her and he frowned. The boy that seemed to be smitten with her was shifting a little awkwardly from foot to foot, looking hesitant to depart.

Elle smiled brightly at him and nodded her head, confirming that she felt the same.

Liam and Elle both watched as Jason disappeared into the crowd, the amount of people there easily swallowing him up.

"Having fun? You look very lovely this evening, by the way," Liam told her, that last sentence coming out before he could stop it.

Her hands occupied, Elle nodded and mouthed *thank you* to the Alpha. His hands were still working her wrist, so she couldn't really jot her thanks down.

Watching her lips round out to form the words, Liam knew he was in trouble. Big fucking trouble.

***

"Elle, watch this!" piped up a small voice. It belonged to a little girl in a lavender baby doll dress with white leggings underneath. The knees of them were stained with grass, and Elle hoped they weren't permanently ruined.

The little girl couldn't have been more than five, but she ran for a bit and then did a perfectly executed cartwheel.

Elle smiled brightly, clapping her hands together and watching as the little girl ran over to her for a congratulatory hug.

Casey – who was four and a half years old, thank you very much

– giggled and squealed a bit as Elle caught the girl as she tried to jump into the air for her hug.

Another small voice piped up, a close friend of Casey's, and pleaded with Elle to watch her as she tried to best her friend in the apparent cartwheel competition.

Liam watched from afar, amused, while sipping a soda. He had seen the little grouping of children grow from two, to six, to ten little ones. When the first two children had come over to ask to play with her, Liam had almost been certain Elle would say no. To his surprise, she had gone off with the tykes to the edges of the party where there was space, and they had been playing together until the children had decided it was time for an all-out acrobatic war. Round-offs, tumbling, and cartwheels for the past half hour, Elle reacting like each tumbling pass was an Olympic-worthy floor routine.

"Fuck, you have it bad," a deep voice said, coming up from Liam's right and startling him.

"What? What do I have?" Liam asked Trace, who was smirking at him from a few feet away.

"You've got the hots for your mute little she-wolf," Trace said, raising his brows. "You know, the one you've been shacking up with since she got here."

"Bullshit," Liam growled, his voice sounding less assertive than he had intended.

"If you say so," Trace said, his voice making it all too clear that he didn't believe his Alpha one bit.

"I'm just making sure-"

"Making sure that she doesn't speak to any other males?" Trace interjected. "Like that Jason guy? He's watching her, too."

Liam's eyes quickly darted around the crowd, searching for Jason. He was on the opposite side of the fire, watching Elle interact with the toddlers, and smiling.

Prick.

"Elle already has a mate and it's not Jason," Liam said, low enough for only the two of them to hear. "He'd be wise to steer clear and wait for his."

"But he's a male wolf," Trace said. "Hormonal and single, ready to mingle and all that."

Liam could feel the irritation skittering across his skin like hives, and found himself wanting to rip the eyes from the sockets of any of the men who were gazing on her with anything more than friendship on their mind.

"You, on the other hand, are mateless and free to choose a Luna from any of the unmated she-wolves," Trace reminded him, as if he needed it. Trace was getting to be as bad as Blake. Acting like a bunch of amped up matchmakers, the pair of them. And don't get Liam started on Colleen. That girl could take first prize in a meddling competition.

Another few cartwheels, and the parents of the kids came over to wrangle up their children. More than a few of the toddlers wanted to stay and hang out with Elle, but she gave them hugs and promised them she would play with them again, and soon.

As Elle walked back over to where Liam was standing with an irritatingly amused Trace, Liam found himself immediately standing taller, rather than being in his usual slouch he had when forced to attend Colleen's shindigs.

"Tired?" Liam asked as a yawning Elle walked over, attempting to stifle it with the back of one slender hand.

She waved her hand in a *so-so* type motion and glanced at Liam's hand, eyeing up his soda.

He immediately walked over to the coolers and grabbed a Mountain Dew, popping the tab and handing it over to Elle. She smiled gratefully and mouthed her thanks again.

Fuck, that mouth.

He shouldn't have been looking at it, but he couldn't seem to help himself. A now familiar twitch behind the zipper of his pants made him sigh with irritation at himself. Trace was right, though Liam wouldn't admit it. He didn't know what it was, but he was just as smitten with her – if not more so – as Jason was.

Fucker better stay away from her, he thought before he could stop himself.

Trying to divert himself from the situation in his pants, he mindlinked with his enforcers, trying to find out if anything had occurred since he had last checked in. It had only been half an hour, but he kept his link open so he would be first to know if the situation changed.

The head enforcer allowed that there was nothing new to report, and the scent of foreign wolves was almost gone with the slight breeze. He would send more out to search in the morning, but until then he was calling it a night, except for the recently amped up security patrols around the perimeters of the territory.

"The kids seemed to have taken a liking to you," Trace told Elle, a wickedly flirty grin on his face. He could afford it as he was single, and he wanted to goad his Alpha a bit. A push in the right direction, as he saw it. Just like Colleen was wont to do lately in regards to Liam's fascination with Elle.

Elle shrugged, took a sip of her soda, and looked off toward the woods. It reminded Liam again that there was possibly a search party looking out for her, a fact that he would have to let her know. ASAP.

Liam shot a look over to Trace, one that would have sent any other wolf cowering away. But this was Trace. He lived on the conflict he started. It was his meat and potatoes. The fucker.

"Well, when you're ready to go, I'd like to have a chat with you before bed," Liam told her, causing Elle to raise a worried brow in his direction.

"It's nothing, I'm sure," he told her, though he wouldn't lie if she asked. She deserved the truth.

Elle looked to be deep in thought for a moment before she nodded to herself. Her chin lifted in the direction of the Alpha's home and she looked at him, signaling she was ready to go. It was like ESP, the way the two could communicate, and it left even Trace a little awed at their silent understanding of each other.

Perhaps there was more than just a sexually frustrated Alpha male under Liam's leather jacket and full-sleeve tattoos. Something more...well, just *more*.

Saying goodbye to the others as they passed, many of the wolves watched as the Alpha followed the diminutive female towards his home, Trace shaking his head in confusion and amusement.

The party would continue on for several more hours, fueled mainly by alcohol and hormone-driven wolves. Babies would probably be conceived that night, and the thought of that made Liam both elated and morose. He wanted his pack to thrive and grow, and newborns were a way to do that. But knowing he may never have that for himself sent a twinge of pain into his heart. He didn't look like Dad-material to the naked eye, but he had so many qualities of one inside. At least he hoped he did.

Once they entered the house, Liam escorted Elle into his study on the first floor. She had never been in there before, and as soon as the light was turned on, she looked around.

The room wasn't dirty, merely untidy. She never went in there to clean since he always had it locked. It wasn't that Liam didn't trust her, he simply locked it out of habit. And since Elle respected his privacy, she hadn't thought to bring it up with him.

Papers littered his desk everywhere but on his trusty laptop, a newer model MacBook Pro that he kept shut down unless he needed it. Powering it on, he spoke as he typed his password onto the screen with lightning quick stabs at the keyboard.

"I know your wrist is sore still or you wouldn't be holding it so gingerly," Liam told her, not looking as she rubbed at the sore muscles. "You can type though, on this. It will be less stressful on you until your wrist feels better."

Elle nodded, stifling another yawn. Her day had started early, as it usually did, and she had cooked a few meals ahead for the weekend. Colleen had mentioned going to the mall, and she didn't want the Alpha to go hungry if she were gone for a meal or two.

Liam gestured to his desk chair and Elle took a seat, typing out a question before looking back up at Liam who was watching the words appear on the screen.

What did you want to talk about?

Liam stood there, contemplating for a moment on what he had to say.

"There have been foreign wolves scented on the outskirts of the territory," Liam told her, watching her still at his words. "We don't know to which pack they belong, but this hasn't happened before in my tenure as Alpha. I can only assume it can mean one of two things."

You think they're looking for me.

Liam hesitated briefly, knowing Elle would think of everyone but herself first, and possibly try to flee.

"That's the most likely scenario, but don't worry," Liam told her quickly, placing a firm hand on her shoulder. "I've upped patrols on the perimeter, and the foreign wolves seem to have gone. They probably won't return."

Elle wasn't so sure. If it was Jeremiah, the man was stubborn as hell and didn't give up that easily. He could sift through the same areas and not find what he was looking for a hundred times, only to go back and try for one hundred and one. She typed her response.

I should go. If they find me here, they'll take me and punish you and your pack. I would go willingly, but I can't have anything happening to your pack – not when you have been so hospitable.

"You're not leaving, Elle." His tone was firm. Almost a command, and she dropped her head a bit until her chin hit her chest.

Fuck.

"I'm sorry," Liam said, his voice soft. "I didn't mean for it to come out so forcefully. It's just..."

Damn it. What was it just? Just that she was still recovering? That she deserved to have a stable foundation and strong pack behind her? Or was he being selfish and keeping her here for...him? He thought it was probably a little bit of everything, although he had to admit he felt it was heaviest on the selfishness aspect.

"You aren't fully recuperated yet," he told her, only giving her part of the reason she shouldn't leave. "Besides, I've placed you under pack protection. Nothing can happen to you without my say so."

Her head shot up to his, eyes dilated and wide.

But...I haven't even taken your oath. I want to when you will allow it, but maybe it's best if I don't. I can't be the cause of ill will between neighboring packs. This isn't your problem. It's mine.

Liam immediately shook his head, denying her words.

"If I felt it wasn't worth it, I wouldn't have placed you under our protection," Liam told her. His fingers dug into the skin on her shoulder as if to keep her rooted there. With him. He had been afraid of her running, and that's just what he was afraid she would do now.

"Promise me you will stay here, Elle," Liam implored. "I'll make this work. I may have to speak with Jeremiah or something eventually, but we will figure this out. *You're not his.* He made sure of that the first time he laid hands on you in anything but a loving manner."

Elle's eyes were wide and frightened, and her whole body shifted, facing him. Her mouth opened with only one word.

No.

She said it silently, but it held the gravity of a thousand *no*s.

No.

No. No. No.

"Yes," Liam said, and watched as Elle's face crumpled. Despair. Fear. He couldn't help but feel her emotions any more than he could help it if he was experiencing them himself.

He also couldn't help himself from reaching out and pulling her small body into his and feeling her pain as she trembled in his arms.

Chapter 8

"Say it. Say my name."

"Leeeeeee..." Her voice petered out like a diminishing howl on the wind.

"Uhm," he pressed. *"Lee – uhm."*

Her nose crinkled as she thought. How was it so hard for one to make sound? Her voice had taken on a raspy quality she hated. She had been told it was nearly musical before her injury.

"Uhhhhmmmm."

"Good. Now try it together," Liam prodded.

"Leeee-uhm."

"Much better," Liam said as he gave her a genuine smile.

Over the weekend, Elle had not been able to hit the mall like Colleen had wanted. Liam had been afraid that she would be seen since it was apparent to him that her old pack was most likely looking for her. Though the nearest mall was over half an hour away, he didn't seem keen to press his luck.

Instead of shopping, Liam had downloaded some documents on speech therapy and started to work on getting Elle talking again.

At first, she was only able to try for a few minutes at a time before her throat would feel too sore. By Sunday afternoon, she was able to put more time into it, and though the sound was still raw, she was able to speak in monosyllables.

Elle's voice was throaty and untamed, coarse and unsteady, but it held Liam's rapt attention, especially the appendage currently covered in blue basketball shorts and a pair of boxers. Christ, it was like she was speaking directly to his dick.

"Lee-uhm."

Each time she said it, his cock stirred and he had to bite back a groan.

"Again," he told her, praying the next time she said it, it wouldn't send a rush of blood to his groin. He had to become immune to it at some point – right?

Wrong.

After twenty more minutes, she was trying to pronounce

Colleen's name. Liam had hoped a change of noun would set things right, but it was useless. It seemed that no matter what she said, whether it was a name, or if she suddenly decided to recite the Gettysburg address, it would have the same effect on him. The effect he might get if she had stripped down to nothing and sat on his lap to grind her pussy against him.

He cringed at his own thoughts. His dick was betraying him and needed a good spanking. Not that he hadn't tried that. Numerous times. It...didn't really help. If they didn't stop practicing speech therapy for a bit, Liam was likely to whip his dick out and start stroking it right then and there.

He blamed Trace. And Colleen. And Blake. They had all planted the seeds, though he had a feeling they would have been sown anyway without the meddling of his closest friends.

"Let's take a break. Drink some water," Liam told her, handing her a half-full, lukewarm bottle of the beverage. All the speech therapy materials he had downloaded had urged that cold water may cause her to strain her vocal cords, and suggested room temperature would be better for her healing throat.

Elle sat on the couch in the living room, her eyes surveying the space. She looked like she was thinking, and when Liam came back to her with a fresh bottle of water, he asked her about it.

Can we rearrange the room or something? I have an idea that will keep the glare off the TV during the day.

"Sure," Liam said, blinking at her. "Any other reason for moving the place around, besides *fenging your shui*?"

She cocked her head and frowned a little.

Well, I'm bored. There's only so much cleaning and cooking one can do before going out of their mind.

He supposed that was true. Even with the diversion of an iPod playing while she puttered around the house, she had to be dying of boredom doing the same thing over and over again. It had to be mind-numbing to the extreme.

"Want to help me with some paperwork?" Liam blurted out without thinking. He seemed to do a lot of that around her. "How are you on math?"

Her brows hiked up to mid-forehead in surprise. Usually, Blake helped him, but he was entertaining Colleen as she nursed the world's longest hangover.

I know two plus two equals four, but I'm no Archimedes.

Liam smiled reassuringly at her.

"You don't have to be," he told her. "You just need to know how to use a calculator and be able to write. As long as you can do those two things, you'll be just fine."

Elle nodded and followed Liam to the home office. He was helping her so much it was only fair that she returned the favor, no matter how small the gesture.

Plus, he wasn't half bad to look at.

She blinked, not knowing where the rogue thought had come from, and shook her head at herself to ward away her unwanted thoughts.

Clearing her now sore throat, she brought her drink along with her and hoped she didn't suffer a case of the dropsies when she got into his office. Water, laptops, and calculators were not a clever mix.

It seemed the work was easier than Elle thought, and soon she was doing calculations and balancing the pack checkbook like she'd been born with a pocket protector in one hand, a balance sheet in the other.

Her handwriting was neat, and Liam asked her to make out checks to places like *First World Title* and *Remington Mortgage Co.* When she asked what the checks were for, Liam answered quickly.

"Most of my money comes from properties I own and rent out," he told her. "Some were bought outright at short sales and auctions, and others I went through lenders. These checks we're filling out now are all commercial properties I own in the tri-state area. I prefer the commercial sites. Less chance of someone bailing on rent money, and the owners of the businesses tend to be more careful with the properties I lease to them."

One check stood out from the rest. It was made out to Arden Collier. Elle picked it up and raised a questioning brow in his direction. She didn't know if she was being too nosey, but Liam hadn't told her to stop prying as of yet.

"Ah, that's for my sister," Liam said. "I started up a college fund for her kid – or kids. She's only got the one now, but I assume she'll probably become pregnant again any time now."

It was gone in a flash, but Elle noticed the downcast look that whipped across his face. Her frown resurfaced and she grabbed her notepad again.

You should go to The Claiming next year. I think you'd make a great dad, but that's not happening until you find someone.

She slipped the pad over to him and hoped he didn't cut her with a look, tell her to mind her own fucking business. She was only trying to help.

Instead, he sighed, looking out the window.

"I don't think I'll find what I'm looking for at The Claiming," he told her. "If I ever find it at all."

***

"Sir, we've checked the perimeters of all the surrounding packs," the warrior told Jeremiah, whose face had grown colder the week since he had first started searching for his mate. In that time, he had nearly strangled a few enforcers, taken out his rage on the furniture in his bedroom, and punched a few holes in walls when he realized he was out of beer in his fridge.

Jeremiah gave him a passive wave before speaking.

"Keep looking," he told the man. "She has to be out there somewhere. Dead in a ditch or shacking up with another pack, I know she can be found."

"Yes, Sir."

The man left Jeremiah alone with Carter at his side.

"What's up your ass, Jere?" Carter asked as soon as the warrior had left. "I would say it was lack of pussy, but you're an Alpha and you can get it anytime you want."

That was true, but something had fucking changed. Jeremiah was now convinced that Giselle was alive and well and out there somewhere, probably having a good laugh at his expense because she had slipped through his fingers and off into the great wild yonder.

"Nothing," Jeremiah said, lying through his teeth.

"Bullshit."

The Alpha stood, his body towering over his oldest friend.

"Truth."

"You fucking miss her," Carter stated, jaw twitching with irritation.

"Only because of the bond," he excused, waving his friend off.

"Maybe, but you do," Carter said. "When's the last time you hooked up with a female since you started searching for her?"

I haven't, Jeremiah thought, his molars grinding as he bit down harder on his own teeth.

"I'm fine, just fucking dandy. Couldn't be better," the man told him.

"Is it because you can't get it up without Giselle being nearby?

That you don't know where she is?" Carter taunted, against his better judgment. But he had pretty much had it by now. The Alpha was acting like a lovesick fool, and, to be honest, he was a fool that didn't deserve the love of his mate. Not after all he did to her whilst she was still his.

"Carter..."

"I don't understand you, man," Carter continued. "You could have been marked and mated with her by now. Possibly be pregnant with your firstborn. Instead, you took her station – something that is not her fault, mind you – out on her with your fists because you think being mated to an Omega makes you look weak."

"Easy for you to say," Jeremiah spat. "Your mate is someone of stature. Mine-"

"Was a kind, caring female who would have done anything to please you," Carter finished. "Instead, you tossed her aside, hoping you could overcome the bond someday so you could pair with a female of your choosing. One with status in the pack. You should have just rejected her, Jeremiah. Let her be free and choose an unmated female if that's what you wanted. You should-"

"But I wanted my mate!" Jeremiah growled out. The words surprised him, even more so when he realized that they were true.

"And you still do I see," Carter said, his voice low. "And for what it's worth, I hope you never find her. She's better off that way."

Carter left the room quietly, closing the door firmly behind him and hoping, *praying,* that wherever Giselle was, she was safe and being cared for.

***

Liam paced the floor of his bedroom late Monday night. He was dressed for bed, but his mind was running rampant with unwanted thoughts. Thoughts he didn't desire to have but hijacked his mind anyway until they were all he could think of.

The foreign wolves. No one had heard from them since the previous Friday, and that made him nervous. It was the old adage. Keep your friends close and your enemies closer. Not that they were enemies, per se. But he was pretty certain what they wanted, and he was determined to keep it from them. Whatever the cost.

It made him think he should arrange a meeting with Jeremiah. Tell him to call off his dogs, so to speak. He was afraid, though. Afraid of saying too much – or maybe not enough – to keep the man from snooping around where he shouldn't. Maybe he would go see him the next day. He had to head into town anyway to drop off the checks to be mailed. Jeremiah's pack was on the way there. He could simply contact him and set up a time, warn him off, and pop down to the post office to send out his checks. Simple enough.

And then there was Elle. If he was honest with himself, he'd admit she consumed most of his waking thoughts. And some of his naughtier dreams.

Okay, a *fuck-ton* of his dreams.

And he always woke up rock solid and having to take a wicked piss. It was irritating, and he'd usually have to rub one out just to get his dick to behave so he could find some damned relief. For both his arousal *and* his bladder. Otherwise, he'd have been pissing up at the ceiling. His aim wasn't all too steady with his dick twitching like it was first thing in the morning.

Elle had done well over the past several days and was able to speak names and some simple words. She was coming along fast, faster than he thought she would, and he was starting to relax more. He didn't have to rely so much on body language and facial expressions, not that he paid any less attention to them now. In fact, he paid more attention to them and it was making him cranky and sexually frustrated. He was tired of having to take breaks during the day so he could find some relief for his ever-present erection.

He left the house early every morning, but even so, he could smell her lovely scent everywhere. It was a heady mixture of jasmine and freesia, and he could smell it on the clothing she had washed, folded, and laid out by his bed every few days. It was distracting as hell. Distracting and alluring.

Even as he paced, he could hear Elle walking around her room just a door over. Her small steps sometimes scurried, and the sound of the iPod he'd had Colleen get for her over the weekend and had given her earlier today was soft and inviting. He just wanted to walk into her room and silence her steps with a heated kiss. First her lips, then her neck, her tits, and finally lower...

At one point he realized he had been padding back and forth across his plush rug for over an hour and the music next door was turned off. No sounds of steps. Elle must have gone to sleep.

He finally sat down on his mattress, welcoming the soft squeak of the springs beneath his ass. It was familiar, normal, and outside the bounds of everything new he had been feeling recently.

He covered himself in the duvet and realized...he could smell her there too. She must have washed the sheets for him recently, and he wondered if he should start laundering his own things. Sure, the house would probably be knee-deep in suds the first time he attempted a load, but he'd get used to it. Eventually.

Liam was close to finally passing out when he heard a door open down the hall and small, soft steps. He scrunched his eyes tighter and tried to ignore the pull to get up and investigate, but ended up losing the battle when the sounds faded off into the distance.

If he was ever going to get any sleep, he needed to make sure everything was okay. She hadn't sounded distressed, but something in him told him that she wasn't any sleepier than he was.

He moved toward the stairs, hearing the soft pitter-patter of feet below him. It caused his heart to race and he took a few steadying breaths before making his way down the stairs.

At the bottom, he walked into the kitchen to find Elle heating up the teapot, a box of chamomile tea sitting on the breakfast bar.

"Couldn't sleep?" he asked, causing Elle to jump slightly.

"N-night...m...mmm," she attempted to say, getting frustrated a moment before stomping her foot on the ground.

"Easy," Liam said, moving toward her. "The words will come. Was it a nightmare?"

Elle nodded, gaze drifting to the ground.

"They wake you up?"

Another nod.

"I almost wish I had nightmares," he told her absently. "Nightmares come with sleep. I could deal with the dreams. This fucking insomnia...not so much."

"Tea?" The word came out faultless and clear, as clear as he had ever heard her sound.

"Sure."

Liam had never been much for tea, so he was merely capitalizing on the company that came with it.

Elle got out another mug and placed it on the bar before Liam. He grabbed two teabags and placed them in the mugs as she went to grab some milk, a few lemon wedges, and some honey.

"N-not...b-b-both," she said to him, cutely stern as she pointed from the lemon to the milk. "C-c...ur..."

"It'll curdle," he finished for her. She simply nodded back at him and then got a spoon and a spare saucer for their teabags.

It was quiet all over the territory this late at night. Most everyone was asleep except for the patrol, which was miles away on the outskirts of the land. The silence didn't bother either one of them, and the increasing sound of the tea kettle coming to boil was the only thing out of place at that time of night.

"Does this help – the tea?" Liam asked.

She wiggled her hand in a *so-so* gesture.

Sometimes.

He heard the word as if she had spoken it, though that was impossible since she hadn't taken the oath and opened herself to the pack mindlink in the process. But he heard it anyway and nodded his head.

"Worth a shot," he said, more to himself than to her.

After their tea had been steeped, drunk, and the resulting dishes put away, they both climbed the stairs. Liam hoped sleep would find him, whereas Elle hoped the soothing brew could keep away the terror.

As they both made their way to their rooms and stood at their respective doors, Liam stopped and turned around. Elle was standing there, staring at the doorknob like it would come alive and take a bite out of her. He watched her shiver for a moment and place her hand on it, turning it slowly as if there were armed robbers on the other side.

"Want to chat a bit before going to sleep?" Liam asked, walking over toward her. He was hoping that conversation would relax her enough so she could find sleep. Maybe even tire himself out since having to endure mindless chatter was tiring in and of itself for him.

Elle looked up at him, doe-eyes sorrowful and insanely large in the dimly lit hallway.

Liam thought she would say no, but she only nodded her head and opened the door wide.

Walking over to the bed, she climbed under the covers and patted the bedside for Liam to sit down. It was his house, after all, his sister's old bedroom, and he should feel as comfortable anywhere in his home as she had at her parent's.

"Tell...sister," she said, looking around the room.

"Tell you about my sister?" he asked, to which she nodded. "Not much to tell, honestly," he admitted. "Her name's Arden, and she's about two years younger than I. She found her mate around the same time I did and moved away. Colorado."

He continued to speak, regaling her with stories of his childhood, explaining some of the rules of living at Plumbrook, many of which she was aware, and explaining more about some of his closest friends, Colleen, Blake, and Trace.

Liam spoke for a long time, not knowing when her eyes had

finally closed.
    And not remembering when his did, either.

Chapter 9

She woke up warm. Much *too* warm. A long arm was draped across Elle's waist, giving her the illusion of-
Wait – *what?*
Blinking her eyes open, she took a long sniff of the air. *Liam.* She remembered that she had fallen asleep after Liam had started talking about some of the pacts he had made with neighboring Alphas in his tenure, but she didn't remember anything after that. Not even the hint of a dream.

A gust of hot air blew across her cheek and she shivered. Not out of fear or air temperature, but from something else. An emotion she couldn't quite put her thumb on. Once the proverbial thumb got close, the word skittered away, evading her.

At least Liam had fallen asleep outside of the duvet. But he was draped across her body like a skin-tight outfit, or a cheap off-the-rack suit.

Sliding her body out from under his was more of a task than she anticipated. She was not keen on him waking up before she got dressed, brushed her teeth, and started breakfast. Talk about awkward.

And what time was it anyway? Looking at the clock, she was surprised she had slept so long. It was half-past nine, an hour the back her eyelids hadn't seen in years. Of course, waking up to a nightmare and then her tea and conversation with Liam had chipped away at some of her usual bedtime hours.

When she was free of the bed – and Liam's arms – she walked quietly over to the bathroom, placed her mussed up hair in a sloppy bun, and proceeded to brush her teeth.

She made a mental list of things that they would need to buy. They were running low on eggs, so unless she started laying them herself, Liam was going to be stuck eating Cheerios or Fruit Loops tomorrow morning.

Downstairs, she cracked a few eggs and put the burner heat on low, adding a pat of butter into the frying pan and whisking the eggs vehemently, like they had somehow personally offended her.

Coffee was ground and perking, the scent of which usually woke up the Alpha, who craved his caffeine.

"Morning," Liam said from the door, voice groggy with sleep.

"M-morn-n-ning," Elle replied from her place at the stove. She kept her gaze fixed on scrambling the light-yellow mix.

"Sorry about last night," Liam told her on a yawn. "Must've dozed off. I knew I was dull, but I didn't think I could bore even myself to sleep."

Elle smiled and turned around.

"Iss...o-kay," she told him. "Y-your...home... your...b-bed."

"You're getting good," he told her approvingly. "And it's your bed now. I bequeath it to you. It's not like my sister's going to send for it, and I didn't actually pay for it. If you really wanted to be picky, it's my parents' bed. Their hard-earned dough purchased it."

Liam had never mentioned his mother and father, and Elle could only wonder why.

"Where...are p-par...rents?" she asked.

"Dad became an elder with The Council, so he stays close by their settlement," Liam told her. "It was a hassle for him to fly back and forth, and he's getting too old to be driving there and back. Mom, of course, went with him. They're in Colorado, like my sister, so there's that."

Elle nodded and flipped some bacon, another necessity from the store that they needed. Her mind made the mental note while Liam's voice rang out in the background.

"I'm heading into town today," he told her. "Have to drop some mail off. Is there anything you need?"

She told him in stilted words. Bacon, eggs, bread, and milk.

"I'll grab those things on the way back from town," he promised, and started to sit down at the breakfast bar.

After eating, the two parted, Liam heading to his bedroom for a shower, Elle to her own room to start her morning routine. They were both showered and ready for their day within half an hour.

The staircase needed dusting, Elle noticed, and she decided to get going on that, moving to the hallway closet where the cleaning supplies were always kept. A Swiffer duster, a rag, and some lemon-scented furniture polish later, she was ready to tackle the upstairs first, passing by Liam as he left his room.

"Eggs, milk, bread, and bacon, right?" he asked, stopping Elle with a firm hand to her shoulder.

"R-right," she said, nodding up at him.

"Okay, I can remember that without writing it down," he told her.

That's when something happened.

Liam leaned in, his lips close to her temple and, for the briefest of moments, Elle thought he was going to kiss her there. But it only became a swift brush of his lips against her skin and she blinked, wondering if she had imagined it.

"S-see you later," he stuttered, shaking his head as if perplexed with himself.

Which, by the way, he was.

***

I almost fucking kissed her, Liam thought the whole way toward Blackriver.

After ridding himself of the delicious fragrance of Elle on his body and clothing, he had called Jeremiah, requested a meeting, and then centered his thoughts back to the same five words. *I almost fucking kissed her.*

It should have felt surreal, but the idea of it had come so naturally to him, that it almost ran across as an afterthought. It had been as easy as breathing, getting that close to her. If he hadn't seen her flinch just slightly, he would have followed through.

"Bye, honey. I'm off to work. Kids, you be good for your mother." Then a kiss on the cheek, forehead, or temple. Completely domestic and utterly unlike him. He hadn't kissed anyone before leaving the house like that since Cecelia. Blake, or even Trace sometimes goaded him, requesting a kiss before leaving his office, but they were always silenced with one of his infamous glares, walking quickly away when they saw he meant business.

"Un-fucking-believable," he muttered to himself, shaking his head for the millionth time that morning. Pretty soon his fucking brain was going to start rattling around up there, he had shaken it so much.

Liam patted the envelope in his hand, a large manila one, containing all the checks Elle had filled out for him and handed over for him to sign. Her penmanship was pretty and very legible, whereas his closely resembled something some henchman from Hell might have scrawled for some virgin-sacrificing ritual. Or a doctor's handwriting. Lord knew what those symbols on those prescription pads even meant.

Liam slowed his car down on the outskirts of Blackriver and waited for the three men ahead of him to approach his vehicle.

"Name?" a tall, burly male asked while leaning over at the level of

Liam's head. Liam drove a dark green Mercedes-Benz AMG GT R, low to the ground. The ogre standing next to his car practically had to fold himself in half to get a look at Liam.

"Alpha Liam Stark," he obliged. "I have a meeting with Jeremiah Bluth, your leader, I presume."

"Kent?" the man called to one of the other males.

As in Clark Kent – Man of Steel? Liam quipped to himself, groaning internally that he couldn't just say it out loud.

"He's good. The Alpha is expecting him," Kent told him. "He can pass." *Thank you, Superman.*

The Jolly Green Giant nodded and stood up to his full height, backing away from the car and gesturing for him to pass.

"Last house at the end of the road," Goliath called after him, his voice booming out so that most of the pack could probably hear him.

Liam nodded, though he doubted that the man saw it. He waved his hand out the window in acknowledgment, and drove on a bit faster.

After a few minutes, he pulled up to the last house on the road. It was blood-red with dark blue shutters, a sprawling two-story monstrosity. Liam's eyes darkened as he put the car into park and stepped out of the vehicle.

He grabbed his manila envelope, not wanting to leave it in his car, though he locked the doors behind him. He was on enemy territory, for lack of a better term, and he hoped his increased blood pressure didn't give Jeremiah any reason to think that this wasn't just a friendly visit.

"Liam," a voice called out from the front porch. "I was told you were here. Come in."

The man's voice was gruff, and the dark circles under his eyes made Liam smile internally. Maybe the man was having a harder time without his mate than Liam had suspected. He hoped for damned sure he was. Served the fucker right.

They stood in the kitchen for a minute while Jeremiah offered Liam a beverage.

"Just water, please," Liam said. "My... housekeeper filled me up on coffee this morning." His lips twitched up at the word "housekeeper", a little amused with himself.

"What brings you here, Liam?" Jeremiah asked, getting out a bottle of water for his guest.

"I was just concerned is all," Liam stated in a measured tone of voice. "My patrol has told me that some neighboring pack was searching the land just beyond my borders. Since you're the closest one, I was wondering if it was you and yours."

Jeremiah tipped his head back, taking a deep draught of water before speaking.

"It was," he told his guest. "We've been looking for someone."

"Who?" Liam immediately asked. "Maybe if I see them I can let you know."

"No one of importance," Jeremiah said waving his question away.

Liam's eyes flashed. No one of importance? His mate didn't matter to him? *Un-fucking-real.*

"Male or female?" Liam pressed. "If I see any strange wolves around, it would to be good to at least get a gender or a description."

"Why do you care?" Jeremiah asked, beady little eyes scrutinizing Liam's. "It's not like we have close ties. Why would you help me?"

"Well, if you're looking for someone, I can only assume the person might be dangerous. Is that not so?"

"She's not fucking dangerous, she's-" Jeremiah stopped his angry outburst and did his best to school his features.

"So...a female," Liam said, raising his brows. "A love interest? Maybe one of your flavors of the week? I know how you love your women. Many of them, and not always one at a time."

"She's not-"

It was almost too easy for Liam to goad him, though Jeremiah couldn't have suspected it. These were all simple questions, one's anyone would ask.

"Well, have you found your little female?" Liam asked. "It makes my patrol antsy to have that many foreign wolves skirting our property, and you've made them quite anxious."

"I...no, I haven't found her, and we've not stopped looking," Jeremiah admitted grudgingly. "We are done searching your area, though, and I doubt we'll be back. We've decided to look north, towards Canada. We feel she may have doubled-back to the northwest."

"Well, good luck on your search." *Not.* "I hope you find whoever it is you are looking for." *I hope your whole body burns for days on end, just like you burned your initials into Elle's soft, creamy skin, you sick fuck.*

"Is that all you wanted?" Jeremiah asked, suspicion engraved in his words.

"That and your assurance that your search party will not cross pack lines," Liam said. "I would hate to have a blood feud on our hands when I'm forced to imprison one of your wolves. That is, if one was stupid enough to trespass."

Liam held the manila envelope in his hand, waving it in the air before he went to take his leave.

"Wait!" Jeremiah called out, his voice strangled, so different than the tone from only moments ago. It sounded desperate.

Liam looked back, blinking as the man came closer to him, his nose tilted in the air.

Jeremiah's eyes flickered between Liam's face and the envelope in his hands.

"What's in there?" Jeremiah asked, his tone edging on dangerous.

"Just some paperwork. Some checks I have to send off," Liam said. "You know, business things."

"Why does it smell like a female?"

"I had my housekeeper help me yesterday with the books," Liam told him, feigning impatience. "She's just as good with numbers as she is in the kitchen. Now if you'll-"

The envelope was ripped from Liam's hands and Jeremiah dug into it, looking crazed as his hand stuffed the checks into his face, searching for the scent that had, until now, evaded him so completely.

Before Liam could think to run or even panic, Jeremiah's hands stuffed the checks back into the envelope and dropped it to the ground. His face was in Liam's in half a second before his hot breath hit the cooler skin of Liam's cheeks.

"Where the fuck is she?" Jeremiah roared. "Where is my mate?"

Fuck.

Liam gave one slow blink.

Jeremiah worried him, but he was only mildly afraid of what of the man could do. He wasn't true Alpha blood, and he never would be.

"She's safe from you, you sadistic asshole," Liam answered, his voice gravelly and deep.

"She's mine!"

"*Was* yours, I would say," Liam said, breaking their eye contact with a quick blink. "If you truly wanted her, you wouldn't have done what you did to her."

Jeremiah let go of Liam to take a small step back, shocked.

"You know nothing." Jeremiah sounded confident, but it didn't translate to his eyes. They wavered, unsure.

"I know more than you think," Liam decreed quietly. "She was quite forthcoming with the extent of your...*hospitality* while residing here at your house."

"She's an Omega." As if that was some sort of explanation.

"And you're a black-hearted, egotistical fool," Liam spat back at him, his blue eyes blazing and becoming darker at the same time.

"She's mine to do with as I please."

"She's a person, not property for you to maul and destroy," Liam told him. "If you didn't want her, you should have rejected her. Let her have a chance at a different life. A better one."

"I want her back!"

"You'll get nothing from me," Liam stated firmly. "She has my pack's protection. One wrong move, even a toe over the line into my territory, and it's war."

Jeremiah's eyes widened, the pupils dilating furiously.

"You'd risk a war for some strange wolf? An Omega?" he asked. His jaw twitched as he spoke.

"I'd risk it for someone as innocent as her," Liam said with a nod. "You can let her go quietly, or you can try your hand at beating me. It's up to you. I warn you now, though. I have told my Beta where I am and he is expecting a call from me in..." He checked his watch. "Fifteen minutes. If I don't call, he is poised to attack. Attack and *win*." It was an easily fabricated lie, but one that came quickly to Liam.

Jeremiah's eye twitched. Then his jaw. He was biting back a snarl when something came to his mind. No one would risk their people for the sake of someone else unless...

"You plan to take her as your Luna?" Jeremiah barked the question out, though it sounded more like a statement in Liam's ears.

Blinking, Liam thought quickly about it. It would free Elle from Jeremiah, take care of his Luna problem, make the pack stronger, and solidify the protection orders on her. It was a win-win. If Elle was on board, at least.

And, Liam had to admit, he did want her as his. Badly.

"And what if I did?" Liam asked, deciding to play his cards close to his vest for the moment.

"You'd never get away with it." Jeremiah sounded certain. "You would have to attend The Claiming with her and be paired up from there. And you couldn't guarantee she wouldn't be claimed by another."

The man sounded so sure of himself, it was all Liam could do not to laugh at him.

"You forget that my father is an Elder," Liam said. "I could call in a few favors, have them make an exception. They would do it once I let them know what she has gone through as your mate. The doctor who treated her and the wolves who found her would have my back. You'd be lucky to keep your pack by the time I was through with you."

Liam could almost see the wheels turning through Jeremiah's thick skull. While the Elders usually didn't intercede between the packs unless it was absolutely necessary, they would take the information Liam gave them and could have Blackriver watched, infiltrated – possibly disbanded. It was known to have happened before. Not in a while, but it had occurred.

"Fuck!" Jeremiah roared. Liam's lips curved upward slightly. "You better watch yourself, Liam. Watch your fucking back good."

"I plan to," Liam said smugly, tasting the bittersweet victory of his win over the man. "I know you better than you think, Jeremiah. I know your strengths, your weaknesses. I know when to push and when to pull. I also know that this won't be that last time I see your ugly face. But the next time I do, it may very well be with a marked Luna who could have been yours but wanted – and deserved – so much better."

Without another word, Liam grabbed his envelope and stalked to the door. He heard the sound of glass shattering just before the door slammed shut behind him.

***

Liam stopped at the store after dropping off the checks in the first blue USPS mailbox he saw. They stank of Jeremiah's greasy paws, and he was glad to be rid of them. He picked up the groceries they needed at the house, feeling, all the while, like he was being watched. He knew it was only his own damned anxiety working itself out, but he still took it to heart and warned Blake of his meeting with Jeremiah. Patrol was alerted, though that was only as a precaution. He knew Jeremiah would bide his time and work out a plan. It wasn't the last they'd hear of him, though.

What worried him most was talking to Elle. He didn't want to scare her with the news that Jeremiah now knew where she was. She had promised she wouldn't run, but she was selfless and would do anything to keep Plumbrook from having to face outside adversaries. Especially ones she had brought almost to their door.

Liam tried to think of the most sensitive way to break the news to her. He wasn't well-versed with delicate, and thought that maybe having another female with her might help. Colleen was too brash though, and she was the only other she-wolf that Elle truly trusted, aside from Dr. D'Amato maybe.

"Fuck," he muttered to himself as he got into his car. "Fuck fuck fuck *FUCK!*"

He slammed his hands against the steering column, the material of it groaning beneath his clenching fingers. His forehead met with the wheel as he breathed in deeply. All the adrenaline from his meeting with Jeremiah had worn off long ago, and all the worry was setting in now.

If Liam had been as selfless as Elle, he would have found another pack, far away, that would accept the would-be Luna and have them protect her. It would come with a risk, but it would keep her far away from Jeremiah's greasy mitts. Across country, if need be. But...he couldn't find it in himself to do that. She was barely comfortable in Plumbrook and was only just learning to speak again. Was becoming whole again.

He turned on the car, pressing the button to start it and peeling away from the store, gravel bits flying everywhere in his wake.

***

Elle listened as Colleen nattered on about seemingly nothing. She was more interested in the music coming from the iPod she had set up on the mantle of the fireplace. She was glad it was a working fireplace. There was nothing homier than having a working flu during the cold winter months. And it made her think of her old home at Blackriver. The one her parents still lived in.

"Are you listening to me?" Colleen asked, ripping Elle from her thoughts.

"No." She had less of a stutter. She was getting better quickly, and that made her smile.

Colleen laughed.

"Well, I have to admire your honesty, even though I've been trying to get you to pay attention for the past half hour," Colleen said, teasingly.

"S-sorry," Elle replied with a smile. "Wh-what were you...s-s-saying?"

Okay, any phrase or sentence longer than three words was still a trial, but it was a distinct improvement.

"That guy Jason at the bonfire," Colleen started to say. "He's been asking about you, wondering how you were doing."

"He was nice," Elle said with a shrug.

"And very interested in getting to know you better," Colleen continued. She watched as Elle's nose crinkled.

"He's a g-good f-friend," Elle stated.

"You're not interested?"

Elle shook her head.

"Is there anyone else that catches your eye then?" Colleen asked, digging.

Elle wasn't good with lying, so she simply stayed quiet.

"Your silence is all the confirmation I need," Colleen stated, smiling. "Who is it? Is he cute?"

Elle's face flushed, and she wiped the sweat from her brow. Maybe Colleen would think all that red on her face was from doing chores. It was not necessarily hot out as it was still fall, but working around the house could cause her to sweat just as easily in the mid-'70s as it did in the dead of summer.

Colleen continued to bother her about who she might be interested in until Elle's face was fire-truck red and she was stuttering worse than ever.

Someone save me, she thought moments before the front door opened and a harried-looking Liam strode into the house with purpose.

***

The longer Liam drove, the faster he pushed the car. He knew Jeremiah's game, how the man thought out his battle plans carefully before deciding on a course of action. Just like his father. He had been the same way when he was younger. He had plotted, from beginning to end, working out the discrepancies, the risks, the possible outcomes of every move. Jeremiah was a force to be reckoned with when he was plotting something.

It only made Liam more anxious, more eager to get home. Make sure everything was okay – that *Elle* was okay.

Because he had made up his mind. He wanted her as his Luna. And he hoped she was agreeable to it. Otherwise, it would be difficult to keep her safe, even with the pack protection. If she was his Luna, the pack would be sworn to protect her by default, just as they were sworn to protect their leader, their Alpha.

The drive home seemed to stretch on for eons. He tried getting in touch with Blake or Colleen through the mindlink, but they were both turned off. He'd have to fucking speak to them about that, but until then, he let his heart beat an unsteady pattern in his chest, his blood racing through his veins. With worry. And it was probably only going to be the start of it.

He knew no matter what, the true bond of a mate never faded, not at least until that mate died or marked another, but he knew for certain that that would never affect Elle. Not *his* Elle. She would never go back to Jeremiah, of that he was certain.

Unless...

Unless it was between giving herself back to him and saving his pack. Then...*then* she might.

Fuck.

She wouldn't.

She couldn't.

And she damned well shouldn't.

The next ten minutes drew out like he figured the last minutes of a man's life would on death row. Agonizingly slowly, he would imagine.

He finally skidded to a stop in front of his home and launched himself from the car like his ass was lit on fire. He ran up the steps to his door and opened it quickly, not caring if the wall behind where the door slammed cracked or splintered.

"Elle." His voice came out in a relieved, raspy sigh. She was safe. For now, at least.

He knew Colleen was in the room, could smell her, sense her, but his eyes were only on Elle. Red-faced and slightly sweaty. Colleen was there in the background, suddenly talking to him. He paid no attention to the words. They were garbage. Unnecessary noise as far as he was concerned.

Jeremiah knows you're here.

The only way you're safe is with me.

Be my Luna, please.

A dozen other starting sentences bounced around in his mind, Colleen's voice playing a grating counterpoint to his thoughts. He wanted to silence her in some way so he could think and not have to focus on drowning her mindless drivel out. There was only one way to do that.

Slowly, his feet moved forward. Once. Twice. Again and again until he was walking over to Elle's small figure as it stood in the doorway of the kitchen, a confused expression etched on her face.

"Wha-"

"Don't," Liam said, his forefinger coming up to her lips to stop her words. "Don't say anything."

Then his lips were on hers, warm and inviting. They moved against hers slowly and he heard Colleen shriek for a moment and then fall silent.

Finally.

But it wouldn't have mattered. The only thing he could really hear was his own blood pounding in his head. A dull roar that kept everything out but what he was feeling. And it was a lot. Emotions long since buried stirred deep inside him. Deep, deeper until all he could feel was her lips on his, his hands cradling her cheeks as her mouth slowly opened for him.

His tongue slid slowly inside, touching hers. She tasted citrusy, like lemonade, and smelled like heaven. As always. He could also smell his own familiar musk on her, and his chest seemed to vibrate with a groan. He liked his scent on her, that deep, woodsy sandalwood.

His tongue stroked hers gently and she gave a soft moan of her own, her hands coming up to rest on his chest. They stayed there, not pushing him away, but not pulling him closer either. Almost tentative.

His hands skimmed her jaw line and then through her hair where they stayed knotted in her dark brown locks.

Liam didn't want to stop kissing her, but he knew Colleen was still in the room, probably orgasmic with glee, the fucking meddler.

Slowly, he pulled away, his eyes searching for any signs of trepidation in Elle's. They were wide, but not scared, not uncertain. He didn't even blink as he spoke out loud.

"Get out, Colleen," he said, the command stern but somehow still gentle. "I need to speak with Elle. Alone."

He didn't even listen as she spoke while getting up from the couch she was splayed out on. He waited for the door to swing shut behind her before rising to his full height above Elle.

"I have news," he told her. "And a plan. I need to know if you're...amenable to it."

She nodded *go ahead* before taking an audible breath and swallowing over the lump of nerves in her throat.

Chapter 10

One of Liam's hands moved from Elle's face to her waist. Then the other. Only seconds had passed, and the only things that had changed were their positions and the look in Liam's eyes.

Uncertainty. Fear. And...something else entirely.

"I met with Jeremiah this morning."

Elle flinched, attempted to step backward, but Liam's hands only pulled her closer to him.

"I was trying to find out whether or not he would be coming back around this way to search the perimeter," Liam explained. "I figured it might have had something to do with you – was almost positive. I was right."

Elle's face crumpled, mouth opening wide to say something.

"Go," she rasped. "I...have to...go."

Liam stood firm. "You promised me you wouldn't run," Liam reminded her sternly, a determined gleam in his eyes.

Elle shook her head. "He'll find me."

"He already knows you're here," Liam said softly.

Another flinch, and panic filled Elle's eyes. Her legs felt weak, like sun-warmed rubber.

"He could smell you on the checks I went to mail this morning. He was...livid. Demanded I give you back like you were some toy I had stolen from him," Liam said.

Elle started to squirm away from him, shaking her head.

No. She couldn't go back...could she?

"I have a plan, though, that will make sure he can never hurt you again."

Elle stilled, her eyes wary and confused, but hope lit a faraway ember in her eyes. It was buried deep, deep in them, but it was there. The smallest trace of longing filtered through.

"He can't take you if you are marked by another," Liam ventured, his voice low and almost luminous. "If you were to be claimed by another wolf, he would have no right to you at all."

Liam watched Elle as she grew even more confused, her large eyes blinking back up at him.

"For this to work, for you to be free of him, I would have to mark you." Elle's breath caught, and she stopped breathing. "You would be my Luna and mate. He would have no right to you and the whole pack would be behind you. I have already put a protection order on you. Our mating would only reinforce that order."

"We...w-we would-"

Liam just nodded his head, cutting her off. "I'd be lying if I said that if this situation wasn't hanging over our heads I wouldn't have wanted this, but even if you had come onto my land with no baggage, I would still have wanted you for myself."

One of his hands moved slowly up on her back, splaying out possessively on the fabric between her shoulders. It stayed there, steady and unmovable.

"Tell me you don't want this, don't want me, and I'll find some other way," Liam said. "You'll still have my protection and the pack's, but I will find something else we can do to keep him from getting to you. I know people and have friends in high places. I can make something happen."

There was a trace of sadness in his voice, and the uncertainty in it unlocked something in Elle's throat.

"Are...you certain...you want me?" she asked, as if dubious of his claims.

He smiled gently, his hand rubbing up and down on her back, the one at her waist moving around to the small of it and holding her in place.

"Very much so. Elle, since the first night you were in my home, I knew there was something different about you. At first, I couldn't place what it was. It took me only a few days to realize that *you* were different. Quiet but brave, abused yet still strong. Next to my closest friends here, I trust you more than anyone. It's not common for me to become close with strangers or for me to trust someone I haven't known for the majority of my life. But I know your secrets as you know mine. I thought it would hurt to tell you, but I only felt...relief. You didn't judge me, didn't show pity. You understood, and that's what I needed."

"Not your fault." Now Elle sounded stern, and Liam fought back a smile.

"It doesn't make me feel any less like blaming myself for not seeing what could have happened sooner." They both knew they were talking about his deceased mate and the guilt he still harbored. "It gets...easier after a while, but the guilt still gnaws at me from time to time."

His hands came back up to cup her cheeks, and her eyes fluttered closed for a moment, enjoying the tender caress before she opened them back up. Her gaze didn't falter this time.

"Okay," she simply stated.

"Okay you'll let me mark you? Become my mate?" he asked. His eyes lit up, a steelier grey than the usual startling blue they normally were.

"Yes, I'll do it," she said, a small smile spilling onto her face.

"And you're certain?" he asked, looking into each of her eyes like he was searching for a deeper answer there. "You won't back down? Once I mark you, you will go into heat within a few days. Will that be a long enough time to come to terms with this? With us? Once you are marked, you will sleep in my bed with me. I won't force anything, but I won't be able to be away from you either."

Elle nodded slowly. That was what she had expected from her first mate. "I'm certain," she told him.

Then, her legs flew out from under her as she yipped, and she was being pulled up into a bridal carry as Liam walked them both swiftly toward the stairs.

"W-where are we g-going?" she asked, blinking in surprise.

"To my room," Liam told her, voice firm. "I wish to mark you now since you are so sure. You will bleed some, and I don't think standing in the kitchen with your shirt off is how you'd want to do this."

It...made sense. It was just so sudden.

Elle's heart began to beat double-time in her chest. It suddenly felt like what should have when she had waited to be marked by her true mate, though obviously, that was not the case. This was a twist. No true mate bond, but there were indeed feelings there, even if she had tried to bury them deep.

Once they were in his room, he sat her down on the edge of the bed, his hands at the hem of her shirt. Liam was looking at her with an *are you still sure about this* look on his face. Elle simply nodded and blinked as her t-shirt was whipped over her head and she was suddenly sitting there in only a bra and shorts. Her arms immediately went to cover her small chest.

"Don't," he told her softly. "You are perfect no matter what size you are, though you are filling out nicely now that you are being fed well." He leaned in and his lips found her ear, nipping the lobe and sending an enticing shiver down her spine. He pecked at her neck slowly and dragged his tongue down to the crease where her neck and shoulder met. The perfect spot. He sat down beside her.

"Are you ready?" he asked between kissing and licking at the spot he desperately wanted to sink his teeth into.

"Y-yes." It wasn't a stutter from her damaged vocal cords, but one of desperate, overwhelming desire.

His teeth sank into her skin, just hard enough to pinch at the flesh, but not hard enough yet to mark her. He groaned as his tongue flicked out against her skin to taste her. It was salty, yet sweet underneath.

He slid the strap of her bra down a bit to keep it from being soiled and let his incisors sink deep into her flesh. Warm blood spurted out from the wound and Liam took a deep drag as he groaned out. One suck and Elle's whole body was quivering. It seemed to simultaneously relax and become as tight as a coil all at once and a soft whimper followed by a moan left her lips as she felt her nipples pucker.

Liam dragged his tongue over her skin to seal in the bite and he shifted his body, pulling her onto his lap so that she was astride him.

"Now...mark me," he told her, baring his neck eagerly for her. He was breathing heavily and Elle could immediately tell why. He was rock hard beneath his tight jeans. His hands came down to steady her hips, digging into the flesh through the layers of clothing.

Elle's tongue slid over her lips, her eyes placing the spot where her bite would go. She leaned further into him, rubbing against his length and drawing out a hiss from him purely based on her movements.

"Shirt," she said, reminded him he was still over-dressed. He nodded and pulled it up and over his head. Then there was only her thin bra between their skin and his hand moved back to cup her ass, keeping her in place. He pulled her even closer, his hard length rubbing against her sex, and Elle moaned as her body moved closer and molded to his.

Without thinking, she let instinct take over and felt her canines elongate before slicing into his flesh.

"Shit!" His pelvis drove upward into hers, rubbing against her clit through her shorts. She was sure she was soaking through the layers, but it didn't seem to matter as her teeth sank in, sucked, and then her tongue slid across the bite to heal the wound.

A hand at her bra strap undid the clasp and pulled it off her body.

"I need to feel you," he said, the words coming out harsh and desperate. "I won't take you. Not until you're ready. But I want to touch your skin as much as I can."

Elle said nothing, her breath hitching as his hands came back to the front of her body, thumbs brushing lightly against her nipples. They tightened further and her hips ground against him in response.

"Fuck..." He was hard as granite, diamond even. His groin once again met with her sex, the friction making her clit quiver. She mewled helplessly.

"That...that feel good?" he choked out. "Christ, you make me so fucking hard, Elle."

As he ground his cock against her he took her lips again. The kiss was slower and hungrier, his tongue sweeping into her mouth and teasing hers. His hands cupped her breasts, thumbs flicking over the sensitive buds. Swallowing her moans as he tasted her, his mouth then kissed her lips, chin, neck, and collarbone. His eyes flickered to her mark, watching as it became more defined. It was a flower – *no*, a blossom. The perfect, deep rose of a plum tree blossom. He vaguely wondered what his would look like, but his lips were so close to taking in a nipple he pushed the thought away.

There...one rosy pink tip was hard, elongated, just begging to be taken into his mouth. He closed his lips around it with a suck and felt Elle shiver and arch her back. He traced the areola, sucked it back in, stroked it with the flat of his tongue and felt how completely her whole body seemed to respond to his, not just her sex. Her toes clenched and he drove his pelvis up into her again and again.

Shit. I may come in my pants like a fucking kid if I keep this up, Liam thought to himself as his cock throbbed painfully, and strained against Elle's perfect little body. It had been years since he had felt a woman's soft, pliant form against his, or felt anything but the touch of his own hard hand on his dick. He couldn't wait until she was squeezing him with her hands, her mouth, her pussy. The thought made him even harder and he gave a grunt as he rolled his hips into her again.

Elle let out a soft cry, her core clenching. She didn't know what he was doing to her, but she begged silently for it to continue. She felt ready to burst into flames.

"Elle, sweetheart, do you hear me?"

"Yes," she breathed.

"Do you want me to keep going? Make you come like this?" He moved against her again.

"Yes. Please. It feels...you feel so good," her voice rasped.

He rubbed against her again with a quick thrust. She moaned, her head tipping back as his mouth closed around her nipple again.

"H-how...do I know if I've c-c-ome?" she asked, squeezing her thighs together. She circled her pelvis against his again, greedy for friction.

"You've never had an orgasm before?" He sounded surprised. "I thought that Je – your ex-mate would have-"

"He...only *his* p-pleasure...m-m-mattered."

Her tummy felt tight, as if a molten ball of lead had settled there and was doing its best to weigh her down. Liam's lips worked at her nipples, his hips pumping up harder. All of the sudden, his own pleasure didn't matter as much. Getting her there seemed to be his goal. To give her what no one else ever had.

"Do you want to keep doing this?" he asked on a groan, dick twitching. "I can finger you or lick your pussy. Get you coming on my face."

"Don't stop!" she cried out. She was so close. The friction was just right, not enough, almost too much. It was difficult to tell which.

Liam could smell their mixing arousals, hers heavier than his own. He was sure she was soaking wet beneath those tiny shorts she had on. It took everything in him not to find out with his hands or his mouth, but he was pretty sure she would flood them both by the time he got her coming for him. He let go of another grunt as he circled his hips against her, rocking up into her. His cock throbbed heavily.

"You feel amazing," he said, his lips against the skin of her breasts. He had her wound up so tight she was nearly rigid in his arms.

"Close..." she murmured.

"Oh, love. I can't wait to have you coming on my cock when we mate," he told her. He relished the hot friction of her pussy rubbing against him. "Damn...you're gonna make me make a mess of myself."

"I'll do...laundry," she muttered. "Just...come with me. Please."

He growled, his hips bucking up towards her. He was right there on the precipice. His face wore the same strained expression as hers, but it was so fucking beautiful. Hollowed out cheeks, thick lower lip that he bit down on as he rubbed his body against hers. Even his usually perfectly angled brows as they knit together in concentration were poetry. All. Beautiful.

And perfect.

And she was his. He had wanted her, and she had found herself wanting him right back.

"Oh...fuck, Elle!" He cried out as he hurtled closer to release. "Come with me, my angel."

Come she did. His words, the tortured groans he gave, the friction – they all combined to wind her up and set her free. All the tingling warmth from her orgasm spread from her groin to her toes, her head, making her call out a garbled version of his name as they both tumbled over the edge.

As they sat there entwined, Elle sprawled on his lap with their breaths mingling and combining, she became a puddle of mush. Warm, gooey, satisfied mush.

Their breathing slowly settled, his arms wrapping around her, keeping her from sliding off his lap onto the floor until they both felt the need to move.

"Baby, I love you sitting on my lap, but I'm gonna need to get cleaned up," he told her, his lips to her ear. "And I'm pretty sure you soaked right through your shorts."

She nodded silently, testing the floor with one wobbly leg before placing the other one down. Liam stood up after her, gripping her hips and pulling them close to his body.

"I'll let you have the shower in here," he told her, breath fanning over her forehead and cheeks. "I'll take the bathroom in the hallway to shower. Then we'll move your stuff into my room and go downstairs to cook."

He pressed his lips against her forehead, pulled back, and started to unzip his pants before pushing them off his hips.

Elle's eyes averted and Liam smirked a little. Even half-hard as he was, the man was packing. He took off his dirty clothing, used his t-shirt to clean himself up a bit, and tossed them into the hamper. Then he walked out of the bedroom to the hallway bathroom, completely naked.

Chapter 11

Liam spoke on his cell phone while his hands skated lightly over the bruised flesh of his mark. Like Elle's, it was a plum blossom, but his was just the fresh buds on a sturdy branch.

"Yes, I understand it was a risk to mark her without consulting you first," Liam spoke. He was standing in front of the mirror in his bedroom, caught between looking at his mark and smelling the wonderful fragrance of the chicken and rice Elle was cooking downstairs. "But Jeremiah, he was – well, is *still* – a cruel bastard who would stop at nothing to take her from me."

'You do understand that she is his mate and he will most likely try to get her back anyway, son?'

"He is not her mate," he snapped back at his father's voice over the phone. "I have marked her as mine. She has no want of leaving here and no want of him as her mate. He...he marked her with silver, beat her bloody, and almost killed her. You can understand why she would be hesitant to go back to him. Frightened to, to speak plainly."

A sigh through the phone told Liam that his father didn't like what he heard, but that he was going to go to bat for his son with The Council.

'Do you have proof of his crimes?'

"Photographs, yes," Liam said. "She was also found by my Beta, Delta, and Gamma. She was nearly dead when they ran across her. She also has a scar with Jeremiah's initials on her back. Done in silver."

A hiss crackled through the phone.

'He would brand her with silver, but not with his own teeth? That is cruel.'

Liam nodded to himself, agreeing. "Will you speak to the other Elders? Let them know this was an emergency? Even if she was to go to The Claiming, she would be too frightened to attend. She is...wary of people except for myself, Colleen, and the pups. Strangers would be so much worse. I need you to secure an exemption for me."

There was a moment of silence on the other end of the line before his father sighed.

'Do you love her?'

Liam blinked as he blew a breath out. "I have feelings for her. The first true feelings I have felt for anyone since Cecilia died. If that is the beginning of love, then yes."

'Do you need me to send someone there to check on things at Blackriver?'

Liam shrugged, though he knew his father could not see it.

"It couldn't hurt, though it will probably only anger Jeremiah more," Liam responded. "For someone who was quite adamant on not having an Omega as a mate, he was awfully clear on wanting her back."

'Stupid man. He has feelings he cannot reconcile and takes it out on his mate because she is not of stronger blood. I'm glad you know better, Liam. Sometimes the best mates are those that are opposite you. They temper you, your anger, your frustrations. They make you well-rounded. Does she do that to you?'

Again, Liam was silent. He didn't know what it was about Elle, but it was *something*. He tried to describe it as best he could in the simplest manner.

"She makes me feel whole again," he simply said.

'Then I look forward to meeting her. Your mother, too. Hell, I may even drag Arden with us when we visit. I'm sure she wouldn't believe that you were actually happy unless she saw it for herself. After...after Cecilia died, I was certain I wouldn't have heard you speak of another woman this way. Even if this relationship is young, it has plenty of time to grow. I look forward to witnessing it.'

The two men said their goodbyes a few minutes later, Liam's father promising to call him when word came back from the other Elders. He would have his work cut out for him in order to convince them that the marking was a necessity, but once they were shown the proof of the claims of abuse, he was certain they would agree with him.

"Elle?" Liam called out, walking into the kitchen to the sounds of sizzling chicken and boiling water.

She looked over at him, smiling.

"Almost done," she said. "When will...the others be here?" Her face twisted oddly, like she couldn't believe the words came so easily from her mouth.

She was cooking not only for Liam and herself that night, but for

Blake, Trace, and Caleb, along with Colleen who wouldn't take no for an answer when Liam told her it was a private meeting.

"Twenty minutes or so," he told her, coming up from behind her and digging his fingers into her hips. He pulled her back to meet his body and curled his arms around her stomach to rest there.

"Dinner should be ready in 15," she said. Her voice was stronger, not wavering as it once had been.

"You're not stuttering," he observed, lips pressed against her head in a smile. "I'll have to ask Evelyn if it has anything to do with the marking. Mating with an Alpha *does* have its advantages."

Elle smiled and stirred the rice and vegetables.

"Or you're just an outstanding speech therapist," she said. "You may have missed your calling." She was teasing him and he grinned again into her hair.

"I brought the last of your things into my room and spoke with my father," he told her, pressing his firm body against hers. Hard. She always made him hard. If he was smart, he'd have stepped away from her, but their bond was still forming, and that tether that attached the two souls was making itself known in any number of ways. "He will speak with the other Elders, but once we send him proof of your mistreatment, he says they should have no trouble in approving this odd pairing, even if you didn't attend The Claiming."

"It is unusual," she said, stirring the rice again. Almost done.

"Yes, it is," he agreed. "For one to take a mate when they are already bound to another is one thing, but to have that other mate brutalize and-" His voice caught. "It's almost unheard of, especially in an Alpha. They are known to be most protective of their kin."

"Did Je—did he know you were planning on taking me as your mate?" Elle asked softly, her form stiffening slightly.

"He had an inkling I would say," Liam told her. "I certainly allowed that it was a distinct possibility. He...well, he didn't take it very well."

"Too bad." Her tone was bitter, jaw locked tight as her throat worked to swallow over the hard stone forming there.

"Hush," Liam murmured, holding her tighter. He could feel her struggling to relax. "He won't get to you. Not once we've mated and the whole pack is officially behind you as their Luna."

"Is there...a ceremony?" she asked, stilling with the question.

"Usually, but we will keep it small this time. I know you are not fond of attention, but I will be announcing the mating at the next meeting for the entire pack. You'll have to be there, but you won't have to say or do anything. It's just a formality. The pack will be pleased to have a true Luna again. It's been years since my mother left, and I believe most of them thought I was never going to take a mate."

"Has anyone...offered themselves to you?" she asked.

Liam shrugged, not caring. "A few. None that I would have taken as a serious partner. The most diligent was Sheila. She bothered me for a whole year after Cecilia died. She still attempts to seduce me every once in a while, but for the most part, she leaves me alone."

"I'm sure when you glare daggers at her she cowers."

"She deserves every ounce of my indignation," Liam said bitterly. "She was Cecilia's best friend growing up. Waited a whole two weeks after her death before making bedroom eyes at me."

Elle winced. That was tacky. She couldn't blame the lust the woman probably felt for Liam, but after only two weeks and with your best friend's grieving mate? Downright unbelievable.

"Does she have a mate?"

"No clue, not that I care. If all the pack females were to perish for some reason except for her, I still wouldn't take her. She's conniving and manipulative. The last type of person I want as a partner."

They were quiet as Elle continued to cook, taking the rice off the burner and stirring it with seasoning that made it a rich yellow color.

"What's that?" Liam asked.

"*Sazon*," she explained. "I put it over the chicken as well. It's good seasoning."

A hard knock on the door broke them up a bit and Liam went to the door. After opening it, he was surprised to see it was Colleen and Blake. He cocked a brow.

"How is it that you didn't just walk in like you usually do?" Liam questioned pointedly at Colleen.

"I didn't know if you two were getting cozy or anything in there," Colleen said, stepping into the house. "Smells good. Hey Elle!"

"Hi Colleen," Elle called, looking over her shoulder and smiling at the woman.

"You're not stuttering!" Colleen beamed.

"I know."

"How-" Colleen started to ask.

"I'll explain in a bit," Liam said, ushering his guests to the dining room table. "Eat first, questions later. Alpha's orders."

Trace and Caleb came by in the next few minutes and sat down, watching the silent Elle dish chicken onto a serving dish, vegetables onto another, and a heaping bowl of seasoned rice into a huge serving bowl.

"Oh, wow. This is really good, Elle," Colleen said, swallowing a bite of chicken. "What did you use?"

Elle told her, letting her know the seasoning could be found in the ethnic aisle at the grocery store. They ate in relative silence, once in a while praising Elle's cooking, making her face flush happily. Liam smiled every time her face tinged pink at their words. After the plates were all cleared, Liam stood from his seat and leaned onto the oak wood table.

"I'm taking Elle as my Luna," he announced, no preamble needed. "I've already marked her."

Colleen squealed and Liam rolled his eyes. The woman had no volume control and an unending amount of enthusiasm.

"I knew it!" she said, flipping Elle's hair back from her neck to look at her mark. "I'm planning the Luna ceremony! It's going to be-"

"Small and intimate," Liam finished for her. "Just a small gathering of wolves. Elle doesn't want anything flashy or big."

"Lee, she's gonna get "big" even if she doesn't have a big ceremony," Colleen said with a smirk. "Everyone knows Alpha's are large in the man bits department."

Liam's face flushed this time. Elle already knew what she was dealing with, and she looked off into the distance beyond the bay windows.

"She already knows, doesn't she?" Colleen guessed, her face lighting up. "Did you two already mate or-"

"Col, baby," Blake interrupted. "Not your business, and certainly not the time to bring it up."

"Right, I'm zipped," Colleen said, miming zipping her lips and tossing out the key.

"If only," Trace grumbled, rolling his eyes.

"That's not all," Liam said, moving forward. "As you all know, Jeremiah Bluth, formerly of Plumbrook, is her rightful mate. We all know how that turned out." His eyes scanned the group, who all nodded back. "He also now knows that Elle is here."

There was a chorus of cursing, muttering, and *how did this happens*.

"I went to visit with Jeremiah this morning about his close proximity to our pack borders," Liam continued. "He smelled Elle on some documents, and now he's aware of the fact I intend to keep her here with us. I also made him aware of the fact that it was a definite possibility that she would be my Luna. He wants her back and has said as much. To mate or to torture? That I do not know. But as I have marked her and she has agreed, he will not have her."

Liam stood up tall from his bent position and walked over to Blake.

"Set up a meeting for the whole pack for this Sunday afternoon," he told Blake. "I will make the announcement of a new Luna then. Trace, I need you in constant contact with patrol. They will need to be reinforced and doubled in case of attack. Caleb, I will need you to start training the younger members of the pack. I don't *want* to do it, but it may come down to using them if Jeremiah is stupid enough to attack. Anyone 16 and above is to train, male and female, all the way down to Omega."

They all muttered their acquiescence, their eyes cast down as their Alpha commanded them.

"They will not touch the Luna of Plumbrook," Liam announced loudly. "They will not get my mate."

***

Liam's bedroom looked strange to Elle, not at all like the room she was used to sleeping in. It was more masculine and smelled of Liam's heavenly, musky aroma. Sandalwood and spice.

Slipping off her clothing, she stood in her panties and bra before grabbing a silky pajama set. It was light pink with short shorts and a camisole-style top. It was something that Colleen had picked up for her when she had gone shopping.

She could still hear Liam on the phone with his father, though she couldn't tell what they were discussing. Instead, she grabbed a book that she had been reading and pulled the comforter and sheets down on the bed to slip under them. They were cool against her skin and she shivered a bit.

Elle couldn't tell how long she had been reading for before she realized the house was silent of chatter. She dog-eared the page she was reading and put the book down onto the nightstand before pulling the covers back over her body and closing her eyes.

All was silent except for the swish of fabric and Liam's heavy footsteps on the wood. Then the stairs. They walked slowly to the bedroom door before the light from the hallway caused Elle to open her eyes just slightly and look at the figure in the door. It was definitely Liam, and he turned off the light in the hall and silently slipped inside the bedroom.

"You awake?" he asked, his voice soft.

"Yes."

"I usually sleep naked or in boxers, so I hope you don't mind if I wear just the latter in bed with you," he told her.

"Liam, you made me come earlier today by dry-humping me, then stripped yourself naked in front of me," she told him wryly. "I think I'm okay with whatever you do or do not wear to bed."

He chuckled. "You were uncomfortable when I stripped, though."

"Well, it was the first time seeing you naked and you're...well, even only half-hard you were huge," she told him, thankful the light was out so he couldn't see her blush.

"Did...did Jeremiah ever-" his throat caught on the words.

"He made me go down on him," Elle said softly. "He took me in the ass. He liked the pain it brought to me. He never wanted to give me anything that would bring me pleasure."

There was a growl. Liam's.

"I don't regret it, being marked by you," Elle told him. "If only my true mate could have been as kind, as giving as you are, I-"

"No more talk of Jeremiah," Liam told her.

"You brought it up."

"I shouldn't have," he said tossing his jeans into the hamper. "It still smells of sex in here."

"I can put the hamper downstairs."

"Wouldn't matter," he told her. "It's on the sheets. It...it's making me hard."

He climbed onto the other side of the bed and slid under the sheets, cozying up behind Elle, his firm chest pressing against her back.

"I can change the sheets if you like," she offered, feeling his erection as it pushed up against her ass.

"Hmm...that wouldn't matter either," he told her, his lips at her ear. She closed her eyes. "You're in bed with me and that alone is enough to get me rock hard for you."

Elle forced herself to be brave, turning over so she was facing him.

"I can...take care of that for you," she told him softly.

"Elle, no," he told her, frowning. "You will never have to do anything with me you don't want to, and I don't want you to feel compelled to either."

She looked up at him, his dark lashes fanning over the deepest blue eyes she had ever seen.

"And what if it's what I want, too? Would you deny me the pleasure of bringing you pleasure?"

Liam hesitated, his lips opening slightly as if to speak. He wanted nothing more than her hands on his body, her mouth – but he didn't want it to feel forced. Not after Jeremiah.

"I'm following you, Elle," Liam told her, cupping her chin and then kissing her softly on her lips. "If your hand or your mouth on my cock makes you happy, I'll let you have at it. But don't feel the compulsion to please me just because it was something you were forced to do before this. I don't want that, don't want you in any way associating me with *him*."

Her lips brushed against his.

"But I want to," she whispered lightly, drawing a tortured groan from him.

"Fuck, you are a tempting little minx," he told her on another deep groan.

She smiled at him as if he had complimented her.

"Take off your boxers," she said, her voice soft and a little raspy. "Please."

"Shit," Liam muttered, pulling his boxers off and tossing them to the floor.

"I'm not that good with my hands," she told him. "But I'm quite skilled with my mouth and my...tongue."

Liam was so hard he could chop wood with his dick.

"Lay on your back for me," she ordered him softly.

Watching him stretch his hard body out across the bed, Elle felt a pang deep in her sex. He was in the perfect position to mount him, to place her legs over him and sit down, take him deep inside her.

The thought startled her. She hadn't felt anything but dread when thinking of sex since Jeremiah took her after the first week she had been with him in his bed. Only fear had bloomed when she thought he would mark her, mate her, make her his completely. None of that existed here, in Liam's bed. It felt odd and so right at the same time.

Grabbing the bull by the...balls, Elle did straddle him, first bringing her mouth to his, kissing him deeply and letting his tongue slide into her mouth to tangle with hers. His hands dug into her hips, kneading the flesh there and sliding up to cup her breasts. His thumbs brushed her nipples, pulling them into points and then up to her face, cupping her there as their mouths moved against each other's.

"Elle," he whispered huskily, his eyes opening as she pulled her mouth from his.

Her lips dragged down his chin, over his collarbones. Soft and wet, her tongue flicked out at a nipple, then the other before winding a path down his trim torso. Liam's stomach quivered, tightened, and her fingers skimmed the path of her lips as she went.

Face to face with his cock, which was rigid against his taut abdomen, she looked up at him. He was larger than Jeremiah, though she could have guessed that from earlier that afternoon. It would be a task to take him all in, but not an unpleasant one.

Her tongue darted out, tasting the head of his dick and drawing a hiss from Liam. She swirled her tongue around the flared rim of it, taking in the salty tang of pre-cum dripping from his tip.

"Hell!" Liam growled out once her warm lips wrapped around the crown of his cock.

She sucked at his head, feeling it strain and twitch between her lips. She slid lower. Lower. Taking in inch by inch of smooth, hard...

"Mmm," she moaned around him, sending a flurry of nerve endings to fire up under Liam's skin. Heat sizzled in his veins and his fists clenched at the sheets at his sides.

Her hands raked down his thighs, gentle at first, then harder before bringing one hand up to cup his balls. They were tight, drawn up already, and she knew it wouldn't take long for him to come.

Her hand fisted him at the base of his cock, gripping tight in slow jerks, coming up on his shaft as her lips glided upward in tandem. Mouth sliding up and down with her hand, wet with her saliva, she moved faster over him, bringing him close, so close until he was barely holding back.

"Elle, sweetheart – I'm gonna fucking come," he rasped out.

She gave no sign of hearing him except to move faster, bringing him even closer to releasing. Her mouth hummed around him again, and she felt him grow more rigid in her mouth.

"Baby, you gotta – oh, shit! Gotta move before I...oh, fuck," he choked out.

Her hand and head were moving urgently up and down him, coaxing him to come, to spill inside her mouth as her tongue flattened against him, barely able to move as it wrapped around him again and again.

"Elle...love," he pleaded, almost sounding pained. She moaned around him again and her hand planted firmly on his thigh, squeezing slightly. She looked up at him, his face tight with pleasure, his jaw twitching with barely contained desire.

"Elle, move away now if you don't want my load shooting straight down your throat." His voice was thick and he was barely able to push the words out.

She kept sucking at him and he couldn't hold back.

He shot deep in her mouth with a cursing groan and felt as her throat closed, again and again, swallowed every drop he spilled. When he was done, he took long breaths, shivering as he felt her lick him clean.

"Better?" she asked, looking up at him from his pelvis, her tongue flicking out to catch one last drop.

He didn't speak, only pulled her up to him so she was atop him, straddling him again.

"Fuck, you're amazing," he told her before kissing her deeply, desperately. "Never came so hard and fast my whole life. Not even..."

His voice trailed off. It wasn't the time to speak of previous mates, deceased or not.

"That couldn't have been very enjoyable for you," he told her, kissing her lips again, softer this time. Almost placating. "You didn't get anything out of it."

"Says you," she said, smiling down at him. "You taste good, not like..." And she too faded out.

They lay in silence, her soft, light body up against his as he stroked her back.

"Elle, I..." He paused briefly, choosing his words. "I want to taste you, too. Want to have you come in my mouth, taste you on my tongue."

Her eyes met his, a little confused.

"You mean...what *do* you mean?"

"I want to eat your pussy, baby," he told her, running his hands through her hair. "I'll make you feel good. It...it's not tit for tat. I really can think of nothing better right now than to have your thighs wrapped around my head while I sucked your sweet little clit up between my lips and tasted you."

She squirmed on him, aroused.

"I've...never done that," she told him. She wasn't saying no, nor were the words indicative of a yes, and the question drew out the awkward silence in the room.

"I'd like to be the first," he coaxed. "Right now."

She thought for a moment and spoke.

"Okay," she said.

He immediately flipped them over, pulling her camisole up her chest and over her head as he did so. His mouth immediately latched onto on one of her nipples as he sucked it in. Her hips rolled, gyrating against him as his mouth hungrily worked her breasts between his lips with head-spinning suction on them. As he sucked, he pulled off her bottoms, panties along with them. One, then the other nipple was teased before slowly working his mouth across her belly, licking a line down to her lower abdomen.

His nose drank in the heady scent of her arousal before he parted her sex with his thumb and licked a slow line up her slit. She shivered and he did it again, enjoying her response.

"Liam...wha-oh!"

His mouth sucked at her clit, bringing it into his mouth while his fingers played with her hole.

"You're so wet for me," he murmured before lapping at her again, pulling every ounce of her enjoyment into his mouth. "And so, so sweet."

That was a pleasant surprise. She tasted sweet, like strawberries. And he dipped his head down to thrust his tongue inside her sweet cunt, enjoying not only her flavor, but the grip her walls had on him. She would be perfect once they mated. Tight, warm, wet. His dick twitched again, rousing from its dormant state to half-awake. He cupped his balls, squeezing them to try and remind they already had their turn. This was for Elle.

Her hips rocked against his mouth, smearing her wetness over his face as his tongue darted in and out of her. Wrapping his arms around her thighs, he pulled them over his shoulders, letting him feast deeper inside her before flicking back up to her clit. He swallowed, pulling her taste into his throat, groaning as his tongue lashed back and forth on her clit, up and down, side to side.

He pulled her fleshy little bud into his mouth again with a pop and her hands darted to his hair, soft and silky. She moaned and her hips moved faster, faster, chasing her release.

"Liam," she moaned, her hands weaving through his hair, tangling and pulling gently at the strands. He didn't respond, only adding suction, causing her to cry out. Her moans got louder, fanning out across the room until she was practically bucking her hips up into his face, so close to her release she could scream.

"Li-oh, I'm coming!" she cried out as her orgasm washed through her, spreading from between her hips outward in heavy waves of pleasure.

He licked her slowly through her orgasm, feeling her tiny, quivering clit pulse against his tongue, making him wish she was squeezing his cock. Liam crawled up her body, placing kisses on her skin as he settled between her bare thighs once more.

He kissed her mouth once, twice. Again, until she was almost breathless with need and he rolled onto his side, running a gentle hand up and down her body between her chest and lower abdomen.

"You want children, right?" he asked, his head cradled in his propped-up hand.

"Yes, I love children," she said. "Always have."

"How many would you like me to give you?" he asked. His hand lingered on her flat belly. He hoped the answer wasn't just one. Or two. He hoped she wanted lots.

"As many as I can handle," she said with a smile. "I don't have a number in mind, but I'd like at least three. Or maybe a better answer is, *as many as it takes until you get a son.*"

He chuckled. "A son would be nice," he said. "Someone to take over when I'm done being the boss. I'm just glad you want more than two. I always wanted a big family even though it was only my sister and me growing up."

"How long do you want to wait to start having them?" she asked, rolling over to face him and cradling her head in her hands.

"I wouldn't want to wait at all," he said honestly. "I know you're young, only 18, Elle, but I'm 24 and I was ready to have kids years ago with my first mate. You know how that turned out. Even if she had taken her medications, it...the types of meds she was on were not very conducive to procreation. Too high a risk that one of the babies would have issues from the meds. Defects. I feel like I've been waiting forever." He shook his head. "I don't want to wait, but I will if you want to."

Elle looked up at him, pondering his words.

"I don't want to wait either, though I know I'm young," she said. "My mother had my oldest sibling at 19, and I know I can handle it. And I have you to help out, right?"

Liam smiled down at her before pressing his lips to her forehead.

"I'm not the type of man who expects his woman to bear his children and then leave her to raise them alone," he told her. "I want to be a part of their rearing, a part of their lives every step of the way. If I fuck up, I fuck up. The more kids we have, the less chance I have of repeating the same mistakes. If you want three babies, fine. If you want a hundred...well, I'll see what I can do about that."

Elle laughed, a musical tinkle of giggles that lit up Liam's face in turn.

"But for now, I'd like you to do me a favor tomorrow," he said.

"What's that?" she asked.

"Promise me you'll try?"

"Of course," she responded. "What is it?"

"Promise me you'll try and sing for me."

Chapter 12

Waking up warm and cradled in Liam's arms, Elle noted that she was still naked, still bare. His left hand was cupping her breast while the other was pressed against her flat tummy. Its position made her think about the conversation they had the previous night before going to sleep.

As comfortable as she was, her bladder begged for relief and Elle was able to slip out of bed with minimal disruption to the Alpha's sleeping position.

Closing the bathroom door behind her, she relieved herself and washed her hands, deciding to brush her teeth before turning on the water for a shower.

As soon as the soothing heat of the water hit her skin, she sighed. She tested her vocal cords by gently humming. The sound was a bit rough, but only because it had been a while since she had attempted to sing, and it was morning. Her voice was always a little throaty when she first woke up.

Sometimes while at home in Jeremiah's house, she had hummed a little or attempted to sing, but she was usually too frightened that he would come home unannounced and yell at her. Anything seemed to set him off. Humming, singing, speaking. Even a sigh could get him to cut a glare at her if it was ill-timed enough.

Settling on a tune to try to sing later, she hummed the melody lightly, not wanting it any louder than the steady thrum of the water hitting the floor of the shower. She closed her eyes and tilted her head back, wetting the front of her body and letting it soak up the heat. When she turned around, she dropped her head to her chest to let the water run over her back.

"What are you humming?" Liam's voice asked, making Elle jump slightly in place. He was standing, completely naked, at the other end of the walk-in shower and watching her.

"Geez, Liam," Elle breathed. "You scared the hell out of me."

"Sorry," he said, smiling. He didn't look sorry at all, and she frowned at him.

In response, he moved closer to her in the shower and cupped her ass, pulling her toward him. He ran his hands up and down the soft skin of her rear, making his cock twitch against her stomach.

"What's the song?" he asked, kissing her on the forehead.

"*Not A Day Goes By*," she replied. "It's from a musical originally, though it's been covered by other singers as well. I used to sing it a lot. It...it has different lyrics for different times in life. Some of them good, some – not so great. I would just change the lyrics to whatever I was feeling at the time."

"How can a song have different lyrics?"

Elle placed her arms around Liam's waist. "When it's first sung in the show – part one I guess you could call it – it's about a breakup. Husband and wife getting divorced and the woman is bitter. He cheated and they have a child together. All she wants to do is forget that she loves him, but she can't. The child reminds her every day of her love for him, and it kills her over and over again."

Liam said nothing, his face inscrutable, eyes blinking as he watched her.

"The second time it's sung, it's at the couple's wedding. It's much more...happy, I guess, and looking forward to their life together," Elle explained.

"He cheated and she forgave and married him again?" Liam looked confused.

"No," Elle said with a smile. "The show is done in reverse chronology. It starts in the present day and moves back in time."

"What? That sounds ridiculous."

Elle shrugged. "It was the only way to get a happy ending maybe?" she suggested with a shrug. "I don't honestly know why they did it backwards. The beginning of the show is a party that starts out great and ends with the breakup of his current marriage. The man marries twice, neither female sticking around because of his...ways."

"Ways?"

"Yeah. If you start from the beginning – or rather the end of the musical – it's full of hope for his future," Elle said. "A miracle in the sky. Sputnik, the Russian satellite. Things...happen after that to tear that hope apart. It's about a trio of friends who become successful at writing musicals, but it revolves around one man in particular. He becomes so successful that he loses sight of what his dreams used to be. He sells out, loses his friends, his self-respect, his wife – basically everything that used to mean anything to him. He realizes too late that he's screwed up everything by making the media and the public happy. And he's no longer happy – or true to – himself."

"Hmm, sounds familiar," Liam posed.

"Yeah," Elle said with a sad smile. "Some men don't know how good they have it until it's too late."

Liam cupped her face, kissed her lips slowly, and pulling away gently.

"The day I start taking you for granted, I want you to kick my ass," he told her. "Or have Blake do it. I would never hurt my best friends purposely, but if you see me acting like a dick, I expect you to call me on it. Deal?"

She smiled back up at him. "Deal."

They spent the rest of the shower touching, kissing, washing each other's bodies, shampooing, and conditioning until the hot water started to turn cold. Turning off the shower, Liam tossed Elle a big fluffy towel and grabbed one for himself.

After drying and dressing, they checked the time. 10:00 AM. Liam was amazed. He'd slept longer and more deeply than he had in years.

Elle was still humming, though it was a different tune. She cracked the fresh eggs he had bought the day before and started to briskly whisk them so they were a uniform light-yellow color.

While Liam made coffee and got out milk, flavored creamer, and sugar, he listened to the song she hummed.

"Can you sing me the other song? The one from the shower?" he asked, silencing Elle.

"Sure," she said. "I mean, I can try."

Elle cleared her throat and hummed a few notes, testing out the key she wanted to sing in. After a deep breath, she started.

From beginning to end, Elle sang in a low, wavering voice. She was tentative at first, growing more confident with each word and phrase, and by the time she was halfway through, Liam understood that she was singing the sadder version of the song. It melted his heart and uplifted him in turn, until her voice finally faded away.

There was a pause at the end, Elle looking down at the omelet she had created without thinking before adding a generous helping of cheese and tucking one end over the other. She eventually flipped it and took it off the burner, setting it aside.

"I hope you like vegetables in your omelet," she said quietly. "Onions, peppers, some mushroom. I was...I got so into the song that I forgot to ask."

"I'm sure it will be delicious," Liam told her, his voice equally as soft. "And that song – you sang it beautifully. With…so much heart. I felt I understood every emotion behind it as if I'd written the words myself."

Elle smiled over at him, nodding.

"Thanks."

She plated the rest of his breakfast and set it on the counter in front of him. He gave an appreciative moan with the first bite.

"How do you get the eggs so light and fluffy? My last housekeeper burnt the edges and the eggs felt like a lead weight in my stomach after eating her breakfast."

"A little bit of milk goes a long way," Elle told him from the stove. "Do you want me to cook up more bacon or sausage?"

"This is perfect," he told her, scooping up another forkful of eggs and vegetable and eyeing the crispy bacon next to it. "And I don't have much time before I have to meet with patrol. All has been silent on the borders, but I don't want them slacking due to lack of action."

"I thought Trace was taking care of that," Elle said, adding some vegetable to her own omelet.

"He is, but it doesn't hurt to show them I'm serious by making an impromptu appearance," Liam said. "Keeps them on their toes if they know I'm sniffing around. Not that they're lazy. They just get complacent."

Elle hummed a response. She could understand that. She felt she could relate, staying at Plumbrook for the weeks she had. She was equal parts happy and scared, the latter because she never knew when the other shoe would drop, and Jeremiah would somehow get to her.

"Hey, what are you thinking about?" Liam asked before taking a sip of his coffee. Her face had fallen and her eyes had become unfocused and crinkled with concern.

"Lots of things." She shrugged. "I'm happy I can sing again – and without getting hit. Scared that he knows where I am. Terrified that he'll do something to my parents or brother to force me to go back to him."

"He hit you because you sang?" Liam's voice was gruff, angry.

"He hit me whenever I did something that made me happy," she explained. "He would take his iPod with him to work so I couldn't listen to it after he broke mine to bits. It had been a present from my parents a few years back for my birthday."

Liam's hands gripped the edges of the bar until the wood beneath his fingers groaned with the force. Elle looked back at him and quickly plated her own omelet.

"Hey," she said as she walked over to him with her food. Setting the plate down, she placed herself so she was between his spread legs and put her hands on his chest. "Liam."

He grunted, his fingers flexing and the material beneath them groaning. He was going to break the damned table if he kept it up.

"Don't look for trouble," she said, knowing he was about three seconds away from bolting out the door to find Jeremiah and beat him to within an inch of death. "It'll most likely find us soon enough."

Liam blinked rapidly, took a few calming breaths, and pulled Elle by her waist until she was flush up against him. Closing his eyes, he breathed in her scent, the light flowery mix calming him little by little. His locked jawed tensed, then released.

"You should eat while your omelet is still warm," he said.

"Not until you've calmed down," she replied, her hands now running through his still-damp hair.

"We can do both at the same time," he declared, and stood up from his chair.

He moved her along to the dining room and went back for her coffee and plate, bringing a napkin with him. He sat down at the table and patted his lap. Elle looked at him and sat down gingerly on it, as if she would break his legs with her weight. He, in turn, pulled her into his body until she was against his chest, her head snuggled into his neck. One hand kept her firmly planted on his lap, the other went to the plate in front of him, scooping up a bite of her omelet.

"Eat, sweetheart," he told her. "You sitting close to me will calm me, and me feeding you will allow me to concentrate on something other than ripping Jeremiah's fat arrogant head off his body."

She thought about that and opened her mouth. Warm, fluffy egg with some veggies and cheese were thoroughly chewed before she swallowed. They sat there for a while in silence, him feeding her until her plate was empty while he sat breathing in her aroma of freesia and jasmine. By the time he was done feeding her, his head was cool, calm, and he was ready to meet with patrol.

***

Trace blinked as Liam strode toward the group of wolves he was speaking with. They were all in human form and had been listening intently to him until his head had turned to see their Alpha coming towards them.

There was not only his movement, but a strange sound. Liam

was...humming? Impossible. Liam hummed as often as he smiled, which was an occasion as rare as hen's teeth.

But, no. He was humming *and* smiling. He looked happy, and Trace lifted a brow as the Alpha walked toward him.

"You either fucking mated with her last night, or she has a great set of hands," Trace whispered to him, smirking.

He sniffed at the Alpha who pushed him away. The smile, though, stayed firmly in place.

"You don't smell any different, so I'd say she probably has wonderfully capable hands," Trace said, laughing.

Trace was not as close to Liam as Blake was, but they were still good friends. They joked and talked smack while they worked out at the gym or on the training field, though nothing would ever compare to Blake and Liam's close brotherly friendship.

"None of your fucking business, dog," Liam said with a smile. "Just because you're not mated doesn't mean that you get to live vicariously through me."

"Don't need to live vicariously through you," Trace told him. "I get enough pussy to make that grin of yours pale in comparison. So tell me, did she need both hands to get around the Alpha's thick cock?"

"Fuck off," Liam said, his mouth twisting a bit. "Besides, you don't need hands at all if you know what to do with your mouth."

Trace's eyes widened slightly, surprised. "You dirty-"

"I'm not discussing it any further with you," Liam said, cutting him off. "I've said enough and I'm here for more important matters."

Liam walked away, inspecting the line of patrol that would be leaving at 12 PM sharp for their rounds. He walked up and down the row, glad to see that Trace had more than doubled their number.

"Alpha, permission to speak?" asked one of the newer additions to the patrol. He looked to be barely 18, 19 at best.

"Granted," Liam said. "What is it, Andrews?"

Moving a step forward, the young man looked down at his feet, baring his neck as a sign of respect before looking back up.

"Is it true the pack will have a Luna soon? That you have found a mate?" the man asked.

Liam looked at the man. The kid had balls, he had to give that to him.

"We will discuss that at the next meeting this Sunday," Liam stated bluntly before turning to the rest of the group. "Anyone else care to check in on my love life, or can we get started?"

There was a mumble of responses, none of them wishing to impinge upon the Alpha's personal life until the man deemed them worthy to hear the details.

"Good," Liam said. "Now let's begin."

***

'The Council was understanding about your impromptu marking, what with the evidence you sent along. It was...shameful, to say the least.'

Liam's father sounded tired. That worried Liam, and he asked him about it.

"What is it? I know there's something more you're not telling me," Liam said, his voice gruff.

'The Council was split down the middle whether or not to send one of their own to Blackriver.'

"I don't care if they send someone or not," Liam told him. "My pack can handle Jeremiah and his pack of savages." Though he knew it was unfair to lump them altogether with the deceitful and cruel Alpha, he couldn't honestly help himself.

'I'm not honestly too worried about him coming after Giselle.'

"Elle," Liam corrected possessively.

'Right. As I said, I am not so much concerned that he will try to steal your mate. I am afraid of what he'll do to her relatives. She has a brother and parents there still, does she not?'

Liam's face was grim. Elle had said she was concerned about this same thing just the day before. Between that and the fact her heat should be coming on soon, he didn't know which he was more concerned about.

Your dick, he thought to himself. *You're more concerned about getting your dick wet. Admit it, you horny perv.* If his inner wolf had been able to speak, he could have sworn that was exactly what it would say to him.

"Yes, her parents and her brother still live there," Liam said with a sigh. "Her brother is a doctor, so they may let him be since war could come, but it will be only a matter of time until they try to use her parents in some way to bring Elle back into the fold."

'Perhaps not. If Jeremiah does something idiotic like imprisoning her parents, it would only be a matter of time before the brother would go looking for them. It would look bad on the Alpha if both daughter and parents went missing in such a short span of time, so there's that.'

"True," Liam said, breathing out a cleansing exhale. "And though her parents are a lower station at Omega, someone would certainly notice them being gone. Her father is a teacher, after all."

'It would be easy enough to ask for a leave of absence for a teacher, so do not let that fact ease your mind.'

"What if Plumbrook asked for assistance themselves?" Liam asked slowly. "What if it wasn't so much a reconnaissance mission to Blackriver than helping a pack who requests it? A pack in good standing, mind you."

His father hummed, thinking.

'Could work. Send the request our way and I'll have it delivered to the head of the Council. If he doesn't approve your request, I'll come myself – say I'm taking some time off to visit family. It wouldn't be a total lie.'

"Yes, but if you went to Jeremiah and told him you were there as a part of the Council, you could lose your standing amongst them. They could brand you rogue if they thought it prudent."

'Don't make me laugh, boy. I may have only been doing this for a few years, but I still have all my wits about me. I can tell them I'm part of the Council so long as I don't ask too many questions. Maybe request to see Elle's parents as we both have mated kin. They'd be asinine to deny that request.'

That could work. As long as his father minded his P's and Q's, maybe everything would turn out alright in the end.

***

When Liam got back to his home from his office in the Packhouse, he immediately smelled something delicious. He heard something as well. Elle humming again. Pretty soon she was singing instead.

The house was hot inside since the stovetop and the oven were both on, and Elle fanned herself with a newspaper Liam had discarded that morning. He hadn't had a chance to finish it like he usually did, but he wasn't so much worried about the world around him as he was much more focused on the trouble most likely coming to find him.

As Elle finished her song, she bent over to check the food in the oven and Liam spoke.

"Is...was that Taylor Swift?" he asked, cocking his head at her. His sister had this album, and at one point listened to it nonstop.

She looked back at him, stopping the cute sway of her hips to the music she heard only inside her head.

"Yes...yes, it was," she told him, waving the newspaper back and forth like a fan as she stirred the noodles aimlessly. "It's called *Blank Space*."

Watching her fan herself, Liam walked toward her.

"Would you like me to open the windows? They can be sticky, especially with this muggy weather."

"It's okay, I don't mind," she told him. "Food should be done soon anyway."

Liam walked over to see what was brewing in the large pot of cauldron-like proportions. Corn on the cob. No wonder she had used the largest pot available in the house. She could have practically crawled inside it her herself, it was so large.

"What's for dinner?" he asked, replacing the glass top to the large pot.

"Stuffed pork chops, corn on the cob, and butter noodles," she told him, taking the noodles off the burner so they wouldn't dry up.

"Smells heavenly," he told her with a smile before planting a soft kiss on her cheek. The difference in height was staggering. Liam, at his last recollection, stood 6 foot 6, and Elle barely topped 5 feet 1 inch – 2 in sneakers.

The alarm that signaled the pork chops were done went off just as Elle grinned up at him, and she immediately turned the oven off, grabbed a couple of oven mitts, and pulled the door open.

A searing wave of heat came out in a chuff and Elle quickly grabbed the food, placed it on the stovetop and went to get plates.

The air cooled slowly in the house throughout dinner, though Elle still felt hot as ever. She had turned on the fan above the stove to pull the heat up and out of the room, but she still felt like a charcoal briquette.

They were both quiet as they ate, Elle trying to cool herself by drinking lots of ice water, and Liam blinking over at her every few moments as her newspaper-fan waved back and forth.

"I think the fan in the kitchen is broken. It's hot as Hades in here," she finally said, blowing out a puff of hot air.

Liam blinked, his eyes narrowing a bit in speculation.

"Babe, it's nice and cool in here now," he told her, placing his knife and fork onto the plate.

"Are you kidding? I'm sweating bullets, Liam."

Liam's nostrils flared and he took a deep sniff before clearing his throat.

"You may be 'sweating bullets', as you say, but I'm telling you that has nothing to do with the room temperature in here," he told her.

"What?" She seemed a little perturbed, and her lips turned down in an adorable frown that, with the combination of her scent, had Liam's dick hardening in his jeans.

"You're in heat," he told her, getting up from the table and placing his plate in the sink. "It starts slowly, but pretty soon you'll be in pain, sweetheart. We need to mate before that happens."

"Shit," Elle mumbled beneath her breath. No wonder she felt like she was being broiled alive. She was surprised her skin wasn't as red as a lobster.

"Come on, angel," Liam told her, pulling her up from her place at the table. "I'll have just enough time to get you good and ready." He smiled down at her. "As you know, an Alpha's cock is a force to be reckoned with."

Elle gulped past the nervous lump in her throat and nodded. She wasn't nervous for anything except for the actual penetration. If his size wasn't so daunting, she would have spread her legs wide for him days ago.

Trace! Blake! Liam barked through the mindlink at the two of them.

'Sup?

Liam rolled his eyes at Trace's informal greeting.

Blake! Liam yelled louder through the link.

Fucking...dammit, Liam, you cock-blocking son-

Shut it, Blake, Liam told him before he could lose his temper. *Elle is in heat. I am not to be disturbed unless the territory is being invaded or the Packhouse is going up in flames. Got it?*

Yes, Alpha, they both said.

Finally. Maybe he'll be less crabby if he's getting pussy on the regular, Trace grumbled, still connected to the mindlink.

Link's still open, assclown, Blake told him.

Shit! Sorry, Alpha. Trace sounded contrite.

Not my fault you're such a whore, Liam told him. *I'd rather fuck my mate over anonymous, temporary pussy any day of the week.*

Amen to that, Blake said before cutting himself out of the link.

Assholes, Liam thought to himself.

I heard that! Trace growled out angrily.

I'm glad, seeing as how you were meant to, Liam threw back.

"Everything okay?" Elle was looking up at him, worried. The sweat on her brow had doubled, and she looked ready to pass out.

"Everything's fine," he told her, moving them along quickly with the gentle nudging of his right hand against the small of her back. "Just had to tell Blake and Trace I would be...indisposed."

Elle's face reddened ostensibly, and Liam at first wasn't sure if it was because of her heat, or the fact that those two probably knew they were going to mate within the very near future. Her next words confirmed his suspicions.

"The-they know what's going on?" she asked. Liam watched as a drop of sweat slipped down her face, dripped off her chin and onto the fabric of the light-yellow t-shirt she wore.

"They do," Liam confirmed. "But if it makes you feel any better, I cockblocked Blake at the same time."

Elle's lip twitched up in amusement. He was right. She did feel a little better knowing that she wasn't the only one that was about to get laid.

"You're still a virgin, right?" he asked her as they crossed the threshold to their bedroom. Elle had mentioned Jeremiah preferring to take her anally, but he wasn't sure about other penetration. Elle nodded at him and her breath came in short, raspy pants. Liam's smile widened. "Good. I mean, I know this isn't what you had originally thought your mating would be like, but I'm glad Jeremiah didn't take your pussy."

That's mine to take, he added silently in his head.

Her hand came up to his chest and Liam could feel it instantly through his shirt. She was burning up.

"I don't regret this, and I won't," she told him. "I'm glad he never tainted me. I'm glad I'm rid of him. It led me to you."

Liam's chest warmed and became full before he picked Elle up to his height. She wrapped her legs around him just as his lips came down on her neck, teasing her mark with soft nibbles of his teeth against the sensitive flesh there. Her mark had fully healed, but it would always be the most sensitive part of her body, save her genitals. On the other side of that, if anyone else besides her mate tried to touch her there, it would be painful. A mate's mark was sacred.

Liam turned and sat himself on the edge of the bed, already starting to pull her shirt from her body by the bottom. When he tossed it aside, Elle gasped, her head falling back as another blistering wave of heat ran throughout her body.

"Liam! Please touch me!" she begged, her voice breathless and strident. "It's the only thing that makes the pain better."

He quickly removed his shirt and tossed it aside, pulling her chest against him as he reached around to unsnap her bra. She was finally starting to fill it nicely and the more generous swells heaved with every movement of her chest. He turned them both over and onto the bed, Elle beneath him, her hips squirming and a rivulet of moisture trickling down between her breasts.

"Fuck, angel," he said as he looked down at her for a moment, drinking her in but putting space between them.

"Liam," she whimpered.

"Shit...sorry, sorry." His voice was a soft coo, completely unlike the dominant Alpha he was. "I know it hurts, but I just had to look at you." He took a breath, exhaling slowly before closing his eyes for a moment. When he opened them back up, they were a surprising amber color instead of sparkling blue. His wolf was peeking out.

"You're fucking gorgeous, Elle," he told her, inhaling the heady musk of her arousal with a heavy breath, his lids fluttering closed again. When he opened them back up again, they were blue with a hint of grey. "Jeremiah was a fucking fool to let you go. And I'm one lucky bastard to have caught you." He lowered his head, sucked a nipple into his mouth and felt it harden against his tongue.

"Liam, please!" she cried out as she squirmed beneath him. She needed more of his touch. She needed everything he could give her.

He pulled away and quickly unbuttoned her pants, pulled them from her body in one swift movement and taking her panties with them. Her pussy glistened in the soft light of the room, making his dick throb and swell. He looked back at her face, breathing heavy.

"You trust me, angel?" he asked, voice bordering on a growl.

She nodded. "With my life. I wouldn't be here if I didn't."

The warm glow of her words lit up his chest like a match to a candle wick. In the wake of the soft glow, he lowered his mouth to hers and pulled her bottom lip into his mouth, groaning as he felt his dick get even harder. It had already felt impossibly hard beneath his black jeans.

"I'm going to make sure your pussy's one hundred percent ready for my cock, sweetheart," he told her, letting go of her lip slowly as he pulled back from her, dragging his teeth.

"Then I'm going to mate you so thoroughly it would be a miracle if I didn't have you soon pregnant with my child."

Chapter 13

Liam buried his face between Elle's thighs, groaning before lapping at her clit. She immediately felt cooler to the touch, though still sweaty and heated.

"Fuck...your pussy smells divine, sweetheart," he told her and sucked on her labia for a moment before thrusting his tongue inside her. Again, she felt her body temperature drop a bit, though it was still uncomfortable in the grand scheme of things.

Pulling his tongue out of her, he situated her in the middle of the bed and shucked his jeans and boxers off before crawling once again between her legs. He looked up at her as he blew on her clit, causing her to shiver slightly.

"I'm eating this pussy until you come on my face, angel," he told her, again blowing gently across her sex. "Then I'm gonna take you nice and slow until you're used to me." He really didn't want to hurt her. The woman had been hurt enough, even for several lifetimes.

Elle started to nod her head, but just as his tongue met with her clit again and he sucked on it slowly, he fluttered his tongue against it before adding more suction. Elle threw her head back and Liam immediately felt her get wetter, hotter, though her skin was starting to cool from his touch.

The vibration of a groan against her sensitive flesh caused Elle to arch her back again and she ground her pussy onto his mouth.

"Don't be quiet, angel," he told her, pulling away for a moment, the heat of his breath licking at her core. "There's no one in this house to hear you but me and I need to hear your moans and cries."

Her sex clenched at his words and a soft mewl spilled from her lips as her head tilted back. He took her clit back into his mouth and sucked gently on it at first, adding suction and rolling his tongue around it. Her legs shook and tried to come together, but Liam used his large hands to keep her thighs held wide for him, though he tossed one of them over his right shoulder and planted a hand on it to keep her steady. With his free hand, he took one finger and parted her inner folds, feeling her quiver against the thick digit. Penetrating her slowly, it easily slid inside.

God, she was so wet. It made his dick harden further until his balls ached. With renewed vigor he knew he had to speed up, get her coming for him so he could fill her and take away the residual pain of her heat.

"Come on, angel," he commanded her between hard flicks of his tongue. "Come for me." He continued to flick his tongue against her, the strokes harder against the underside of her clit until she released with a gush over his lips.

Elle's accompanying cry echoed out in the room and was only softened when Liam's large hands stroked her thighs, soothing her receding burn.

With one last lap of his tongue, he crawled up her body, kissing the flesh of her torso on his slow journey upward. When he got to her neck, he bit softly down on the flesh of her mark and heard her gasp audibly. It was more sensitive now and would be even more so after they mated.

His hips moved against her, his cock sliding against the wet flesh of her sex before he grabbed the base and pointed it directly at her center.

"We do this and you are mine for life, Elle," he told her, dominance dripping from his words. "My life for you. If J—if he tries to take you from me, I have every right to take his life to spare yours. Are you sure you're okay with that?"

His cool blue eyes pierced hers, looking for any hint of trepidation. When he found none and she nodded back at him, he pressed the tip of his cock against her, feeling the muscles of her pussy straining against him. He parted her slowly, reveling in the feel of her tight, wet warmth. The difference in her body's core temperature was almost immediate, and he buried himself slowly to the hilt inside her.

"Ah...fuck, Elle," he groaned out once he was seated completely inside her. He felt like he was being sucked into her from the dick on in. Moving wasn't an option, her grip was so complete, and he sucked and lapped at her mark, hoping to relax her a bit. When she finally did, he pulled slowly out of her before pushing himself back in.

"Baby, you need to let me know how you want it," Liam told her, kissing her neck again. "Harder, softer. Faster, slower. I need to know so I don't hurt you and so that I can make you come."

She bit her lip and nodded her head frantically, moaning when he hit a spot deep inside her with the crown of his cock.

"Is it right there, angel? Is that that spot where it feels the best?" His dick rubbed her there again, causing a moan to spill from her lips.

"Y-yes, Liam," she told him, and he groaned as she said his name.

He slowly started to pump his hips faster, Elle's moans continuing to allow him to read her body, let him figure out what got her off, what was too much. With long, dragging strokes, his hips angled more and he hit her g-spot dead on. A few thrusts had her on the edge, and when she crashed over it, he could feel the drag of her pussy as it convulsed around him. It was almost enough to toss him over the edge of bliss as well, and he groaned into her ear before smoothing her hair back with his hands and kissing her lips. It was his method of distraction from coming too soon.

As he devoured the rest of her post-orgasm moans, he felt her arms wrap around his neck, coming up from his chest and over his shoulders to settle, tangled in his smooth black mane.

"Shit, angel," he grunted out. "You make me want to slam into you and claim what's mine. You are mine, aren't you, sweetheart?"

"Y-yes," she moaned out slowly, her hips rising to meet his as her eyes closed in bliss. "Yours. Always."

He groaned out again and felt his balls drawing up tight against his body. "Fuck, sweetheart, you're gonna make me come." Nothing was hotter than his little mate gladly submitting to him.

Her hips tilted and met with his as he continued to rock his body against her. He couldn't help but speed up just slightly, and Liam watched her face as he moved faster. Then more. And more. He was soon taking her harder than he thought he should, but there was no sign of any pain or hesitance on her face or in her sparkling eyes. While his hips slammed into her at a brutal pace, he tried to read her every emotion like a book. Each bite of a lip, every flutter of her eyelids, even the way her mouth opened minutely before taking in a deep, dragging breath.

"Tell me if it's too much, angel."

"No," she said immediately. "More. I need more."

His dick jumped inside her and he thanked his lucky fucking stars he had found her. He planned on keeping her always, ex-mate be damned. He would crucify Jeremiah before ever letting him have her. The sadistic bitch deserved far worse in his opinion.

Liam threw his hips into hers and felt as her legs shook and she started to swell and tighten around him. She was too fucking sweet, so wet, and damn it if he wasn't well on his way to being completely enamored with her.

"Oh...shit, Liam!" she cried out as her body tightened around him again. "I'm coming!"

He felt the first contractions of her sex around his dick and cursed. There was no way he wasn't going to follow her with the way she was milking him. He felt himself swell and then spill out into her, emptying the contents of his balls inside her with hot jets of his ejaculate. He let out a strangled sound from deep within his chest.

Liam thrust a few more times into her as he floated on the remnants of his release. Then his forehead rested against hers as they both fought to regulate their breathing. He was still hard as a brick inside her, though he could feel himself slowly deflating.

Rolling off her body, he pulled her with him until she was half on him, her head tucked away in his neck and his hands moving slowly over her arms, hips, and thighs.

They both came down slowly until their breathing regulated. The tenuous bond that had been formed when he marked her swelled and consumed them, and Elle couldn't help but kiss the mark she had given him on his neck. His dick instantly stiffened again, half-hard as it already was.

"Angel, you might want to steer clear of the mark," he told her softly with a chuckle. "Keep teasing me like that will get you good and fucked again."

Elle's body stilled for a moment before she did something unexpected. She bit gently at Liam's mark and rubbed her left calf up against his now fully erect manhood.

"You asked for it, sweetheart," he told her before quickly rolling them both over so he was planted between her legs, his hips grinding up against her slick sex. Elle moaned, her eyes fluttering shut as she rocked against him in response.

"Is that what you want? More of my dick?" he asked as the head of his cock rubbed enticingly up against the hard edge of her clit, causing her to utter a wildly intoxicating sound. Something between a whimper and a purr. She let out a small mewling "yes" and continued to squirm her hips beneath him.

"Can't hear you, baby," he told her, smirking down at her. "I want to know if you want my dick again."

"Yes, Liam. Please," she begged, her hips picking up a frantic tempo. He was so close to being inside her, the tip of him mere centimeters away.

"As my mate wishes," he said and grabbed a hold of his length before teasing the head up and down her slit. When he had her wanting and pleading with him, he pressed up against her, feeling her flesh strain against him. With the first thick inch wrapped tightly in her warmth, he leaned down and kissed her lips.

"Dear – fucking...sweet Jesus," he muttered. "I wish I could say this will be longer than last time, but with the grip you have on me that's debatable. You make me fucking lose myself when I'm inside you."

Her hips moved and he was encased even further inside her. Liam groaned out and moved his lips from her mouth to her neck, collarbones, and settled lower as he captured a nipple with his mouth.

Elle's hips bucked upward and Liam sank down further into her with a grunt.

"Oh, fuck me," Liam swore and clenched his eyes shut. Being inside this woman was almost too much for him. She had his dick standing at attention every second of the day with the slightest cock of a hip, the minutest trace of a smile. "I'm going to take you from behind in a minute. Have to, sweetheart. But, shit, you just feel too fucking good around me." He pulled the other nipple into his mouth and sucked deeply on it, rendering it solid as stone.

He continued to stroke slowly in and out of her as he feasted on her breasts. Elle's hands gripped his hair and pulled slightly, the touch of pain only turning the man on even more.

"Fuck, Elle," he gritted out. "I need you on your hands and knees now. Roll over and give me that ass."

She gazed up at him with a startled look and Liam knew where he went wrong.

"I'm not going to fuck anything but your pussy, baby. No need to fret. I just want to see your ass move while I take you from behind."

She rolled over willingly for him after that, getting on her hands and knees before him. The pale, smooth flesh of her cheeks begged for his hands, and he used one to skate over her skin gently while the other grabbed his cock and centered it at her entrance. As he pushed into her from behind, his hands gripped her hips and pulled her back to him. She felt deeper this way, and much tighter. Liam pushed her thighs together and straddled her hips, relishing the even tighter feel of her pussy around him. He then gently pushed her upper body down so her chest was against the mattress.

She was a sight. All soft curves and that sexy as fuck moan she gave every time he pushed his cock deep within her. It made him want to lose his ever-loving mind. He pumped his hips into her slowly, letting the drag of his cock press lightly against the sweet spot inside her. It riled her up a bit, and pretty soon she was squirming, begging for more.

"Please, Liam," she begged, her voice muffled a bit from the bed sheets.

"Harder? Faster? Tell me what you want, little mate."

She let out a whimper, and her sex fisted around him, making him hiss out tightly.

"Everything," she finally told him, her voice breathy. "Faster, harder. I want it all."

Oh, you're going to get it all, he told her through their newly formed mindlink. He saw he surprised her as her head snapped to his, eyes wide and unblinking. *You want my dick that badly, sweetheart? Then you're going to get my dick. Deep. Gonna fill you up so good with my cock and come that you'll feel me for a week.*

Elle moaned and closed her eyes, her body relaxing a bit at his words.

Yes...please, yes. I want it, she said to him in kind.

A feral growl was ripped from his body and his fingers dug into the skin at her hips.

"You got it, angel," he told her aloud. "All of me."

He sped up his thrusts and felt it as soon as he pegged that sweet spot inside. She immediately became tighter around him and so he angled his hips and rolled them to hit her just right in that same spot. He wanted to have her coming. Every orgasm he pulled from her, every moan, and every plea, was his.

Pretty soon he was throwing his hips into hers, slamming against her ass as her moans permeated the room, only louder this time. One orgasm. Two. He was well on his way to granting her a third when his own balls started to tighten and he felt himself losing control.

"Fuck, angel," he rasped out. "Come for me one more time. I'm about to fill you up real good."

As impossible as it seemed, her sex clenched at him even tighter until they were both crying out their release. Hers was a soft, musical wail, his a deeper, growling groan.

When the last jet of hot come was spent and emptied out into Elle, Liam stroked her trembling thighs and pulled out of her. He got up from the bed and walked over to the en-suite bathroom and started up a hot, soothing bath for them both. He knew she would be sore, for she had taken a whole lot of him in just one night. He really shouldn't have been surprised that his new mate was his perfect match. Sometimes the unexpected turned out to be utter perfection.

Maybe that supreme being in the sky knew what he or she was doing when they made these two cross paths.

After the bath was filled and fragrant with suds from a sweet-smelling bath oil, Liam walked back into the bedroom and looked down at Elle on the bed. Her eyes were closed, but in no way she was asleep. He could hear her mind still working as he prodded it with his own. She was recuperating. The bath would indeed help.

Leaning over, he smiled as Elle's eyes blinked open when he picked her up from the bed in a bridal carry.

"Where are we going?" she asked into the curve of his neck.

"We're going to take a bath. Together," he told her. "I'll try to be good when I'm in there, but I can already feel my cock getting harder by the second. Are you too sore for more?"

"I'm a little sore, but not much," she said, almost sleepily. "A bath sounds nice right now."

Bathroom sex sounds even better, Liam thought to himself and immediately felt his dick harden and point straight up. It nudged at her skin and she froze before shaking with silent laughter.

"You won't be laughing when that cock's buried deep inside you in a few minutes," he growled out as he moved them both into the bathroom.

Liam lowered her into the hot water and got in after her. He spread his legs and pulled Elle in between them, her back snugged up against his fully engorged length.

After he washed her body, she did him, and ended up stroking his cock until he pulled her to straddle him and pierced her sore pussy with his thick spear of flesh once again.

"Shit, baby," he growled out. "Told you I didn't know if I couldn't *not* take you in here. Fuck!"

Still, he had her coming twice more before he finally found his release. A shower set them to rights before they both headed to bed to sleep.

***

Jeremiah had been trying to take an after-dinner nap when he felt the remainder of the mate bond with Giselle snap. At first, he wasn't quite sure what it was, but when he tried to reach out with his mind, he was met with a silence he hadn't felt since before meeting Giselle.

His Giselle.

It didn't matter that Liam had tried to claim what was rightfully his. Unless Jeremiah was dead, a part of that bond would always be there, ready to take over the muted, lesser bond of a chosen mate.

Still, he had felt the snap, and he knew what it meant. He had not only marked her, but mated his female as well. It didn't sit well with him, and he was up and scrambling out of bed before he could think.

Carter! his voice blared through the mindlink to his Beta. *Get your ass to my house on the double!*

He could hear the soft response of the cowed Beta and knew he was frightening him. Everyone cowered under his command, even his closest and oldest friend and second in command.

When Carter arrived at the house, he was out of breath and looking like he had done hours of winding sprints prior to this. Jeremiah cut him with a glare.

"He's fucking done it," the Alpha bit out. "Not only has that usurping bastard marked her, but mated with her as well."

There was a pause as Carter took a deep breath and exhaled slowly.

"How do you know?" he finally asked, his voice low and deep. He *had* his mate and didn't know what the loss of one would feel like.

"I could feel it, the moment he took her. It-" He cut himself off as a wave of unwanted emotion balled itself up and lodged in his chest and throat. "The moment he claimed her as his, I could feel the remnants of our weak bond snap. I can't...I can't feel her or anything."

It was almost enough to make his friend feel sorry for the poor fool. He could tell he was much more attached to Giselle than he wanted to be. Or at least more than he would admit to. It was as natural as snow in winter or the heavy thunderclouds of summer. She was his mate, and whether that was now untrue, he would always feel the loss of that bond tremendously.

"Permission to speak freely, Alpha?" Carter requested in a tired monotone. He needed his voice devoid of emotion for what he had to say. He couldn't risk making it seem like he was on anyone's side but Jeremiah's.

"Permission granted," Jeremiah said begrudgingly with a low grunt.

"Do you actually care for Giselle or do you just want her because of the bond? If you don't care for her, you should leave her be and take a woman to mate at next year's Claiming ceremonies."

"That bastard took what's mine!" Jeremiah snarled, his head whipping around to meet Carter's gaze. "It doesn't matter if I love her or not. She is mine to do with as I please and I will have her back!"

Carter closed his eyes, giving up. If Jeremiah couldn't admit to his slightest feelings now that she was mated to another, he would never admit to them. The man was a lost cause in matters of the heart.

Maybe it was because he didn't have one.

Or – maybe it more because he didn't *want* to have one. At one point his father had loved, and look at where it had gotten him. A dead mate and a fucked-up son in the bargain. It was somehow easier to do things his way now. It wasn't pleasant, but it kept people and things in their places. And kept him from feeling the emotions he so desperately wanted to be rid of.

"Send out a group of warriors to find Jackson Kincaid," Jeremiah said staunchly, his Alpha command heavy in his tone. "Have them bring him to me and tell Jackson...tell the bastard I have a proposition for him."

"But Jackson-" Carter protested.

"Do it now, Carter, or it will be your life for refusing your Alpha's command."

The man had literally lost his fucking marbles. They were scattered, never to be seen again possibly.

Carter bowed and showed his neck in submission before turning and walking slowly out the door of the Alpha's home.

***

A chorus of songbirds greeted the morning at Plumbrook the next day. It was surprising as it was awfully late in the Fall for them to still be hanging around. The milder weather was to blame, but certainly all of them would see to seeking warmer climes by Halloween, possibly sooner.

Elle stretched her limbs and found the bed to be empty of anyone but herself. Blinking over to the alarm clock on the nightstand, she saw it was 10 AM. She had slept for a solid ten hours, a feat she had rarely accomplished before. Granted, she loved her sleep, but eight hours was usually her limit. By then she would be up and chirping happily along with the birds in her own musical manner.

As she sat up, she realized she was still nude from the night before, having been too tired to pull on her normal sleep apparel. She got out of bed to put on some panties and a tank top.

Liam. The man had some serious stamina. It made her blush a little to remember how she had begged and pleaded with him, though it had only seemed to serve to turn him on even more.

Life was a lot different now than she had thought it would be six months prior. Though she couldn't see her parents or her siblings, she found herself grateful in this new home, and with a new mate – a handsome and loving one at that. It was all so surreal that she found herself wanting to pinch the skin on her arm to see if she would wake up and find herself back at Blackriver with Jeremiah and still a slave to his sexual whims.

No. That would be too cliché. Like something you'd read about in some fairytale.

"Angel?" a voice called from the doorway. Liam stood there with two large, greasy bags of food in his hands.

"Liam," she called, smiling back at him. Her stomach growled as the scent of food permeated the air.

"I wanted to make you breakfast but I'm shit in the kitchen, so I went out and got us something to eat," he told her.

"Smells good," she told him. "What is it?"

He promptly told her while taking out each dish. A Colorado omelet, bacon, sausage, and hash browns. Each were delivered jokingly with the pomp and circumstance worthy of a 5-star restaurant.

Liam grabbed them plates, trays, and utensils, and they dug into their food right there on the bed. They ate in silence for a bit, though Liam watched her with scrutinizing eyes. When they were three-quarters of the way done with the food, he finally spoke.

"How are you feeling this morning?" he asked. "Any aches or pains?"

She surreptitiously flexed her limbs and shook her head. "Only slight, like you might get after a moderate workout at the gym," she told him. "Otherwise, everything is standard."

Liam nodded, swallowing another bite of bacon.

"We'll be announcing you as Luna at the meeting tomorrow afternoon, though some of the wolves on patrol seem to already be slightly aware of my finding a mate."

"I don't have to do anything, do I?" she asked, a forkful of egg stopping mid-air on the way to her mouth. It jiggled and fell to her plate, the fork following behind it loudly.

"Just have to be there and let me introduce you," Liam told her. "You met a lot of the pack at the bonfire and the parents of the pups are already quite taken with you." He added a kind smile to that remark. If there was anyone in a pack you wanted on your side, it was the parent of a pup. They were notoriously protective of their young, and Elle had won over the children without even trying.

"Colleen wants to take you out later on," Liam said, his lips straightening into a thin line. "Something about pampering, or mani-pedis or something. Probably just a ruse to find out more about our mating. That woman..." he trailed off.

"She is quite nosy," Elle agreed with a cock-hardening giggle. "But she's a good person." She paused. "Or maybe she wants to know how big an Alpha's dick really is."

Liam looked at her and smirked.

"I have no shame in that department," he told her. "You can boast all you want on my account in regard to my dick, angel."

They finished their breakfast and Liam cleared their things, putting the dishes in the washer and tossing the debris in the bin.

When he got back upstairs, Elle was already in the shower and singing, this time a song he was more attuned with. It was one that was popular when his sister was still living at home. Arden may have had a weakness for Taylor Swift, but her true love was Bruno Mars.

He recognized the Mars/Travie McCoy version of *Billionaire* and smiled. It didn't surprise him that she sang it, for she had gone from having nothing to a true home. When she morphed from one song to the next, he listened hard for the words. She sang Adele with none of the gritty rawness of the professional's voice; Elle's was too sweet to compete, but it still stirred something in him. The words. It had to be the words.

She sang *Send My Love* from beginning to end without stopping, as if the words were ingrained in her, or she had written them herself. He wondered if she knew how true those words were, in fact. Apropos to this situation they found themselves in.

"Angel," he called to her once she was done with Adele. "Colleen should be here in half an hour. Blake just told me she's getting ready and should be coming over soon."

What Blake had really said was that Colleen would be there in 15 minutes. Due to her lack of timeliness, Liam had merely added an extra 15 because it was more than likely when she would arrive.

"Okay!" she called from the shower, and then started to hum something else. It sounded like *Rockstar* by "A Great Big World".

She seemed more in tune with songs from a few years ago than anything popular today. He made a mental note to buy her a new iPhone as well. He had already replaced the iPod Jeremiah had broken. If *he* didn't want her to have it, Liam would make sure he would supply her with it.

The song changed, and Elle started to sing. This time, Liam wasn't happy with her selection. *Unpretty* by "TLC". He didn't stop her from singing, though. That's what Jeremiah would have done, though the content of the song wasn't what he would have liked to hear. The title said it all.

She seemed content enough as she sang, and when the water turned off and she took over humming something else, he sighed and gave her some privacy to change.

Since it was Saturday, he wouldn't necessarily be going into his office so he had the majority of the day to himself. Elle would be out with Colleen for a good portion of the day, and though he thought she was beautiful just the way she was, he wasn't going to tell her not to go. He just hoped she didn't make any radical changes to her appearance.

Elle bounced down the steps in sneakers, a fitted t-shirt and some Capri pants that almost fit her small stature like regular pants.

Liam looked over as she descended the last step and he walked over to her, leaning down to capture her lips with his. He breathed in the heady scent of her through his nose, and felt himself stiffen below the belt. Biting her lip gently, he plunged his tongue into her mouth in a dominating kiss. All tongue, teeth, and lips, he had to adjust himself in his pants as his other arm curved around her waist and cupped her ass in his large hand.

"Knock knock!" a voice called out as the front door opened.

"Fuck," Liam muttered. He had forgotten to lock the door behind him on the way back with their breakfast.

"Hey, lovebirds," Colleen said, grinning cheekily at the two of them in their tight embrace.

"The one fucking instance when you're on time," Liam mumbled to himself, though he was sure that Colleen heard.

She had and paid him no mind. Colleen was used to the older, grumpier version of Liam, so though his outlook on life had changed a bit, she was still ready for any emotional reaction from him.

"You ready to go?" Colleen asked, looking over at Elle.

"Yeah, just let me just get my purse," Elle said, and walked over to the dining table where she had a tendency to leave it.

"You don't need your purse," Colleen told her. "This is my treat and it'll only get in the way. Leave it for now, and we'll get food on the way back."

Elle shrugged her shoulders and followed Colleen.

"Wait!" Liam called to her before she left the house. He stalked toward her and pulled her into his body before planting a deep kiss on her mouth. She opened it for him and let his tongue tangle slowly with hers before he eventually pulled back. "I'm going to have a few of the warriors follow you. I don't trust Jeremiah not to try to take you while you are off pack territory."

She nodded at him, a frisson of fright traveling up her spine and making her heart beat double-time.

"I understand," she told him.

"Be safe," he told her and pecked her lips once more before letting go.

Chapter 14

"I have a question," Colleen announced as they drove along the country highway towards one of the larger human towns just south of Plumbrook.

"I'm not telling you Liam's penis size," Elle said immediately. Her eyes glanced in the direction of the car following them. There were two warriors in a large black SUV behind them.

"Not what I was going to ask, but good to know," Colleen said as her lip twitched in amusement. "We all know Alphas are large. *Everywhere*. I was actually just wanting to make sure this was what you really wanted. I mean, it's too late to take it back, but I'd feel better knowing that you are all-in with Liam. He can be a difficult man to know. I can only imagine he'd be even harder to love."

Elle didn't hesitate. "I'm positive, Col. I was given a cruel Alpha mate in Jeremiah so I know I can handle whatever this odd coupling throws at me. It's just...I'm not with the one that was originally meant for me. I don't regret becoming Liam's mate – not at all. I'm just concerned about what this means for the pack."

"You think your old mate is going to come for you still," Colleen deduced shrewdly.

"I don't think. I *know*," Elle told her. "I may be years younger than Jeremiah, but I've had years of living at Blackwater to see what he was like from the outside. And I've had six months of living with him. I've seen what he can do from both perspectives. He puts on a good show for the pack as a whole, but knowing what he's like behind closed doors is – *and was* – eye-opening. He orchestrates things. He never gets his hands dirty when he can get someone else to do his dirty deeds for him. He's sly and selfish, and though he has everyone thinking he is looking out for them, he isn't. If it was between himself and the pack as a whole, he would choose himself over them every day of the week and twice on Sundays."

"What does his Beta say?" Colleen asked, for once relatively quiet as she listened to Elle speak.

"He doesn't agree with everything Jeremiah does," Elle said. "He calls him out on it, but only up to a point. Carter and

Jeremiah...they've been best friends for years, but I think Carter is only in it just to keep up appearances. I don't think...if the chips were down, Carter wouldn't-" Elle stopped herself and shook her head. "Certain things – unless Jeremiah used his Alpha command – he just couldn't bring himself to do."

"He's a good guy?"

"I owe him my life," Elle said with a nod. "If it weren't for him, I'd still be with Jeremiah. I'd still be miserable."

"You'll make a good Luna, Elle," Colleen told her. She was being serious for once and the look on her face was steely. Determined. "Liam is a good guy. A bit prickly until you get to know him, but he has a good head on his shoulders and his heart's in the right place. After his...after Cecilia died, he was impossible to reach. He hated outsiders, didn't trust anyone but the people in the pack. When Blake, Trace, and Caleb found you, I thought for certain he would kick you out immediately. Blake knew you weren't a threat, but Liam...I don't know how you wormed your way into that block of ice he calls a heart, but I'm damned glad you did."

"Packs are always strongest when they have an Alpha and a Luna," Elle said with a small smile.

Colleen laughed and shook her head.

"They are, but it's not that," the older woman told her. "Liam's one of my best friends. We grew up together, me and him. Blake, of course, as well. You've changed him, Elle, and that's a good thing. He hasn't been this happy in years and it's definitely not just the toe-curlingly good sex he's probably getting now."

Elle's mouth twitched a little, her face turning slightly pink at Colleen's words.

"He's almost back to where he used to be before everything started going bad with Cecilia," Colleen continued.

"What was she like?" Elle asked, curious about her predecessor.

"She was a very pretty woman," Colleen told her. "Thick mane of red hair, deep brown eyes-"

"No. I mean as a person," Elle interjected. She had already seen the photos. Photos didn't say what type of person Cecilia was, and Liam, as her mate, would have only focused on the good parts of his other half.

"She was...different," Colleen said with a shrug. "She was like an onion. You had to peel back the layers. She let people only see the outer layer most times, the pretty surface she had."

"And when you peeled back the layers?"

"Harder to say," Colleen told her. "Her...with her mental illness, it made it difficult to figure out what was her, and what was the psychosis talking. She could be kind and caring one moment, and the next...It was like she was a completely different person. On the medication, she was a bit better, but she lost all her vibrancy. She became just a shell of a person. I know I give Liam a lot of shit, but it hurt to see him when he was dealing with her and her sickness. He did everything for her and with her, but he wasn't...he wasn't *there*. I don't know how else to describe it. It was like he was just going through the motions. Making her eat, making her bathe, forcing her to get enough rest. Then after she died, he just...he became cold and distant. Until you."

Colleen smiled over at Elle. "You woke something up in him that I was afraid was going to be dormant forever," Colleen told her. "We tried to get him to pick a mate, but the more we pushed, the more he struggled against us. Liam's always been a bit of a rebel. Tell him to jump and he'd walk just to spite you. I didn't think he'd ever make a move on you, though I knew he wanted to. And I knew you'd be good for him and said as much. You're everything his old mate was not. Level-headed, giving, compassionate. I don't say these things to make it sound like Cecilia was a bad person, it's just that, with her troubles, it was hard for her to focus on anyone but herself. I mean, how could she have taken care of a pack when she didn't know word one about taking care of herself?

"Cecilia wasn't mean like Jeremiah, and she *did* love Liam," Colleen continued. "But with all her issues, it was difficult for Liam to care for the pack properly. All his focus was on her. He was certain it wouldn't always be that way, that she would take her medications regularly and, voilà, she'd be all better. But mental illness is with you for life. It...it's probably best that she isn't *here* anymore. I'm not saying that I'm glad she's dead, but if she were still around, this pack would be weak, with a leader whose primary concern was whether or not his female was medicating, or if she was on the verge of suicide again."

"Fate," Elle said solidly. "I have to believe that this was all fate." She shrugged her shoulders heavily as they drove past a sign that told them the mall was only five miles away.

"We're shifters, so of course we believe in fate," Colleen said. "We have soulmates, people who are literally our other halves. We have to believe everything comes down to fate."

Elle agreed and nodded her head. She just hoped her fate was taking a turn for the better.

***

Colleen made Elle get the works. Mani-pedis, a haircut, seaweed wrap, and a facial. She also made sure Elle looked the same, only better. She wanted her to be Elle 2.0 for the meeting the next day. It would be difficult enough for her to have all eyes on her, a relatively new and strange wolf, and when she was introduced as Luna, it would be with scrutinizing eyes.

Many people at Plumbrook remembered the type of man Jeremiah Bluth was – both before and after the death of his sister and mother – and Colleen hoped that would be enough to appease the doubtful, the unsure of the pack.

As they got massages – done by female masseuses – Colleen decided to bring up a new topic. It was difficult to speak as the two humans in the room would probably have been frightened that they were giving deep tissue massages to dangerous werewolves. Wolves and humans coexisted peacefully, but there was always a bit of a stigma in regards to the two-natured. Therefore, Colleen made her best attempt at speaking in code.

"Halloween is coming up soon and you – well, someone of your position is supposed to organize any of the gatherings the, uh...the *community* has," Colleen told her.

"I'm horrible at that type of thing, Col," Elle told her, feeling whiny. "I wouldn't know the first thing about throwing a party."

"That's what I'm here for, silly," her friend told her. "I love doing it, but you'll have the final say. I can't promise not to go overboard, but I'll try to reign in my more outrageous tendencies."

Elle wondered what an "outrageous tendency" could portend, and figured she probably didn't really want to know. Fireworks or pyrotechnics, probably.

"So, what does this entail? Costumes? Bobbing for apples? A haunted freaking hayride?" Elle asked.

"Well, since this is the first time in a while we've had a Lu-uhm, had *you*, we should make it special. Maybe make it like a couples-themed costume party," Colleen explained.

"What – like Romeo and Juliet? Sonny and Cher kind of stuff?" Elle asked. It was an interesting idea, rife with possibilities.

"Exactly," Colleen told her happily. "Maybe you can come as a queen and Liam as a king."

"That sounds like it might be too much," Elle said. "I like the idea of a couples-themed party, but let's not get silly."

"Up to you," Colleen said, sighing in relaxation. "I think it's a damned good idea though, seeing as you are...well, who you are."

Later, during the ride home, Elle thought more about the costume party. Liam would probably have a shit fit before dressing up in tights and playing Romeo to her Juliet, so she was trying for something a little more subtle.

Richard Burton and Elizabeth Taylor. Mick Jagger and Jerry Hall. Antony and Cleopatra. John Lennon and Yoko Ono.

No. Definitely not that last one. John died horribly and Yoko was blamed for the break-up of The Beatles. All sorts of bad juju was associated with the two of them.

Elvis and Priscilla Presley. Now *that* one had some potential. Minus the rhinestone jumpsuit, Elle could see Liam dressed in leather and denim and singing *Jailhouse Rock*. Well, maybe not singing. That didn't really seem to be his thing, but she could definitely see him with a gelled pompadour with a little sneer on his lips. His pink, *kissable* lips.

Yes. That was what she wanted to do. And Elvis had been dubbed the King of Rock. Close enough to royalty. She believed Liam could appreciate that. Smiling to herself, Elle looked out the window. She saw the following black SUV in the side view mirror and her smile faded. No matter what happened, her past was never too far behind, taunting her.

***

Liam had kept busy while Elle was away. He had been to several stores in a town and had come home to find Elle still gone. He mindlinked with the guards he had following them, and they had told him they were on the way home from the mall. Everything had gone as smoothly, just as Liam had suspected it would. He didn't expect Jeremiah to strike so soon, but he wasn't taking any chances either.

He mindlinked with Trace and had him assign warriors to keep an eye on the Alpha's home. Close enough to see everyone who came and went without the benefit of hearing anything. Trace told him that it was as good as done and there would be two wolves assigned to each entrance, four in total.

The front door of the home opened, and the quiet steps of his mate made him smile.

"Angel," he said as he moved toward the sounds. He looked her up and down, and was pleased to see she was still his Elle. Her hair was a few inches shorter, but still long and silky. Her face was the same, unmade and open, the blue of her eyes still sparkling brilliantly. The rose color on the apples of her cheeks deepened when he cupped her face and kissed her lips gently.

"Your hair's so soft," he told her as he ran his fingers through it.

"I got the split ends cut," she told him and placed her lips on his again.

"Looks beautiful," he breathed against her mouth. "I'm glad you didn't cut too much off." He played with the ends of her hair until Colleen interrupted with a loud cough.

"You can call off the hounds, Lee," she told him. "We're back on pack territory, and they're still out there looking like extras from *Men In Black*."

"Got it, Col," Liam said without looking at the woman. "I missed you," he told Elle.

"Oh, God!" Colleen exclaimed loudly, rolling her eyes. "If you two weren't so completely adorable together, this would be completely nauseating."

"Goodbye, Colleen," Liam told her firmly, a command in his tone.

"Fine, fine," she said as she placed the bag she was holding down near the front door. "Elle, that shampoo and conditioner they used on your hair is in the bag. I'm out of here. Think about what I said for the party."

Liam waited until Colleen left and spoke.

"What party?" he asked, still holding onto Elle. His hands had left her face and he was holding her against him by her hips.

"Halloween," she told him. "It's in two weeks."

"Ah, forgot about that," Liam said, laughing softly. "Colleen loves Halloween. It's her favorite holiday. What is she doing this year?"

"A couples-themed costume party," Elle said. "And I had an idea for us."

"Yeah?" He tucked his head into her neck and breathed against her mark. It made a burst of gooseflesh pop up on her skin and she shivered.

"Yeah. Colleen wanted us to go as King and Queen, so I thought, why not?"

"Please tell me you're not talking royalty in tights," he said, a groan slipping out.

"Not in the least," she told him, smiling. "I have a better idea. Not all royalty comes with scepters and crowns."

"Color me intrigued, little mate," Liam said, lifting a brow at her. "What did you have in mind?"

"Leather for you, a bouffant for me," she told him.

There was a short pause as Liam pondered that. "Okay, I give up. What does leather and big hair have to do with kings and queens?"

"Elvis."

"Elvis." He looked like he still didn't get it.

"The King of Rock," she reminded him. "Elvis and Priscilla Presley."

"Ahhh." A moment later he frowned. "You're not putting me in a studded jumpsuit à la *Viva Las Vegas* or anything, are you?"

"As much fun as that would be to see, no. I'm thinking more along the lines of *Jailhouse Rock*-type Elvis. Much sexier than bell bottoms, butterfly collars, and horrible facial hair. Do you think you can do that?"

"Can do, angel," he told her, and placed a small kiss on the corner of her mouth. "Can do."

***

"What's this?"

Elle was just finishing up the last of their dinner and had added some garlic bread to the stove to cook along with the meaty lasagna she had made.

"Open it," Liam said with a smile.

Elle looked askance at him, and stuck her hand in the red bag sitting on the kitchen counter. There were two boxes inside, and she used both of her hands to pick them up.

"An...iPhone *and* an iPad?" she asked, looking up at him, confused. "I already have an iPod, Liam."

The reminder made him smile. She used the hell out of the iPod he had gotten her, but she didn't have a phone or tablet.

"And now you have a phone and tablet," he told her. "The phone is just like the one I have, and the tablet is so you can download any books you want. Here." He handed something over to her. It was smaller. A credit card with her name on it.

"I ordered it for you," he told her. "It's attached to my account so you can have some way to pay wherever you go."

"Liam-" she started to protest.

"Hush," he told her, his fingers pinching her lips together gently. "Once you accepted me as your mate, you accepted everything about me. Whether that's money, or a car, or having to deal with my sweaty socks at the end of the day, it's yours and I won't hear a word against it."

He waited for a moment to let that sink in, and when he saw her shoulders relax slightly, he knew she had relented.

"Fine," she told him. "I don't need these things, though."

"But I want you to have them," he replied. "If I could, I'd give you everything you ever wanted. But that seems a bit unrealistic, so we'll stick with just this stuff for now."

"And I don't need a car," she told him.

"For now," he said as he walked away to get washed up for dinner.

As he washed, he thought that he was glad she didn't want a car yet. Cars could drive far, and he needed her to be close. Having her out with Colleen and the security detail was pretty much his limit on distance from her. If she didn't have to meet with the pack the next day, he would have told her – no, *pleaded* with her – to stay home. He would never order her around like *him*.

They had a semi-quiet dinner, Liam only telling her a little bit about what to expect the next day.

"Lots of the pack didn't think I'd ever take a mate," he advised her, taking a sip of his water. "There have been a few…offers from females, but I never took any of them seriously. Oh, and Sheila will most likely be there."

"Who is Sheila again?" The name sounded familiar, and she wondered where he had mentioned her before.

"Cecilia's old best friend. The one who tried to get me to take her to mate as soon as Cecelia was gone," Liam reminded her, frowning. "She's a nasty piece of work so try and steer clear of the bitch. She'd befriend you just to stab you in the back quicker than you could blink."

"Did you…ever, well…"

"God, no! With Sheila? I'd rather cut my dick off than be with her," Liam told her. "She is the worst type of creature. Two-faced and shallow. She's pretty enough to look at until you see what type of person she is underneath."

"Is she mated now?" Elle asked. Liam simply shrugged.

"I have no idea what is going on with her," Liam told her as he took a bite of his garlic bread. "I rarely speak to her and when I do see her, I usually walk in the opposite direction. Even small attention gives her the impression that I'm interested in her."

"That's – well, that's sort of pathetic," Elle said, her mouth twisting. "Doesn't she want to find her mate? The one meant for her and her only?"

"She's the type who thinks she doesn't need a true mate. Or at least not one who is just any old rank-and-file wolf," Liam told her. "She prefers powerful men and wants to be the powerful female behind the man. I doubt anything but another Alpha would make her happy."

"She sounds like the female version of Jeremiah," Elle pondered and finished the last bite of her lasagna.

"She does, doesn't she?" Liam sounded almost amused. "She's no Omega, but she doesn't come from Alpha or Beta bloodlines either. At least, I don't think she does. I honestly haven't thought enough about it to figure out what she is."

Elle wasn't looking forward to meeting the woman and hoped she steered clear of her. It would be smart for Sheila to stay away from the Alpha and his female. Especially as they were so freshly mated.

After dinner, Elle and Liam cleaned up in the kitchen together and decided to take a bath in the jacuzzi-style tub. Elle put her iPod onto the docking station and hooked it up to the Bluetooth speaker for some music before slipping into the hot water.

"I like this song," he told her as Jason Mraz sang about not giving up.

"Really?" Elle asked, her head turning to look at his face. "I would have pegged you as listening to rock anthems or alternative music."

"It's all the leather," he told her, smirking slightly.

"And the tattoos," she said agreeing.

"You like the tattoos," he challenged, and shifted his hips. "It makes me look like a badass and you love it. It turns you on."

Elle smiled and rotated where she sat to face him. When her legs were folded on either side of his hips and she was straddling him, she smiled before giving him a small kiss.

"That's true," she admitted. "I love all your badassery, especially the tattoos."

"Badassery?" he asked, lips quirking up a bit.

"Badassery," she asserted with a nod.

His hands came down on her ass and he squeezed.

"I like *your* badassery as well," he told her and gave another squeeze to her cheeks. "And your tits," he said as he leaned forward to suck a nipple into his mouth.

Elle's back arched, pushing her breasts into his face.

"And pussy," he said around her nipple and traced a line down her ass to dip a finger into her slippery slit. "And that beautiful, sexy heart of yours," he finished and pulled her mouth to his.

They were all lips and tongue. A hint of mint from brushing her teeth after dinner could still be scented and tasted as he stroked in and out of her mouth.

Liam's cock had been stiff since Elle had gotten undressed for him in the bathroom, and it was now wedged between their bodies, the tip leaking with his excitement. He shifted his hips more and lifted her ass into the air. He was poised beneath her and groaned into her mouth as the tip of his cock strained against her hot center. She lowered herself, the first few inches of him slipping inside her and causing that warm glow to light up his insides again.

"I never want to stop doing this with you," he told her as he lifted her again. She came down and took a little bit more of him inside her.

"Then let's not ever stop," she told him, her mouth whispering it against his lips.

He cursed in response.

"Sounds like a fucking phenomenal idea to me," he told her and thrust his hips upward, forcing her to take more of him. "If I have to get a nanny when we have pups, I'm making sure I can take you whenever the spirit damn well moves me."

"Nanny?" she asked.

"Yes," he told her and rolled his hips as he entered her again. "When I get you pregnant, I'm looking for a fucking nanny so we can never say we're too tired to have sex with each other."

"Pregnant?" Her brain seemed a little slow today. With his cock inside her, rubbing her walls the way it did, she was rendered stupid.

"Yes, and it's happening," he told her with another pump of his hips. "The sooner the better."

Elle moaned and rotated her hips in delicious counterpoint to his.

"You want that, angel?" he asked her, and watched as her tits bounced on impact. "You want my cock to fill you up with my babies?"

Her mouth opened, his words causing the knot in her stomach to tighten even further. She could only let out a strangled moan as their hips moved faster.

"What was that, love?" he asked, and thrust up to meet her again. "Can't hear you, sweetheart. I wanted to know if you are ready for my cock to fill you over and over again, make you ripe with my children." Her hands gripped his shoulders and her face looked down on his. He was completely serious, the hopeful look in his eyes saying everything for him.

She found she wanted that too. Wanted it badly.

"Yes. Yes, I do," she told him, and felt his dick jump inside her as he groaned. "I want that. Please give it to me."

They stopped talking and moved together, her hips coming down on him faster and harder, his meeting with hers until they both found release.

"Fuck, Elle!" he cried out as the last of his orgasm was spent with a jerk of his hips. He rocked against her, his pubic bone rubbing her clit and tossing her over the edge once more.

"Liam!"

His name on her lips. It was enough to render his dick solid enough to break through concrete again, but he found he wanted to take her on the bed this time.

"Angel, I want you again, but I need you in our bed," he told her. He pulled himself upright and watched as the warm water slid slowly down her body.

Yeah. Concrete. Metal. He could have chopped through pretty much anything right now with how hard he was.

He took a towel and wiped her down quickly, then set to drying himself off. As soon as they were rid of that top layer of moisture, Liam pulled her into the adjoining bedroom and pushed her gently onto the bed. He crawled in after her and placed himself once again between her legs.

His cock slid between her slick folds as his lips pressed against the skin of her mark. Elle arched her back and her chest pressed against his. His dick jumped up from where it slid.

"Shit, angel," he groaned out as he fisted his cock to center it near her entrance. "I'm not even in you yet and I'm ready to come." He slid his way inside slowly and felt the drag of her sex around him as she welcomed him in. Liam put his lips over her nipple, sucked it up until she moaned loudly for him. He retreated from her, trying to calm his libido with the agonizingly slow pace he set himself.

"Fuck, you feel so good around me, sweetheart," he choked out. "It's like your pussy was made with my cock in mind." He angled himself to hit her in just the right spot, the head of his dick brushing over her front wall and causing Elle to clench her muscles around him, her body tightening for a moment.

"Yes," she breathed out, her eyes fluttering closed as she felt him retreat from her again before pushing back inside of her.

Their motions were smooth, the movements almost symbiotic as they met together in the middle, each of them shifting their hips in time with the other. His mouth came down on hers, his tongue sinking slowly into her. He swallowed the soft, sexy sounds she gave, as if they fed him.

"Liam," she murmured against his lips. "So...close. Need more."

He bore down and angled his hips even more. He knew he was hitting her in the right spot when she clenched around him and gasped, her fingers branding themselves into the flesh on his shoulders with the bite of her nails.

"Angel," he murmured, and pressed his forehead against hers, breathing in their mixed scents. Sex, freesia, a deeper musk reminiscent of the forest. They all mingled in the air and spurred him on, his hips almost slamming into hers as he chased her pleasure. First hers, then his.

The tension forming in her stomach tightened even further, and with it, her hips. Elle's thighs started to quiver and Liam growled. He was losing it, losing himself inside her. Luckily, she was close to coming and he powered on, adding an even larger roll of his hips as they crashed into her.

"Oh...fuck," he groaned as he felt her tighten up around him. "Angel, you need to come for me." He was done. About to fill her up. And it appeared all she needed was the push of his words.

She cried out as the pulse of her sex contracted and released around him in steady waves. He bit down on his lip and then her neck. He couldn't help it. The need to mark her again was absolute, and though he didn't draw blood, it still caused her to cry out again, the sensitivity of her mark making her hips buck wildly beneath him as they both rode out their peak.

The aftermath was all tangled climbs, heavy breathing, and soft, slow caresses.

"Do you want a boy or a girl?" Liam asked once he was laid on his back with Elle tucked into his side, her long hair a splash of dark color against his chest.

"For a firstborn?" Elle asked. "I've always wanted a boy first. Then a girl."

"Any reason?" he asked, though he liked that idea as well.

"I liked having an older brother," she told him as her fingers traced a soft pattern on his chest. "He was always there for me, protecting me. I want the same for our children."

Our children.

His chest swelled and the heat there stirred again, causing the warmth of it to expand to his belly, his throat.

"I want the same," he said, and kissed her forehead. "I was the older brother to Arden, though she sometimes acted like the roles were reversed. When I found my first mate, she had all eyes on her. Wanted to make sure she was worthy to be Luna of the pack, worthy of me."

"Did...did Arden approve?"

"Not at first," Liam said. "She knew Cecilia was friends with Sheila and she couldn't *stand* Sheila. She had that bitch's number from the start. Arden was very perceptive so – though at first she was reluctant – she soon got over it."

"Colleen said Cecilia was nice but needy," Elle said. "It sounds as if someone like Sheila would have taken advantage of a friend like that, and maybe Cecilia was...too good a friend to see all her faults."

That was pretty accurate description of his former mate. It would have taken something huge for her to have seen Sheila for who she truly was. But Liam was tired of living in a past that he couldn't change. The past he longer *wanted* to change. He was happy in the here and now, and said as much in his own way.

"I always hated thinking about these things, but I think...I think I'm glad about the way things turned out. I'm not happy that people have died and suffered to achieve this, don't get me wrong. I am just content with the way things have turned out. I didn't have the mate pull to you as I did with Cecilia, but somehow this – what we have now – is worlds better."

"Everything we go through shapes who we are," Elle returned. "A year ago, I was timid. Meek. The only singing I did was in my bedroom or for my family. I would have never been able to sing for anyone else. Having to go through what we went through, both you and I, it made us stronger through trial. I don't feel like an Omega anymore because I'm not. When I accepted your mark, something changed. I'm not who I once was, but I'm still me. Does that make any sense?"

Liam thought about that before speaking.

"I think it makes perfect sense, sweetheart," he told her. "You're mine as I'm yours, and that makes us something different, something more."

She was quiet for a moment.

"I like more," she told him.

"I like it too."

Chapter 15

Liam couldn't help but love up on Elle over the next 24 hours before the meeting. It was as though he was trying to soak up as much alone time as he could until he made the announcement and had to share his Luna with the rest of the pack.

At one point they were sitting on the couch with Elle in between his legs, Liam's head in her neck and watching TV. There was nothing that interested Liam on the television, but Elle seemed content enough to watch old reruns of *Friends* and laugh.

"Haven't you seen this show before?" Liam asked as his lips traced slowly over her skin.

"Yes, I have, but this episode is one of my favorites," she told him. "Monica's head gets stuck in that stupid turkey and Chandler admits he's in love with her. How can you not love that? It's funny and sweet."

Liam's arms curled around Elle's waist and he pulled her further into his embrace. His breathing was a bit rapid and Elle wondered if he was alright. Before she could ask, there was a knock on the front door.

Liam swore softly and muttered something, but Elle got up and went to the door. Blake and Colleen were on the other side of it, and Elle let them into the house.

They all went into the living room to see Liam, who was sitting in the same position she left him in and looking petulant.

"Hey, Liam," Blake said as he took a seat on the couch perpendicular to the one Liam was sprawled out on.

"You guys want anything to drink?" Elle asked, making as if to go toward the kitchen.

"No, thanks," Colleen said. "If we do, we know where to go to get something."

"Liam?" Elle asked, raising her eyebrows in question.

"No. Just get back over here, angel," he told her with a *come-hither* motion of his hand.

She went to sit down next to Liam who stopped her with a hand and pulled her onto his lap instead. That seemed to amuse Blake and cause Colleen to grin widely and snicker.

"So, what do we owe the pleasure of your visit?" Liam asked as he settled Elle comfortably on his lap again.

"Just wanted to go over business before the meeting later," Blake told him.

They talked for a bit about smaller issues, the new patrols, more training, until they got to the crux of the meeting. Liam and the new Luna.

"After Cecilia, they're going to wonder how you got a mate without having to attend The Claiming," Blake warned him. "It's unheard of that this could happen. They're going to ask questions and you need to figure out what you're going to say."

Liam looked like he didn't know how to respond to that.

"I'll just advise them that The Council okayed it," Liam said gruffly. "That should be good enough for them."

"But it won't be, Lee," Colleen warned him. "And if you don't say anything about why this happened, you're just going to fuel even more rumors."

"So far, only the patrol and warriors are aware of something wrong, and stories – incorrect ones, mind you – are being spread," Blake said.

"What are they saying?" Liam asked.

"Rumors of war on the horizon, rogues, even hunters," Blake advised with a shrug. "The usual. Trace has kept his ear to the ground with patrol, and they are wondering if this has anything to do with the word that you have gotten yourself a mate."

"Not exactly the way you'd want your Luna to be introduced," Colleen offered up. "They don't want one of their leaders to be the cause of war or the reason they have to keep a closer eye on their children."

"This isn't Elle's fault," Liam groused. "They shouldn't blame her for the increased security. That's on me."

"But they might," Blake said. "The only way to correctly handle this is to explain it to them. *Everything*, Liam. The good, the bad, and damned ugly."

"No!" Liam growled out. "They don't need to know why she left her old pack and why I've taken her to mate. That's none of their damned business!"

"Liam," Elle said softly. "I don't mind that they know. You said many of them remember Jeremiah and know the type of person he became. If I tell them what happened, it can only be-"

"This is your private business," he interjected. "None of their damned concern as far as I can see. You're mine. We've marked and mated, and you're their Luna. That should be enough."

"They all know you had a mate before," Elle reminded him. "They're going to wonder."

"Let them," he said gruffly. "Anyone who has a problem with things as they are can deal with me directly."

***

Hours later, Elle was searching through her closet for something to wear. She was debating between a yellow A-line dress and a long, asymmetrical flowered one when Liam came into the room.

"Which do you think?" she asked him, holding both options up for Liam to inspect.

"To wear to the meeting?" he asked. He honestly couldn't care less. She could wear a paper sack and still be as pretty as a picture.

Elle nodded in response.

"That one," he said, pointing to the asymmetrical maxi dress. "And keep your hair down, angel. It looks gorgeous falling over your shoulders like that."

Elle smiled, her face tinting a delicate pink at his compliment. She put back the other dress and hung up the one she would wear near the front of the closet before grabbing fresh underthings.

Slipping into the shower, her heart seemed to become very aware that the meeting was only an hour away. An hour. Sixty minutes. She didn't know how many seconds, but they were too short by at least half. Her nerves got the better of her and she stood still in the hot water, trying to allow the soothing heat to calm her anxiety and work the kinks out of the muscles in her tensing back.

"Elle, angel, what's wrong?" Liam asked as he opened the door to the bathroom all the way. "I could hear your heart starting to race. Are you nervous?"

She nodded her head but couldn't speak. She knew he couldn't see her, but the words just wouldn't come no matter how hard she tried.

Liam opened the sliding door to the shower and slipped inside naked just as Elle looked over at him. The look on his face softened as he realized just how anxious she was.

"Liam," she said when she finally found her voice. "I need to shower and get ready. We have no time to fool around in here."

"I promise to be good just this once," he said with a gentle smirk. "Just let me wash you. It'll calm you and make me feel better as well."

She nodded her head shakily and let him take care of her. Shampoo, conditioner, bath gel. He worked her whole body over until she was a pliant puddle of mush in his hands and her heart wasn't making a desperate bid to escape her chest.

They both got dressed and left the house within fifteen minutes of the meeting. It was to be held in the basement of the Packhouse, as always. The room was a semi-furnished and utilitarian space that had a raised platform at one end of the hall. Liam made his way immediately to it and took a seat behind a long table.

Elle surveyed the room. It had hundreds of folding chairs set out in neat little rows, and Blake, Trace, and Caleb were walking about the room, talking lowly with one another. Caleb, she thought, looked over at her for a brief moment and then refocused his attention back on Blake.

"Angel," Liam called. He gestured for her to come to him, and when she went, he again pulled her down on his lap and tucked his head into her neck. He breathed in deeply and Elle knew he was trying to calm himself. She wasn't the only nervous Nelly in the group it seemed.

She ran her hands through his silky locks and heard him utter a soft groan.

"Baby, I love when you do that, but you might want to stop," he told her softly. "I really would prefer to emcee this meeting without sporting wood."

Elle giggled softly and put her arms around Liam's neck as he pulled her even closer to him on his lap.

He was amazed. Amazed that he felt this strongly about someone without having the mating pull first. He had often pitied humans who could not shift or feel the draw produced by the mate bond, but no longer. It seemed that the love the humans felt could be just as deep, just as profound, and that fact made him immensely happy.

Members of the pack started to slowly filter into the room. At first, Elle tried to pull away and sit on the seat next to Liam, but he wasn't having any of it. He kept her seated on his lap until the room was buzzing with excited noise. Noise he was certain was probably all about the little female stuck to him like glue.

Precisely on the hour, he reluctantly helped Elle off him and stood to his full height next to her. He only needed to clear his throat once for the room to become silent. Nodding once to all the shifters in the room, he opened his mouth.

"As you can see, I have news for all of you," he told the room. "I have taken a mate, a chosen one, and wish to officially welcome her into the fold."

All eyes were on Elle as she stood next to Liam.

"Many of you have seen her around or spoken with her before," Liam continued. "Those who have not, I would like to formally introduce you to Giselle Stark, née Kincaid, formerly of Blackriver pack."

A muttering went around the room as people spoke softly to each other. Liam allowed it for a moment before continuing.

"I know you have a lot of questions as to how this may have happened, but I assure you that I have The Council's blessing and was given full waivers to attend The Claiming due to...special circumstances."

He looked all around the room as if in challenge. Everyone was still, stricken silent, until one young man cleared his throat and stepped forward.

"Sir, how is it you were able to pick your chosen without attending The Claiming ceremony? Such a pairing is unheard of." The young man in question seemed befuddled. He was not being insubordinate, just curious.

"I'm afraid that's all the information I can tell you at this time," Liam told him with a stiff jerk of his head. "The details are not anyone's business, save the people involved, and will not be discussed. Just suffice it to say that I am happy with my new mate, and your new Luna, and I hope you will be as well."

There was a bit of chatter, people wondering why there was so much secrecy behind the mating of their Alpha. Elle looked to Liam, who was frowning slightly at the pack as a whole. A lot of them seemed to mention Liam's father as being the go-ahead for the odd mating, and one female looked up at Liam and smiled a slow, secretive grin before stepping forward.

"Don't you think it is the pack's right to know a little more about their Luna?" the female asked. "What about her mate? What of him? We all know about your previous mate, Alpha, but what about our new Luna's?"

Elle watched as Liam's jaw ticked and became hard. His blue eyes turned cold as steel as his face took in the woman's countenance before he drew a slow, deep breath.

"As your Alpha, Sheila, I would warn you of becoming impertinent with me," he told her. "Her past is as a member of

Blackriver Pack in good standing. She was an Omega there, which she would gladly tell you. Anything aside from that she would share with you herself in time."

Liam looked over at Elle, his gaze softening on her.

Sheila, the one Liam had warned her about, looked like she wanted to say more. Immediately, it made Elle's proverbial hackles rise, and she opened her mouth to speak.

"My mate had already rejected me, in a sense, before I came to Plumbrook," Elle announced loudly. She could see Liam watching her from her periphery, his fists tightly coiled as she spoke.

Elle scrutinized Sheila. She was the typical Barbie doll. Long, wavy blond hair and sparkling blue eyes. Too much makeup and an air about her that Elle didn't like. This one would be catty, two-faced. She wore those characteristics like she wore her layers of expensive MAC foundation.

"The man I knew as my mate for six months did nothing but try to wear me down and break me," Elle continued, her face feeling flushed and hot with her indignation. "He saw me only for my rank in the pack and nothing more, and though he did not outright reject me, his actions spoke volumes. He abused and attacked me, nearly killing me before I was able to get away. So, to answer your question, Sheila, my mate was no mate at all, but a sick, twisted fool who was completely undeserving of me."

Elle stepped back a bit, not realizing she had come forward while speaking. The room was silent, all eyes fixed on her. Elle forced herself not to look down, but straight ahead, meeting the eyes of those in the crowd who looked back at her in awe.

"Does that answer any questions we might have about our new Luna?" Liam asked after clearing his throat.

Silence greeted him for a moment before he decided to speak again.

"Now, if you-" Liam began.

"Who was he?" Sheila asked, interrupting. "Who was your mate? Why did being mated to an Omega matter so much to him?"

Liam's face darkened and he went to speak.

"If my previous mate was anyone but who he was, I wouldn't tell you," Elle said, her voice muted yet strong. "It would be none of your business. But since he is...who he is, I feel obliged to share."

Her eyes scanned the crowd and then Liam's face. His eyes softened as he watched the roll of her neck as she swallowed her nerves down.

"My old mate was Jeremiah Bluth, Alpha to Blackriver."

Chapter 16

"Angel, you didn't have to do that," Liam told her as he helped strip her from her clothing after the meeting later that night.

"It was only fair to let them know what could be coming," she advised him. She unhooked her bra and tossed it in the hamper. "It would be different if Jeremiah wasn't an Alpha, but he is, and that puts the whole pack at risk."

After Elle's revelation, there was a lot of alarmed noise and it took Trace, Blake, and Caleb a while to calm the group. Sheila had somehow slithered away and was not to be found for the remainder of the evening. Like a cockroach, she had scurried off once the light had hit her full-on.

People had much to say about the possibility of attack, and most seemed to be wary of their new Luna at first. Elle had sighed, thinking it couldn't be helped. It would have been worse if she hadn't said anything at all and the pack as a whole was unprepared. Many people spoke of the possibility that Jeremiah would try to come and take her and destroy the pack, though once Elle advised them – in detail – of his true persona, there was not one person that could hide their shock. It was unimaginable that a mate – an Alpha mate at that – could treat their female in such a fashion. For any who had doubts, Elle showed them her scar, the one that was etched into her back for the rest of her life. The one that simply said **JB**.

That seemed to cause a chain reaction in the group. Instead of fear, it caused outrage. Outrage at a man many of them knew, but hadn't seen in many years. One of the head warriors, a middle-aged man that went by the name of Jerome, spoke to the group, and promised them that his warriors would do their best to keep their Luna safe. He knelt and bared his neck in submission and respect. Without fail, all the warriors followed suit. Patrol promised to be resolute and unflappable in their guarding of the borders, and showed their fealty as well.

Liam was pleased, though most wouldn't have been able to tell from the look on his face. The only visible change was that his eyes became slightly brighter and he gave them a tight nod in thanks.

After that, there wasn't much else to discuss and the group disbanded for the evening.

Many of the parents of the young came up to Elle and expressed their loyalty to her. Elle hugged all the mothers, nodding and shaking hands with the fathers. She knew as a newly mated female – no matter who the man was – Liam would not want her to be intimately touched. A handshake was about all his possessiveness would be able to take.

"You're right," Liam told her. "I just...I didn't want them to see you as a victim. A survivor, yes. You don't want – nor need – their pity. You are strong, Elle. Stronger than most."

"People *want* something to fight for, not just the notion of something," she said. "If they knew, *really* knew, what Jeremiah was like, they would be more likely to fight willingly for the pack."

She was right and Liam knew it. He didn't like the fact that they were now all aware of the pain and humiliation she had gone through, but knew what she did was ultimately the proper thing to do. Still, it stung to see the looks of indignation and pity coming from the pack toward Elle, and he wished to remove it from his memory forever.

"My father and mother want to meet you," he told her, changing the subject. "I spoke with them this morning and they want to come next week for about a month to visit."

"Will Arden be joining them?" She was curious about what Liam's sister would be like.

"No," he told her as he pulled the duvet back from the bed. "She is pregnant again and her mate is a very cautious and overprotective man. We can Skype with her though, if you'd like to speak with her."

"I would," she said, and slid into the bed next to Liam.

He opened his arms and she went into them willingly, his hand coming to rest on the small of her back before breathing in a sigh.

"You were brave to speak so plainly today," he told her.

"I wonder where Sheila slithered off to after trying to make me uncomfortable," Elle wondered aloud.

"Wherever the vermin of the world seek shelter, no doubt," Liam said with a huff. "That female is vexing."

"She's plastic," Elle said bitterly. "All looks and no substance."

"You're...are you jealous?" he asked, tipping her head up to his with a finger.

"No. Well, yes, but not really," she told him honestly. "I mean, I know you don't want her, but she damned sure as hell wants you."

"She wants what she cannot have," Liam told her. "I have no want or need of anyone but my mate, and you, my angel, are it."

She snuggled further into his chest and he placed his lips to her forehead before pulling her flat against his body. He was warm, and hard, and...well, *hard*. Her one thigh slid between his legs and rubbed up against him. He grunted briefly, his hips shifting forward slightly, adding more friction.

"It really doesn't take much, does it?" she asked softly with a chuckle.

"Have you seen you?" he asked, laughing with her. "You're perfect. Soft. Gentle. You know your worth and you show it. That's very fucking sexy."

"You just want to get off," she told him, her lips twitching up.

"I want to get you off first, though," he told her, and rubbed his erection against her clothed sex. "Can't help what you do to me. Your hands on my body, that gets me going every fucking time."

He flipped her on her back and pulled up the old t-shirt she was wearing. It was one of his and he thought she looked better in his clothing than he did, honestly. He exposed the skin on her stomach and placed his lips just above her belly button in a long, sweet kiss. His mouth moved lower, and his fingers hooked into her panties before pulling them down slowly.

Liam could already smell the thick musk of her arousal and he hardened further in his boxers. Her pussy was like velvet. Smooth and soft, and he wondered if she was just freshly shaven or had gotten a wax with Colleen the day before. He couldn't help but ask.

"Did you...did you get a wax yesterday?" he asked as his tongue dipped between her lips to lap up the moisture there.

"Y-y-es," she said as she breathed out. "Much...easier than shaving."

It had hurt like a bitch though.

"I like it," he told her, and sucked her clit up into his mouth before letting it go. "So...soft."

He lapped at her for a bit, his tongue fluttering against her. The rolling of her hips morphed into a rocking motion as she sought more purchase against his tongue. Liam started to use his teeth, nipping at her sensitive bud before sucking at it.

"Liam!" Her hand pushed him away. It was too much, this delirium. His mouth, his teeth especially, had the knot in her belly forming rapidly. It was so tight it almost hurt.

"No, angel," he told her between quick licks at her sweet cunt. "I want you to take it, feel it all." He added more friction, more suction. It had her thighs quivering around his head and he hummed as he sucked her into his mouth again.

"This is what you do to me," he told her from between her legs. "Make me feel so good it fucking hurts."

Her hips began to rock against him again in earnest and the moans she was giving were causing his cock to swell and drip with his pleasure. He pressed himself against the bed to relieve some of the ache.

Sliding a finger into her, he stroked the front wall of her sex slowly. It made her pulse around him and he added another finger. Then a third. She was giving off delicious, cock-hardening sounds that had him wanting to fist his dick. Or shove it so deep into her they'd become permanently attached.

Elle's fingers filtered through his hair and he noticed the slight pick-up of her hips' movement and change in breathing.

"Liam," she choked out. "Oh, God! I'm...coming!"

And when she did, she came hard. Harder than ever before. He felt it against his tongue, his mouth, in the quiver of her clit against his lips. Her orgasm was accompanied by a loud wail as she climaxed, and he sucked and lapped at her to the very end.

Once her legs and body had relaxed, he kissed a slow line up her torso, taking special care of her breasts as he licked and sucked at them. His mouth eventually pressed to hers, and she could taste herself on him.

"Angel," he choked out, his voice tight and deep. "I need you, need to be in you."

She nodded her head. She needed that too. So badly she burned.

The tip of his cock strained against her as her arms wrapped around his strong shoulders. He fused his lips to hers as he pressed gently inside her, welcoming the hot, wet embrace of her pussy.

Fuck. The smooth sleekness of her sex against him was like a dream, and he felt himself unraveling all over again for her. The way she hugged him just right inside her, the taste of her lips as they moved against his – both were perfection. And the way she was squeezing him so tightly just now...it had him hard and tight, just ready to erupt.

"Angel, you keep fisting around me like that and this is going to be over way too soon," he told her on a grunt.

"C-can't help it," she murmured, her eyes fluttering open and shut. "Feels too good."

"*So* good, baby," he reiterated with a roll of his hips into her. He grunted. "So fucking good."

His large hands framed her face as he kissed her again and again, never getting enough of her mouth, of the steady stream of moans he kept swallowing down. Even when his hips started to move faster, harder, he was tasting her lips like he was devouring a seven-course meal after having fasted for a week.

"Next time," he said as he pumped himself inside her. "I want you on top. First riding my face, then riding my cock."

She nodded frantically at him, eyes shut, her body going tight and taut at his words.

"Yes," she whispered out. "But...I'll want to suck on you first."

Her eyes opened a bit, the lids still heavy, and Liam's gut clenched. Yes. He wanted that. Wanted that badly. His dick in her mouth. In her pussy. Both hot and wet and utterly perfect.

Liam shifted his hips, looped his arms around her legs so her pelvis was tilted more for him. He went deeper this way, hitting all the spots inside her that had her coming. And he needed her coming. He was coming dangerously close to emptying his balls into her and he wanted to feel it as she squeezed him dry.

His strokes became harder and longer, the head of his dick scraping against the front wall and hitting her g-spot dead on. He felt it went she gripped him tighter and he gasped. It was a short, startled breath that had his dick swelling, his balls drawing up tight.

"Oh fuck, sweetheart," he groaned. "Tell me you're close because I'm about to bust deep inside you at any moment."

She squeezed around him again and moaned.

"So...so close, Liam," she moaned. "Please...just like that."

Her hands clenched at his shoulders, dark crescents appearing as her nails sank into his skin, the bite only riling him up more as he felt the first steady pulse of her sex.

"Come for me, angel." It sounded like he was commanding her, but it was really a plea. "Come on, baby. Get there for me."

Her body tightened, her hips thrusting upwards to meet him as she cried out her release. Her legs shook, the soft flesh quivering as she contracted around him. With the first steady pulse of her climax, Liam let go. Hips jerking, he groaned into her neck as he felt every nerve ending and synapse fire across his skin. It spread like a ripple along his flesh and joined the warm glow in his chest as it fanned out to his fingers and toes.

He laid there atop her, balls deep still, and breathed in. Out. In.

Everything. She was everything. And she needed to know that from him. And she would.

Soon.

***

Bright and early that following Monday, Liam got up to find Elle already up and just fresh from the shower. He propped himself onto his elbows and watched as she ran a cream-colored towel over her wet hair before using a brush to comb through her long mane.

Immediately, Liam got up from the bed and slipped on his boxers. He walked up behind Elle and plucked the brush from her hand. Looking at him in the reflection with a questioning tilt to her head, she looked confused.

"Let me do that," Liam said as he set about running the brush through her hair.

He sectioned off quarters of her hair and brushed the long locks from root to tip, marveling at how soft her hair was.

"Your hair – it seems softer than before," he remarked as he pulled all of it together and ran the brush through it a few more times.

"It's the shampoo and conditioner I used," Elle told him. "I liked how it felt after the stylist did my hair so I bought some to take home with me. Or rather, Colleen did."

Liam forced himself to stop brushing and wondered if she was going to blow it dry or let it dry naturally. He wanted to ask – hungry for every detail of Elle as he was – but he didn't think she would ever blow dry her hair. It was too damned silky soft to ruin it with the heat of a dryer.

"What do you want for breakfast?" Elle asked as she got up and searched her drawers for something to wear.

"Surprise me," he told her and went off into the bathroom to grab a shower for himself.

By the time he was done, the smell of bacon permeated the air and his stomach had started to protest loudly. He padded down the steps and into the kitchen to find Elle at the stove, flipping bacon, scrambling eggs, and – of course – humming to herself. Liam walked up behind her and placed his hands on her hips before leaning down to kiss her on her neck.

"Good morning," he mumbled into her ear in his deep voice. "That smells good."

"Mornin'," she said back as she leaned into his touch. "There's coffee brewing and the bacon should be done in a minute. You want cheese on your eggs?"

He had barely heard a word she said he was so caught up in the fresh scent of her. Coffee...something about cheese.

"Hmm?" he asked as he breathed her in yet again.

"Cheese. Are you listening to me, Liam?" she asked, looking up at him to find his eyes closed and his breathing slow and deliberate.

"Yeah," he mumbled. "Cheese, sure. How does your scent smell better than anything I've ever experienced before?"

"We share a bond now," she said shortly. "Of course, I would smell good to you. You've marked and mated with me so-"

"No-" he interjected. "Even before that. Your scent intoxicated me. I found myself hard all the time when I was near you. Still do, in fact." He pressed his crotch up against her ass to prove his point and she swatted at him playfully.

"Quit distracting me or I'll burn the bacon," she told him, smiling. "Grab yourself a cup of coffee and sit down. You're in the way."

Properly chastised, Liam stood back, laughing at her gentle scolding. He grabbed a cup of coffee for himself and poured a glass of orange juice for her. Elle looked back and frowned at him.

"Is that for me?" she asked, pointedly looking at the tall glass of orange juice.

"Yes, ma'am," he told her. "And before you say anything, I don't think you should be drinking coffee, which is why I didn't pour you a cup."

"What? Why not? I always drink coffee," she asserted while she plated a few strips of bacon for Liam along with some cheesy eggs.

"Because I've been inside you raw for the past few nights – and some mornings – and it would be unwise to have too much caffeine if you happened to be pregnant right now," he told her mildly.

He had a point, but Elle thought he was jumping the gun a little. Or, well – a *lot*.

"Why don't we wait until we actually know anything before limiting my caffeine intake?" she bargained. "It's only been a few days and the odds of me being pregnant are still pretty slim-"

"Slim, but still there," Liam cut in. "They say the first few months of pregnancy are the most important when it comes to limiting your caffeine intake and I would prefer to play it safe rather than sorry."

Elle sighed, but knew the man had a point. And it's not like she had asked him to wrap it up. If she was pregnant, it was as much her fault as it was his and she should take some responsibility for that slim possibility.

And it wasn't like she didn't want to have children with Liam. She did. But she was young, only 18. Granted, her mother had been young as well when she started to have babies, but this wasn't normal society and it was almost to be expected for the Alpha and Luna to start trying for an heir right away.

"You're not rethinking having children with me, are you?" Liam asked, his eyes piercing hers plaintively, trying desperately to read her thoughts.

"No, not at all," Elle said with a sigh. "I guess, I just didn't think things through. It's fine. I'll drink the OJ and pretend it can give me that caffeine high I so desperately crave."

"Sorry, angel," Liam said apologetically. Elle had come over to give him his plate of food. "I just want to make sure both you and our future babies are healthy."

"And happy?"

"Well, that goes without saying."

"I want to take you out somewhere this evening," Liam told her as soon as they had both finished their breakfasts. He was halfway out the door to head to his office when he decided to mention this.

"What? Where?" she asked.

"On a date," he told her, and gathered up his keys, cell phone, and wallet.

"A date? Don't you think it's a little late to be trying to woo me with candlelit dinners and moonlight strolls?" she asked, amused.

"It's never too late to show my lady a good time," he said as he walked up to her, picked her up by her waist and gave her a hard, hungry kiss. "Be ready by 6."

With that, he placed her back on the ground, winked, and walked out the door, leaving Elle shaking her head at him.

***

Colleen came over for a bit once Blake left to help Liam and the two women started to make plans for Halloween, a short couple of weeks away. Elle wasn't surprised to find her friend had plenty of ideas about the party.

"We're having it inside," Colleen said. "Basement of the Packhouse."

"Why? Wouldn't it be spookier if we did it outside and hung white sheets in the trees and dummies with nooses around their necks from the branches?"

"Yes, but it's also cold out at the end of October. More importantly, it's more secure to have it inside now that we know that Jeremiah is aware of your general proximity," Colleen told her dutifully. "Liam will have a fit if we have it outside, so I'm just looking out for you. He's going to be all possessive male around you anyway, especially when he knocks you up."

Elle looked at her, wondering if Colleen knew they were actually sort of trying. The twinkle in her friend's eyes bespoke of her suspicions.

"How-" Elle began.

"Please," Colleen interrupted as she rolled her eyes at her. "He couldn't keep his eyes off your stomach all night last night. I thought he was trying to Jedi-mind-trick you into becoming pregnant. Plus, I know Liam. He was so excited when he met his first mate, he started trying to have kids right off the bat."

"What happened?" Elle asked.

"Cecilia became too ill to conceive before they could," Colleen said. "The meds she took – they weren't conducive to a healthy pregnancy. Liam was crushed."

Elle looked down at her flat tummy. Having kids seemed to mean a lot to Liam and Elle made a promise to herself not to fight him when it came to things like not drinking caffeine and limiting her intake of mercury-laden fish.

Changing the topic, Elle decided to distract herself – and Colleen – with what Liam had said that morning about a date.

"Liam wants to take me out somewhere," Elle told her. "Any idea what he's planning?"

"Not a clue," Colleen said honestly. "That boy isn't exactly an open book. He could be taking you away for a weekend in Paris and I'd not have a clue about it. And trust me, I've tried cracking that nut before. He's as closed off as anyone I've ever met."

"I don't know what to wear," Elle admitted. "I've never dated before, though we're kind of going about this ass-backward."

Colleen grinned. "I think it's sweet that he wants to take you on a date," Colleen told her. "He's never formally dated anyone before. Not even before Cecilia. He was always waiting for his mate. He didn't want to be one of those guys that screwed a bunch of women – sow his wild oats as it were – before settling down to become a family man."

"I'm glad," Elle said fervently. "Jer-my ex-mate didn't even stop fucking other women after he found me."

Colleen sighed.

"I'm so sorry, Elle," she said softly. "You don't deserve that and he certainly didn't deserve someone like you. I don't think he realizes that just because a mate isn't the same rank, it doesn't mean that they aren't just as strong as someone of his stature."

"I know," Elle said. One side of her lip twisted down in a frown. "For the longest time, I thought there was something wrong with me. After the first beating I didn't know what to think. At first, he was able to control it and keep the bruising to areas that couldn't be seen. After a while though, he got careless and Carter...Carter saw what was going on. I owe him everything. He's the one that got me out and dumped me practically on your doorstep."

Colleen leaned forward, curious.

"How did he help you get away?" she asked, her natural curiosity mixing with concern.

"He almost got me killed," Elle said with a bitter smile.

"What? How-"

"It's not like that," Elle said on a sigh. "He and I both knew that even though Jeremiah had no plans of marking me, he wouldn't let me go either. The bond wouldn't allow it. Carter said the only way I'd be free was if I died. He said I...I had to do something so horrible that Jeremiah would lose control. So, one day when I was cleaning, I dropped his mother's ashes on the ground along with the ceramic urn they were kept it. I did it on purpose, knowing he would go out of his mind. He was livid. Literally flipped his shit. He beat me until I was almost unconscious, then shifted and tore my body apart with his claws. He was sure I was as good as dead and he had Carter take me off pack territory to make it seem like I'd gotten lost and was killed by rogues or the elements."

Colleen shook her head, angry tears forming in her eyes.

"Well, I'm glad you're here, Elle. You and Liam – you're good together. I could see it from the start. Liam...he doesn't take kindly to interlopers and when I heard he had a foreign wolf staying in his house, I knew you had to be something special." Colleen looked off in the distance for a bit, thinking. "It makes it almost a shame that we can't all pick our mates. I certainly wouldn't have chosen Blake as my first choice. I had a horribly insane crush on Caleb for the longest time before I turned 18."

"Caleb?"

"Yeah, Liam's Gamma," Colleen said, nodding her head.

"Why Caleb?"

"He's cute. I grew up with both Liam and Blake," Colleen said. "At 17, I would have thought mating with one of them would be nearly akin to incest. They were like brothers to me. Imagine my surprise when I found out Blake was my mate. I almost stopped breathing." She laughed softly at the memory.

"How did it happen?" Elle asked, almost dreamily. Her and Jeremiah's meeting was anything but romantic, and she wanted to live a little vicariously through Colleen's quirky little love story.

"It wasn't all that special," Colleen said, eyeing Elle. "But I suppose it was probably worlds better than your story, so I'll spill."

"My birthday is in August, and my family and I usually would go to the Adirondacks and go camping – live off the land. It was a family tradition to do that every summer around my birthday. That year, though, we had to go a little late because my idiotic younger brother was forced to attend summer school that year. He had failed a class – English, of all things, honestly – because he kept skipping. Anyway, we ended up having to go a few days after my 18th birthday that year, and I had been busy since my birthday packing up all my camping gear. I didn't get to see Liam and Blake a lot because of that. I got a text from them wishing me a happy birthday and all, but that was pretty much about it.

"Well, I'd had a growth spurt a few months before, and my damned Sasquatch feet went up a size. I needed new hiking boots and the piece of crap car my mother had handed down to me decided to take a dump just at the same time I was getting ready to head into town to get some new boots. Liam was busy with his father, and Trace and Caleb were with him. Blake was taking care of his younger sister, Miriam, who was 12 at the time, so he was the only one I could call. He brought along Miri and a toolkit to see if he couldn't figure out what the problem with my car was. I saw him coming from down the road a bit with Miri before he got close enough to smell me.

"It was actually pretty hysterical. He was so surprised that he dropped his toolkit on his foot and ended up cussing up a storm. His little sister threatened she'd tattle on him for swearing so much, but he paid no attention. He limped up to me once he was able to walk and kissed me right then and there."

"That's sweet," Elle said with a grin.

"Oh, trust me. It gets even better," Colleen said with a roll of her eyes. "When he couldn't fix my car – it needed a new battery, apparently – he took me to town to get the new boots. He stood over me at the store like he was the Secret Service and I was the president's daughter. When he asked what I needed the new boots for and I told him, he refused to let me go on the camping trip without him. I think he was convinced I'd get eaten by a bear or a mountain lion."

"I bet that went over well with your family," Elle pointed out, her grin widening as she giggled. If Colleen's family was anything like their daughter, she was sure that year's camping trip had been a colorful event.

"My mom was fine with Blake coming, but my father absolutely refused to let him join. My mom tried to convince him to let Blake camp with us, but Dad was firm. No campouts with mates. We could mark each other and mate when we got back."

"Did Blake get to go with you in the end?" Elle asked.

"Well, my Mom was the tipping point." Colleen shook her head at the memory. "She told my father that if I couldn't take my mate, then maybe he shouldn't be able take *his* either. Of course, she meant herself. Mom was pretty firm when it came to ultimatums. She said if Blake stayed behind, she and I would as well. Dad finally gave up, but insisted Blake sleep in a tent with my little brother."

"Did the two of you sneak out in the middle of the night and have some romantic rendezvous?" Elle asked. Knowing Colleen, she wouldn't have listened to her father. Or, at least, she would have pretended to and gone behind his back anyway.

"Of course! We didn't mark each other until after we got back from camping, but it was a close thing a few times. My father would have gone full-on wolf if Blake had marked me before we got home, so I'm glad we waited."

After that little break, they went back to planning the Halloween party and Colleen was tickled pink at Elle's idea for her and Liam to go as Elvis and Priscilla Presley.

"Lord! That's fucking perfect for you two!" she practically crowed. "I have no idea who Blake and I are going as. He wants to stick with what he knows and be Jake and Bella from *Twilight*, but I think he just wants an excuse to stick a fake tattoo on his bicep and walk around half naked. The man has no imagination."

"*Twilight*? Really?" Elle asked, sounded pained at the cliché. Sparkly vampires and Native American shifters aside, the whole franchise was pretty idiotic.

"I know," Colleen said, rolling her eyes. "I wanted to be a little more imaginative, so if you have any great ideas, lay them on me."

They both tried to come up with some ideas for a good while, but, in the end, fell short. "Well, I'm sure we'll think of something," Elle said, getting up from her seat on the couch. "You hungry? I'm starved. Want a sandwich? We can plan and eat at the same time that way."

That sounded good to Colleen, and she followed Elle into the kitchen to help.

Chapter 17

"What place is this?" Elle asked as she looked at the brick facade of the building in front of them. There was a faded sign hanging at the front, but it was hidden in the shadows and could not be read easily.

"It's the Norfolk Tavern," Liam said with a grin. "It doesn't look like much on the outside because the building is so damned old, but it's got great food and live entertainment on some nights."

"What – like live bands and stuff?" Elle asked, her face brightening. She loved live music. Well, music of any sort, really.

"Yeah, sometimes," he told her and placed his hand at the small of her back. "No bands tonight, though. They sometimes have game nights and other forms of entertainment, but we'll just have to see what's in store this evening."

In all actuality, Liam already knew it was karaoke night at the tavern, but that wouldn't start until 8 PM and they had plenty of time for a leisurely dinner before the fun really began.

They walked in and were immediately seated by a peppy hostess. Since most of the people waited to dine until the night's entertainment came on, the place was only half full, mostly with small families or couples starting out a date night at their favorite watering hole. The place seemed to be half tavern, half family dining. It gave the establishment a down-home sort of feel.

Elle ordered a lemonade and Liam took a beer. He needed a little liquid courage to try to convince Elle to sing karaoke later on that night.

They both ordered after scanning the menu briefly. Elle chose a chicken dish while Liam requested the poached salmon and T-bone steak platter. With all the freshwater rivers in the area, their seafood dishes were some of the freshest to be had.

They talked about their day over dinner and Liam was pleased to note that Elle was more receptive to his ideas about avoiding caffeine and certain seafoods. She even mentioned picking up some folic acid at the store the next time they went.

Liam couldn't stop smiling and before he knew it, it was 8 o'clock and the emcee for the night was coming out to offer some entertainment for the evening. A TV screen and some large, nondescript black machine were rolled in from the side of the small stage as Elle looked over to Liam with a crinkled brow.

"What's going on?" she asked, pointing discreetly up to the lone man on stage. He didn't have anything but electronics at his disposal, and a line of people had formed near his side at the small fold-up table there. People were looking at what appeared to be a binder and pointing at it frequently.

"It's karaoke night," he told her, taking a sip of his beer. "I thought it might interest you and maybe you could grace us with your presence on stage in a little bit."

Elle paled as her mouth opened wide, trying to form words.

"I-I-I can't do that," she stammered, sounding horrified. "There are...*people* here. With *ears* and stuff." She paused. "And food that can be thrown."

"Yeah, that's usually how karaoke works, angel," he said to her, still grinning. "People drink too much, go up on the stage, and sing off-key. Think of it this way: most of these people can't sing a lick but will try to just for the fun of it. They'll either have too much to drink and not even remember this evening or be blown away by your sheer presence."

"They'll boo me. Maybe throw ripe fruit," she said, frowning.

"They wouldn't boo someone as beautiful or talented as you," he told her, putting his hand out to cup hers on the table. "But I'll tell you what. I'll go up there with you and we'll do a duet. That way my horrible singing will make yours sound even better. They can throw the ripe fruit at me instead."

His eyes were laughing, but Elle could see what he was doing. He was trying to pull her out of her shell a bit more. She loved to sing, but only did so alone or – more recently – in Liam's presence.

"I...well, I just-" she stumbled over the words.

"Say yes, baby," he cajoled softly, voice husky, and leaned forward so his lips were barely touching hers. She whined.

"You don't fight fair," she told him, relenting. That caused a sly smile to lift his lips.

"Never said I did," Liam said as he got up and walked over to the short line by the emcee.

Elle whimpered as she saw Liam go through the song list and then write his selection and name on the growing list of performers. Maybe if she was lucky the place would catch fire before she was forced to sing whatever song Liam had picked. She doubted she would know it. He seemed a more rock anthem type guy, and she was more pop.

"What did you pick?" she asked anxiously when he arrived back at the table.

"You'll know it, don't you fret," he told her, correctly deducing her worries. "My sister has the same tastes as you musically and blared her radio morning, noon, and night when she was living at home."

Shit. She had sort of been afraid of that. He had mentioned liking some of the songs she had downloaded on her iPod the other day. They weren't exactly his type of music, but he knew some of the words and most of the melodies.

Fuck. She felt trapped and sent a silent May Day to the heavens. She needed a true-blue miracle of God to get out of this mess.

"You're not going to give me a hint?" she asked. She was becoming slightly aggravated with him. This was an emotional coup d'état, and she was the target. The bastard.

"Only if you're *lucky*, baby," he told her and winked.

They watched as performer after performer came up to the stage. Most were horrible and off-key, but had fun trying to sing. Some were okay and could even carry a halfway decent tune. There were a couple who could actually sing pretty well, and they made Elle even more nervous.

Liam's hand came down on her knee to stop her leg from bouncing up and down with her barely contained anxiety. She was full of so much nervous energy, his touch almost had her rocketing up from her seat.

"Angel, we're up next," he told her at the halfway point of *Sunday Bloody Sunday*. "No one's expecting anyone here to be professional. It's all for fun anyway. Don't be so nervous."

"I don't...don't sing in front of people," she choked out.

"You sing for me," he told her. "And I'll be up there. Just pretend it's just me and you in the room."

"At least tell me what we're singing," she begged. "That's half of my nerves right there."

Liam smiled and relented.

"*Lucky* by Jason Mraz with Colbie Caillat," he told her.

That did, in fact, make her feel a bit better. She knew the song well, and it was a pretty simple tune. It was nothing too showy either. Elle blew out a semi-relaxed breath and closed her eyes.

Once the applause started for the singer on stage – he was actually pretty decent – her heart rate picked up, and she glanced nervously over at Liam.

He rubbed the back of her hand with his thumb and smiled over at her.

They were called up to the stage, and Liam made sure Elle got there without tripping over her own feet. That was a feat in itself since she was pretty sure she had left her balance back at the table somewhere.

They both grabbed a mic and Elle smiled nervously at the crowd before looking at Liam. He didn't seem nervous at all, and before she could question that, the first bars of the song played.

Liam picked up the words right away and Elle...she was completely shocked. The man could *actually sing*.

And he sang directly to *her*. Somehow that made her nerves give way and she let the melody wash over her and the joy of performing come to the fore.

They sang the entirety of the song together and Elle almost completely forgot they were surrounded by strangers in a pub watching them. Possibly armed with ripe fruit.

Liam gave her a small smile and a soft kiss to her lips at the end of the song and a burst of applause could be heard. It jolted Elle out of their little two-person bubble. She laughed and buried her face in Liam's chest as he held her close.

"Encore!" someone yelled, causing Liam to smile. The request caught on even after Elle started to bring the mic back over to the emcee.

The man at the table handed it back to her with a grin.

"No way," he told Elle. "Your adoring public is waiting on your encore, little lady."

"Well, we got to give the public what it wants, don't we, baby?" Liam asked as he came up behind her and tried to pull her back to center stage. She was reluctant to go, but the adrenaline buzzing in her veins didn't allow for any more nerves, and she relented.

"Hey, what do you want to sing?" the emcee asked, and Liam thought quick, still pulling Elle back onto the stage.

"*No Air*," he told the man.

"Jordin Sparks and Chris Brown?" the man called back.

"That's the one," Liam said. "You know it, don't you, angel?" he asked Elle.

She nodded back at him and her lip twitched slightly. The emcee was quick, and a slow beat started as soon as they hit the middle of the stage. This time, Elle started the song. Again, she focused on Liam, the way he sang to her, the interchanging lyrics responding to each other's on a deeper level.

By the end of the song, Liam had tilted her head up to his with his hand, and gave her a soft, slow kiss which caused a round of rowdy catcalls to join the even heftier round of applause.

More shouts of "encore" were heard, and this time it was Liam that shook his head and declared his show business days were over.

"No way," he said into the mic. "But maybe my little angel here can give you a taste of her solo career. What about it, baby? One more for the road?"

Elle looked at the buoyant grin on Liam's face and nodded slowly.

"Okay, but just one more," she said into the mic. "And I get to choose this time."

She walked over to the emcee who introduced himself as David. He was the son of the owner of the Norfolk Tavern, and karaoke nights were his favorite. They were a little rowdier with drunken singing and loud boisterous off-key anthems, but the aura of the place on those nights was ultimately one of fun, and David seemed to live off that raw vibe.

"*Real Emotional Girl*? Never heard this song before," he mused as he read her selection.

"It's not a contemporary piece," she told him with a shrug. "My mom and Dad had an old Randy Newman album with it on there. I remember this was one of my mother's favorites songs."

"Alright, well let's hear it, songbird," he told her. "The natives are getting restless and I think the rest of the people that signed up aren't too willing to follow you and your man's performance out there."

Elle walked back to the stage and cleared her throat before she spoke to the crowd.

"A lot of you probably don't know this song," she said. "But it was one of my mom's favorites and, recently, it became one of mine as well."

She saw that Liam was watching her intently, leaning forward in his seat.

The first piano chords played, and it was like she was at home again in her parents' living room, listening to the album with her mother.

Emotion dripped from her every word, particularly when she

sang about meeting someone who broke her heart and made her hesitant to love again. And then, how it made her lose herself inside herself. It made Liam want to reach out to hold her, tell her everything was okay; that what they had was better than anything he had ever experienced before – even the love of his true mate.

When the song ended, it was silent. The applause came slower, almost hesitant to begin. It was just as heartfelt, but it seemed the crowd felt a bit of what she was feeling: a little heartbreak, a little sadness, a little homesick.

But it was still beautiful.

And Liam was walking swiftly towards her. Before she could move toward the steps to leave the stage, he was pulling her off it and into his arms. Her feet gently hit the floor and his hands framed her face, thumbing away tears she'd had no clue were there until Liam brushed them away.

"Liam?" she asked, an uncertain question in her voice.

"Hush, angel," he told her softly. "That was beautiful, but so sad."

And he fucking hated it in a way. He was so happy that she was here, and with him, and all his, but he hadn't thought really deeply about how much she was probably missing her family.

He held her gently, the applause slowly fading away before he walked them back to the table. He tossed twice as much money than they needed to pay onto the table. Liam didn't care. It would have been worth a small fortune to see Elle be so fearless as she was when she opened herself up to sing that last song. She had made herself vulnerable in front of complete – yet adoring – strangers. They walked out of the tavern in utterly comfortable silence.

"Hey, songbird! Sir!" a voice called out as Liam and Elle started making their way towards where their car was parked. Both turned around and saw David, the owner's son, running toward them. They waited for him as he slowed his pace and came up to them.

"Listen, that was some of the finest singing I've heard at this joint in a while," David told Elle. "You too, man," he said to Liam with a nod.

"Thanks," Elle said, flushing prettily.

"I don't have much time in between songs, so let me just say this," David said, a little out of breath. "We have a piano night here on Fridays. It's not very popular since people want to hear more than just background noise. Anyway, I was wondering if you'd like to sing for it. I play the piano and we could work something out, drum up some clientele. We would pay you of course, and there are tips if things go well. Just think about it and let me know, yeah?"

The man handed her a business card with his name and number on it, giving him the title of "Artistic Director" of the Norfolk Tavern. He then turned around to head back inside.

Liam took the card from her and, after scrutinizing it, put it in his wallet before freezing in place. He stood completely still for a moment until Elle placed a hesitant hand on his chest. His pupils dilated slightly, and he looked down at her in fear.

"Angel, we have to hurry," he told her and pulled her towards the car. "Something's happening at home. We're under some sort of attack."

Chapter 18

Liam didn't know what to do. If the territory was under attack, he was only bringing his mate closer to the battleground. Still, he couldn't *not* help defend his land and people. And the truth was, it was probably due to Elle that this was happening at all. This was unprecedented.

What's going on? Liam demanded of Blake through their link.

The intruders smell like rogues but seem to be more organized. It's like they're looking for something. Or someone, Blake told him.

"Shit," Liam muttered and pressed his foot harder on the gas pedal.

"Liam?" Elle asked as she grabbed the "oh shit" handle and hung on for dear life. "What's going on?"

"Rogues," Liam said shortly, and took a sharp turn blindly. "Blake said they seem to be looking for something. They're not...fuck, they aren't acting naturally."

"Me? Are they looking for me?"

Liam looked over at her and couldn't lie. Not to her.

"I don't know, angel. Maybe," he said. "I wouldn't put it past Jeremiah to enlist rogues to get you back. It seems like the sort of underhanded, cowardly shit that sick fuck would pull."

"Maybe I should-"

"No!" It came out almost like a snarl. "Don't say it, baby. Don't even think it. You go back there and you're as good as dead. Or worse."

He was right, but Elle felt her lips tremble as a set of hot tears rolled down her face unchecked. Liam's hand fell to her knee briefly before he needed it to take another sharp turn.

Blake kept Liam abreast of things and then mindlinked with the head warrior to meet him at his house in five minutes with a few of his men. He had to go back to help with the fight, but he wasn't leaving Elle alone either.

"When we get to the house, I want you to go with the warriors that will be meeting us there," Liam told her stiffly. "They'll keep you safe until this...thing is over with."

"No, I can-"

"Elle, please," Liam requested quietly. "If you were there trying to help, it would only distract me. Since you may be who they are looking for, it will be harder for me to protect you when they catch your scent. Please. Just do this."

Elle nodded her head but was still unhappy. She was sure that there was more she could do, even if it was just to act as bait for the rogues.

How many are there? Liam asked an exhausted Blake when they were about two minutes away from the border of Plumbrook.

We're down to ten left, Blake told him with a gasp. *There was twice that number that somehow snuck past the border when patrol was starting their rounds.*

I'll have their fucking heads, Blake. Patrol is supposed to keep this kind of shit from happening!

I know, Liam. I know, Blake responded in kind. *But we don't have enough men to surround the entire place. Even with the increased numbers on patrol there was always a chance they could get through.*

Keep at least one of them alive. Kill the others, Liam told him. *I want to know what they're doing here. We haven't had an attack in years. This is very suspicious.*

Blake agreed, and gave orders to keep a minimum of one rogue alive for now. The others were to be hunted down and killed.

By the time Elle and Liam had gotten back to the house, only a few of the interlopers remained. The other seventeen had been killed by the warriors, Blake, Trace, and Caleb. Many of the pack involved were still shifted, sniffing the ground uneasily, and whining deep in their throats at the unfamiliar scents.

Two warriors walked into Liam's home, following their Luna and Alpha as Blake mindlinked Liam to say he had the last three rogues in the cells.

Liam gave orders for the warriors with him not to leave the house unless ordered directly by him, and kissed Elle on the cheek before letting her go into the bedroom to get ready for bed.

As Liam stalked down to the cells, an underground property about fifty feet into the woods behind the Packhouse, he linked with Blake again and told him to meet him there.

"Any casualties?" Liam asked when Blake arrived, winded and a bit worse for wear. He had several claw marks across his torso that were halfway to healed, and his grey t-shirt was utterly ruined, not that he cared.

"No fatalities and only a couple of severe chest wounds to some of the warriors," Blake told him on a long exhale. "Doc D'Amato says they'll live."

"What. Fucking. Happened?" Liam snarled out, all his earlier joy from the night out completely disintegrated into red-hot fury.

"Don't know," Blake said. "Patrol was just heading out when they heard snarling and smelt the stench of rogue. They were able to get some of them before they got close enough to the houses, but half of them got away and started sniffing around. They acted like they were searching for something. You'd have to ask them what it is, though. We got three of them underground chained in silver, so you can ask them yourself."

Liam nodded and pulled the door to the underground cells open with one large hand. He skinned quickly down the stairs and didn't bother to greet the guard at the bottom. He simply moved past without a word until he was face to face with some of the filthiest mugs he had ever seen.

"The first one of you who talks, won't get a week of torture before I rip your head from your neck," Liam said, not mincing any words. "Now who has anything they'd like to say?"

A soft cackle greeted his ears and he snapped his head to the last cell on his left.

"You!" Liam growled out, moving towards the cell in question. "What's so fucking funny, mutt?"

"So, you're the man who has Jeremiah all hot and bothered about taking back his little Luna," the man said with a sadistic little grin. "He never said you were such a tall drink of water, though. I'm surprised."

"Jeremiah all but rejected his mate," Liam gritted out. "She was practically dead when we found her and would have died soon after if we hadn't gotten her help."

"Still, the little bitch is his female," the man said, his rotting yellow teeth peeping out as he smiled. "She is his to see to. If he wants her dead, she would be dead."

"She's mine!" Liam decreed, his eyes changing to the amber hue of his wolf's. "I claimed her and she is *my* mate! Jeremiah can choose someone else to be his Luna."

"But he doesn't want another Luna, you idiotic boy," the man told him. "He wants *her*. Oh, he won't admit that to anyone, but it's as plain as day. He won't give up until one of the three of you is dead.

My money is on the Omega. She'll probably try to do something stupid and heroic and get her ass killed in the mix."

"Don't," Liam warned him. "Elle wouldn't do that. She's smarter than that."

"Elle, you say?" The man sounded suspicious. "I thought her name was Giselle."

"Her name could be Mud and it wouldn't matter to you, vermin," Liam bit out. "I assume that Jeremiah put you and your gang of mutts up to this. What did he promise you? Money? A place in his pack?"

"Oh, I don't need the money myself," the man told him. "And I could give two fucks about being in his pack. What I really wanted is retribution."

"Retribution? What for?" Liam asked, confused. The man had surprised him.

"Little Giselle there – your mate? She's my dear, sweet cousin," the man told him. "My name is Jackson Kincaid and Giselle's father is the reason I was made rogue in the first place."

***

"Halt! Who goes there?" a voice called out as soon as they could smell the scent of the foreign shifter.

"It's me," the other voice called out. "I wish to speak to your leader."

"Who are you and what do you want with our Alpha?" asked the man. He looked to be in his early twenties with wide shoulders and a trim waistline. His stature was tense, though he knew the person was not a filthy rogue.

"That, I cannot answer," said the stranger. "Just let him know someone is here to meet with him. Someone with a common purpose and a proposition for him to consider."

The man nodded his head at the stranger and linked his superior to get in touch with their Alpha. The stranger was soon let through and presented with the leader as he shifted from wolf to human at the edge of the forest.

"What is it you want with me?" the man asked as he pulled the basketball shorts up his legs.

"I want to see if we can't work together on something," the stranger said. "In the end, if things go well, we both get what we want."

The man looked at the stranger for a moment, scanning their features to test for any lie in their words.

"Okay," the man said. "I'm listening."

***

'I'll be coming tomorrow, first thing in the morning,' Liam's father said into the phone. *'Since it's not safe there, I'm leaving your mother here. She's sad she will not be able to meet your mate, son, but it's for the best.'*

"I understand, and I don't want Mom in danger as well," Liam said. "If it wouldn't be physically painful for me and bother me to distraction, I would have sent Elle to you in the mountains so Jeremiah wouldn't be able to get to her."

'The rogue wolves...they admit it was Jeremiah who sent them?'

"Yes," Liam reaffirmed. "We caught their leader and it's...it's not good. Not only is he a hired rogue, but also one of Elle's cousins."

His father swore loudly over the phone and Liam had to agree wholeheartedly with every cuss word that spilled forth.

'He's fucking family to her?'

"Yes," Liam said.

'But...but why?'

"He blames Elle's father for getting him exiled from Blackriver pack. He won't say why, but it had to be serious for a family member to turn on one of their own blood."

'Fucking ridiculous. What kind of soap opera pack is that boy running over there?'

"I don't know, but the man obviously isn't in his right mind," Liam said shaking his head. "I haven't told Elle everything, but I wanted to let you know before you decided to come visit. Didn't know if you'd still be keen to."

'Oh, I'll be there, you'll see. I can't wait to meet my daughter in mating in person and kick Jeremiah's scrawny ass from here to the Atlantic for trying to take her from you. That fucker better watch himself or he'll be made rogue and I'll disband his fucking pack.'

"Easy, Pops," Liam said with a small smile. When his Dad got worked up, he had a colorful way of talking. "He's mine to fuck up since he's after my mate."

'How is Elle doing anyway? Is she okay with your stubborn ways? Have mercy on the poor thing for having to deal with your ass twenty-four seven.'

"She's great besides this damned clusterfuck that happened this evening." Liam paused. "Listen, Dad. I've got to go and see her. She's probably worried sick. We weren't at home when the attack happened and she's feeling responsible for it."

'Alright, kid. I'll see you tomorrow. Have Caleb pick me up this time. You know I hate fucking driving, and Blake and Trace both drive like a bat out of hell. Gonna give me a coronary one of these days.'

"Fine. I'll let Caleb know your itinerary as soon as I go see Elle," Liam told him.

Liam walked out of the study in his home and locked the door behind him. He made his way toward the stairs and took them two at a time. He was met with the two warriors he had left Elle with at the top. They were standing outside the bedroom looking a little like statues in a museum.

"You may go," Liam told them. "But I want two warriors stationed at each entrance of this house until our enemy has been dealt with. No one is to come in or out of this house without my say so. Even if it's Blake, you mindlink me or something. Blow fucking smoke signals for all I care. No one comes in or leaves without my knowing. Got it?"

The men replied with a "yes, Alpha", and walked down the stairs to take their position on the front porch of the home. Pretty soon, the back entrance would be covered by another two warriors as well as the four that were watching the house from afar. Eight pairs of eyes on the house at all times. Sixteen keen werewolf-enhanced peepers. A few lines of defense to get through. It wasn't enough for Liam to feel truly confident in his mate's safety, but it was a fucking start.

***

"Elle, sweetheart. You awake?"

Liam bent over the huddled form of Elle, whose body was curled up in a fetal position on their bed. She looked no bigger than a child with her small limbs, minuscule curves, and long, inky black hair covering her face in a silky-smooth curtain.

"Liam?" Her muffled voice called out softly.

Liam smiled and pulled back her hair gently so he could see her face.

"Is everything alright? Are they gone?" Elle asked, blinking up at him.

"Everything's being taken care of so don't you worry," he told her as he sat on the bed next to her. "There were three rogues left, but they're all in the cells under lock and key."

"Good," Elle said as she pushed off the bed to sit up. "Did they come here for me?" The hesitation on his face was enough to answer the question.

"Yes, angel. They did."

Elle sighed and buried her face in her bent knees.

"Is everyone okay? No one died, right?" she asked, her voice muffled again, this time by the flesh of her thighs.

"Everyone's fine. Just a few flesh wounds is all," Liam explained. "Elle, I have to talk to you about something. It's important."

"What is it?" she asked, pulling her face from her knees and looking at him.

"Do you have...or rather, do you remember a relative of yours by the name of Jackson Kincaid? Maybe a cousin?"

Elle frowned, her brows crinkling in the middle with her concentration.

"It...sounds familiar – like I might have known someone by that name when I was quite young. Why?"

More hesitation.

"There's a man in the cells who says he's your cousin. He said his name is Jackson, and claims to have your last name," Liam told her. "He told me that Jeremiah hired him and his group of rogues to find you and bring him back to him. The man...he seems unhinged in his mind."

Elle thought a bit, worrying her lip with her teeth before opening her mouth to speak.

"My father had a brother named James," Elle said. "He's dead now, but I remember Uncle James had a few kids. Two boys and a girl. Their mother, my Aunt Cindy, stayed with us for a while after Uncle James was killed. One day, she up and vanished along with her kids. I was quite small at the time, maybe only six or seven years old. Two of the kids were older than I, the oldest being about 14 or so. I remember asking my father about where they went, but he always got this...this *look*. Like he was angry at them for disappearing. He told me that Aunt Cindy went to live with some other relatives on the west coast, but I always wondered. Maybe it was one of her children and they really didn't move west. Who knows?"

"Do you know at all if there was any bad blood between your family and theirs?"

"Not that I'm aware of," Elle said. "If you hadn't mentioned it just now, I probably wouldn't have even thought about them. It was over ten years ago."

Liam sat back and wondered if "Jackson" was a right old fraud or if the man was speaking the truth. He was incarcerated for the time being, so it didn't seem reasonable that he would lie. He had no reason to, but still...

"Can I go see him?" Elle asked, pulling Liam from his musings. "Maybe if I saw him, I'd recognize him and-"

"No!" The answer was vehement. Liam didn't know why, but that sounded like a horrible fucking idea right about now. Call it instinct, call it being an overprotective Alpha male, but he just knew that would somehow be a bad idea. "It's disgusting down in the cells and the men reek of filth. And it's a little...well, it's currently a little bloody down there. I had the guards...take care of the other two men."

Elle didn't have to ask what "taking care of" consisted of. Though she was a peaceful person in general, she didn't feel sorry in the least bit for their demise. They wanted to take her and, as a result, wounded some of her pack.

"Good," Elle said, her voice almost a low growl. "I hope they rot in hell."

Liam's brows rose in surprise and he fought back a chuckle. She was becoming protective of the pack, which was a good thing.

"My father will be here sometime tomorrow," he told her, trying to bite back the chuckle bubbling up in his throat. "But because of the attack, my mother will be staying at home. I'm sorry you won't be able to meet her, but my father is looking forward to making your acquaintance. He's most taken with you already. Threatened to kick Jeremiah's ass for us. I told him I'd think about it – just to humor the man a little."

Liam spoke a little more about their increased security around the house so Elle wouldn't be surprised in the morning, and asked that if she needed to leave the house for any reason, to mindlink with him so he could arrange for her safety.

"That's not really going to be necessary, is it?" she asked. "What if I'm only going over to Colleen's?"

"You'll be escorted everywhere until this...this situation with Jeremiah is taken care of," he told her. "That's one of the reasons my father is coming. As a member of The Council, he has the rights to cross onto any pack's territory. If you'd like, he could take a message to your parents for you."

Since Liam had gotten her the iPhone, she had been trying – in vain – to rack her brain. She wished she could remember her parents' cell phone numbers. Since everything was stored digitally these days, it was more difficult to remember phone numbers, unless it was your own, of course. So far Elle could remember the first five digits of her mother's phone number, but the rest was a blur.

"I'd like that," Elle told him as he finally slipped into bed with her. "I don't know if I should say much or just let them know that I'm safe. What do you think?"

Liam thought about that. If Elle had been his own kid and had gone through all those atrocities with her fated mate, he'd probably be breaking down the door to Jeremiah's home once he found out she had been hurt by him.

"It's probably best to just let them know that you're safe for now," Liam told her. "If your father gets wind of the type of mate Jeremiah is – or *was* – I fear for his safety."

"True," Elle said, her lips pulling down in a frown. "He might try to fight him if he finds out how I was treated." She sighed. "I do wish I knew who this Jackson guy is though. I feel like if I saw him, I might recognize him, or at least see some similarities between him and my Uncle James."

"You don't remember what any of the kids looked like at all?" Liam asked as he pulled Elle into his arms. After the day they both had, he would forego any loving just to be close to her and listen to her breathe.

"No," Elle said. "Weird, right? I can remember Aunt Cindy and Uncle James, but the kids...it's like their faces are a blank."

"Did you get along with them?"

"I think so," Elle said with a small shrug. "I mean, I don't remember having any fights or anything with them, so I assume that we were cool. But I don't remember any of the fun we must have had either."

They laid in silence for a while and after a bit, Liam thought Elle must have fallen asleep. He sat there thinking and finding it odd Elle remembered so little about her cousins. Maybe she was wrong and had been younger when they had left. What one might remember at six, would be that much blurrier at four or five.

"Liam?"

"Angel, I thought you had fallen asleep," Liam said and placed his head into her neck.

"I know you don't want me to meet with this Jackson, but I'd like to," she told him. "I have a feeling that if I could just see him, everything would fall into place. Maybe that's ludicrous, but it's...it's just a gut feeling that I have."

"I...I'll think about it," he told her grudgingly. "I don't like it, but I'll try to keep an open mind."

That was untrue. He hated the idea of Elle even being in the same zip code as Jackson. If he had the ability, he'd drill a hole to the center of the Earth and drop Jackson in it so he could rot there. Or burn. Or melt. Fuck...wasn't there magma, that lava shit, in the center of the Earth?

"Go to sleep, baby," Liam told her and closed his eyes. "It's been a long fucking night for both of us."

Neither of them said anything more, and soon Elle was breathing deeply, eyelids fluttering in the throes of a hopefully peaceful REM cycle.

For Liam, after the threat to his loved one, it took him much longer to find the solace of sleep.

***

"You must be Elle," the tall man said to her. "Such a tiny thing you are, my dear. How'd you end up with my giant of a son?"

Elle liked Liam's father immediately. Conley Stark was an older version of his son. He stood at Liam's height of six foot six and had the same jet-black hair and startling blue eyes. The only difference was the smattering of grey the man maintained in his long, slicked-back mane of hair.

"Be careful of his big feet, sweetheart," he told Elle, going in for a hug. "He may squish you like a bug under those damned things."

Liam rolled his eyes at his father from behind his back. Then Conley picked up the small woman and gave her a nice hard squeeze before setting her back down. Elle squeaked out at the bear hug, and immediately felt dizzy when set on her feet again.

"Pop, try not to break my mate," Liam told him. "I promise I would care for her just the same, but your whole visit would be moot if you ended up squeezing her lungs flat so she suffocated to death."

"Nonsense, boy," Conley said. "I've come to visit you and your lovely girl here just as much as I've come to kick some Blackriver ass. Speaking of asses, I was sorry to hear about your past, Elle. It's a nasty type of wolf who would treat his mate as such, and I'm certainly glad you found my boy here. He's a little rough around the edges, but he's alright."

"Yeah, so-" Liam attempted to interrupt.

"Quiet, son," Conley interrupted. "Let me get to know my new daughter in mating. I can talk to your insubordinate ass any day of the week. So, tell me, dear, how old are you?"

Elle was amused and embarrassed, but found herself answering every one of Conley's questions, even the ones bordering on ridiculous. Liam played host and got his father and Elle drinks as the two chatted amiably. He couldn't help the small smile tipping his lips as he heard his father ask Elle all about her life at Blackriver and her journey to Plumbrook.

"Elle, I'm heading over to Blackriver in the morning," Conley explained. "Liam mentioned you wanted me to give a message to your parents?"

"Yes, I wrote up a note," she told him as she pulled it from her pocket. It was folded up so it was the size of a business card, and she handed it over to Conley. "I thought it best to write them a note instead of just having you tell them I was safe. With the note, they'll know it's really me. From the handwriting."

"Wise decision," Conley told her. "I know I'm an Elder in The Council, but it's always best not to trust strangers. They don't know me from Adam and such."

"Pops, you gonna continue to interrogate my girl or can we have that chat now?" Liam asked his father. He wanted to speak with him about his trip to Blackriver the next day. Liam wanted him to have some security as a precaution, and his father was acting like it was unnecessary.

"Back off a bit, boy," he told his son. "You get this sweet little thing for the rest of your life. Let a father get to know his new daughter a bit before you start aggravating me about "necessary precautions" and how your old man can't take care of his own damned self."

Liam gave up. The man was impossible to reason with. Though his father was probably going to talk himself hoarse pretty soon, so there was that.

Elle chatted a bit more with Conley and then begged off, stating she needed to get started on dinner. As soon as Elle was humming away in the kitchen, Liam escorted his father back to his study to have a talk.

"I'll be fine without a God damn army battalion behind me, Liam," his father told him gruffly.

"Two warriors is not-"

"It's two too many, but as I'm willing to compromise just to shut you up, you can send Caleb with me," his father told him.

"What's it with you and Caleb? You got some sort of bromance going on with my Gamma?"

"Yeah. We bond over old 80's rock ballads and leave curlers in our hair overnight before giving each other mani-pedis," his father said, rolling his eyes so hard that he thought he caught a glimpse of his own brain. "I like Caleb. He's unmated but not a complete whore like Trace. Blake's got his motormouth mate Colleen, and heaven forbid if anything happened to him over at Blackriver. She wouldn't have to stab me to get even, she could just talk me to death."

"Fine," Liam said. "I'll send Caleb with you. But if he starts complaining about having to babysit your geriatric ass-"

"Geriatric, please! I got more game on my worst day than you got on your best," his father told him. "But do me a favor for your octogenarian old Pops here."

"What's that?"

"Make me a grandpa before I wither away from old age," he teased his son.

Liam just smiled.

"At least there's something you and I can agree on."

Chapter 19

"A pleasure to meet you, Alpha Bluth," Elder Stark said to Jeremiah with a curt nod. It was difficult for him not to want to up and whip the boy until he bled. "I hope my visit isn't an inconvenience."

Jeremiah blinked his irritation away. He knew what the man was probably there for, and he knew his son had probably gotten him up to speed with what was going on. He hadn't heard from the rogues he had sent to bring Giselle back to him, so he assumed they were either dead or had flaked out on him. Either was a definite possibility.

"Not at all, Elder Stark," Jeremiah said with a gruff jerk of his head. "As I have important business to attend to, I will have my Beta see to your needs during your...*visit*."

Jeremiah nodded at Carter, who stepped forward to give the older man a tour of their facilities.

"Beta Carter, at your service," Carter said with a nod once Jeremiah stepped away. "But you can just call me Carter. I'm not much on titles."

"I'd like to see the hospital ward and clinic first, if you don't mind, Carter," Conley said, all business. "I hear you have made many improvements since I've stepped down as Alpha of Plumbrook."

"Indeed," Carter said as he started to walk away from the Alpha's home and toward the center of the community. Caleb, Conley's silent shadow, followed. "We've gotten two more doctors, young ones, that you might be interesting in speaking with."

"Oh?" Conley's brows rose in interest.

"Yes," Carter agreed. "Dr. Elia Bailey and Dr. *Chase Kincaid*." He said the words heavily, with meaning.

"How interesting," Conley said slowly. "I know a few Kincaids. Perhaps it would be wise to visit with the family for a spell as well."

"And perhaps you could also tell me how Giselle fares at Plumbrook," Carter said, his voice but a whisper. "This is hush-hush, but I was the one to help her flee from Jeremiah."

"I know," Conley told him, equally as quiet. "She told me you were one of the good ones, though that you went against your Alpha is a bit of a shock."

"He was killing her slowly, Elder," Carter said. "She wouldn't have lasted much longer here. Jeremiah, no matter how he acts, would never have marked and mated with her. She was a plaything to him at the time, nothing more."

"And now?" Conley asked, his brow raising again.

"He – the man claims the same, but acts in utter contrast to that. He's...it's like he's become unhinged," Carter admitted. "He doesn't wish for anyone – not even me – to know he is in love with her."

"In love? A poor way of showing his affection for his female," Conley scoffed under his breath.

"I agree," Carter said. "It's why I helped her escape. She...he...it's so fucked up, pardon my French. The whole damned situation riles me up. We are meant to care for our women, not treat them like debris. Does...well, your son – is he being good to her?"

"Exceptionally good from what I am gathering," Conley said. They were almost at the clinic. "He lost his true mate a few years back, as you know. I honestly didn't think he would pick another to – well, to replace her, for lack of a better term."

Carter nodded.

"Good. I'm glad I helped then," he said. "But Jeremiah...he's not going to give up until he gets the girl or one of the two of them winds up dead. He's obsessed with getting her back no matter the cost."

"Surely there can't be much of a pull left towards her now after she's been marked and mated," Conley said.

Carter shook his head.

"It's more of a principal thing with Jeremiah. He saw her first, so she is his. She'll always be his in some way. He just takes it to unnecessary extremes."

"I – I saw the initials carved into her back," Conley said, his voice sounding equal parts irate and sorrowful. "It's treacherous. The girl's not fucking cattle to be branded and hoarded."

Carter couldn't help but smile sadly in agreement.

"I couldn't agree more, Sir."

Carter then ushered him into the clinic for a cursory look at the place.

***

"Mr. Kincaid, I'd like you to meet Elder Stark of The Council." Carter made introductions to a startled Roger Kincaid.

Conley stepped forward with his hand out to shake.

"Mr. Kincaid, I would first like to point out, the pleasure is all mine," Conley said. "And that I come bearing news of your youngest daughter, Giselle. Here."

He produced Elle's small note. A small business card-shaped piece of folded, college-ruled paper was in his hands, and he dropped it into Roger's outstretched fingers. The man opened it and read the first few sentences before gasping.

"Mary!" Roger called out to his wife.

"Rog? What is it?" a voice called from the second floor of the home.

An older version of Elle came down the steps hurriedly, her tiny frame billowing in a long-sleeve t-shirt, chucks, and jeans.

"Look at this!" the man said, and they both leaned in to read the letter.

Dear Mom and Dad,

I wish I could tell you more than that I am safe where I am. I needed to leave Blackriver for reasons I will tell you at a later date. But be assured I am being cared for, and the man who gave you this note has seen this for himself.

I know it will drive you to distraction to know I am somewhere out there in a place unknown to you, but it was for my safety that I left. That's all I can really tell you. I have found someone else. A second chance, if you will. If you can, please give the man who brought you my letter your phone numbers. It may not be safe to call and my old phone was left at Jeremiah's. I will leave my phone number at the bottom of the page but I will probably not answer unless I have your numbers first. I can't risk it.

Please don't ask Elder Stark any more about me. If I think it's safe, I will tell you myself.

Love,
Giselle
(315) 267-8842

"It...it's her handwriting," Mary Ellen said, her voice almost awed and sounding a touch watery.

"And it...it sounds like her as well," Roger agreed. He looked up at Conley. "How do you know my daughter and when did you meet?"

"I'm afraid answering those questions would be unwise at the moment," Conley told him in a serious tone. "If things right themselves, then before long you will have all the answers you need. But not a moment before. Your safety and the safety of your daughter depends upon it. Just trust me."

"This reeks of Jeremiah's hand in it," Roger snarled. "He's behind our daughter going missing, isn't he?"

"As I said, there is much I cannot discuss, and that is one of those things, but I promise you she is well cared for and happy where she is," Conley told her father.

"I...I hadn't seen her for a while before she left," Roger said, the dark, purple bruises under his eyes as plain as day. "And when we wanted to see her, we were always pushed back by either Jeremiah or his Beta."

"Just doing what my Alpha commanded of me," Carter said from his spot in the corner of the Kincaid's small home. Caleb was standing mute next to him, eyes everywhere.

"He is also your friend," Roger said to him, almost sternly. "Surely you could have spoken with him, gotten him to let us see our daughter."

"It wouldn't have been allowed," Carter said. "Just take what Elder Stark has given you. Respond to her if you will."

"Of course," Roger said and walked over to the kitchen to grab some scrap paper and a pen from the small drawer to the left of the microwave. He wrote for a moment, scribbling a few words to his youngest child, and handed it over to the Elder. "Tell her to call us. Any time, even if it's 3 AM. We want to speak with her badly."

"You have my word that I will give this to her," Conley said as he nodded and tucked the note in an inside jacket pocket where it couldn't fly free or fall out. "Just wait for her to contact you and don't – whatever you do – don't make her feel bad for leaving. It was not her wish. It was a necessity."

***

"Elle, angel, he'll be fine," Liam told her and pulled her to him on the couch.

"But what if he's not? What if Jerem-"

"He'll be fine," Liam reiterated firmly. "I sent Caleb with him as a precaution and the old man's smoother than blown glass with his words when he wants to be. Makes me sound like an awkward,

bumbling fool sometimes, but – well, don't tell him I said that. He'll never let me live it down."

Elle sighed and continued to worry. Liam pulled her onto his lap so that she straddled him and kissed her lips.

"Do I have to thoroughly distract you in order to get you to stop fretting?" he asked. Elle rolled her eyes at him.

"Distract me, or distract *you*?"

"Why can't it be both?" Liam grinned.

"And maybe I can worry and be distracted at the same time," she told him, countering his argument.

"Not if I'm doing it right," he told her. "I'll have you moaning my name in minutes. Hard to have you thinking of my father's safety when my cock is sliding balls deep into you and fucking you incoherent."

Elle leaned down and kissed him, her arms wrapping around his firm shoulders as she melted further into him.

"You make a good case," she told him. "But I'm still worried and nothing you can do can stop that from happening."

He studied her for a moment before smirking just slightly.

"Challenge accepted," he told her, and pulled her against his body until there wasn't an inch of space left between them.

He ground his pelvis against her.

"You..." Elle began.

"Already hard, baby," he spoke against her lips. "That's what you do to me and it's all for you, angel."

He unzipped his pants, took out his dick, and stroked it for her a few times.

"I..." She was speechless as she watched him.

"Unless you follow that with the words, "*want your cock*", I'm not listening," Liam told her.

He pulled her long, bohemian style skirt up a bit and pushed aside the panel of her panties before he played with her slit, pulling moisture up to rub at her clit.

"God, I don't think I want to see you in anything but a skirt or dress after this," he told her as he circled her sensitive little bud slowly. "Such easy access when I want to have you panting and coming for me."

"Liam," she whined, her legs trembling.

"What, baby? You ready for my dick already?"

Fuck, she was wet. Already. Dripping. He was going to be soaked by her when he finally got inside.

Just how he liked it.

He moved her so her wet pussy was hovering over his dick, an inch or two from sliding right into her.

"Come on, baby," he murmured enticingly. "Ride my dick. I know you want to. Your pussy wouldn't be dripping for me like this if you didn't."

Inch by thick inch, she sat down on him until he was fully seated inside her, cock twitching. He pulled her head to his so he could kiss her lips and he circled his hips so she could feel him everywhere inside her.

"Oh yeah, that's it," Liam groaned out as he felt Elle clamp down around him. "Squeeze that cock, angel."

She lifted up slowly, churning her hips when she came back down.

"Fuck, yeah." His groans made her want to speed up, but she knew he needed slow at first. She did too.

"That's it. I'm making it a house rule for you to always wear something with easy access to your tight little cunt," he told her as his hips thrust upward to meet with hers. "Your pussy's too good...not to..." He trailed off as she sat down on him again.

Soon, she was being bounced on his lap and making these adorable soft mewls that had his dick wanting to spit.

"That's it, baby. Take it," he told her as he met her thrust for thrust. "Take this dick deep for me."

He circled his hips and felt her squeeze and get tighter around him. Though she was still mostly clothed, her tits bounced in time with their thrusts and Liam had to keep himself from leaning forward to bite at her nipples through her shirt.

"Well, shit!" a voice exclaimed. "Taking my advice on getting me some grandchildren quite seriously, aren't ya, son?"

Chapter 20

Elle squeaked and toppled off Liam's lap. Liam immediately grabbed a throw pillow from the couch he was seated on to cover his dick.

Too late.

His father nodded approvingly.

"Good to know the family gene for large cocks was passed down to you too, son," Conley told him and looked over to where Elle was hiding most of herself behind a throw pillow. "Mazeltov for taking that on, my dear."

Elle groaned into her pillow and tried to make herself as small as possible. If she had her way, she would just up and evaporate into thin air.

"Dad, for crying out loud-"

"What?" Conley asked. "It's not like I haven't seen a dick before and she's all covered up, which was wise since you decided to get intimate in the living room. It's not my fault you left your front door unlocked. How was I to know what I was walking into?"

Liam ran a frustrated hand through his hair and prayed to God his father left the room before he started plotting his murder. Patricide? Was that the word?

"I'll just be in the kitchen if you need me," Conley said. "Feel free to mosey on upstairs to, uhm, finish yourselves off and all that. I expect grandchildren immediately, and with what I've seen here, I'd expect them soon."

"Just kill me already," Elle mumbled into her pillow.

"Later," Liam said lightly. "I haven't come yet and neither have you."

Elle threw her pillow at him, tossed her hands up in the air, and walked up the stairs to their bedroom.

***

"My father brought this back from Blackriver," Liam told Elle, who was lurking in the bathroom after taking a warm, yet unsatisfying, shower.

She grabbed the small piece of paper from him quickly and

opened it up.

"He did it! He saw my parents!" She beamed at him and he returned the smile. "These are their cell phone numbers! Liam, I can call them now!"

"I know, angel, but remember to be careful," he warned. "Too much information could lead to someone getting seriously hurt. And when, not *if*, you do call, make sure it's at a time they're sure to be home or away from the rest of the pack. Dad said they've been missing you. He spoke to their Beta as well. Carter."

Elle immediately frowned.

"I hope they were cautious as to where they spoke," she said.

Elle. Forever worrying about everyone else.

"He said they were, and I believe him," Liam said. "My father wouldn't put a good guy like Carter in jeopardy. Not when he's the one that ultimately led you to me."

She jumped into his arms with a squeal and he stumbled back, startled at her sudden enthusiasm.

"Carter saved you, Elle," Liam told her. "My father and I will always be forever grateful to him." *Especially me.*

"And *you* saved me," she told him, tilting her head up to look him in the eyes. "You took me in when I had no place in this world, gave me a home, some security, your devotion. Those things are important as well and without them, I don't know what I would have done."

"Well," Liam said through a breath. "You saved me too. You gave me something that's mine again. Something to live for, to fight for." He paused. "And someone to love. I love you, Elle. I might have loved you the first time I met you, I don't know. But I know it now, and I never want you to ever doubt it."

He kissed her as her eyes widened at his words, pushing her up against the wall of the bathroom. Her legs squeezed around his hips as his tongue slipped into her mouth. The kiss started out slow and quickly grew feverish, needy. His stiff length pressed against her sex and the heat there mingled with hers.

They needed less clothing. *Now.*

Liam quickly unzipped his pants and pushed them down over his hips before pulling her dress up to her waist. He slid her panties to the side and pulled her body higher until the tip of his cock was pressing hard and ready against her slick entrance. He let her down onto him slowly as she sighed a moan into his mouth. His cock slipped further into her, inch by thick inch. Once she was seated, his lips unlocked from hers and he looked her in the eyes.

Fuck, he loved her. Loved the way she moaned for him, loved the way she worried. He even loved the way she had gotten so embarrassed in front of his father before. It was fucking adorable, the way her cheeks stained crimson at being caught in the act. Yes, it had been embarrassing for Liam as well, but his father also had walked in on his son masturbating before. There was nothing more mortifying than that, even if it had been ages ago when Liam was still a young teenager.

"Liam, I-"

He cut her off.

"Don't say it if you don't mean it, angel," he told her and pulled out, leaving only an inch of his dick encased in her. "My ego is strong enough to withstand it if you don't. It...it's better if you only say it if you mean it. I'm already there, but if you're not, understand that *that's okay*."

She shook her head at him. "I do, though," she told him. "I do love you. I don't know if it's the bond or something else, but I love you, am *in* love with you. And thank you for saying it. I don't think I would ever have the guts to say it to you first."

He smiled down at her and gave a slow, steady stroke into her.

"I wanted to say it days ago but, shit happened," he told her. "Rogues, your stupid fucking alleged cousin. My father coming...I guess it – those weren't the right times. But I owed it to you to tell you how I felt. I want to say all the words to you, and I-"

"Liam," she interjected, her voice soft.

"What, angel?"

"Shut the fuck up and make love to me," she told him, her eyes rolling back while her lashes fluttered.

Liam could only smile.

"With pleasure."

***

After Liam fucked her against the wall of the bathroom, in his bed, and over the desk in the corner – just for good measure – he realized he was starving. He looked at the clock and was astonished to see it was after 8 PM. He hoped his father knew how to cook grilled cheese or something. He didn't need his mother nagging at him that he wasn't feeding the old man.

Apparently, the inability to cook ran through the male Stark genes.

"Baby, are there any leftovers from last night still in the fridge?"

he asked as he leaned over to kiss Elle on the cheek.

"Should be, unless your father ate it," she mumbled to him. "Does he like Chicken Parmesan?"

Fuck. His father loved it.

"Yeah, it's uh...one of his favorite dishes."

"I'll get up," she said, pulling herself upright from the bed and ready to cook him something fresh.

"Don't bother," Liam told her. "You're tired and I can make a sandwich. You want one?"

"Sure. Do we still have turkey?"

"Think so," Liam said. "Mayo, some lettuce and cheddar?"

She moaned.

His cock stirred.

"Sounds good," she said.

Fuck. Now he was hard again. Just from that cute little moan she gave.

He adjusted his hard length and walked out into the hallway, hoping his father was in his bedroom already.

He wasn't.

"Have fun getting that all out of your system?" his father asked as Liam stepped off the last stair into the living room.

"You didn't listen," Liam stated. At least he hoped to God he hadn't.

"The hell I didn't," his father exclaimed. "Wolf hearing, remember? This place isn't exactly soundproof. You need to work on your dirty talk, by the way. Hackneyed if you ask me."

Liam rolled his eyes to hide the frisson of embarrassment he felt.

"Whatever, old man," Liam said. "Quit listening to me or I'll make you wait for grandkids."

"Please. With the amount of semen you probably pumped into that poor girl, I'd be surprised if she didn't have triplets. Nice stamina by the way."

"Pregnancy doesn't work that way," Liam said, flustered. Why were they having this conversation again? He was so glad his mother wasn't here to witness this. "You want anything to eat? I'm making sandwiches or I can heat up some leftovers for you."

"I already ate," Conley told his son. "Your girl's a good cook. Chicken parm the way it was meant to taste."

Figured. The man could probably sniff out a good chicken parm at fifty paces.

"I told her I loved her," Liam said, opening the fridge door to grab the sandwich fixings.

Well, at least that confession stopped his father from speaking more to him about sex. There was only so much a man could take in a day, and Liam had overshot it by a fucking mile.

"You did." It wasn't a question. "Good for you, kid."

"That's it?" Liam asked as he took out some bread. "No *but did you mean it?* or *did she say it back?*"

His father shrugged.

"It's not half as interesting as talking about your sex life," Conley told him. "Plus, I could already tell you love her and she probably said it back. I can tell that she does love you. I'm just surprised that you couldn't."

"I hoped," Liam said with a shrug. "And she did say it back, in case you were wondering."

"Well, let's pound it out," Conley said, shoving a fist at his son. Liam looked at it like it was a newly discovered species of cockroach.

"What?"

"Pound it out, you idiot," Conley said, pausing. "Jesus Christ, pound your fucking fist against *my* fist. It's called *pounding it out.*"

"I know what it means, I'm just surprised an old fossil like you does as well," Liam retorted.

"Bah...Arden's mate's always saying shit like that to his kid," Conley said. "Got it from him. Makes the little one giggle like crazy. Thinks it's fucking hysterical or whatever. Speaking of hysterical, Caleb said something about having a Halloween party. Colleen's doing, I'll bet."

"And Elle's," Liam said as he smeared mayo onto a piece of bread. "Since events are something Elle's not that great at, Colleen's helping her out. She lives for that shit."

"What you going as to this shindig? It's this Friday, right?"

"Yeah. Elle had a good idea, at least," Liam said as he plated some chips to eat with the sandwiches. "She wants us to go as Elvis and Priscilla Presley."

His father looked at him.

"60s or 70s Presley? 'Cause if I see you in a bejeweled one-piece, I'm taking pictures and blowing them up for your mother. She'll laugh herself silly."

"60s, of course," Liam said, rolling his eyes. "Not even Elle could get me into a bedazzled one-piece with a neckline down to my belly button."

"She probably could," Conley argued lightly as he grabbed the bag of chips and threw some into his mouth.

"Yeah, you're probably right," Liam admitted. He'd probably do a lot of stupid things he never thought he'd do for Elle.

"Well, it's good that you're self-aware," Conley told him with a grin.

"Quiet, old man," Liam told him, cutting him with a glare. "Don't even deny that you'd do the same for your mate."

"Yeah, but I'm old and can blame it on my advancing senility."

Liam sighed and shook his head. There was no winning with this man.

"Just don't tease Elle about walking in on us before or...anything that happened after that," Liam told him. "She's embarrassed enough. You don't need to make it widely known that we spent the last several hours up there trying to knock her up with your grandkids."

"Ah! So, you *are* trying," Conley said gleefully. "I can't wait to tell your mother. She's gonna be fucking thrilled."

Liam went to respond, but let it slide. Whenever he told his father to do or say something, the man usually did the exact opposite. It was time to quit while he was ahead.

Instead, he took the two plates, two bottles of water, and went back upstairs to his tired, hungry, and probably chafed mate.

***

Liam inspected himself in the mirror. He had on dark blue jeans, a striped black and white shirt, and a jean jacket on. He was Elvis à la *Jailhouse Rock*. Elle had coiffed his hair in a ridiculous-on-anyone-but-the-King pompadour, and had to use nearly an entire bottle of hairspray on his head to keep his long hair in place. He was certain he had the stuff up his nose and under his fingernails. The shit made his scalp itch, and Elle nagged at him not to touch her masterpiece.

"Liam, stop it!" she yelled at him. "You're going to ruin your hair!"

"I can't help it," he told her. "You used up half that crazy bottle solely on my head. It itches like hell."

"I have ten times the amount of hair you do," she scolded. "How do you think I feel?"

That was true enough. Elle had teased her hair into a moderate bouffant and was now using the rest of the spray to get it to stay. She wore cat's eye makeup and a light pink, shimmery lipstick she had purchased the day before when she went shopping.

"How does this look?" she asked. Liam looked her up and down. She would have made a hot 60s chick any day of the week, but he was irritable and grumpy at the amount of follicular torture he'd had to endure, and it showed.

"Well, the hairstyle is ridiculous, but you can rock it better than most," he told her.

"What a rave review," she said, rolling her eyes. "It was the style back then. I'm not looking to have it revisited. It's a Halloween party, for Pete's sake. Act like The King and not like a grumpy old goat."

"I'll try not to bring the party vibe down," he told her petulantly as he struggled not to thrust his fingers through his helmet of hair as he was wont to do. How the hell did these guys function without being able to thread their fingers through their hair when they got irritated?

"Good," she said to him. "Then I won't have to bring out the big guns if you start getting all brooding and sullen."

"Sullen? And what are the big guns? You going to tempt me with your sweet pussy if I act like a good boy?"

"Nope, but I was thinking of withholding it if you didn't start cheering up already," she told him. "Have fun for once, Liam. Even your father looks like he's going to have a blast."

His father, much to his chagrin, had decided to go as a Bond villain. The one with the scar below his eye, sans the feline. Felines didn't generally take too kindly to being around this many wolves – or anything of the canine species in particular – even if there was one around to be had. Animals just fucking *knew*. When Liam had asked his father why he chose that particular character, his father had simply shrugged and said, "chicks dig scars".

It was maddening. It was like dealing with a horny teen and not his middle-aged father. Who the hell was the adult in this equation?

"Fine, I'll have fun. Be happy," Liam said, his eyes rolling to the ceiling. "Even if it fucking kills me."

"Drama queen, er...King, or whatever," she said lightly.

"Just *The King*, baby," Liam said, doing his best impression of Elvis. Needless to say, it fell well short of the mark.

"Even your Elvis is drab," she told him. "Try a little hip action, get into the swing of being The King."

"I prefer all my hip action happening with fewer people watching us," he told her with a smirk. It was as close to The King as Liam could get, apparently.

"Ugh, you're impossible," she told him, giving up.

"You don't say that when I'm deep in you," he told her and came up behind her to press his hips against her ass. Hard. As always.

"Lee!" she scolded.

"Ugh, I think that did it," Liam groaned. "You called me Lee just like Colleen does. I immediately wilted."

"So, *Lee* doesn't do it for you?" she asked, snickering. "This is important information I will mentally file away to ruminate on at a later time."

Liam groaned again.

There was a knock on their door.

"What the hell, you two?" Conley's voice blared through the wood of the door to their bedroom. "I know you two ain't doing the nasty in there or else I'd have heard it, so what's taking so damned long?"

"Who calls it "the nasty" anymore?" Liam asked lowly, mostly to himself.

"Old farts like me and pre-teens," Conley answered, having heard his son. "Now move your asses before I come in there and interrupt your little pow-wow."

That got them moving before the man walked in on them yet again.

***

"Just stand there and look confused. It's easy," Elle instructed Colleen, who couldn't figure out how her costume as 'Bella' from *Twilight* fame should look. She was pretty much dressed normally, though she had gotten herself a long brown wig. She had yet to adopt the dopey look on Kristen Stewart's face that had two supernatural males drooling over her somehow. Maybe she had too many brain cells to pull it off.

Colleen opened her mouth and tried to widen her eyes.

"No. Now you just look confused and constipated," Elle told her. "Stick with your regular face and just hang around Blake. They'll get it once they see he's shirtless and has a round stick-on tattoo on his arm."

Blake, of course, was wearing khaki shorts and had stuck the round tattoo on his bicep to try to look like the third spoke in the love triangle between human, vampire, and werewolf.

"You should have had my Dad come as Edward from that shitty movie," Liam told Colleen. "He's pale enough and thinks he's pretty enough to try to pass himself off. Get him some plastic fangs and he'd be good to go."

"They don't have fangs in the movie," Colleen told him. He just replied with a shrug that indicated he couldn't care less.

"Whatever," Liam said and took a sip of beer. It was obvious he wasn't a fan of the franchise.

They'd decided to have the party deejayed by one of the older teens, and Elle was pretty surprised. There was a nice mix of songs that showed he was in touch with music from the contemporary all the way back into the 70s. It allowed almost everyone to find a song they liked to dance to.

Dancing Queen started to play and Colleen's eyes lit up in the darkened room.

"Shit! I love ABBA!" she cried and pulled Elle along with her to the dance floor. Elle couldn't help but laugh and follow along. ABBA was a guilty pleasure for her as well. That band knew how to write a damned catchy tune. It was the earworm of all earworms for Elle, though she preferred *Mama Mia* over *Dancing Queen*.

Some of the older members of the pack joined them on the dance floor and the younger generation walked off, some of them with pained expressions on their faces.

Yeah. ABBA wasn't for everyone. Though Blake and Liam were quite entertained.

"God, I hate this album," Blake said to Liam. "Colleen likes to play it while she cleans. She says it motivates her to get her work done, but she mostly just uses the Swiffer duster as a microphone while she sings in front of the mirror." He paused and shuddered. "Trust me, it's not a pretty scene. Col can't sing for shit."

"You love her anyway," Liam said as he watched Elle and Colleen dance together with a small smile on his lips.

"Just like you love Elle," Blake told him. Liam only glanced his way, not denying it. "I can tell. Everyone here can if I'm not mistaken. Hell, I think if the decorations could talk, they'd fucking agree."

"And?"

"And nothing," Blake replied. "The pack is pleased. Happy to see you happy finally. Your dad seems to be pleased as well."

That was true enough. Conley adored Elle, even if he had seen her in a somewhat compromising position earlier that week. He treated her like a daughter. Like he treated Arden. She was as much part of the family to him now as she was to Liam. And he loved that his father took to her so well. Especially after Cecilia.

"He is," Liam said, still watching Elle dance with Colleen. They were laughing as much as they were dancing, if not more. "Treats her better than me, at least."

"That's 'cause she *is* better than you."

"Shut it, Blake." He paused. "I already know that."

The song came to an end and Colleen and Elle looked to be arguing about something on their way back.

"...I'm just saying, if you had to pick a vamp, I'd pick the hot Nordic looking guy," Elle was saying.

Colleen shook her head vehemently.

"No way," she replied. "Bill is tall, dark, and handsome. Mysterious and brooding. Erik just screams of danger."

"And that's hot," Elle retorted with a smirk.

"What are you two fighting about?" Blake asked.

"*True Blood*," Colleen explained while jabbing a thumb in the direction of Elle. "She thinks Erik, the vampire sheriff or whatever he is, is much hotter than Bill."

"Because it's true!" Elle cut in, standing her ground.

"Christ," Liam said as he shook his head. "Vampires? Really?"

"There were werewolves in the show as well," Colleen said.

"*Hot* werewolves," Elle added. Liam looked at her and she shrugged her shoulders. "Joe Mangia-whatever-his-name is, is pretty fine."

"They're fictional," Liam said.

"Played by real people," Colleen added, not helping.

"Yeah, but didn't he marry that lady with the inexplicable accent?" Elle said, her mouth twisting in distaste.

"Who cares what she says? That Eva something-or-other is hot as well," Blake said. Colleen cut him with a glare. "Oh, what? You can drool over some freaky-ass vamp and I can't say when a woman is fine? Double standards!"

A slow song came on and Liam pulled Elle toward the dance floor before the argument got out of hand. *Crazy For You* by Madonna was playing now, and he wrapped his arms around Elle's waist as they swayed back and forth in place.

"Erik, the blond vampire in *True Blood*, eh?" he asked.

She shrugged. "He's good looking. "

"And?"

"You get to see his dick once on screen," she mentioned blithely.

"Go on."

"It looked...small, but it could've been shrinkage. He *was* sunbathing in the snow."

"Yep, that would do it," Liam said and almost laughed. He pulled her tighter so no space separated them. Honestly. Arguing about fictional characters. It was...too much.

"Are you having a good time?" she asked him. He had pretty much stayed on the sidelines, sipping a beer and chatting with people in the pack.

"The best," he told her, and curled his arm around her waist further.

"You don't seem like it, *King*," she said smartly. "You've been standing in the corner chatting with Blake and Caleb – or Trace, wherever he is."

"He wandered off with some female," Liam told her. "I can't wait 'til that boy finds his mate. He's gonna wish he wasn't leaving so many damned brokenhearted females in his wake. He's like an F5 tornado of sex."

"Does Caleb have a mate?" She had never seen him with anyone and she remembered the little crush that Colleen admitted to having on him when she was in her teens.

"Not yet, but he's a bit more...discerning with who he goes to bed with," Liam told her.

They were quiet for a bit as they rotated slowly to the rhythm of the song.

"Did you ever...after Cecilia?" Elle asked. "I mean, it's okay if you have, but I was just wondering."

"No, not after Cecilia," Liam said. "I...I couldn't bring myself to touch another female. Not until you. And Lord knows I tried fighting that. Do you know how difficult it is to go to sleep and wake up with a raging hard-on every fucking day?"

Elle laughed and tried to bury it in Liam's chest.

"Hey," Liam said, tipping her head to him. "Don't hide from me. I want to see your face as much as I can while I can." He brought his head down to hers and sucked on her lower lip before scraping his teeth against it in one slow drag. She was too short, though, and he picked her up so that she was at his height. As the kiss ended, he set her slowly back down on the floor and cupped one cheek with his hand.

"Mind if I cut in?" a voice asked from behind Liam.

Liam didn't even turn to address the voice.

"Yes, I do mind, in fact, Sheila. I'm here with my mate and have no desire to dance with anyone else."

"Fine," Sheila said, her voice taking on a hard tone. "But she isn't really your mate. Your true mate's gone."

The bitch was blunt. And rude. And a right old pain in Liam's ass.

"She *is* my mate, just as much as Cecelia was. More so, even," Liam gritted out. He was starting to lose control of his temper and Elle frowned. Leave it to Sheila to ruin everything.

"He told you to leave," Elle said to her. "He may not have said it outright, but a mentally impaired ape could have read between the lines quicker than you."

Sheila's face turned red with anger before her eyes narrowed and she stomped off into a random direction of the room.

"You would have thought once I took a woman to mate she would leave me alone, but I see she's as pigheaded as ever." Liam shook his head.

"What are you going to do?" Elle asked.

"Ignore her for now," Liam said. "If it happens again, I'll deal with it differently, maybe send her away or something."

"What? Make her rogue?"

"I'm not that malicious," Liam said, shaking his head. "It's a tempting thought, but no. She has relatives in Ohio. I could exile her there and hope that when – or *if* – she comes back, it's with a little more grace and civility."

Elle snorted her derision.

"When pigs fly," she said.

"Hmm...a flying Trace would be a bother," Liam said offhandedly. "Are you almost ready to go? I want to bury myself in you tonight. Soon. The King needs an heir."

"You ever think of anything outside of impregnating me?" Elle asked with a raised brow.

"What was that?" He pretended to be deaf. "I couldn't hear you over all the loud thoughts I have of you moaning my name as you come."

Elle's lips twitched and tugged, fighting her smile as her cheeks bloomed roses.

"Let me go say goodbye to Colleen and Blake and then we can get going."

Chapter 21

"Mom? Is that you?"

"Giselle, dear," her mother's soft voice breathed. *"It's so good to hear from you finally."*

"Sorry it took me so long," Elle said into the phone. "It's been hectic here and this was the first time I had free that I knew you wouldn't be around anyone."

It was 10 PM the following Monday night. Her mother always – *always* – used Monday nights as this time to do laundry. Even now, Elle could hear the dryer running in the background like white noise.

"You could have called me at 3 AM," her mother told her. *"I would have taken the call no matter what."*

Elle knew that, but she also knew that once they spoke, it would be emotional and that her mother would take hours to get back to sleep if she cried. That, or eat her feelings.

"I know, but I'm asleep well before then as well," Elle told her. It was a half-truth. She was *usually* asleep by then, though sometimes Liam kept her up that late. The man was insatiable. Like he had stored up his sexual stamina for years waiting for her.

"I know there are certain things we're not supposed to ask, which is why you're not calling your father's phone instead. Am I right?"

Her mother was on the money. Her father would have drilled her with questions. Questions she couldn't answer. At least not yet. Someday, though...

"You're right as usual, Mom," Elle told her. "I wish there was more that I could say, but just know this: I'm happy. I'm healthy. I'm...not with Jeremiah anymore. I – I've got a different mate now and-"

"Different mate? How can that be, Elle? Isn't your mate Jeremiah?"

She knew she shouldn't have said anything. But this was her mother. *Her. Mother.* The woman who labored for hours when giving birth to her. If you couldn't trust your mom, who could you trust?

"It...didn't work out," Elle said. "We're better off this way."

"But the mate pull-"

"All but gone," Elle interjected. "I feel almost nothing. He never marked me or anything, so there was nothing to lose in regards to the bond."

"You were with him for six months, Elle! How could he not mark you?"

And how could he go without announcing me as Luna for six months? Elle thought. *Think, Mom, think.*

"Geez, I *know*, Mom," Elle said. "Quiet down, please. There's no need to get excited. This is...my mate now is much better than Jeremiah. He's...he's everything you would want in a son in mating. I promise."

"Who is he, or can I not ask?"

"Mom, if I answer that, I say too much," Elle said. "He's not...low ranking like you and me."

"Is it...is he another Alpha? What about his mate?"

"His mate is gone. Dead. Years ago, so there's no harm in us being together."

"But Jeremiah-"

"He'll come after me, I know," Elle said on a sigh. "But, it won't be for the right reasons. Not now, not ever."

"What's that supposed to mean?"

"Mom, I can't stay on for much longer, but I did want to ask you something," Elle said. Silence greeted her. "Do we have a relative by the name of Jackson Kincaid? Who is he?"

She heard her mother breathe in. Then out.

"Jackson is your first cousin. Your Uncle James' son. He...he's not a good person – at least he wasn't when I knew him. He acted alright at first, but he was rotten. To the core. If you ever meet him, stay away."

"What? Why? What did he do?"

"Just – just be safe, Giselle. And stay away from Jackson if you ever meet him. I...I have to go now. The dryer's almost done, and I don't want the clothing to wrinkle."

The line cut off and Elle knew she had to meet this Jackson. Even if everyone in her life warned her away from the man.

***

Elle thought of ways she could get to see Jackson the next day. She didn't know if Liam had requested total solitary confinement for the man who was probably her cousin, but she didn't think he would have thought to tell the guards to order them not to let her into the cells.

At least Liam would be gone for a few hours having to deal with some business in town. Blake was pretty much in charge. Conley...well, Conley was doing his job as an Elder and was visiting another neighboring pack. It would have been suspicious had he only come to upstate New York and visited Blackriver. He would be gone several hours as well.

After Elle took a shower, she put her long hair up in a messy bun to keep it off her neck. A pair of jeans, a t-shirt, and jacket were donned, and she walked to the door after mindlinking with Liam that she would be heading over to Colleen's.

Two warriors followed her to Colleen and Blake's home. They looked a little like Secret Service as one walked in front of her, the other staying behind. She felt somewhat ridiculous. In the middle of the day, with members of the pack out and about. Jeremiah would have been crazy to attack right now.

As she made her way over to Colleen's, she hoped to God that the woman would be sympathetic to her need to see the man in the cells. She didn't know why, but it seemed imperative, now more than ever, to meet with him. There was something missing to his story, and she was determined to find out.

Her guards left her at the front porch at Colleen's and stood on either side of the door while Elle knocked. The smiling redhead opened the door and Elle was ushered inside with a hug and some well-meaning chatter.

"Col, stop." Colleen's incessant rambling was giving her a headache and keeping her from saying what needed to be said. "I have to go down to the cells and speak with the prisoner. I don't know how much longer he'll be alive. I need your help."

"What? Why?" Colleen questioned. "Can't your two bodyguards out there escort you?"

Elle shook her head. "They'll try to clear it with Liam first and Liam doesn't want me to see the man they have."

"Why not?"

"The man...he says he's related to me, though I don't remember him," Elle explained. "He says he came here to bring me back to Jeremiah because he wanted to get back at my father for some wrong he did to him."

"You don't know what happened?"

"No, I can't remember anything from when I supposedly knew him," Elle said helplessly. "It's like there is a big gaping hole in my memory. I mean, I was young, yeah, but I have many memories from before my aunt came to live with us with her children. I don't understand why I can't remember anything about them." *Or him.*

"And you think meeting with him will jog your memory?" Colleen guessed.

"I'm hoping so."

"Why not leave it be? I mean, how memorable can a kid's shit be? Maybe he pushed you down the stairs or pantsed you in front of your childhood crush. I honestly can't see what good it will do to meet with him," Colleen told her.

"Please, just help me get away from those two oafs outside so I can visit with him. Just for a few minutes," Elle begged.

Colleen pursed her lips and shook her head.

"I should say no," she said. "I think there's probably a damned good reason that you should leave this well enough alone, but...I can't. You're my friend, Elle. My best friend outside of Blake and Liam, and if you think you need these answers, I'll help you."

"But...how?"

"Leave that to me," Colleen said with a wink.

Colleen, ever the hospitable Beta female she was, invited the two warriors into her home. She got their names – Eli and Warren – and invited them inside for something to drink and a snack. She made a killer apple pie and offered them some while practically pushing Elle to one of the back rooms of the house.

"Go out this window and head straight to the tree line," Colleen whispered to her. "There's a large oak tree with a walnut tree near to it. You'll be able to tell because all the nuts have already fallen off and are crunchy under your feet. Smack dab in the middle of the two trees, there's a door in the forest floor. That's where the cells are."

Colleen practically pushed her through the window, and Elle dropped to the ground. There were only a couple of feet to fall, but she still landed off-balance and wobbled. When she was completely upright again, she walked swiftly towards the woods, looking for a large oak next to a walnut tree. There were several oaks in the woods along the tree line, but only one walnut tree, so it was relatively easy to find.

"Bingo," Elle breathed out and walked to the space between the two trees.

Hollow. And the ground had some give when she bounced on her feet a bit.

Getting onto her knees, Elle searched for the handle Colleen had told her about earlier. It was covered by leaves and a pat of moss, but once she found it she stepped back to pull the heavy door open to get inside.

It was dark, and she heard a slight cough come from somewhere down below. A dim light could be seen reflecting off the stairs heading down.

Mustering up all the courage she could, she started to walk down the steep set of stairs and saw that once she was at the bottom, the hallway went on for some time before it veered off to the right. When she turned to the right at the end of the hallway, she saw two men standing guard near a cell door and the sounds of cackling laughter could be heard from beyond them.

"I would recognize your scent from anywhere," a deep voice rumbled. "Good to see you again. *Cousin.*"

***

"Giselle! Wait up!" Lena's small, kittenish voice called out from behind her.

"Come on up here! It's great!" Giselle called from the top of the ladder. "Daddy made it for my birthday."

They were soon in a largish tree house that Roger Kincaid had spent many hours laboring over. When asking what his daughter had wanted for her seventh birthday, Giselle had said, "a tree house", without any hesitation. It was easy enough to make for an educated man like Roger.

"I'm hungry," Aaron whined. He was the youngest of her Uncle James' kids at the age of 5. Lena was 9, and their oldest brother was 14. Since he was a teen, he didn't hang out with his younger siblings much, preferring to hang around with kids his own age.

"I'll go get some snacks," Lena said and started to descend the ladder Giselle's father had built against the wide tree trunk in their backyard.

"I'm coming too!" Aaron piped up, and followed after her sister.

"You want anything?" Lena called back over her shoulder at Giselle.

"Nope. I'm good."

"Be back in a few," Lena called and started to speed-walk back to the house.

Giselle kept some of her favorite toys in the treehouse now. She had spent many hours in it since her father had built the house for her, and she had slowly made it into more of a toy house than a tree house.

There was a small radio that ran on batteries if she wanted to listen to music, and a tiny TV set that she hadn't figured out how to get a signal on. Still, it was her little home away from home and she practically lived in it the past month since it's grand unveiling.

Heavy footsteps up the ladder outside signaled that her cousins were back.

Only they weren't. Not the ones she was expecting, anyway.

"Hi, Jackson," Giselle said as she turned the power on for the radio. She liked listening to one of the oldies stations and "Blue Moon" was in the middle of playing when she tuned it in to the right frequency.

"Hiya, squirt," he said, using his nickname for her. Giselle had always been smaller than average for her age, so the nickname had stuck after he first used it.

"Stop calling me that'," Giselle scolded. "I'm much bigger than the last time you saw me."

"You're still a squirt to me," Jackson said as he moseyed over to where she was fiddling with the radio. "Whatcha doin'?"

"Playing the radio and waiting for Aaron and Lena to get back. Aaron was hungry."

"Aaron's always hungry," Jackson told her. "He's gonna be a big guy when he gets older. Takes after..." He trailed off. His brows crinkled, as if in distress.

Yeah – his dad. The man that died and landed his mother with three kids on the Kincaids' front doorstep.

Not that Roger or Mary Ellen Kincaid minded. Family was family, and unless they did something unforgivable, you pretty much had to deal with them.

"Your dad," Giselle said. "I get it. I'm sorry he's gone."

Jackson shrugged, acting as if it was no big deal.

"He's gone. It's done," he said. "No need to dwell on the past, I say."

"Yeah, but – he was your dad," Giselle said. "You don't get another one."

"It's cool, kid," Jackson said. "Just drop it already."

Drop it she did. Jackson always closed up when the topic of his father came up. That or he simply just walked away. Hiding.

"Want to play Barbies with me?" Giselle asked, trying to cheer her cousin up.

"Naw, I've got better shit to do." He paused. "In fact, I have a better game we can play."

"What is it? Monopoly? Life?" They were two of her favorite board games.

"Those are kids' games," he said offhandedly. "You want to play a grown-up game with me instead?"

Giselle's brows puckered. Grown-up games to her were cards. Like poker, or perhaps Trivial Pursuit.

"Is it fun for kids?"

"It's fun for all ages, kiddo," Jackson said. "But you have to do something first."

"What's that?"

"You have to take off all your clothing to play this game."

Jackson was her cousin. Family. He wouldn't do anything bad to his family.

Would he?

Chapter 22

The sudden memory was so potent, so devastating, it almost dropped Elle to her knees. Her breath came out in rasping exhales and wheezing inhales as she fought wobbly knees to move forward.

"Luna-" one of the guards started to say.

"What is your name?" Elle asked him, cutting him off.

"It's Adrian," he told her, completely at odds with himself on what to do. The Alpha hadn't said that their Luna could not visit the prisoner, but he hadn't sounded like he was kidding when he said that the man was to be kept in complete solitude from other wolves either.

"Adrian," Elle said, thanking God her voice sounded stronger than she felt. "This is my cousin, Jackson. I am not going to let him go free because he has done far worse to me than anyone else ever has." Even Jeremiah, in a sense.

"Little cousin," croaked Jackson. "So good to see family in this hell hole you call a cell. Do you realize how many rats infest this...place you call my new domicile?"

Elle moved forward and spoke directly at him. She hoped those rats bit his dick off in his sleep. Poetic justice of a sort.

"I'll call the Orkin man as soon as I've said my piece," she told him coldly, blinking once.

The man looked horrible. He smelled even worse. She wondered how the guards in charge of him could even come within twenty feet of the man. It was obvious that he hadn't bathed in a very long time.

She was caught between her pity for the guards' sensitive olfactory receptors and the little bit of joy Jackson might take from even a cold shower to scrub away the layers of grime.

"Then please, have at it, squirt." The man had the audacity to smile at her.

"You abused me when I was a child," she told him.

"That is not news to either of us." He didn't deny the fact of his trespasses.

"You took advantage of a family member."

"Again, we both know this," he said, as if disappointed in her idea of conversation.

"Why?"

The man – *animal* – shrugged at her as if he couldn't find it in himself to care less.

"I was bored," he said.

There was a pregnant pause.

"Not good enough," she told him.

He thought deeply, his eyes wandering to the ceiling before speaking.

"I've always had...urges that most men do not suffer from," he said. "Even in my early teens I knew there was something wrong with me, something not quite right. The day...the day my father died, he had found out we were being exiled from our pack."

"Why? Why were you being exiled?"

"Me, of course," the man said, looking at Elle as if she was stupid. "I had molested a small child and the Alpha had found out. Since I was still considered a pup, there was no way my family was going to leave me. It would have been cruel-"

"As cruel as the molestation of a child?" Elle interjected, unbelieving. Again, the man only shrugged.

"It most likely would have meant my death if I was made rogue as a pup," he told her.

"A just verdict for a person as foul as you." Her eyes narrowed in on him.

Jackson continued as if she hadn't spoken her disdain.

"The Beta found me with the girl I...*touched*." Elle scoffed at his words. He was downplaying his part to the best of his abilities it seemed. "He went to the Alpha and spoke with him. He was a different man than your Jeremiah, little wolf. He was a good man, and knew what was right and what was wrong. When my father returned home that night, we were turned out of our house. We were left with nothing. My father couldn't believe I would do such a thing and went into a rage when we were exiled. He went into a hysterical state and had to be...*put down*. Like a rabid dog."

While Elle felt bad at the loss of a parent – *anyone's* parent – there was little else she felt for him at that moment. She was too numbed by the shock of her own sudden memories, disgusted by them even.

"Why do you have something against me? Why me?" Elle asked. The man looked over at her and smiled. Elle growled back.

"My mother and siblings came to your family at Blackriver. We were desperate," Jackson said. "Your parents knew very little as to why my father went berserk. They just knew that we had been exiled and made rogue. Your father pleaded with your Alpha at the time, and he reluctantly let us in. After all, it was my father that went insane and not us. He just didn't know why.

"After you and I had our little *game*, I convinced you to be quiet about it and, for a while, you complied. But kids like you can never stay quiet for long and you ended up telling your mother what happened. Your father had a talk with the Alpha and he kicked us out. Even if your mate is a complete shithead, it doesn't mean his father was altogether loathsome, squirt."

Elle ignored the implication of Jeremiah as her mate and plowed on.

"So, you blame my father for getting your family kicked out a second time? Is that why you agreed to kidnap me for Jeremiah?" Elle asked.

"Of course, that was part of it," he said. "The money helped as well. You see, I found own my mate at age 19. I knew I might not make it out of this alive. I wanted the money for her, so she could start a new life somewhere else if I were to be killed."

"Noble, but you are still a despicable creature," Elle told him bluntly. "I pity the female that got paired with you. To think she chose life as a rogue over rejection of you and a stable family life. Does she know of your proclivities towards young females?"

The man shrugged.

"She may have an inkling," Jackson simply said.

Disgust tasted like bile in the back of Elle's throat. It was rancid and heavy. Acidic.

"And yet...she stays with you," Elle responded with shock.

"Females will believe what they want to believe," he told her. "From the look on your face when you walked in here, I would say you had blocked quite a few memories yourself. If Ellen wishes to look past some of my foibles, it is because she cannot imagine a man she loves to be capable of such atrocities. Or at least she believes that I have changed my ways. For her."

She didn't want to admit to the shock of seeing him again, the visions, the memories. She didn't even want to acknowledge them to herself right now. She could do that later, on her own. When she was alone, preferably.

"Jackson Kincaid," Elle said stiffly. "Your crimes are indeed atrocious, and you show no sign of regret or remorse for your victims. You are hereby found guilty of the following crimes: conspiracy to kidnap, attempted kidnap, two counts molestation of a minor, and assault of a minor."

"Playing judge and jury, little wolf?" Jackson asked, snickering. "Will you be my executioner as well? It's only fitting. One generation to the next. Your father certainly condemned us."

Elle hesitated. Could she execute the man before her? Lord knew he deserved it. The things he had done, the easy way he had talked about them. Abominable. Deplorable.

Before she could think, she laid the last blow on him.

"I, Giselle Stark, Luna of Plumbrook, find you guilty of the above charges," she told him firmly and took a deep breath.

"I sentence you to death by *Blood Eagle*," she decreed and, before she could see the shock register on his face, did a quick 180 and walked out toward the stairs leading to clean air and freedom.

***

Alpha. We have lost your mate.

It was one of the wolves he had set to guard Elle, and Liam immediately growled at their incompetence.

What the fuck happened? he snarled back through their link.

She went to visit the Beta's female. We were invited in and she fled while we were...busy.

Liam would figure out what "busy" meant later. He had to find Elle first and demand to know why she slipped away from her guards.

Go and search the grounds, Liam demanded. *I will head back to the house and try to pick up her scent from there, if she hasn't already made it back to the house.*

He got a reply of, *Yes, Alpha,* and cut the link, standing up from his work desk and moving towards the door. He knew that if she was sneaking around, she would most likely ignore any attempt at him linking with her. Liam's hand met with the cold metal of the doorknob and turned it. He found Trace on the other side, about to knock on the door of his office, and Liam pushed him aside as he walked right past the man, heading toward the Packhouse's front entrance.

"Liam!" Trace called.

"Not now," Liam said shortly, huffing his displeasure at being waylaid by his own Delta.

"But it's about Elle," Trace told him. Liam immediately stopped and did an about-face back to him, grabbing him by the cuff of his shirt and lifting him from the ground.

"What about her?" Liam growled as his eyes shifted to the amber orbs of his wolf.

"She was seen in the cells with the rogue. Jackson," Trace told him, cowering under his Alpha's fierce presence.

Liam let him go and immediately turned around.

"But she's not there anymore," Trace told him before Liam could walk three steps. "She left a few minutes ago. One of the guards there linked me and said she had left. He...he said she...she laid down a death sentence on the rogue." Trace paused. "By *Blood Eagle.*"

The fuck?

It was unlike his little Elle's sweet nature to hand down such a punishment as that. *He* certainly wouldn't have even handed it down. It was bound to end up as weeks of unbearable pain until the man succumbed to his significant injuries.

Blood Eagle. He never would have thought to use that. It was more of a torture device and slow death for a wolf.

Used first by the Vikings, *Blood Eagle* was a sacrifice they used where the condemned person was laid naked on his stomach before each of his ribs was broken. The bones were then pulled through the skin and bent up towards the sky, resembling bloody wings. Even with a wolf's swift healing capabilities, it was difficult to generate enough energy to fix it themselves. Even the stamina of a rogue wolf – who was sometimes used to getting by on little sustenance – wouldn't stand a chance.

Blood Eagle? What was Elle thinking?

So, Liam left his Delta in the Packhouse and went searching for his mate, hoping to find her in the first spot he looked.

Their home.

***

Liam seethed. He'd yell at Colleen and the guards later. All he could focus on was the sound of weeping coming from somewhere inside his home.

Once Liam had stepped over the threshold of his house, he heard it. The soft wails of his mate. The sound tore at his heart, and he followed her scent to the second floor, down the hallway, and into their bedroom.

He eventually found Elle in a lump of blankets on the bed. They almost swaddled her like a baby. The shock about her surprise death sentence took a backseat as he moved over to the side of the bed to sit down.

"Elle," Liam called softly to her. "Angel."

She continued to sob under innumerable layers of comforter until Liam had to dig her out, pick her up, and place her on his lap. His shirt was instantly saturated as she sobbed into it, smearing tears and snot all over it.

"What happened?" he asked quietly as he rocked her back and forth gently. He had let her calm a bit before speaking, and she was down to sniffles and the occasional hiccoughing sob.

"He *is* my cousin," she said through her watery voice. "He...he..."

She couldn't verbalize it, so she told him through their mindlink. Monosyllables. Visions. Liam shuddered against her.

And as she spoke to him in his mind, anger flushed crimson on Liam's face, and if Elle hadn't been on his lap he would have stood and stomped off to the cells to exact justice on the scum. *Elle's* style of justice. He was less surprised by her death sentence now than he was before.

"That fucking..." Liam couldn't find words in his vocabulary that would be close enough to what he was feeling for the rogue. He only wished the man had died before this. It was painfully obvious that remembering her abuse had stirred up long dormant emotions again.

First Jackson. Then Jeremiah.

The poor woman had been through enough.

Liam was determined, now more than ever, that she would never be hurt. Not ever again.

***

"*Blood Eagle*, baby? What were you thinking?" Liam asked when Elle had finally calmed down long enough to verbalize words out loud again. The shock of her meeting with Jackson had her almost reverting back to her mute state. It had scared the Alpha for a bit.

"I was thinking of the cruelest ways for a person to die," Elle told him softly, shrugging. "I used to watch a lot of the History Channel, and I remembered seeing a special on Vikings and the sacrificial customs of them. It just...popped into my head."

Liam shook his head again, in awe of his tiny mate. Death by guillotine would have been more her style, if she could even be thought as having one. It was quick. Painless. Easy. Set a basket on the ground, sharpen the blade, *thunk*, and you're done. *Blood Eagle* – for lack of a better word – was inhumane.

"Can I take it back? Do something else? He's already dead anyway." There was no way Liam was letting the man go, and he had forfeited his life by trying to abduct his woman and the pack's Luna.

"You can," Liam said as he nodded to her. Then he shook his head again, smiling slightly. "But you gave the guards something to talk about, I'm sure. It'll be all over Plumbrook by nightfall how unforgiving and unyielding you are. You'll be a legend." She grimaced at him, pained.

"But as Luna, shouldn't I be fair and unwaveringly kind?" It's not like there was a fucking handbook on the role.

"Yes, but you also should be able to make tough decisions when you are able to," Liam told her. "It shows your strength. Once word gets out as to what sort of wolf the man is and what he has done, you'll endear the pack to you even more. If there is one thing they cannot abide, it's causing harm to a child, no matter what the circumstances. It's well within your rights to go about your original terms, though." He doubted she would.

"No," she said quickly. "I spoke without thinking. I don't regret finding him guilty. He as much as admitted to everything he did and he showed no remorse for the things he has done. I think we should make it quick, painless. Once he is gone, his mate will feel it, may even try to come after us. If we make it quick, she may not try to take us all down in her rage. She is already...*somewhat* aware of his past misdeeds."

"I doubt, after the severance of the bond, she will be able to do much of anything," Liam said. After all, *he* would know. The cutting of the mating bond was painful to the extreme.

"Sorry," Elle said, wincing.

"No, you are right," he told her. "I'm – I'm over what happened years ago, and I'm happy with my life now. I...I don't think I ever would have been this happy with my true mate." His admission tasted like guilt, like shame in his mouth.

"But you would have loved her just the same," Elle said, certain. Liam nodded.

"I would have, but I would have been a weaker leader," he admitted. "An Alpha's mate is meant to be just as strong, even if not physically, as the Alpha. Cecilia was weak, both emotionally and physically."

Elle let that thought linger, and paused before clearing her throat.

"What do you suggest?" Elle asked, getting back down to brass tacks.

"Guillotine," Liam said in a low rumble. "Quick. Easy. Relatively painless. Then we send Jackson's head back to Jeremiah as a message."

"And that message?"

Liam looked at her, catching her azure gaze with his steely one.

"He's not getting you back. Anything he throws at me gets tossed back into his court dead, or damned close to it."

***

"Holy shit," Conley breathed as Liam caught him up to speed later that day. His father had been visiting the Shadecreek Pack, the Alpha being an old friend of his from diaper days.

"Yeah," Liam said softly.

"That little mate of yours is tougher than nails," his father said admiringly. "And she'll make one hell of a mother to my grandkids."

It was back to that. All Liam needed now was his father asking how progress on that front was going.

"How is the sex life? Plentiful?"

Oh, God.

"Jesus Christ," Liam muttered. It was his worst nightmares come true.

"What? Be fruitful and multiply and...however the saying goes after that," Conley told his son. "Your sister is on her second. You should at least be halfway done with your first."

"We're...we're working on it," Liam said vaguely.

"Morning, noon, and night?" Conley asked. "When your mother and I were trying we-"

"Good God! Don't finish that sentence!" Liam exclaimed, eyes bulging in his panic.

"What?" Conley asked, feigning innocence. "It's not like you don't know where you came from, boy. Your mother and I may have only had the two of you, but we were pretty fucking active otherwise."

"This...is a fucking nightmare," Liam voiced out loud as he groaned. He needed to hear about his parents' active sex life as badly as he needed a frontal lobotomy or a penectomy. "Okay, old man, any more sex talk out of you and I'll stop trying for pups."

"Probably too late to stop now anyway with the way you two go at it," Conley said. "Anyways, your old man will be out of your hair relatively soon."

"Why? What's up?" Liam asked, thankful for a reprieve from sex talk with his father.

"Your mother's been bothering me since I left," Conley said. "She says she misses me, but I really know just what she misses." He gestured pointedly down to his crotch before Liam closed his eyes and took a deep breath. "The D." As if he had needed to say it.

And they had been *so* close to getting past the sex talk.

"Elle is asleep, so I'm going to hit some take-out joint for dinner," Liam said after a beat. "Will you be okay here with her, or should I ask Caleb to babysit your ass so you don't try and bully her into a quick pregnancy with your horrible sex stories?"

His father blew out a quick gust of air.

"We'll be fine. Stop worrying," Conley told him. "I promise not to bring up sex and babies, and the two of you doing whatever nastiness you get up to in your bedroom there when you think I'm not around."

"Hey!"

"I said I'd not talk to *her* about it," Conley told him. "*You're* fair game as far as I'm concerned. It's a father's God-given right to make his children supremely uncomfortable. I'm just executing my authority as sperm donor."

"I regret inviting you into my territory," Liam told him as he picked up his keys from the bowl near the doorway.

"Hey, it used to be my territory too," his father told him accurately. "Without your mother and I, you wouldn't have a pack to control."

"Chinese?" Liam asked, ignoring him.

Conley nodded.

"You know what I like, kid."

***

The Norfolk Tavern was crowded when Liam took Elle there next. They didn't see any sign of the owner's son, but that was just as well. He would probably have bothered Elle about joining him on Piano Night, and Liam wasn't ready for her to spread her wings – in that sense – just yet.

At least not until the problem of Jeremiah went away. For good.

And Liam didn't know how to do that without creating an all-out war between the two packs. Not something one took to lightly.

After his father's departure back to the mountains in the west, Elle had been bored staying at home. Liam decided to take a few guards with them to the Norfolk Tavern this time to guard the perimeter. He wanted the time alone with Elle outside of being at home with her when he could.

And he had a few surprises in store for her as well. One he knew she would like, and one he *hoped* she would.

David, the owner's son, suddenly appeared on the stage to a

smattering of applause. Most of the people in attendance seemed to take his presence at the piano for granted, and David nodded toward Elle after his eyes lit up a bit when he saw her. As there was no lust in them and only interest, Liam would let the man live. For now. After all, he was human and there were laws against such things.

David gestured her over with a twitch of his head and Liam followed Elle as they made their way past the tables surrounding the stage.

"Elle, have you thought of what I had to say last time you were here?" David asked quietly as the crowd around them murmured a bit.

"I-" she began.

"It's been a bit...hectic at home right now," Liam told the man. "We've talked about it, and she would be willing to consider it after we have some personal matters squared away."

Well, Liam said that in a more diplomatic way than Elle ever could have. She nodded in agreement with Liam. David's face fell, but he brightened after a moment as he thought of an idea.

"Well, why don't we try a song or two now? Just to see how an audience takes to you on Piano Night?" David asked.

Liam nodded at him and looked over at Elle. "You want to give it a try?"

"Sure," she said, sounding anything but confident. "I don't have a lot memorized, but I have a few things I keep in my back pocket."

At that, Liam stepped back to his table, and David and Elle talked a few minutes before he brought out a microphone and placed it in front of the baby grand piano that took up much of the stage. He stood behind it and spoke to the audience.

"I know this is Piano Night, but I thought we'd try something different this week. I hope you like it," he said.

He stepped back to the piano and started a slow, melancholy tune.

I'm With You by Avril Lavigne lacked something in the acoustic version, but it was still damned good and the audience appreciated the talent. Elle sang with a raw edginess as the last several stanzas faded away into applause. Wolf whistles soon followed with loud requests for an encore.

Elle smiled softly and David said something that even Liam couldn't hear over the din of the crowd. Once the applause died down, however, it was apparent that the requests for an encore had gotten through and they were starting a new song. This one was better suited to the piano. It was another song by Avril Lavigne. *When You're Gone.*

Somewhere during the applause for the second song, Elle's head turned to the side of the stage as if she saw something. Shock registered before Liam realized what she must have seen. A small smile tipped his own lips and he watched Elle's mouth form the word *Mom* before he walked to the stage to escort her down. Instead of walking her back toward their table, Liam moved them toward the newcomers.

Roger and Mary Ellen Kincaid.

Sneakily, he had used Elle's phone late one night to contact her parents to try to set up a rendezvous on neutral territory. Norfolk Tavern was the first place he thought of as it was far enough away from both packs to garner the least amount of attention.

He was only able to get them to agree to a meeting when he swore them both to secrecy on his name. He already knew from Elle that her mother had guessed she was with another Alpha and she was game, but it was harder for her father to come to terms with it.

"Mom?" Elle asked before embracing the older woman who was standing next to a handsome older gentleman with glasses.

"Elle, baby," her mother cried. "It's so good to see you again!"

Chapter 23

The group was deep in their conversation when the food arrived. Elle had been so intent on talking with her parents that Liam had ordered for her, knowing what she liked.

"I still can't tell you everything," Elle told her. "But at least you see me and see that I'm happy."

The smile on her face was wide, breathtakingly beautiful, and if it had been anyone but her parents, Liam would have been jealous of the person – or persons – that made her that gleefully happy. But he knew how much she had missed them.

"And you, Liam," her father said, a bit gruffly. "You are an Alpha."

Liam nodded and took a sip of his beer. Elle had introduced them officially soon after embracing her mother and father.

"Yes, sir," he said respectfully to his father in mating. "Plumbrook, but as you know, that is on the QT."

Her father looked doubtful, if only for a moment, before continuing.

"Gis – I mean Elle," her father began.

That was another thing. They were to speak about her only as "Elle" so that word didn't get back to Jeremiah. Liam smelled no foreign wolves in the place beside themselves, but there were ways to mask a scent through witchcraft and the like.

"She told her mother of your previous mate," Roger said to Liam. "I was sorry to hear of that. Very painful. I remember my brother's wife after he passed. Inconsolable she was."

"Yes, it was a very difficult time," Liam said somberly. "I didn't ever think I would get a second chance, even if it was with a chosen mate instead." He paused. "My first mate was...unwell and would have weakened our pack through me. I – I honestly can't say I wished for a different outcome as I have Elle here, but I can say I wish things had been different."

"It's not as rare as one thinks, getting a second chance," Mary Ellen said. "If one's mate has passed on, or both sides have chosen another, then and only then can a secondary bond to another take place as a *true* second chance mate. Until Jeremiah takes another female to mate or dies, he will always have a bond to Elle." She sounded worried at that, and glanced over at her daughter.

"We can only hope for a peaceful resolution to this conflict," Liam said. "I vote for no bloodshed, but…Jeremiah has already tried to take Elle back."

This was something he hadn't mentioned to the Kincaids during their phone conversation. He hadn't wanted her father to go berserk and try to ram down Jeremiah's door without thinking of the repercussions. The Kincaids both looked at him, her father's face a storm cloud on the horizon.

"What do you mean?" he asked, his voice a bit unsteady.

Liam told them everything about the rogues and let Elle take over after he mentioned imprisoning Jackson in the cells.

"Why didn't I remember what I went through as a child?" Elle asked her mother, who glanced at her father anxiously.

"It…the child psychologist said that might happen," Mary Ellen told her daughter. "Sometimes reliving things makes us put a block in our minds against the – well, the more traumatic things we experience. When a few months went by and you started to ask who Jackson was when the doctor started to talk to you, it was apparent that you had built up your own set of defenses mentally."

"She tried to bring them back out, but you were stubborn," her father told her, almost proudly. "As you were happier without the memories, we figured it was just as well that you hid them from yourself."

"Jackson is being executed tonight by guillotine," Liam told the table softly. The piano music coming from the stage ensured that no one would hear them. They all flinched at his words.

"Guillotine?" Mary Ellen asked, surprised. Liam shrugged at her. It did sound a bit medieval, but death by execution was ugly no matter which way you sliced it.

"It was better than your daughter's death sentence by *Blood Eagle*," he told them.

They both blinked over at their daughter. They seemed surprisingly familiar with the term.

"It was a decision I made under…under duress!" she exclaimed as low as she could. "I took it back. Not that the bastard deserved my mercy."

Liam placed a steadying hand on her mid-back and rubbed soothingly.

"Relax, baby," Liam told her. "No one's judging you."

Mary Ellen looked from her daughter to Liam, her eyes glistening with happy tears when she saw his calming gesture working on her. It was the calling card of a strong bond between mated wolves.

"You sounded beautiful up on stage," Mary Ellen told her daughter, in order to get past the weepy display. "Would you sing again? Now?"

Liam was sure the audience would like another song, but he wasn't sure if Elle was ready for one. When he looked over at her, he saw a wide smile take over her face. He stood corrected.

"Of course," she said. "As long as David is okay with me taking center stage again."

Elle got up and walked over to David at the piano. She waited for the song to play out before going up to him. Immediately, David told the audience he was taking five and conversation started up amongst the patrons, including the Kincaids and Liam.

"You're good for her. I can tell," Mary Ellen said to Liam. "Old fussy britches over here thinks so too. He's just too Papa Wolf to admit it out loud though."

It meant a lot to Liam to have her parents' approval. It wasn't necessary at this juncture, but he was glad to have it nonetheless.

"You hurt my daughter, I won't care if you're an Alpha," her father said, almost growling. "I'll put your ass in a sling nonetheless."

Liam nodded, understanding. He'd be the same with his kids when he had them. Before he could say anything back to the man though, a static pop from the microphone took them by surprise and the whole table's attention was focused onto the stage again.

David began to play again. It was another slow tune. Liam immediately recognized it after the first few words as *Flashlight* by Jessie J.

People who had them took out lighters, waving them in the air until the hot metal burned their fingers and they laughed at their own stupidity.

Elle finished the song out to applause. If she'd had back-up singers it would have been like a professional performance. The applause didn't last long before David segued into another song. This one was surprising. It wasn't as slow as the other songs Elle had sung, and was a definite rock anthem.

It was *Here's To Us* by Halestorm, an unlikely and risqué selection for a family place. It was met with approval, though, and many in the crowd sang along to the words.

The majority of the audience was singing along with Elle by the end of the song and raising their glasses in a mock toast. Liam beamed when the whole crowd yelled *'Tell 'em to go fuck themselves'* and laughed when they cheered at their own nerve.

"She's great," he heard someone say off in the distance.

"I love this song," another person commented.

"Think she's single?" a male asked. Liam almost snorted.

Definitely not, puny human.

"I saw her with an older couple and a man who has about six inches on you, bro," his buddy said. "I'd steer clear. Even if that's her brother or whatever, the dude's fucking scary big."

His amusement at their repartee took form in a low chuckle at the second guy's advice and he found Elle suddenly back at the table and looking down at him with a cocked head.

"What's so funny?" she asked as she sat back down to finish her plate of pasta.

"Your adoring public, angel," he told her. They either wanted to fuck her or be her it seemed, and he was having none of the former, though he couldn't really blame them. "I'll tell you later." Her father was barely showing his approval of Liam so he didn't want to push the paternal wolf any further by telling her – *out loud* – that she had a few male admirers that weren't keen on just hearing her sing for them.

About a half an hour later, plied with food and drink, the two couples parted ways with promises to keep in touch and more phone calls if they couldn't see each other somewhat regularly.

As they were walking back to Liam's car, Elle hummed.

"You called them behind my back, you sly dog," she accused teasingly.

"Guilty as charged," Liam admitted. "But I didn't just bring you out here to hear you sing and reunite you with your parents. I wanted to give you this."

He pulled a small box out of his jacket pocket. It was dark velvet. He opened it with a whine and a pop. Elle's eyes flew up to his, large and unblinking.

"We are as good as married in our culture," Liam told her. "The bond forged through marking and mating is irrevocable and complete, and it's stronger than any marriage in the human world. The only thing tying humans together is a scrap of paper and their promise to let nothing come between them. That – and this."

He presented her with the ring before pausing and taking a deep breath.

"I know you enjoy performing," he told her. "I could see it in your eyes when you were up there. I don't know when this whole thing with Jeremiah will be resolved, but when it is, you could come here and perform as you wish. With that being said, I don't think I'd be able to handle that without something a human would recognize to signal your being "off-limits". I want you to wear this ring, if you would. As a sign of our love, our undeniable bond to each other-"

"And a physical barrier so no one else tries to claim me for themselves?" she finished with a smirk.

"A little bit," he admitted with a dashing half-smile. "Okay. A *lot*, but even if you weren't going to come here regularly, I still would have bought it for you and wanted you to wear it. So...will you?"

"Yes," she said softly. "Of course, I will. I love you."

Liam breathed a sigh of relief and slid it onto her finger. It wasn't a flashy ring, for Liam knew she would have hated that. But it was symbolic to him. Three garnet plum blossoms – big, medium, and small – with diamond accents in the middle. It was feminine, sweet, and had cost more than some of the flashier rings he had seen when he picked it out.

After the ring was placed perfectly on her hand, Liam cupped her face and brought his mouth down to hers in a long, lingering kiss. Her hands slid around his neck, pouring herself into the kiss as well. He pulled away after only thirty seconds, breathing hard.

"Angel, if I keep kissing you like that you're going to end up conceiving our first child right here in the middle of a tavern parking lot," he told her with a shaky laugh.

"If I haven't already," she told him, laughing.

Her words brought him up short.

"You..."

She shook her head.

"Too soon to tell," she told him. "Though if we keep going at it like this, it won't be much longer."

She may as well have been having a naughty chat with his dick because he certainly was ready to make that a possibility tonight.

"Baby, get in the car already before I lose my shit and take you right here."

Chapter 24

"Jackson Kincaid, formerly of Blackriver and Massena packs," Liam began. "You have been charged and found guilty of crimes against children and the Luna of Plumbrook Pack. You have the choice to speak freely if you so wish. Have you any final words before justice has been meted out?"

There was a soft grumble amongst the crowd of wolves, none of which were pups.

"You may have conquered this rogue, Liam Stark, but you cannot win against Alpha Jeremiah," the man told him calmly. "The bond between true mates can never truly be broken and Jeremiah is set on having her." He paused. "If you wish death on your pack because of my little cousin, so be it. Their blood will be on your head."

The noise from the crowd became louder as many of the wolves found it egregious for him to speak to their Alpha in such a way. No respect, not even for his own flesh and blood cousin.

"If you wish to anger me and discipline you to the Luna's first choice of punishment, please, continue to speak in such a fashion," Liam told him calmly, though he was shaking with anger. "I have no qualms seeing you suffer as you should, wretched creature that you are."

"You would set *Blood Eagle* on me?" Jackson almost sounded amused. "You are certainly the match for my bloodthirsty little cousin." He looked over to Elle who was seated in the front row of seats next to Blake, Trace, and Caleb. "How are you tonight, sweetheart? Enjoying the show?"

"Don't you dare talk to her," Liam growled. "You are beneath her, rogue, and no family to her. Now, if you have said your piece, we will commence with the execution."

"I could talk for a bit more," Jackson allowed. The man was truly vile. He didn't seem to take his own mortality into account at all, much less the pain he was putting his mate through when he passed on. "But I doubt you would like anything I have to say so I will leave you simply with this: Do not count on even those around you for there are some who are not to be trusted amongst you. Those with treasonous intentions."

"He's lying," Blake muttered to Elle. He couldn't believe anyone would want to harm her. She looked fragile but was a proper bulldog beneath her feminine exterior.

"Maybe not," Elle murmured back. She was sure there were one or two she-wolves that would have liked to see her gone so they could take her place.

"Jealous females," Trace said, eyeing a few in the crowd he deemed low enough to wish their Luna dead. Or at least out of the way.

"Bring him to kneel," Liam ordered the Head Guard.

The man pulled Jackson upright and Elle felt her stomach lurch uneasily. She may have been beaten bloody at times, but she had never witnessed a death. Well, not one she knew of. Parts of her mind were still a mystery to her, even after some of her memories had resurfaced in the cells with Jackson.

The Head Guard forced Jackson to his knees a couple of feet away from the lunette, the half circle that would close in around his neck. He then forced his torso so it was horizontal, or parallel, to the ground. The Head Guard then closed the lunette around him and locked it in place so Jackson was unable to move.

Elle fought against the wave of nausea bubbling up from her stomach. She wanted to shut her eyes but knew she couldn't. She needed to show to all the pack that if she was strong enough to lay down the law, she was determined enough to follow through on the sentence.

After Jackson was tightly secured, the guard backed away and Liam stepped forward. As leader, he was to see to every execution, just as he was to render wolves rogue when – and if – he had to. Admittedly, this was Liam's first execution and he was none too keen on exacting justice in such a manner. Violence outside of defending his female and pack was abhorrent to him in many ways. It was one thing to be filled with the rush of adrenaline during a battle, and an altogether different thing when there was no immediate outside danger.

All was silence. Even the woods around them seemed to stop and listen for the blade that would take Jackson's life.

It may have been ten seconds or a full minute, but by the time Liam pulled the rope to let the blade go, Elle was stricken frozen as she watched the blood splash onto the ground 20 feet in front of her. The head of Jackson Kincaid made a thump, then a sickening splat into the basket below it.

***

Elle was mute. Again.

Not in the same way. She just didn't have anything to say about what she had witnessed thirty minutes before. She was no closer to sleep, though Liam wished she would get some rest.

Or at least fucking *talk* about this.

"Angel, please speak to me," he begged softly. Her eyes shifted to his, the same lifeless look in them as she'd had 29 minutes ago.

"What do you want me to say?" she verbalized almost plaintively.

"Fuck, anything. Everything," he told her. "Tell me what you're feeling at least." He sat down on the bed next to her, close enough to touch her skin.

"I...I don't know what I feel," she said honestly. "Some relief, some sadness. Shit-tons of disgust at what I just witnessed. You're lucky I'm not going full *Exorcist* and projectile vomiting split-pea soup."

Liam's own skin turned a bit green at the thought, though he had been feeling pretty sickly right after he had done the deed. Not something he would admit to anyone besides Elle, though. Colleen would have a field day if she found out. Start calling him "Precious" or "Lil' Liam" or something else emasculating and untoward.

"I'm not a fan of the method we used, but it was probably cleaner and less vomit-inducing than your first idea." He gave her a look.

That was true, if not slightly concerning for Elle. She hadn't had a bloodthirsty bone in her body before this and she certainly wasn't feeling the love for execution right now. She blamed her emotions at the time she had spoken with Jackson in the cells.

"Do you think it was true? What he said?" Elle inquired.

"About a treasonous wolf among us?" Liam asked, lips thinning to a line as he thought. "It's a possibility. Which is why I have very few people I truly trust, you and Blake being top of the list. Even Caleb doesn't know everything and I've known him since I was small."

Elle tried laying down, but the nausea kicked in and she quickly shot upright again and walked toward the door.

"Where are you going?" Liam asked as she opened the door to the bedroom and walked into the hallway.

"Getting some hot tea," she called back at him. Mint tea would be nice. Soothing for the stomach. And it was getting quite chilly at night.

After she fixed her tea, she sat in the living room, cupping the mug to warm her cold hands. It was the second week of November and the temperatures had dipped low enough for snow. She looked out the window, hoping to see some of the fluffy white stuff. It would do her good to see it falling right about now. Cleansing somehow.

And it would cover up the scent and sight of blood that was wafting over from behind the Packhouse.

"Elle, babe?"

Her head shot over to Liam and she gave him a wan smile. He was standing at the top of the stairs looking down at her.

"Come sit with me for a bit," she requested of him softly.

He complied and walked down the old stairs, hopping over the creaky one that was next to last at the bottom.

He curled up next to her on the couch and gently pulled her into his body as she held on, with both hands, to her drink. She didn't need a scalding hot beverage to burn the Alpha's babymakers.

"Mint?" he asked, sniffing the air.

"It soothes my stomach," she told him. He stiffened.

"Are you?"

"Quit thinking with your dick," she told him lightly. "I've only been feeling nauseous since seeing the head of one of my family members lopped off. I'm sure this will pass."

He pressed a kiss to her temple and curled his arm around her waist.

"I'll keep my dick in check for the night then," Liam told her softly. "I can't make any promises about tomorrow, though."

He was serious, though Elle laughed at him. She felt him smile against the skin of her forehead.

"That was...it was horrible," she said when her laughter petered out. She was thinking of the execution again, much to Liam's displeasure. "Have you...have you ever had to do that before?"

"No," he said lowly. "And if I ever have to do it again, it'll be way too soon."

"And if Jeremiah-"

"Oh, I will gladly take him down if the opportunity arises," Liam said quickly. "He is nearly as awful as your cousin, angel. And he wants what's mine." He held onto her tightly, as if Jeremiah were a ghostly apparition outside their window, threatening to spirit Elle away.

"A close second," she agreed.

"Do you have any other relatives or acquaintances I should be aware of that are evil incarnate? A mate likes to know these things in order to keep his family safe."

"None that I'm aware of."

"No witchy blood or vampires in the deepest corners of your closet?"

"Ew. No," she said, crinkling her nose. Vamps were not always the good-looking creatures you saw with fangs and killer abs on *True Blood*. And they were repulsive to the many shifter species in general.

"Good," he said and stopped for a moment. "You aunt and her other kids...where are they?"

Elle shrugged and shook her head. "No clue," she said to him. "They've obviously split ways with Jackson. I'm sure he would have mentioned any other family besides his mate to me. He didn't seem to be very close to any of them even when he was younger, to be honest."

"I feel bad for his family," he said. "To...to have to deal with that rogue all their lives, knowing what he was like. And your aunt, praying that none of her other children followed in his footsteps after his father died."

"My other cousins were always good to me," she told him. "I remember playing and having little Aaron tagging along everywhere his sister and I went. I still can't remember her name, though it's on the tip of my tongue."

"She was a few years older than you?" Liam asked.

"Yes. But both she and Aaron would have been too young to have a mate at the time I knew them. I wonder if they are living nearby."

They lapsed into a comfortable silence and listened as the heat kicked on. They had a fireplace, true, but it was so cold they needed central heating this far north.

"I think Trace may have found his mate," Liam said, offhandedly.

"What? How?" Elle sat up straighter.

"Don't know," Liam said. "He was talking to one of the younger females after the execution tonight. He had...a look in his eyes. He was either extremely horny after a bloody head-lopping or she was something special to him."

"It's Trace," Elle said, relaxing. "He'd fuck anything with a hole if it stood still long enough." There was a pause. "Well, not a man, I suppose."

"Oh, but it would be rich if he was mated to another male," Liam chortled. "I have nothing against gay partnership, especially if the two are true mates, but it would be completely ironic for him to be drowning in pussy and then have to take a male to mate."

"Would he reject him if he was mated to a male?" Elle asked.

"Never," Liam told her. "This pack is traditional in that sense. Rejection of a mate is akin to blasphemy. Trace could be made rogue and exiled if he rejected his match without damned good reason."

"Well, we can always hope he'll finally settle down," Elle said, though she had her doubts. From what she had witnessed, Trace could get aroused simply by someone saying the word "wood". It was semi-entertaining to behold at times.

"He will," Liam guessed. "He's never been averse to having a mate. He's just having fun while he still can."

"Didn't you have *fun* when you were younger?" she asked.

"I found Cecilia when I was 21," he told Elle. "Would have found her sooner had she still been here at Plumbrook. Since she went with her father and brother over to Blackriver, it took us longer to connect. I had what you might call a *little* fun prior to that."

Liam was happy he could speak so openly with Elle about his past. He had never wanted to before, even with Blake. Blake, however, knew the amount of guilt Liam had suffered when his mate had died and didn't want to revisit old wounds. He thought they would somehow open up again and Liam – immediately after Cecilia's death – was not a nice man to be around.

"Do you think it will snow soon?" Elle asked, her gaze once again wandering to the window and moonlight beyond it.

"I'm surprised it hasn't already," Liam said. "The mild weather has been a rare treat, but it's finally started to get really brisk – especially at night."

Elle took another sip of her tea and thought. She hoped that whatever happened with Jeremiah would be over before the holidays. She wanted to visit her parents for Christmas at the very least. And Chase, her brother.

If she couldn't, well...she didn't like to think of a Christmas without all her family around her, or, at the very least, her parents.

"I hope Trace finds happiness with his she-wolf," Elle said absently. "If he doesn't treat her well I'll have his nuts as ornaments on our Christmas tree."

"Then we'll have to keep the tree outdoors," Liam told her definitively. "I can't stand the smell of sweaty balls even on a good day. Add blood onto that and I think I might go off the holidays altogether."

Elle smiled.

"Permission to castrate your Delta if he fucks it up with his mate?"

"Permission granted, sweetheart."

Chapter 25

"She's not a virgin," Trace grumped as he plunked his heavy ass in the chair across the desk from Liam. His Alpha only blinked.

"Come again? Who's not a virgin?" This was the weirdest start to a conversation he'd ever had, and he had lived with his father for over twenty years.

"Helene," Trace growled out. "My mate."

So. He *had* found her at last.

"Trace you *do* realize that you're not exactly Mother Bloody Teresa or the Virgin Mary," Liam said while raising a brow in disbelief.

"This...it's different," he harrumphed.

Completely. Idiotic.

"And why is this different?" *Please let this be a double standard type situation,* Liam silently pleaded. He really wanted to lay into him if it was.

"She's...well, she's a *female* for one," Trace blurted out. "Secondly, she's mine! No one else should have had her!"

Thank you Baby Jesus, Santa Claus, and the motherfucking Easter Bunny. Christmas has come early.

"And what does she say about your sexual status? Did you show her all the notches on your bedpost before you got angry with her for having a sexual partner or three before you?"

Trace looked away.

"She's well aware I'm...popular," he simply stated.

"Son, twerking was popular," Liam told him. "Those stupid-ass sneakers with toes were popular. If we're talking ratios for popularity here, you're the fucking *God* of popularity."

"I-"

"Like to get around," Liam finished. "How many sexual partners has she had before you?"

"Two," Trace said, as if he had added a few zeroes after the lone number.

"Well, if you add both your exploits up, you'd get somewhere around 200 or so," Liam told him.

Trace's jaw twitched.

"You know if you fuck up with Helene, I gave Elle permission to extract your nuts through your tonsils," Liam told him.

"She wouldn't," Trace mumbled.

"You *have* met my mate, haven't you? The same one who gave a death sentence of *Blood Eagle* to her own cousin and wants to use your balls as Christmas decorations if you fuck it up with Helene?"

Trace glared at him and Liam sighed.

"What are you going to do?" he finally asked.

"I'm going to find those two guys she slept with and make their future mates very unhappy with me when I rip off their junk and-"

"And what? Do you realize how hypocritical you sound right now? Threatening to separate the two male's cocks so their future females won't have anything to bounce on? Listen to yourself, man. What about when the other men find their mates with some of the women you slept with? They'll want to flay you alive."

"I'm a Delta. They wouldn't dare," Trace said confidently. "The only two females with higher rank are Colleen and Elle, and I've never fucked either one of-"

"Watch what you say, Trace," Liam growled, his eyes flashing amber for a flickering millisecond. "Though I know the chance of you and Elle fucking is nil, I don't want to beat you to within an inch of your life because you said something as stupid as what you're about to spout off."

"My apologies, Alpha," Trace said meekly, chastised.

"Now get the fuck out of my sight, take your mate to bed, and fuck her 'til she forgets those two other men's names," Liam told him. "You'll feel better for it, trust me."

Trace got up, but knew better than to stomp or slam a door in the Packhouse when Liam was working.

Besides, he had a mate to get to. Just thinking about the other two males possibly being around her was utterly distracting.

And, he had to admit, the Alpha was right. Not that he was about to say that to the man's face.

***

"Lucy! I'm home!" Liam called out as he pulled off his winter jacket and tossed it onto the coat rack.

"Ricky! Where have you been?" Elle called, playing into his act.

"I was at de club playing de bongos," he told her and pulled her into a kiss as she walked toward him from the kitchen.

"Is that some kind of euphemism? Playing the bongos?"

He let his hands slide to her ass where he slapped her cheeks a few times in an indistinct rhythm.

"How did you guess?" he asked as he picked her up by her thighs and let her wrap her legs around him, cinching at his waist tightly.

"I'm fluent in the secret language of euphemisms."

He carried her into the kitchen where he dropped her on the counter next to the sink before giving her a proper kiss now that she was closer to his height.

"Hey, baby," he said before sinking his lips into hers and immediately darting a warm tongue into her mouth.

"Hey," she breathed out when they parted.

"You're cooking?" he asked, surprised. "It's Thanksgiving tomorrow. I'd figure you'd be tired of cooking by now."

"I'm not actually cooking right now," she corrected. "I'm baking. Pumpkin and apple pies."

"Two pies only?" he asked. They were having Colleen, Blake, Trace, Helene, and Caleb over for Thanksgiving dinner as well. Blake and Liam could clean up two entire pies on their own.

"Colleen is making a strawberry rhubarb and blueberry pie to bring over as well," she told him before sliding off the counter and bending to check her masterpieces in the making.

Liam smacked her on the ass when she bent over and Elle yelped from her position before knifing back up.

"No pie for you!" she scolded, as if she were the *Seinfeld* soup Nazi.

"How 'bout if I give you a little sugar later on tonight? Does that grant me pie tomorrow?"

"Depends how many times you can make me come," she told him, unashamed.

"What's the minimum?"

"I'm not telling, underachiever," she told him.

"I always shoot for the stars, baby," he told her. "Right before I shoot inside of you."

"You are disgusting," she told him, scoffing.

"You swallow my come," he told her.

"And you swallow mine," she threw back as she went in search of the Christmas oven mitts she had Colleen purchase for her at Target. It was a little early, but she was already in a holiday mood.

"And if these pies taste as good as you, I'll die a happy, tryptophan-sleep-induced wolf."

"I'm slipping arsenic in your slices of pie," she threatened.

"I'd be sick for a while, but I think I'd live through it," he said honestly. Sometimes it paid to have an Alpha's heightened cell-regeneration ability.

In all honesty, Liam and Elle didn't mean a bit of their nastier banter. Unless it was sexual. Elle realized he liked when she got a bit feisty with him, so she upped her sass on occasion to placate his unwavering need.

"So, if you're busy baking pie, what's for dinner?" Liam asked, having had enough of their back and forth for now. "Should I pick up some takeout?"

"No need," she told him. "We have sandwich fixings if you don't mind slumming it for a night."

He didn't. Not when Elle was preparing a feast for them tomorrow. Colleen was sure to come early with Blake to help her, so he wouldn't be lonely without Elle.

At least, not too much.

Elle and Liam had met Trace's little mate, a spitfire of a blond who was only a couple of inches taller than Elle's small stature, but miles ahead in curves. Trace had always gravitated toward the females with a bit of roundness to them, not that there was much he would say no to. If he had gravitated towards celebrities, J. Lo or Kim K. would have been right up his alley, so to speak.

Still, after Liam had had his chat with Trace, he noticed that his Delta bore a mark that was similar to his own, though smaller.

Liam was happy to see Elle filling out as well. Whereas she had been bone-thin when she had first come on Plumbrook territory, she was now a healthy size six to eight, depending on the brand of clothing.

Her breasts had grown as well and filled Liam's hands fully when they were intimate. She had complained of their sensitivity as of late because of the thinner skin after being stretched a bit, but they were so fucking soft and tasted sweeter than honey dipped in sugar.

Fuck. He had gotten hard just thinking about Elle's firm tits. He wondered how much more time they had before the pies were ready. Maybe he could convince her to have a quickie on the couch if she set the timer on the pies.

He moved closer to Elle and ground his quickly hardening cock against her.

"Liam! I have to watch the pies," she scolded, though her legs wrapped around him to keep him close.

"We can be quick," he told her and pulled her away from the

counter toward the living room. "Besides, my father's not here to walk in on us like last time."

"Is the door locked?"

He made a detour as he double checked the locks on the front door. He always kept the back door deadbolted.

"This is gonna be short but sweet, angel," he told her as he tugged his tight jeans down past his knees. "I still have a mission to impregnate you before my father and mother get fed up with us and come here to supervisor our mating. They'll walk in on us in our bedroom just to make sure we're doing it right. My mother's a master at picking locks too. God knows where she learned that talent."

Elle giggled and pulled down her panties. Liam had pulled her pants off before he had sat back on the couch with his jeans around his ankles and looking utterly ridiculous.

And Elle had no doubt Conley would do it. And give tips. The man had zero filter, and even though it embarrassed her sometimes, there was a part of her that sort of liked it.

Elle's giggles were cut short as she was slowly impaled on the Alpha's thick length as it slid home inside of her.

"Liam," Elle moaned out as his hips thrust up into her and he growled. He loved when she moaned his name. Her hips drew up and off him before sitting back down, his own meeting with hers on her slow downward stroke. She gripped his shoulders as her fingernails dug into his skin making crescent-shaped marks.

Liam's fingers found the hem of her shirt and whipped it over her head before taking a hard nipple into his mouth. He traced his tongue around it lightly and then sucked it between his teeth, letting the friction grate against her sensitive skin.

She moaned out as he stroked her with the flat of his tongue and nipped gently at the hardened tips.

Elle clenched around him as he stroked in and out of her, hitting that sweet spot inside her with the perfect angle of his pelvis against hers.

"Shit, angel. So soon?" he asked. She was so responsive to him, particularly as of late. He didn't know if it was the weight gain or something else, but he wanted her to respond to him this way forever, even if it meant having a curvy mate. He would still love every rotund inch of her.

"Yes! Right there!" she called out as he all but assaulted her sensitive g-spot with punishing thrusts of his hips.

"Fuck!" she cried out as she shattered around him in a wave of pulsating squeezes that had him all but spilling inside her as she milked him dry.

"Oh fuck, baby," he growled out and willed himself to last a little longer inside her. When she was this easy to get coming for him, it always had him erupting inside her all the quicker.

"Liam...please," she begged, a quivering mass of soft flesh and bone atop him. "Come in me."

He bit her neck hard as his nuts tightened and drew up, ready to burst. He felt her lips brush against his mark, and with a few more thrusts, he found himself emptying into her with an elongated groan of pleasure.

"Fuck, angel," He breathed against the skin of her neck. "I think I emptied my balls out on that one. If you don't get pregnant with that, I think I'm giving up on trying."

She giggled, her soft body limp against his.

"What if I told you that you didn't have to try so hard next time?" she asked him through her giggles. "Would you fuck me less frequently or with less abandon?"

"Baby, if I ever give you less than my all, I'm having my sac amputated and becoming a fucking eunuch."

That made Elle laugh even harder. Full-on belly laughs that made her separate from him to clutch at her stomach.

"Good, because now you can't tell me you won't touch me when I tell you I'm pregnant," she told him, still laughing.

"What?" He wasn't sure if he had heard right.

"You heard me," she said. "I'm pregnant. *We're* pregnant."

"You're pregnant?"

"Yes."

"With...with a baby?"

"No, I'm having a panda," Elle said, rolling her eyes. "Of course, with a baby. *Your* baby."

"My...you're not fucking with me right now, are you?" he asked, his eyes growing a bit narrow with suspicion.

"I would never do that," she told him. "We. Are. Having. A. Baby," she reiterated slowly to him.

Elle watched as the reality of the situation seemed to sink in. His face slowly lit up with a grin that threatened to split his head in two and he barked out a single, loud laugh that made Elle flinch slightly at its suddenness.

"Baby! We're having a baby!"

Elle nodded at him and pecked him on the lips.

"Congratulations, Daddy," she breathed against his mouth.

He kissed her again, this time taking it deeper for a moment before pulling back.

"Fuck," he breathed out. "I didn't think I could love you more than I did, but...*a baby*? Elle, you've given me everything I've ever wanted. I'm one lucky fucking bastard to have found you."

"Technically, your Beta found me," she told him with a smirk.

"And thank God that asshole doesn't listen to my instructions very well," Liam said. "If he had, you'd be...well, I don't want to think about that." He paused. "A baby..."

It was almost a chant — as if he still couldn't believe it.

His little reverie was interrupted by an annoying buzzer going off in the kitchen.

"Crap! The pies!" Elle scrambled up from her spot on Liam's lap before he could stop her. He didn't give a shit about pies right then and only wanted to hold his world close to him for a moment more.

"We can buy store bought if they get ruined," he protested as she pulled her clothing on quickly. "I'd rather keep you in my arms right now, so fuck the pies."

"Store-bought don't taste the same as homemade!" she protested and scurried into the kitchen amidst Liam's grumbling protests.

Fortunately, the pies weren't burnt and Elle pulled them out of the stove and turned it off. She settled them on the countertop over some potholders to cool.

Liam strode up behind her as she was setting the last one onto its potholder. He was wearing only boxers and had curled his arms around Elle before placing a soft kiss to her hair, then drinking her scent in.

"Have you gone to see Dr. D'Amato yet?" he asked. She nodded, bumping his nose with her head.

"Yes," Elle replied. "She told me I'm about four weeks pregnant. I'm due around mid-July."

"When did you go see her?"

"Earlier today," Elle said. "I've been so tired lately I decided to visit her and she gave me a pregnancy test and then did a sonogram. Look."

She pulled out a small black and white photograph that looked for all the world like a test pattern on an old TV. In the middle, a darker, rounder area could be seen with a little white blip inside it.

"This is our baby?" he asked and took a few deep breaths, his eyes growing slightly wider.

"Yep," she told him. "That little area." She pointed to the dark part of the photo with the white blip. "You can't really tell it's a baby yet, but he or she is in there."

Elle was suddenly dizzy as Liam spun her around and crushed her body into his in a strong, fierce embrace.

"Thank you," he whispered softly into her ear and felt her hug him back.

"You're...welcome?"

Liam smiled before chuckling softly.

"I mean, I never thought I would get to have this," he told her. "The last few years have been uncertain ones for me. I...everyone was always asking me what I was going to do about the Alpha position...if I was going to take a chosen mate or simply give the position over to Blake or another relative. I never...*fuck,* Elle. You've given me so much since you came. You turned a surly, bitter Alpha into an ecstatically happy one. When can we tell my parents?"

Elle smiled and pulled back from him a bit.

"I thought Thanksgiving Day would be a good time," she told him. "You know, something to be thankful for?"

Liam leaned down to kiss her.

"As always, you are right on the money, little mate."

***

"Oh my! A grandbaby!"

Liam's mother started to cry and Conley patted her shoulder gently, an approving and smug little grin on his face.

"Knew you had it in you, son," Conley said with a wink.

They were Skyping on Thanksgiving morning with Liam's parents, and it was bittersweet. She wished she could have told her parents as well, but it was still too risky for them to communicate directly. And if word were to get out to Jeremiah about her pregnancy – it wouldn't be good.

This was the first time Elle and Judith Stark had spoken – sort of – face to face, and Judy had taken to Elle just as well as her mate had. Liam had basically blurted out news of the pregnancy after brief *hello*s were exchanged, and it was all Judith could talk about. Not that Liam minded at all. He was still puffed up with pride over his impending fatherhood. Still, he let the two females talk for the most part, and he and Conley stood in the background of the conversation just watching as Judy gave Elle advice on what to eat, what *not* to eat, morning sickness, and swollen ankles.

"Olive juice?" Elle asked as one point.

Judy shook her head, amused.

"For some reason, it worked better for me than ginger ale or crackers when I was pregnant with Arden," Judy told her. "I had a real hankering for black olives and capers and I could eat a whole tin of them then drink the juice down like it was soda."

Morning sickness was weird.

Since it was still morning and the turkey was already in the oven cooking, they were taking a moment to tell Liam's parents about the baby while waiting for Colleen and Blake to come over to help with some of the side dishes that couldn't be pre-made – like mashed potatoes and the green bean casserole.

"Olives do sound good right now," Elle said. She could feel saliva filling her mouth at the thought. And those little sweet pickles you had at cocktail parties. *Yum.*

Judy just nodded sagely and her eyes flickered to Liam, who was standing in the background.

He sighed and walked out the door before Elle could say anything. Luckily, the nearest grocery store had open hours on Thanksgiving.

And so it begins...

Judith continued to speak with Elle for a while as Conley observed and occasionally gave some input – all of which was dirty. After about twenty more minutes, they had to cut the call short.

"Dear, we would love to talk more, but we are expected at Arden's soon and she is very strict on punctuality. Even with her parents," Judy told Elle with a wink.

"I understand," Elle said with a smile. "Colleen and Blake should be here any minute to help me and I have no idea when Liam will be back. I should probably at least start peeling potatoes and washing the greens."

"We will chat again with you soon, dear," Judith told her as Conley smiled back at them both.

They got off the line just as a knock was coming from the front door. Elle closed the laptop after shutting it down and called out to her guests that she was coming.

"Hey! Happy Thanksgiving!" Elle cried and threw open the front door. Her two front door guards were standing on either side of the door like sentries to some secret military outpost. She had made sure that they were warm, though their increased core temperature guaranteed they would not become a petrified wolf-cicle.

"Gobble gobble!" Colleen exclaimed as she walked into the house with two pies and a hesitant Blake in tow.

"Where's the Bossman?" Blake asked as he kicked the snow off his boots before entering the home.

"At the store picking up some last-minute things," Elle said quickly and escorted the Beta into the living room so he could sit while she and Colleen chatted in the kitchen. "He should be back soon. He didn't have much to pick up."

Blake immediately made himself at home by turning on the television and starting to flick through the channels to get to one of the football games. Once the sportscasters' voices were heard, Blake messed with the volume a bit until he was content.

"So, what haven't you started yet?" Colleen asked.

"Well, I haven't started anything," Elle admitted. "I was busy chatting with Liam's parents. The turkey's in the oven though, and that's half the battle."

Colleen and Elle started to grab some paring knives and set to work on the spuds, quartering them once they were rid of their skins and placing them in a large pot to boil later. They chatted merrily about the upcoming Christmas holiday when another knock sounded at the door.

"That'll be Trace and Helene," Colleen said. "He mentioned that Helene wanted to come over to help as well, and he won't let her out of his sight unless absolutely necessary." She rolled her eyes and Elle knew there was a story there.

"What's his problem?" Elle asked.

"Helene wasn't *pure* enough for him when they met," Colleen said, scoffing a bit. "She'd had a couple of serious boyfriends before and wasn't a virgin. He had a bit of a shit fit about that, but he's over it now."

"That's rich, coming from the king of one-night stands," Elle said in a low voice as she moved toward the front door to greet her guests.

***

Dinner came out better than expected in Elle's humble opinion. She had helped her mother with turkeys on Thanksgivings before, but she'd never had to do it all by herself. Fortunately, Helene and Colleen were there to assist with their opinions and Colleen's not-so-subtle bullying about temperatures and basting.

They were all finishing the last of their meals when Liam abruptly stood up and almost yanked Elle from her seat next to him. It may have been customary for the hosts to sit at either end of the table, but Liam hadn't been able to stand by that tradition. Not when he had a pregnant mate. He was certain to be anxious over her twenty-four seven.

"We have an announcement," Liam said abruptly. "Elle is pregnant."

There was stunned silence. When no one spoke, he repeated himself. "We're having a baby."

There was another shocked pause before Colleen squealed and everyone jumped in place.

"I knew it!" Colleen cried out as she leaped up from her chair. She rushed over to Elle and gave her a huge bear hug until Liam had to remind her that, though wolves were sturdier than humans, they still needed room for their lungs to expand for oxygen to be taken in and transported throughout her body.

"Are you going to find out the sex?"

"Do you have morning sickness?"

"Do you want a boy or a girl first?"

"What kind of question is that? Of course, she wants a boy first! Liam needs an heir."

Helene and Colleen squabbled back and forth while the men congratulated Liam. Even the quiet Caleb was more verbose and grinning at the couple's good fortune. While it was true that an Alpha's mate made them stronger, an heir made the whole pack strong.

"When are you going to tell the whole pack?" Blake asked as he shook Liam's hand before giving him a congratulatory chest bump.

"Honestly haven't thought about it much," Liam said, his smile still wide. "I'm still getting used to the idea of being a father."

"Couldn't have happened to a more deserving man," Trace told him graciously. "And I want to thank you as well for kicking my ass about Helene. I...I was being a stupid, egocentric shithead. And I honestly can't wait to see which flavor that little gal of yours pops out."

"You have a preference?" Caleb asked. Liam shook his head.

"A couple of months ago I didn't think this was possible," he said. "Boy...girl... It doesn't matter. This baby will be loved."

"That's for sure," Caleb agreed with a smile, though it didn't quite reach his eyes. Liam shrewdly determined his single friend's hesitance.

"When warm weather comes, I want you to take a fucking hike,

Caleb," Liam said seriously.

"Huh?" That had surprised Caleb.

"Go on a trip," he clarified. "Find your mate. You're old enough to have found her and I can't keep the Elders off your ass forever. You'll be made to go to The Claiming this upcoming year if you don't get on it."

"I know," Caleb said grimacing. "Maybe if I *did* go, I'd find one there?"

"Or maybe your true mate is still too young to participate," Liam reminded him. "You do remember what happened with that Alpha couple on the west coast a few years back? Messy stuff."

They did remember. It was a black mark on their history. True mate versus claimed mate, with another male also wanting the female in question. Bloody battle and two packs completely liquidated in the process. It ended with the true mates being together, but not until all-out war had been waged and packs annihilated. To make it more interesting, rogues had been thrown into the mix when they had been promised things that no man should be promised.

Caleb nodded after thinking about that. "Once the weather warms, I'll make my way west. I just…I have a good feeling about the mid-west."

Liam figured that when a man's inner beast had a hunch, it was best to go with it.

After things had quieted down, Elle and Colleen went to get the deserts, and everyone was able to get a few slices of their favorite pies. Pumpkin was always a favorite, and thankfully there were two of that particular treat.

The guests all stayed until late that night, celebrating.

And all of them thought that Thanksgiving this year was indeed a particularly joyful and thankful one.

Chapter 26

Elle groaned and put her head over the toilet again as she emptied the meager contents of her stomach into the porcelain bowl.

It was a week after Thanksgiving and the whole olive/sweet pickle diet was not working out well. Not well at all. Oh, they were tasty, but they didn't keep Elle from wanting to bow to the porcelain God at all.

Once the toilet was flushed, Liam came back into the bedroom with some crackers and a ginger ale for her.

"No one told me that impending fatherhood came with a fuck-ton of guilt when your woman is constantly vomiting up everything she eats," he told her, frowning.

"No need to feel guilty," she told him as she nibbled the corner of a cracker. "I wanted this too and knew it was part of the territory. Evelyn said morning sickness is the sign of a healthy pregnancy. It only lasts a few weeks, usually."

At least she hoped it did. There was nothing lovely about seeing your breakfast, lunch, and dinner make an encore appearance.

Elle sipped the cold ginger ale and let her stomach settle before venturing another bite of cracker. At least she didn't feel nauseated anymore and she decided that pickles and olives were probably not going to pass her palate again any time soon. The sweet pickles definitely weren't so sweet when they were accompanied by a round of stomach acid.

Elle sat back on the bed and sighed before picking up the novel she had been reading before bed last night. In the past week – when she wasn't scrubbing floors, windows, and walls, and in general nesting her ass off – she was reading some books from Arden's bookshelf in the next room. The two females had similar tastes, thankfully.

Liam docked Elle's iPod onto the speaker system and played the music low in the background. She liked to have it playing when she read, though why it soothed her so was anyone's guess.

The past week's weather had almost snowed the two of them in, and even with many of the pack shoveling paths between the houses, it was still difficult to get anything done. Just as soon as a path was cleared, the wind blew more snow over it, so Liam had decided to work from home. He had many of his files on a small server and only needed to make sure his Wi-Fi connection was secure to get the documents he needed.

Since he had his MacBook Pro at home, he decided to set up a work station in the bedroom like a lazy lay-about while he monitored his female's bathroom habits. He didn't like seeing her this ill, though he knew it was natural. Liam had interrogated Evelyn D'Amato, who assured him that the morning sickness was not only a passing phase, but a good symptom of pregnancy to have.

After a couple of hours, Elle decided she could go for more food and got up from the bed only to have a dizzy spell. That too was normal, but Liam wasn't having any of it.

"What do you need?" he asked, as he made sure Elle laid back down on the bed. He didn't need her falling down and hurting herself while she was in this condition. It's not like the good doctor could beam herself through the numerous snow banks and walls into their home.

"I just wanted more food," she said as she sighed and opened her book back up. She was used to Liam's constant coddling over the past week.

"Crackers? A sandwich?" he asked. Those were things he could get for her. Ask him to cook a chicken or braise a steak and he'd probably burn the house down.

Well, at least that would deal effectively with the accumulating snow that was making the large home almost invisible through the growing drifts.

"Crackers with peanut butter and jelly," she said, and went back to reading. "And I want chamomile tea."

"At your service, Madam," he told her and left the room with a gracious bow to get her a light lunch.

The snow had stopped falling the night before, but the wind made travel difficult. He was suddenly very grateful that Elle was due in the summertime and not anytime soon. Having to get her to the pack clinic would have been a mean feat in this weather.

Still, Evelyn's cell phone number was on Liam's speed dial. Just in case. He didn't trust just the mindlink to get in touch with her.

He warmed up some water in the microwave and sank a chamomile tea bag in the mug before adding a little honey to the concoction and placing it on a tray with Elle's food to bring it upstairs.

That's when he heard a distinct sniffling coming from the bedroom.

Leaping into action, he hurried to the room, spilling hot tea everywhere on the tray. He opened the door so quickly, it bounced off the wall.

"What's wrong?" he asked when he saw Elle holding the book and crying.

"The fucking bastard only went after her because she was a challenge," she said, sobbing.

Liam was dumbstruck.

Did not compute.

"Who?" he finally asked when Elle didn't volunteer any further information.

She shook the book in her hand as if it had offended her honor.

"This asshole in the book," she told him and the tension in his shoulders released. He thought she had been talking about one of the pack members and he was about to rip a wolf's head clear off his shoulders for upsetting his mate with his petty antics.

"You're crying over a book?"

"Yes!"

"Good grief, woman, I thought something was actually wrong," he told her. "And I think I spilled most of your tea on the tray running in here."

He looked down at the mug and was surprised to see it was still three-quarters full. The tray was a sloppy mess though, and a couple of crackers were soggy.

"It's okay," she said and set the book aside. Liam wanted to grab it and tear it in half. *Stupid book.* But he was sure she would find something else to sob over eventually. It's not like he could throw a fist through the TV because of some idiotic, weepy Hallmark movie she had decided to watch.

Instead, he took a deep, cleansing breath and placed the tray on the nightstand before sitting down next to Elle. She was starting to dig into her food as if she hadn't eaten in a week, though it was very obvious to him with her consumption of calories, that she was indeed eating for two.

He was making a list of things in his head as he watched her. Well, *two* lists, actually. Baby's likes and baby's dislikes. The dislikes list was much longer than *he'd* like. Olives and pickles topped said list.

"I'd like to make the announcement about the pregnancy on New Year's," Liam told her as she shoveled another jelly and peanut butter smeared cracker into her mouth. "It's customary for us to have a party that night and the Alpha always makes a speech when midnight comes."

Elle swallowed thickly as she nodded her head. "Okay."

"Until then, we keep the baby on the down low," he told her.

She gave him a look.

"You do realize that Colleen was one of the first to hear about it," she told him and grabbed another cracker from the plate.

"I had Blake make her swear not to say anything," Liam explained. "My Beta, Delta, and Gamma all have insider information as always, but they are sworn to secrecy about Junior until I make the official announcement. The same goes for their women."

"I wish I could tell my parents," Elle blurted out suddenly after finishing another cracker.

"Why don't we call them later tonight?" Liam suggested. "Or we could go meet them at the tavern again."

Elle shook her head.

"I'm scared Jeremiah will find out where they're going," she said. "My parents honestly don't go out much and it might seem odd for them to visit the Norfolk twice in a month." Her parents were homebodies, much like Elle.

"So, we'll call them after 10 PM," Liam said, making up his mind. "I don't want your parents not knowing when mine are free to be in the loop. It's not fair."

"Oh, life's not fair, Liam," Elle told him. "Above all others, both of us should know that by now."

***

"The snow's too thick to do anything," Carter told Jeremiah as the man paced the study in his home. There was a fire lit in the grate that made the room almost stiflingly hot, and Carter was sweating his nutsac off.

"When is the weather supposed to clear?" Jeremiah barked out.

"It's not the weather that's a hindrance right now. It's the wind," Carter told him. "There's at least two feet of snow on the ground, and don't even get me started on how high some of the snow drifts are."

The snow drifts were up to six feet in places and made the paths almost impassable due to that fact. The hunt for the missing, secretive Luna was on hold.

Not to mention the fact that word had finally gotten out around Blackriver that the Alpha had finally found his mate and was desperate to get to her. The rumor mill was in full swing, and even the inclement weather could not stop it from exploding all around them.

There were several females who claimed to be his mate. They were the same females that made their way over to his house late at night and offered themselves to him fully. Miraculously, all were told to leave or be escorted off pack land as a rogue. It was shocking to Carter when he heard that.

"Jere, Giselle is marked and mated to another. Alpha's move quickly and she could be with child at this very moment for all we know."

A low growl vibrated the very walls of the home as Jeremiah's eyes flickered to the green of his wolf.

"She's mine!" the man snarled.

"And you pushed her away," Carter told him calmly. "I know you haven't been entertaining any other females for a while now and I can only see that as proof that you are indeed in love with your true mate." The Alpha's head shook restlessly back and forth in denial. "Be that as it may, she does not want to be with you anymore. If this...if you had treated her better, you may have had the chance to redeem yourself, but that is not the case. She is happy elsewhere, and you should go to The Claiming this summer and choose another to bear your pups and wear your mark. Giselle...she will not."

"Out!" growled Jeremiah. "She will be mine even if I have to rip off all the heads of the men who stand between her and I! That includes you, Carter!"

"You're being a fool and you know it," Carter told him coldly. "Being an Alpha doesn't always end up with you getting your way. The sooner you realize that, the better off you'll be. Things aren't just yours for the taking. You have to earn them. And all you earned with your abuse was a runaway she-wolf who hates you and is gladly mated to another. You're my friend, Jeremiah, and I hate to see you like this. But until you get your shit together, you'll never see this for what it is. A desperate attempt to win her back. And what would happen if you do get her and bring her back here? What then? You beat her to within an inch of death again? It's deplorable. If you try, Jere, I will try and stop you from hurting her. I don't care what the consequences, but she'll not be hurt again."

With that, Carter walked out of the room quickly, leaving

Jeremiah standing in front of the fireplace, gazing into the flames and wondering where he had gone wrong in his life.

Carter was wrong. He had to be. Jeremiah wasn't in love with the weak Omega. Couldn't be. He was Alpha and deserved a stronger woman in his life. Elle would break like China in his strong arms.

But she survived the beating. Survived and lived to tell about it.

He pondered that for a few minutes. Perhaps the small female was stronger than he had thought all along.

***

Her light-colored wolf's coat helped her remain relatively unseen through the woods. The snow also helped to mute her scent as she crossed the border into no man's land and unclaimed territory.

It wasn't a favorite pastime for her to go gallivanting about in the snowy weather, but this news was urgent enough so that she would fare the bad weather long enough to get to Blackriver and speak with her partner there.

Such a shame that some she-wolves couldn't keep their mouths shut and voices down, she thought sarcastically. After last week's revelation, she had made it a point to go see her friend as soon as the weather permitted. But alas, the snow hadn't abated until the previous night. The howling wind kept most indoors with the exception of patrol, and she knew their shift change was upon them and most of them were either heading back to their homes or were on their way out to start their shift. It was the perfect time to cross the border.

The bag she carried in her muzzle contained two changes of clothing and a winter coat. Just because her increased body temperature kept her from freezing, it didn't mean the cold weather wasn't still a bother to her. She hated to be cold, to be frank.

As cumbersome as the bag was, she kept it gripped in her jaws until she was on the edge of Blackriver's borders and slipped behind a tree to shift into her human and go up to the outposts. Hopefully, one of the wolves there would recognize her and call attention to her friend.

She was in luck today, because the first man she spoke with knew exactly who she was, though not the reason she was there.

"I need to speak with him," she said. "It's urgent. I have news for him and he would not like it if I was delayed."

The man nodded and reached out to the man in question through the mindlink without further ado.

"Liliana will accompany you," the man told her a few moments later. "The pathways are snow-covered for the most part and it is difficult to get anywhere without an escort."

Sheila nodded and followed the raven-haired female the enforcer gestured to. Liliana nodded back at her with a scrutinizing eye and made a "come hither" motion with her hand before walking off in between drifts of snow.

"Are you the fabled mate our Alpha has been so desperate for these past few weeks?" Liliana asked as they walked through a deeper pile of snow that had fallen onto the makeshift path.

"No," Sheila answered. "But I am the key to getting her for him." She paused. "Also, I have an Alpha male of my own that I am determined to make mine."

Chapter 27

The first week of morning sickness and trying to figure out what worked and didn't work, was a right pain in the ass. Once the *dos* and *donts* were worked out, it was not hard to figure out that crackers settled Elle's stomach first thing in the morning while chamomile tea allowed her to go to bed with a restful tummy. Babies were certainly difficult even before they were born.

Soon, though, Elle was able to get through a day without the constant trips to the bathroom to empty her sour stomach.

Colleen brought over ginger root and steeped it in some plain green tea so that Elle had something to settle her stomach between meals, and she iced it to make herself iced tea and added a bit of lemon to flavor it.

When the wind stopped blowing from the seasonal nor'easter, people were finally able to shovel paths between houses and the pups were engaged in constant snowball fights in the backyards. Elle watched it all from her window as she sipped her green tea ginger-lemon brew and smiled.

"My mother's on the phone for you," Liam said as he walked into the bedroom as Elle watched the kids play in the snow. His hand was covering the microphone so he could speak without being heard. "I honestly think she prefers you over me." He shook his head disbelievingly.

"She's just making sure that you're taking care of me," Elle told him. "You told her about the pickles and olives?"

"Yeah, though I don't think she believed me," Liam said. "She swears by it, but everyone's different so..." He faded away with a shrug.

Elle reached out for the phone and Liam handed it to her, looking at it like it was a bomb about to go off. His mother could be opinionated and pushy, and she reminded him of an older version of Colleen, sans the potty mouth.

"Hi, Judy, what's up?" Elle asked as Liam left the room to go back downstairs. He was watching a football game on TV and New England was trying to wipe the floor with New York.

Sunday afternoons were always pretty lazy, and it was just a testament of just how lazy this one was that Liam was hanging out with Trace and Blake while watching the game. Although the snow was still knee-deep in places, there wasn't much else to do but stay inside to keep warm and dry. No one had heard anything from Jeremiah or the Blackriver pack for weeks. It set your teeth on edge to have such silence on that front.

"Your mom talking Elle's ear off about babies and morning sickness again?" Blake asked as Liam came into the room.

"Yeah," Liam said. He honestly didn't mind that his mother took so well to his mate. It certainly would make family gatherings easier, but she was all but ignoring her son. If Liam didn't know how excitable his mother was when it came to her grandbabies, he would have been offended at her lack of attention. "When are you and Colleen going to start trying for a pup of your own?"

Blake raised a brow at him and looked away from the TV before replying.

"Who says we aren't already trying?" he asked. "I mean, we always wanted to have kids, but ever since you announced your own pregnancy she's been chomping at the bit. I'm lucky my dick doesn't need a cast."

Liam grinned. Colleen, of all people, took to any new idea with a passion that so many lacked. She went above and beyond trying, and made things happen. While Blake was content to sit back and take orders from Liam, Colleen was definitely a Type A personality and got things done. The two were an opposite pairing that worked well for the both of them.

"Knowing Col, she just wants to have our kids close together enough so they can grow to become best friends," Liam told him knowingly. It would be just like Colleen to arrange a lifelong friendship years in advance.

"You're probably right, not that I'm complaining," Blake said. "Haven't had this much sex since we were newly mated."

"What about you, Trace? You and Helena going to wait a bit or does she have baby fever as well?" Liam asked.

"Honestly haven't talked too much about it," Trace admitted. "Beyond the *yes, we want kids someday* conversation, it hasn't really come up. Not even after you blurted out you and Elle were expecting."

"Is she pestering you for more sex?" Blake asked shrewdly.

"I wouldn't call it "pestering", but we have had an upswing in the amount of sex we have," Trace allowed.

Blake and Liam looked at each other.

"Baby fever," Blake pronounced.

"No," Trace disagreed with a roll of his eyes.

"You wrapping it up before sticking it in her?" Liam asked.

"Uhm, no."

"She on some sort of birth control that actually works for shifters?" Blake raised a disbelieving brow at him.

"Not that I'm aware of," Trace said, sounding shifty.

"You'll be pregnant soon then," Liam told him as he sat back and slanted a look at Blake.

"I've been pulling out." Trace sounded a bit more hesitant.

"Every time?" Blake questioned.

Trace shrugged. "About half."

"Well then, congrats, *Daddy*," Blake said as he slapped him hard on his shoulder.

"Fuck you both," Trace mumbled as he got up to grab another beer from the fridge.

"Get me one, too!" Liam shouted at him as he walked away. He was certain Trace was probably saluting him with the middle finger.

They sat watching the game for a bit with small breaks to scream at the players and refs for fucking up the calls. It seemed that the Patriots had some insider knowledge or a few of the refs on their payroll every time they played. It reminded Liam of a meme he had once seen on the internet. It had the quarterback on his knees looking like he was giving a blowjob to each of the refs before the game started. It suggested that the Pats were "preparing for the game". It was pretty funny. Since Caleb was a fanatical Patriots fan, Liam had sent that meme to his phone before receiving a slew of angry curse words back at him. Hence, the reason Caleb was watching the game at his own home instead of with his fellow Beta, Delta, and Alpha, aka "the enemy Giants supporters".

At half-time, Elle came down with Liam's phone and handed it back to him.

"Babe, come watch the game with us," he told her as he pulled at the arm that was holding out his phone.

"No, thank you," she said, screwing up her face in distaste. "Last time I watched a game the quarterback received a broken nose and it was off center the whole time he played."

"That was an anomaly," Liam told her. "Besides, that punk deserved it, damned wife beater." He remembered that game well.

"He beat his wife?" Elle blanched.

"Yeah. Well, at least I think it was his wife," Liam said. "Or girlfriend. If that asshole had been a part of *my* pack, his ass wouldn't have been able to complete the season, that's for damn sure."

"Liam would've strung him up by his testicles for a week and then escorted him off the premises as a rogue," Blake allowed.

"A broken nose would have been the least of his worries," Liam agreed.

"Yeah, I still think I'll pass. I want to start on dinner," Elle said and walked into the kitchen to grab some iced tea.

Pretty soon the aroma of Italian food was making the men in the living room's stomachs wake up.

"Baby, did you make enough for some extra mouths?" Liam asked as soon as he heard Trace's stomach give a long, low rumble.

"What did you say?" Elle called out. "I couldn't hear a word of what you said over the sound of your stomachs growling."

Liam chuckled. "Can Trace and Blake stay for dinner?"

"Of course," Elle replied loudly. "I have enough food for Colleen and Helene if they want to come over too." She paused. "And Caleb," she added.

A few minutes later, she walked out of the kitchen and moved fluidly over to the couch to sit next to Liam.

"Thought you weren't watching the game," Liam teased as he placed a hand on her stomach. It was too soon for her to have a baby bump, but he liked to place his hand there whenever he could.

"I'm not. I'm simply sitting here for a while because I need to wait for the lasagna to cook," she told him and rested her head on his shoulder.

"You could always watch me instead of the game," he told her and tipped her head up to his to kiss her lips.

"This is guy time," Trace proclaimed and stood up. "No chicks allowed."

"My house, my rules," Liam threw back at him and went back to kissing Elle's lips.

"You need a man cave in this place," Blake griped. "Poker nights, Sunday Night football, Pay Per View prize fights..."

"I'll take it into consideration," Liam said and pecked Elle on the lips one last time before his gaze went back to the screen. The game was back on.

"Jesus...come on, guys!" Blake yelled at the TV. "Luckily our boys in blue are a second-half team."

The others – with the exception of Elle – all muttered their agreement, though they all knew that was wishful thinking. The Giants were ready to get their asses kicked. *Again.*

***

"I need to go Christmas shopping!" Elle whined as Liam stood firm against her demand to be let out of their home. She wanted to go to the mall, to Target, to...just about anywhere, just so long as she got her holiday shopping done.

"You can order on Amazon," Liam told her.

"It's too late for that! Everything says it will be shipped after Christmas!"

"Give me a list. I'll have Colleen pick up the stuff you need," he countered.

"Some of it's for Colleen and Blake!" she exclaimed.

"Then *I'll* pick up their gifts. Just tell me what they are." The man had an answer for everything. It was truly maddening.

"I need to get out of this house," she told him. "Haven't you ever seen that movie, *The Shining*? The main character went crazytown and tried to kill his entire family when he got cabin fever from staying indoors for too long!"

"You've been stuck inside here for less than a month," Liam told her. "I doubt you'll turn into an ax-wielding maniac if you're cooped up inside for a little while longer."

"I'll find a way to sneak out if you don't let me go," she threatened, narrowing her eyes on him. "You know I can do it, too."

That was the problem. She *would* find a way. Elle was too resourceful for her own good at times and had a way of bending or completely breaking the rules to suit her needs. It didn't help that she looked so damned innocent while conning her way out of – or into – something. It was those damned baby blue eyes of hers.

She felt Liam's will crumbling and poured it on real thick.

"I'll take as many guards as you like," she said, feeling him starting to cave. "I'll go with Colleen and stick to her like glue!"

"I..." Liam started.

"Please," she begged softly.

He found he couldn't say no.

"Fine," he groaned out, utterly at her feet when it came to things she really wanted. "But I'm giving you a fucking entourage of men and you can't go into any stores without Colleen and at least four of my men following behind."

"You mean *our* men," she said and gave him a giddy smile in return.

***

"Wow, I'm surprised he let you off house arrest." Colleen joked, seemingly impressed when Elle had told her she was allowed to do some shopping.

"I think he's concerned I'll be seen by wolves from Blackriver," Elle told him.

"Is that why you're wearing your hair up under that big, stupid, floppy hat and are hiding your eyes behind those sunglasses?" Colleen asked.

"Yep," Elle said without shame. "I also wanted to grab some baby things as well. Not much. Cute clothing that says things like *Daddy's Little Cutie* and *It's all Shits and Giggles Until Someone Giggles and Shits.*"

Colleen laughed, loving that last one.

"I think I've seen that one before online," she said, chuckling as they made their way onto the highway. They had two guards in their SUV, and another SUV with four more men trailing behind them. "Is the whole crowd coming into the mall with us?"

"Yeah, but they'll be following from a distance," Elle explained. "If they're right up on us it'll bring more attention to the two of us."

"Yeah, and then we'll have half the mall following after us thinking you're a celebrity of some sort," Colleen said, snickering.

"Ugh, don't even kid about that," Elle said as she rolled her eyes behind her sunglasses. "It's bad enough being Luna. I can't imagine how people like the Kardashians and such can handle the constant scrutiny."

"Well, if they didn't want the attention they wouldn't have signed up for that ridiculous reality show they have. Or *had*. I don't honestly know if it's still on the air anymore."

"Who cares?" Elle asked. "My life's hectic enough if you ask me."

They were quiet for a while as they thought about that. They said no news was good news, and that seemed to be true enough. But no news was also nerve-wracking as hell. Elle was waiting for the other shoe to drop.

"No word yet, huh?" Colleen asked in an uncommonly low voice.

"None," Elle admitted.

"That's good though, right?" Colleen asked, not sounding altogether certain.

"I don't know. I can't imagine that if he...he *knew*, " she said and gestured to her stomach. "He...well, I think he'd blow his stack. The man's unbalanced to the extreme."

"Still, you're making an announcement at New Year's, right?"

"That's the plan."

"Then there's no telling what will happen afterward if Jackson was right about him having a spy within Plumbrook."

Neither of them could imagine anyone trying to oust Elle as Luna except for a handful of interested females. All social climbers as far as Liam and his inner circle were concerned. A wolf had to be mad not to wait for their true mate unless they had some other agenda.

"Well," Elle said as she sighed. "I'm just hoping to make it through the holidays without any blood being shed."

That wasn't too much to ask for the holidays, was it?

God, she hoped not.

***

Elle was just unpacking the car when Liam came out of the house to help.

"I'll get those!" he called out as he watched Elle pull out a large, unwieldy bag.

"It's not heavy," she protested. "I'm a wolf. I can get it."

But Liam wasn't having any of that. Every one of his instincts urged him to go to her and help and you couldn't have stopped him from bringing the bags in any more than you could have stopped him from pulling oxygen into his lungs by breathing.

"Where do you want them?" he asked when he pulled up to Elle and wound an arm around her waist.

Knowing better than to fight him about it, Elle thought about the question. "Your sister's bedroom. Do we have wrapping paper anywhere in the house? And when can we get a tree? I want to decorate."

"A real one?" Elle nodded her head at him and Colleen came over as well, bouncing up and down.

"Ohhhh! can I help decorate? I've already done my house and you should see it. It's like Christmas threw up all over it!"

Liam wrinkled his nose in disgust as he decided to ignore her holiday vomit comment.

"Sure, I'll let you know when I get one so we can play Christmas music and drink eggnog and decorate and stuff," Elle said, smiling happily.

"Great! You'll need to come over tomorrow and check out our house as well," Colleen replied and wandered back to the truck so she could get back home. "Text me later!"

Liam and Elle carried bags into the house and placed them in Arden's old room in the closet. It also happened to be where he kept things in storage, and Elle eyed a long red plastic container that looked like it could be used for Christmas items.

"Are you going to wrap right away or wait until later?" Liam asked.

"I'm a little tired," she mentioned. "I was thinking of taking a nap. Can we go get a tree afterward?"

"I can have the enforcers cut one down for you. There are plenty in the woods," Liam told her.

"But I want to pick one out," Elle said.

"What's the difference? A tree's a tree."

"I like one that's very fragrant and the perfect shape and size."

"And what is the perfect shape and size?" Liam raised a brow.

"It's…well, it's…it's *tree* shaped, like in a Claymation movie," she told him. He shook his head at her, amused.

"Right, well why don't you take a nap and I'll rope Blake into helping me later on with a tree," he said. "Lord knows you'll probably want one that almost reaches the ceilings downstairs. I'll need the manpower." The ceilings were ten feet high since Liam was quite a tall man. He didn't feel like scraping his head on the ceiling fans every other time he walked through the rooms in his house.

"Okay." She got up on her tiptoes and pulled his head down with her arms so she could peck his lips before pulling back a bit. But Liam surprised her by scooping her up and carrying her bridal style into their bedroom before placing her down on the bed.

He climbed in after her and scooted up behind her so he could spoon her.

"Are you napping, too?" she asked, her voice sleepy as her eyes closed.

"No. I'm just resting a bit."

He settled himself into her body, curving around it almost protectively until he felt a jolt in his solar plexus and his anxiety rose.

Opening his mind, he heard a voice in his head coming through. It was loud, heavy, and hit hard as bricks.

Alpha, we believe we've found the conspirator trying to oust Elle as Luna, Blake's voice came through.

Who? Who dares defy me and my mate? Liam stood up carefully from the bed so as not to wake Elle in her near-slumber.

Sheila. She's down in the cells right now. We found her sneaking back onto the property while Elle and Colleen were away. She was coming from the direction of Blackriver.

Fucking figures, Liam muttered as he shoved on a heavy jacket and started to walk towards the front door. *I'll be there soon. I need to know what she's been doing and who she's been speaking with. How do you know she's the one?*

She's been acting a bit shifty lately and she smelled of foreigners when we caught up with her. Blackriver, if I'm not mistaken, though I've only met with a few of them once. I could be wrong.

Fuck, Liam grumbled. He hoped to God that the bitch hadn't been meeting with Jeremiah. He hoped she had simply found her mate at Blackriver and had been secretly rendezvousing with him. *I'll be there in a few.*

He ended the conversation and started to lace up his winter boots for the trek into the woods. There wasn't a clear path to the cells as it would give their location away, and only the guards and higher ranked wolves knew the exact locale. And Colleen. She seemed to know pretty much everything. Well, everything but who the traitor was in their midst.

Liam crunched through several feet of snow for a while until he came to the area where it was clearer and looked down to see several footprints in the snow before disappearing seemingly into nothing.

He walked over to the area and searched for the knob of the door and pulled. Bits of fluffy snow tumbled down the steps and made traversing the first few iffy, but Liam eventually made it to the ground without breaking his damned neck in the process.

Blake was waiting at the end of the hallway for him just before it veered to the right.

"Where's the bitch?" Liam growled out as he cut cold, cobalt eyes in the direction of the cells.

"Last cell on the right," Blake told him. "We were actually lucky that some of patrol had a hard time getting through the snow. If it had been shallower in places they might have never seen her passing back onto the territory."

Liam didn't want to think about not having found Sheila and he was certain now that she was the one Jackson had warned them of. She was a sneaky, manipulative bitch who cared nothing for anyone but herself. And treason was a damned good reason to lop a wolf's head off. She had some explaining to do.

Liam walked the length of the hallway of the cells. Fortunately,

Sheila was the only one in them at this time and there was no one else but the two guards posted there. Liam motioned for them to leave in the direction of Blake.

Sheila sat in a corner of the dingy cell, her head resting on her knees where they were pulled up to her body.

"What the fuck have you done, Sheila?" Liam asked, watching her flinch at his gruff tone. It was laced with his Alpha command and she couldn't *not* answer it.

"She isn't fit to be Luna," the little she-wolf said. "She's not strong enough."

"She is stronger than most," Liam argued coldly. "She has been dealt a shit hand in life since she was small – not that *you* would know – and she escaped a cruel man who would have killed her before seeing her happy and mated to another."

"She's *his*," Sheila said. "And he will get her back. He'll rid her of the fetus and-"

Liam's resounding snarl sent a shockwave all the way down to Blake and the guards, who winced at the deep, feral sound.

"That baby is my son or daughter – not just a fetus!" Liam growled out. "And how did you know about it? Did someone tell you?"

"I heard Colleen speaking to Blake about it sometime after Thanksgiving. They were saying how it was secret until the New Year's celebration. But *he* knows. I told him."

"You told Jeremiah of the pregnancy?" *Fuck!* Liam thought fast. He needed more surveillance on his house immediately and he linked with Trace to inform him.

I need more enforcers at the house, pronto.

Li—I mean, Alpha? Trace's voice was far away, as if he had awoken from a deep sleep or otherwise not completely involved in the link.

Now, Trace. We've found the leak and she's told Jeremiah of Elle's pregnancy. My child's life is at stake here. I want at least ten wolves surrounding the house at all times.

Got it and I'll take care of it in a moment.

You'll take care of it now. You can get your rocks off another time. Your damn nuts won't fall off from a mere bout of blue balls.

Trace was silent for a moment. *How did you kn-*

I didn't – at least not for certain. Not get to it Trace, before I cut your junk off and feed it to the coyotes.

The link was cut off as Trace confirmed he was moving now, and

Liam went back to questioning Sheila.

"You've told Jeremiah that Elle is pregnant," he concluded, voice dripping disdain. "And what else have you said to him?"

"The location of your home within the pack," Sheila said, smiling grimly at him. "The times patrols come and go. Pretty much anything that will help him get his mate back so you can be free of the useless female."

Liam was about to burst through the silver-coated bars to get to the woman. His whole body vibrated with rage, and Blake started walking towards him before Liam held up a hand to stop him from coming closer.

"I want to gut this bitch, Blake," he told him, voice frigid. "I don't need you getting in the way and hurt you by mistake. Leave it. I'll be fine when this she-wolf is dead and gone."

"You're going to kill me?" Sheila acted surprised. As if she didn't know that treason was a punishable-by-death offense.

"What you've done is considered treason," Blake told her. "Pack law states that treason is a crime punishable by death. We cannot let you go with a warning or exile you as a rogue. You know our secrets, secrets you swore to protect upon your adulthood. If you betrayed us once, what will keep you from betraying us again?"

Sheila's head sank to her knees again with a whimper and her shoulders trembled in fear.

"But what of my family? My future mate? They will miss me." The words were made almost unintelligible by her sobs and the long blond waves of hair falling into her mouth.

"When they hear of your betrayal, your family will surely disown you," Liam told her. "Your future mate is better off without a scheming little cunt like you. You should have thought about all this before you betrayed your leaders and your pack. We are family. When you betray one of us, you betray us all. You are no longer considered *Pack*."

Liam looked over to Blake who was standing mid-way between the guards and the last jail cell.

"I think Elle should be the one to dole out the sentence on this one," Liam said coldly. "She's always been imaginative when it comes to punishments. Perhaps she will want to cut out Sheila's womb first to show her the pain of losing a child and then gut her for the wild animals of the forest to feast upon." He looked back over at Sheila whose shaking had increased twofold. He spoke to her again. "Pray that Elle is feeling generous and grants you a swift death. Lord knows you don't deserve one."

Liam started moving toward the exit as he heard Sheila's wracking sobs intensify.

"I have a mate to get back to," he told Blake. "No food or water for the bitch. We will execute her tonight."

***

Elle couldn't get comfortable. The bed was just as it always was, supremely plush and begging for a body to lie in it to snooze, but Liam was nowhere around so she was not finding it easy to sleep.

Punching a pillow and rolling onto her other side, she tried for sleep again.

Ten minutes. Twenty.

She was just about to give up entirely when a noise from outside caught her attention. It was soft thud – like a sack of potatoes had been dropped onto the wood of the front porch.

Or a body.

The rogue thought made her uneasy and she made her way downstairs, traversing the steps as silently as she could and skipping the next to last one that always creaked coming down.

She was at the bottom when another *something* hit the wood out front. There was no peephole and the only thing that kept her from investigating was the fact that the windows in the front were enormous. If someone was out there, they would be able to see her immediately.

So, she went to the back door and decided to have the enforcers out there check up on what was going on out front.

But no wolves were there. All was still and silent except for the sound of wind whipping through the trees and the creak or two of branches as snow and ice weighed them down.

Elle was not clothed to go outside, so she grabbed a big bulky jacket and the snow boots she had set in the kitchen to dry and walked out in her sweats, t-shirt, jacket, and boots.

The crunch of snow beneath her feet made her wince with the noise at every step before she switched to wading through it like water. She heard no footfalls beside hers, and that relaxed her the tiniest bit. She was still on guard though, and peeked around the edge of the house to see two bodies lying on the front porch, unconscious.

She gasped slightly and reached out with her mind, searching for Liam in the link. Before she could get to him, a hand clamped down around her throat and cut off the air supply to her lungs and brain.

"Good to see you again, *mate*."

Chapter 28

Elle started to quickly choke on her own saliva. Nausea rolled through her gut and she tried to swallow the acidic taste down as it repeatedly climbed up her throat.

"Giselle."

The name tasted like evil coming out of Jeremiah's mouth and she shook her head, warding the sound away.

"Will you be a good girl and come quietly or do I have to tie you up before carrying you back home?"

Tears ran down her cheeks at his words.

No. *This* was her home. With Liam. With their baby. With the Plumbrook pack as a whole. Colleen, Blake, Trace... Their faces flashed through her mind and she screamed against the hot flesh of Jeremiah's hand as it came down harder to stifle the sounds.

She could barely breathe as tears and snot ran freely.

Jeremiah shushed her.

"Quiet, little pet," he said. "Be good and I won't beat you bloody before taking that abomination from your womb and feeding it to scavenger dogs."

The nausea was back and nothing was keeping it from spilling out.

Elle pushed his hands aside and was sick on the ground next to the house. The Mu Shu pork and fried rice she had eaten with Colleen at the mall soon lay in a steaming pile at her feet and Jeremiah instinctively backed away to place distance between himself and the smell of sick.

She heaved and retched a few more times, more tears leaking from her eyes and hitting the snow in hard little patters.

When he felt she was done emptying her stomach, Jeremiah grabbed Elle by the waist and tossed her over his shoulder in a fireman's carry. He cared not that his hard shoulder was pressing against her stomach, and Elle was only glad that she was a wolf and it was hard for their species to miscarry over a little rough treatment.

Later, however...

She couldn't think of that now. She was still on Plumbrook territory and any minute now, someone would smell the foreigners on their lands. Snow muted the smells, but still...

As if on cue, a howl pierced the air and Jeremiah swore as he sped up towards the east, clambering over piles of drifted snow. He almost lost hold of Elle a few times, but was able to steady himself before coming out onto the main road that ran through the center of Plumbrook.

A faraway snarling was heard until the sounds of crunching ice and a car engine came closer, driving slowly over slick, slippery surfaces.

"Hurry up, you fucking idiot," Jeremiah growled low as the silver Audi inched closer to them on the road. Elle supposed Jeremiah's candy apple red Camaro would have been too ostentatious a vehicle to drive through Plumbrook without turning a few heads.

Her head was still spinning, but getting clearer. Her throat seemed clogged and she was unable to speak. Like before she came to Plumbrook. Before...Liam.

A snarling growl was released behind them and a large black wolf leaped at them, Elle only catching a glimpse of it before she fell into a large heap of snow at the side of the road.

The wolf's paw had swiped at her, not leaving any marks, but making sure she fell into something relatively soft before hitting the cold, hard ground. Elle lifted her head and shuddered at what she saw.

Blood. What seemed like gallons of it. Liam's wolf was tearing Jeremiah apart as he lay there, feebly struggling as the large Alpha male ripped at his flesh with its claws and teeth.

"Liam!" she called out to the wolf. They hadn't had a chance to shift and run together in the woods, and wouldn't until she delivered, but she knew instinctively it was him and that he was going to kill the man that was Alpha of Blackriver. It wasn't right. Not like this, anyway. Jeremiah was no rogue. They needed to execute him and place a new Alpha in his stead. Mayhem would ensue at Blackriver if not. People vying for the position. Men dying. Women weeping. "Stop! We need to do this the right way!"

Jeremiah was only a puddle of lacerated flesh as the black muzzle of Liam's wolf turned toward Elle's voice. His jaws were glistening with blood as he licked his chops and grumbled gently, the hint of frustration coming through.

He deserves to die, he said, still in wolf form.

Elle nodded.

"And he will," she told him aloud. "As soon as we put a new Alpha in his place so there is no chaos at Blackriver. It'll be a bloody power grab. My parents are there, Liam. My brother. Place someone in his stead. Then...then he will die."

She whimpered, and though the link to her first mate was all but gone, it hurt her to say so. He should have been hers. Whatever deity or entity had placed the mating pull upon them had deemed it so, and it had once been meant to be. Only...it was not. Mistakes were made. Faith destroyed. Maybe it would have been different if Jeremiah's father hadn't taken over all those years ago. Maybe if she had been born Gamma or above he would have loved her, but this...*this* wasn't love. It was possession. And she only allowed certain people that right. People like her parents. Like Colleen. *Like Liam.* They owned a part of her soul with their love, and what Jeremiah had, this jealousy, this obsession – it wasn't love. Not by a long shot.

Liam howled and stood over the interloper to make sure he didn't move.

He goes for you again and I'm taking him out. Liam's voice was stern in her head and Elle nodded back quickly in agreement.

Blake, Trace, and a few enforcers had run up as quickly as they could onto the scene in their human form. One enforcer placed thick silver shackles over Jeremiah's wrists and ankles, and the other two carried the bleeding man off, away from the scene.

"Giselle," a voice called. The familiar and pleasant tone seeped into her ears and Elle looked back to see Carter, Jeremiah's Beta, standing there next to the silver Audi.

"Carter?"

Liam had slunk off – most likely to shift back and change – while Elle stood up from the snowdrift and brushed the snow from her sweats.

"You were helping him get me?" Her voice was accusatory and she folded her arms over her chest as Carter looked at her and – ridiculously – gave her a slow, wide grin.

"I was, and I wasn't," Carter offered. "He thought I was, but I would have never let him bring you back to his house. As soon as he got you into the car I was going to stab him with this." He pulled out a capped syringe from his coat pocket and showed it to her. "Wolfsbane mixed with silver."

"You were going to kill him?" She was surprised. Jeremiah had been his best friend for years.

"I couldn't let him take you and abort your baby," Carter told her bleakly. "He would have beaten you to death after that. His rage has been...it's been uncontrollable lately. Ever since he found out you were pregnant from that murderous she-wolf he's been speaking with."

"Who?" Elle was at a loss. She didn't know what was going on and why. All she knew was that Jeremiah had somehow found her and was now being sent to the cells where he would most likely be held until he was executed in front of the entire pack.

"Some blond chick, Sharla? Shana? Can't remember the whore's name, to be honest," Carter said shaking his head. "All I know is that she comes from here and she's been thick as thieves with Jeremiah for weeks. Since I didn't know a way to get in touch with you, I made sure that when he came, I was prepared."

"It was Sheila, that bitch," Liam's voice cut in. He had returned wearing thick jeans and an overcoat. He looked at Carter and the hand holding the syringe. "You must be Carter. I have you to thank for my mate. What are you to the man who tried to take my female?"

"Ex-best friend and Beta to Alpha Jeremiah, as you probably figured." But Carter was respectful. "My apologies for this, Alpha. I was only coming along to make sure Jeremiah didn't get any further than that car over there." He pointed to the silver Audi he had come from. "I had one of the doctors – Giselle's brother, as a matter of fact – mix up some wolfsbane and silver for me. If Jeremiah had gotten her as far as the car, he would have died right there instead. Now he will get the public execution he deserves. The shame he deserves for hurting his female. Or who *could* have been his female," he corrected when Liam growled low in his chest.

"As his Beta you will take over the pack at Blackriver," Liam told him quickly. "You are mated, correct?"

"Yes, sir."

"My father is one of the elders in The Council and will be here within the week for the holidays. Until he can make it official, you will take charge of Blackriver. Jeremiah will be dead soon enough for his crimes. Sheila too."

"That mongrel bitch," Carter said, scoffing. "She didn't seem to have any morals. Hit on Jeremiah and me even though she was wanting to be mated to you. No fucking respect."

Liam shook his head. "Sheila's in custody too. Those two will meet their ends tonight. I will lay down the punishment on the

Alpha as it is my right as Elle's mate. Elle," He nodded towards her. "Elle will dole out the punishment on Sheila as all her crimes pertain to the Luna of Plumbrook."

"*Blood Eagle?*" She was kidding and almost laughed when Carter flinched and did a comical double take in her direction.

"The fuck? *Blood Eagle?* That's harsh, little wolf," Carter said when he realized she was joking. "You've changed a lot though, Giselle. Stronger and more outspoken. I didn't know you much before Jeremiah met you, but I do know that he is a fool. You had strength in you this whole time and that man was too fucking stupid to realize it."

"His loss," Liam said and moved towards Elle, cupping her cheek with his hand as he pulled her into his warm embrace. "She's mine. This baby is mine. They always will be and there is nothing that prick can do about it ever again."

"Yours," Elle confirmed as Liam placed a soft kiss on her forehead.

***

"Jesus fucking Christ, Elle! You had me fucking scared when I heard!" Colleen popped up from the ground where she had been tending to the two enforcers lying half-dazed on the ground. Two darts lay next to them on the hard wood of the porch, and one of the men picked one up before twirling it in his hand. He sniffed it.

"Wolfsbane," he muttered and dropped the dart as if it scalded him. "The fucker shot us up with wolfsbane. A fuck-ton of it from the smell."

Elle ordered both of the drugged men into the house where she offered them coffee. They declined, but Elle knew better and brought out a bottle of whiskey instead. Both men looked hesitant before nodding to the drink.

"Straight? On ice?" Elle asked before grabbing two tumblers for the men.

"It's cold as a witch's tit outside," the one man said. "Fuck the ice. I'll take mine straight up."

The other man agreed and Elle filled the two glasses with generous portions as Liam walked in through the back door, stomping the snow from the soles of his boots.

"Jeremiah's in the cells," Liam told her. "No fucking way he's making it out without burning off half his skin trying to get past the silver bars. Can't say I wouldn't enjoy watching that either. I'd like to filet him alive right about now."

Elle dropped the two glasses off to the enforcers and came back into the kitchen, fully invested in grabbing a drink for herself and Liam as well. She moved into his arms and closed her eyes first though, bringing his scent into her nose so she could have her fill.

"Thank you," she mumbled against his chest.

"No thanks needed," Liam told her before cupping her chin to bring her gaze up to his. "Would do that and more a million times over. I mean it, Elle. You're mine. I'm yours. And pretty soon, Jeremiah's going to realize how badly he fucked up with you. That is, if he doesn't already."

"When's the execution?" she asked, nodding at his words.

"Tonight," he told her. "Midnight. It'll be a dual execution. First Sheila, then Jeremiah."

She nodded again and sighed. She really hadn't wanted this to happen, though the man had been cruel to the extreme with her. She really had just wanted him to fade into the background, like a horrible nightmare she had woken up from and faded away with the more time that passed.

She held on tight to Liam as she shuddered to think of, not one, but two deaths occurring on Plumbrook grounds tonight.

"I spoke with Carter. My father is going to place him as Alpha in a week. Until then, Carter will be acting-Alpha and his mate as acting-Luna. Your parents are on their way over as well now that Jeremiah has been caught. Carter said he'd be okay with them transferring here if they'd like, but it's up to them. They don't have to and will always be welcome here. Your brother, Chase, has already said he wants to stay at Blackriver since his mate has family there. He is welcome here anytime as well, of course." Liam ran a hand through her hair and tilted her chin to press a kiss on her lips. "I'll work to set up an alliance with Blackriver. Now that Jeremiah's out of power it will be easier to coexist with them. From what Carter divulged, many of his pack were at odds with their Alpha."

"Not surprising, really," she said. "He was never soft and cuddly like some Alphas." She wiggled her brows at him.

Liam raised a brow. "Are you saying I'm soft and cuddly? I like to think I run things pretty strict around here. Strict, but fair."

"Soft and cuddly when it counts," she corrected as she nuzzled her head into his chest, pressing her body against his as she felt the vibrations of his groan.

"Stop, Elle," he told her on that same groan. "Your parents will be here soon and if I smell correctly, we have guests in the house."

"Frustrated a bit?" she asked, smiling against him.

"You were almost taken by another man," he told her. "All I want to do is take you upstairs and remind both you and I who you belong to. Since that's out of the question, I'll probably merely embarrass myself if your parents come over while I've got a solid bulge in my pants."

"Dear God, you two are too fucking cute," Colleen said with feigned disgust as she walked into the kitchen to grab another drink for the enforcers. They hadn't heard her walk in through the front door. "If I didn't love you both to death I'd be sick to my stomach."

They waited as Colleen refilled the glasses, the liquid almost slopping over the side of one, and brought them back out to the living room.

"Once your parents are gone, I'm totally taking you upstairs with me," he whispered against Elle's lips. "I'd like nothing more than to dive headfirst in your pussy and coat myself in your scent."

"I'd really like that," she whispered back as her lips brushed against his. "But right now, I'm thirsty. I was sick outside and have the most horrible taste lingering in my mouth."

"Orange juice?" Liam asked. He always had a ton of it in the fridge for her since it was now her favorite morning beverage.

"Or pineapple," she said with a wicked glint in her eyes.

"Fuck, baby. You're killing me here."

Liam groaned again and went in search of a little liquid refreshment.

***

At 11:45 PM, the whole of Plumbrook pack, ages 16 and above, was starting to gather out in the meadow behind the Packhouse. Some visitors were there as well, and they stood in the front of the crowd as wolves filed in after them.

Carter stood tall and foreboding in his stance in his black coat with fur lining the hood. His mate stood beside him, her head hung down in shame at her late Alpha's actions. The Kincaids stood next to them, in between the wolves of their own pack and Elle, who was fidgeting in place on occasion.

"Babe, you need a potty break?" Liam whispered to her as she shifted from side to side. He understood her frequent trips to the bathroom were usually to relieve the small bladder that fought for space against her slowly swelling womb.

"No, I'm just...this is harder than I thought." She frowned and looked down at her feet, her eyes closing slowly. Her ex-mate would be coming out in a few minutes and though he was abusive to her, she couldn't find it in her heart to be as callous as he. Even in her worst moments, she couldn't be.

"I understand," he told her calmly. "It hurts that one of my own pack members would go behind my back like this. I can't imagine how you feel. He was your first mate, after all. This has to be difficult."

She looked up at him. His neck rolled with every deep swallow and she could tell he was feeling lost. He knew it had to be done, but once the task was complete how he would feel was anyone's guess. It was one thing to condemn a rogue that had happened upon your territory with ill will; it was a completely different scenario to execute both a mutinous member of your own pack and a fellow Alpha all in one night.

No, it didn't sit well for him and Elle pulled her hand out of her pocket to intertwine with his larger one. She squeezed, nodding slowly as he gently squeezed back.

They all stood there as the silence slowly consumed the space. You could hear a pin drop from a mile away as Sheila was brought out to the wooden platform. A guillotine stood at the ready and Sheila cringed away from it as she shook her head in denial of her fate.

Liam stepped forward.

"Sheila Hathaway, you have been found guilty of crimes against your Luna," Liam's loud voice called from in front of the platform. "You have conspired with an enemy of the pack to engage in the attempted kidnapping of Luna Giselle Stark and in the attempted murder of a fellow pack member. Have you anything to say as your last words?"

Sheila sniffled, looked over at the Alpha with his ranked members, Beta, Delta, and Gamma, along with their mates. Her eyes stayed on Caleb whose eyes were cast down, fixated on the ground.

"Caleb?" she sobbed out plaintively. Elle's head snapped to the Gamma and suddenly she understood. Why Caleb, though he was ripe for a mate, was without one.

Sheila was his mate. His mate and he rejected her. He had to have.

Or had she rejected him?

"I have nothing to say to you," he told her coldly, his words stilted. "I gave you opportunity after opportunity to accept me as mate, but you were a stubborn, vain, and a power-hungry bitch."

His eyes snapped up to hers and Elle could only be glad that she wasn't the one receiving his icy glare.

"How would you feel if your own soulmate preferred the company of another, particularly a friend, and practically a brother? You only look to me now to spare your life," he told her. "I wouldn't. Even if I could, I wouldn't plead your case. This is what you deserve and I accept that. I'm taking up the Alpha on his offer. Perhaps I shall find a second chance mate out there for me somewhere. Someone worthy and not conniving and manipulative as you. If you look for pity, find it elsewhere. I'm done with you."

"Fuck me," Liam muttered, loud enough for only a few in the immediate vicinity to hear.

"Man...that fucking blows," Elle heard Blake say.

Elle herself felt a lone tear almost freeze on her face as she thought of what Caleb was experiencing. She didn't feel bad for Sheila anymore. Her sympathies were for Caleb alone. Not only had she shunned her own mate, but she had also tried to steal another's. She found herself speaking and the words fell cold, hard, and heavy on the ears around her.

"Sheila, you not only conspired to take me away from my home, but you have also neglected your own other half," she said. "As you well know, I had my own true mate before all of this. He was cruel and abusive and he never admitted to our pairing. You are the same type of person as he. You don't deserve a mate, kind or cruel he may be. You deserve death. You will forthwith be placed on the guillotine and die by decapitation."

She had stood forward to speak and Liam looked back at her, wide-eyed but silent.

"At human executions they say 'May God have mercy on your soul'," she said to the quivering she-wolf. "You showed no mercy on me, so why should I wish any upon you? Your kind does not deserve it and yet we give it to you in the manner of a swift death when you would have reveled in my slow one. I will not say it, but I will give you the mercy of the quick death over the agonizingly lengthy one you deserve."

Elle jutted her chin to the Head Enforcer who nodded back, grimly.

Two other enforcers lowered Sheila onto the guillotine. Her weak body barely struggled as she had not been given sustenance and was weak in both body and spirit.

When she was set and locked into place, Elle nodded her head again and didn't even blink when the loud *schunk* of the blade cut through bone and flesh and Sheila's head parted with her body into the awaiting basket beneath.

Elle stepped back into line with the other wolves, feeling as her frigid hand was immediately encased in one of Liam's warm ones.

"You're pretty badass, my little wolf," he told her softly. "As petite as you are, you're somehow scarier than Blake when he gets into an uproar about something."

"She tried to take my family from me," Elle told him softly. "The bitch deserved it."

The soft mumbling in the crowd after Sheila's death increased as the wolves muttered to each other and the guillotine was cleaned and body parts removed for burial. It was a good ten minutes before the crowd was again silenced and a low growl came from the direction of the woods.

"Hands off me, mongrel!" Jeremiah's tone was irate and contemptuous and the enforcers pulling him to the platform had their hands full with him trying to escape.

"You were to drug him with wolfsbane," Liam bit out harshly at the enforcers as the man snarled and tried to pull them off him.

"We did, Alpha," said one who looked to be between 25 and 30 years of age. "We gave him the dosage Dr. D'Amato prescribed and he's still a fucking crazy son of a bitch. You should have seen him earlier. Thought he was going to bust down the cell doors to get out."

"Another dose, Evelyn," Liam ordered. The doctor was prepared and pulled a syringe out of her pocket and walked toward the struggling man. "Give it to Bonham while the others hold him down."

They forced Jeremiah to the cold, hard ground and he was dosed by Enforcer Bonham who was the smallest yet quickest of the group.

Jeremiah slumped and was pulled from the snow-covered ground, finally manageable. They walked him slowly up the few steps and he was put on his knees as Liam walked to within five feet of the platform.

"Jeremiah Bluth, you have attempted to kidnap my mate. She is my family and reason-"

"Mine first! And you killed my sister!" Jeremiah's voice was low and weak and full of raw emotion.

"Mine now. And Cecilia was ill of mind, weak of body," Liam said. "I blamed myself for years for her death, thinking I could have stopped her from killing herself somehow. Forced her take her medications. But there was nothing I could have done to help her. Nothing you could either. It was meant to be this way. I am sorry she is dead. She was my mate. But I will never be sorry for making Elle mine. She belongs here, not with you. You never loved her. You-"

"I did," Jeremiah spoke loudly, voice throaty. "I did love her. I...I still do."

His shaggy head of hair lifted and he gazed over at Elle where she stood next to her parents and Blake.

"I love you, Giselle," he told her. "Carter was right, and I'm sorry. I'm sorry for what I did, sorry for how I treated you, sorry for trying to take you away. Please...believe me."

Elle stepped forward once, the gentle slope of her jaw ticking and Liam was immediately at her back in a defensive position.

"I think you are only sorry you were caught," Elle said to him, her small voice loud in the deafening silence. "I think you're sorry you didn't get the mate you expected. And you're mostly sorry you're about to die, because you are. Your words of love fall on deaf ears. Don't mistake love with obsession, Jeremiah. I don't think you have a single loving bone in your whole body. I don't know how you became this way, but I have to think it was meant to be. You lost your humanity when you lost your family. If that was what broke you...I can understand that. But there are others out there that have been hurt and tortured and...molested. They don't treat others as you do. I don't. I may not have lost a family member as you did, but what I had was just as bad, if not worse. I was assaulted and put in a house-shaped cage by someone meant to protect and cherish me. I was looked upon with disdain by you and with pity by Carter. I was molested when I was young and beaten nearly to death over ten years later, but I'm still here. I'm still here and, pretty soon, you won't be."

Elle looked at Liam for a moment, her love for him shining in her eyes.

"I'm glad I got away from you, Jeremiah. Glad you are the piece of shit that you are," she continued. "You've never shown me any mercy or love, so why should I show you any in return? Only because I am better than you – you with your precious Alpha title and all – are you being shown a quick, painless death. If I was as malicious as you I would have you spread out and gutted so the wild animals could feast on your black heart while you still continued to breathe. You would live for a while, always in agony, always crying to be released unto death. Only because I have a heart am I allowing you to be given a quick death instead of the months of pain you deserve. Save your words of love and devotion for someone stupid enough to believe them. I'm done with all of it. I hope you rot in hell for all eternity until your skin turns as black as your soul."

Liam stepped back a foot and nodded.

"Couldn't have put it better myself, love," he told Elle as she came up to his side. He looped an arm around her waist and pulled her in close before addressing Jeremiah again. "She is my equal, and that's where you went wrong. Born Lunas are everything a pack needs. The nurturer, the protector, the one who keeps harmony amongst the people of the pack. You could have had that with her, but I'm glad you were fool enough not to realize what you had all along. With your death the small string that still ties you to her will be severed and she'll finally be free. Pray now, and quickly, before your brain stops its function when my blade slices through your neck."

Liam walked Elle back to the line and turned them, watching as the Head Enforcer eyed him in question. Thirty seconds went by before Liam nodded, the same firm jut of his chin as Elle had given for Sheila.

Schunk!

Elle blinked, her pulse beating rapidly as she thought, *It's done. It's all over. No more Jeremiah. I'm fucking free!*

An unexpected warmth spread into her chest leaving a large, expanding space where fire snapped and licked at her insides. It made her dizzy with its headiness as the small fragmented string that had connected her to Jeremiah dissolved as it burnt away.

"Fuck...what is that?" Liam's hands shook as he felt it too. The same fire, the same flame. Whatever it was had him looking down on his hands as they quivered for no apparent reason.

And then, what felt like a blooming, sweeping glow took over Elle's body as she felt herself fill with what she could only describe as a white light and some deeper connection she could not readily place. It made her neck burn hot where Liam's mark stood in stark contrast to her pale skin.

"Your mark! What the fuck is happening?" Liam asked her. Elle couldn't see hers, but she saw that something was happening to his.

First, it became larger, like the tree branch was growing before her very eyes in time-lapse. The blossoms turned to fruit – sweet, ripe fruit that hung heavy on the branch.

The blossoms on Elle's mark grew more vibrant and larger as

well, a distinct deep lavender as they twisted and shifted. Gasps could be heard from the crowd and someone yelped a bit when they saw what was happening.

And whatever mystical force that had been there from the moment Liam marked her, grew steadily stronger until he was pressing his body up against hers and sucking in shallow gasps of air with his arms curled tightly around her.

"Fuck! What was that?" Liam asked as soon as his breathing steadied and the flames stopped licking at his insides.

"I...I think I know," a female voice not far off called out.

Chapter 29

It appeared that wishes sometimes came true.

At least Elle's did this time. Her mother and father, though they had decided to remain at Blackriver, were able to come to Christmas at Plumbrook. The house was packed and everyone slept over, including Liam's parents, sister Arden, her mate and little one, and Chase.

Carter was now officially Blackriver's Alpha and he was slowly turning things around. It was a difficult time, but the pack was slowly adjusting. Elle had invited them over for Christmas Eve dinner where he had announced joyfully that he and his mate, Kate, were expecting in another six months.

Christmas was particularly jolly that year and both the Kincaids and Starks got along well on that happy holiday. There was barely enough room and it had Liam thinking if he wanted more children, he'd need to eventually expand the home.

A week later found them at the New Year's party the pack always held to honor another fruitful and peaceful year to come. It was always when people made big announcements and many drank to their good fortune. If one was fortunate enough to be announcing a pregnancy, everyone was always generous in their toasts and happy for the expectant couple.

"Anyone else care to share any good news for the upcoming year?" Liam asked as he lifted a glass to the ceiling in a toast. Three pregnancies and a couple of new matings was enough cheer for many, but they were surprised when Liam spoke to say he had something to add.

"Alright, then if there is nothing else to share, I would like to share my own bit of good news with you," he said with a smile that many in the pack hadn't seen in three years.

Muttering sprung out amongst the crowd as they wondered what the Alpha could say that was important enough to warrant a New Year's announcement. He had never given one before, though he was generous with his praise and goodwill to those sharing.

"As many of know, we are now allied as of Christmas Eve with

Blackriver pack since Elle has kin there and is close with the new Alpha and Luna," he said, gaining several approving nods and murmurs. A few whoops were heard as well as many of the younger unmated shifters saw this as an opportunity to visit and see if their mates were amongst Blackriver's population.

"I would also like to announce that come summertime, there will be a new little face amongst the pups," he continued. "Your Luna and I are expecting and wished to share that joyous news with you tonight."

There was applause and cheering as many were glad to see a possible heir to the pack being born. It wasn't six months ago when they thought their future uncertain with the Alpha's true mate being dead. But a *true* second chance mate was just as good, and sometimes seen as good fortune for an Alpha. Lucky in love was lucky in life for them.

"What's the sex of the babe?"

"Could it be twins Alpha?"

"Maybe triplets!"

The sober and drunk alike yelled praises and congratulations with a few naughtier suggestions on how to ensure a male heir for their next pregnancy if this one turned out female.

"I'll let you know as soon as I can whether we have a future Alpha or not," Liam told them on a laugh before stepping off the picnic bench in the basement of the Packhouse.

Many went up to Elle and Liam to give their heartfelt congratulations and the party continued until many drifted off around 2 AM, sleepy and eager to do a little private celebrating. There were lots of September and October babies born into this pack.

Caleb was there as well, absent in mind as he was.

"Caleb?" Elle walked over to the man who was sipping his beer in a corner of the room.

"Hey, Elle – I mean, Luna," he said, shaking his head as if to rid himself of some unwelcome thoughts.

"Never mind about the Luna bit," she told him. "You're Gamma and you can always call me Elle."

"Fine, Elle," he said. "Congratulations again. I know I already told you when you let it slip on Thanksgiving, but a baby in an Alpha coupling...it's always a special thing."

"No matter who the parents are, it's always special," she said, lightly dismissing her status in the pack. "How are you doing?"

"Fine," he said immediately, his face becoming almost stern. It was like he was trying to convince himself he was just fine with his rejected mate dead these past couple of weeks.

"No, you're not," she told him gently. "But you will be, I'm sure of it. Why didn't you say anything about Sheila being your mate?"

He shrugged at her. "What could I say? My mate was rejecting me because I wasn't the Alpha? That she was a power-hungry, conniving little wench who would rather fuck one of my best friends instead of her soulmate? It's humiliating to even think about, much less share with the world. I mean, *you* would understand, but many others couldn't."

Elle was silent for a few moments, her mind trying to latch onto something that might make the man feel better and coming up with nothing.

"Did you reject her, or was it the other way around?"

"I've known for years that she was my mate," Caleb said. "Felt the pull right away after she turned 18 a few summers ago. She denied the bond and about six months ago, I finally gave her an ultimatum: admit to being my mate and accept me, or face rejection." He paused. "Rejecting someone is painful and...difficult. I suppose she preferred the pain of the rejection over mating with a Gamma."

"Her loss," Elle said stoutly. "I know my experience with a true mate was different, but sometimes these things happen so that you can find something better, someone more deserving of your love. Look at Liam and me. We couldn't be more opposite but we balance each other out nicely, I think. When...when Jeremiah discovered I was his mate, I thought, "finally, I'm going to be loved unconditionally, just like my parents love each other". I had been eager for my 18th birthday since I turned 16 and found my wolf. When I turned 18 and smelt him on the training field, I was both excited and scared. When he came up from behind me to tell me I was his, I was shocked. Within a week, I was devastated. Things change quickly. The mate bond doesn't guarantee love, though the pull helps push the couple together. Finding out from Evelyn that Liam was my true second chance mate was a shock because of how it came about. Who ever heard of a second chance happening before it truly was a *true* second chance?

"I have to believe there is someone out there for you," Elle said. "She may be far away or only over at Blackriver, but she's there. If there is anything I can do to help, please let me know. And come back as soon as you find her and bring her with you. We'll miss our

Gamma while he's gone."

Caleb gave her a hug that she returned for a moment before a growl broke out behind them.

"I realize that you are without a female, Caleb, but steer clear of mine," Liam told him, the growl in his voice edging on playful. "She's cooking a possible Alpha in there and that makes me particularly possessive of her."

"We were just talking about Caleb's trip come spring," Elle said as she wandered over to Liam's awaiting arms. "I suggested he starts local before moving south and then to the west."

"You think he could have a second chance at Blackriver?" Liam asked, his brow quirking up with the question.

"Possibly," Elle said. "Jeremiah kept a tight rein on everyone in the pack and didn't allow much movement to occur off the territory. She could be right there and we wouldn't even know it."

"I'll try there first then," Caleb said. "Lord knows with the new alliance we could use all the goodwill between the packs as we can get. I won't keep my hopes up, though. She could be damned near anywhere, if she even exists."

"She does," Elle said assuredly with a nod and a blinding smile. "I know she does. And she's just waiting for you to come find her."

***

"Are you sure I'm only five months along? I feel like I'm huge," Elle said as Evelyn smiled down at her with the sonogram wand in her hand.

"You're about normal," the doctor assured her. "It's just that you're so petite you look farther along than you are."

Liam kissed Elle on her temple and nervously shifted his feet. It was the day he was supposed to find out if he was having a boy or a girl and he was anxious to know. He honestly didn't care which it was, but he was secretly hoping it would be a boy. He yearned for an heir to take over his pack one day, and he wanted to have the next several months to think up the perfect name for him. Something strong, meaningful. Powerful.

"And you're eating well? No more nausea?" the doc asked, delaying the sonogram, much to Liam's displeasure.

"Haven't thrown up in two months except for the time I ate that greasy whitefish at the Norfolk Tavern that one time. It didn't agree with me, I reckon."

Come on, come on, come on! Liam thought to himself as his foot tapped impatiently on the ground.

"That's fine then," Dr. D'Amato stated and took out some blue jelly-like substance and squirted some of it onto Elle's exposed baby bump. "And I can see we have an anxious Alpha Daddy with us as well today. Are you having any nausea, Alpha dear?" The doctor smiled and looked pointedly at Liam.

"Hysterical." Liam rolled his eyes at the smirk on Evelyn's face. Since becoming mated to Elle, he wasn't so harsh and cold, and many of the pack felt more at ease in his presence. "Let's get on with it already. I want to see what flavor baby my girl has got brewing in her belly."

Elle rolled her eyes at him behind his back and winked at Evelyn. *Let's mess with him a little,* she linked to the female doc.

What do you have in mind? Evelyn asked in kind.

Tell him it's triplet girls or something.

You have to live with him. Evelyn shrugged and made a forced humming sound as she moved the wand over Elle's belly.

"Well...that's interesting," she said out loud.

"What? What's interesting?" Liam stilled and looked at the screen, trying to figure out what was so clear to Evelyn.

"Two...no – three baby girls in there," she said. "Maybe a fourth but I'm having a hard time with this position. No wonder you are larger than most she-wolves, Luna. You're carrying a litter!"

Liam blanched to paper white, his eyes nearly bugging out of his skull.

"Three...girls?" He inhaled and almost choked on air, and there was a rosy redness to his cheeks as Elle stifled a giggle that was threatening to bubble up from her throat. "She has th-three babies in there? Holy crap. I'm gonna be up to my elbows in shit-filled diapers!"

Elle couldn't help it and laughed.

"She was only kidding, Liam," Elle said. "I asked her to play a joke. No need to get upset. Only one baby's in there, I'm sure."

"Yep." Evelyn winked as she spoke. "One healthy baby boy, and one healthy baby girl."

Rolling her eyes, Elle looked at the doctor. "You can stop now. The joke's over. Look, he's already turning back to a normal color." She gestured at Liam.

The pink returned to Liam's cheeks as he took a steadying breath and closed his eyes. "You are so getting spanked when we get home."

"Liam!" Elle's face flushed as Dr. D'Amato laughed out loud.

"I was kidding about having triplets. And quads," Evelyn bit out between chunks of laughter. "I wasn't kidding about twins. You're having one of each flavor, as Liam put it. A boy and a girl. You get your Alpha and a tagalong sister to boot."

"Holy Christ on a cracker! Twins?" Elle sat straight up, trying to distinguish the blobs on the screen. "Where?"

Dr. D'Amato pointed to one circular head and body. "There's baby number one. He's the boy. It looks like he's already protective of his little sister. I'll have to move to get a better view of the girl." She shifted the wand to the side and nodded. "There's baby number two. Definitely a little girl. She's lacking in the man bits department. Or maybe it's really a boy and he's just very *small*."

Liam's brows furrowed a bit as his mouth formed into a straight line.

"No way! Alphas are always packing in the man bits department. No son of mine is going to be small down there. Not possible!"

"I was kidding, Alpha." Evelyn rolled her eyes. "It's definitely a girl you've got in there so calm down before you give yourself a stroke."

"You know what that means though, don't you?" Elle asked. "Two of everything. Cribs, changing stations, one big-ass stroller for the both of them. Two car seats."

"Not a problem," he said, kissing Elle's head. "I got this, babe. You just keep cooking 'em in there like you're supposed to and I'll make sure they each have one of everything on that crazy list I'm sure you're compiling in your head right now."

"Good thing I already have two boobs," Elle said with a sigh, thinking about breastfeeding.

"The babies aren't the only ones thankful for that, babe."

"Liam!"

Chapter 30

"Thank fucking God you're a wolf," Liam said as he slammed Elle up against the door of their bedroom. "If I had to wait any longer because you were human, my nuts would shrivel and fall off. I can't see how the humans have to wait 6 weeks to have their mates after they give birth."

"They...they don't have mates, Liam," Elle told him before his hot, wet lips pressed up against hers.

"Lovers, wives, baby daddies...whatever. They should be given a medal for abstaining from sex for that long."

"You did it after Cecilia died," Elle reminded him as his lips raced over her neck to tease the flesh of her mark.

"Shit, baby. My dick was useless after my first mate died. Might as well have lopped it off and called it a fucking day," he told her as he licked her neck, causing shivers to run up and down her spine.

"Have I mentioned lately how glad I am you didn't do that?" she asked as he bit down on her neck to add a pinch of pain to their lovemaking.

"Mmm...not recent enough it would seem," he said. "Couple weeks, maybe?"

"I've been recuperating," she told him and felt as he teased her nipples with his tongue before sucking on them, one after the other.

It was summer now and Elle had given birth to twins, future Alpha Arsen, and her little lady, Serena. They had both picked the names, and though Arsen wasn't her favorite, it was slowly growing on her. It had been 14 days and 12 hours since Elle and Liam had had sex last, and they had been given the go-ahead from the doctor after a short period of recuperation.

Caleb was still out west, somewhere along the coast of Oregon at last count, looking for a second chance mate of his own. He had decided to start at Blackriver then head west, make his way down the coast and head back via the Southwest, through Texas, Louisiana, and Florida. He was in good spirits when he left and had mostly gotten over his heartbreak over Sheila and her manipulative ways.

Mostly. You never really got over the loss of a mate unless you found and marked a new one.

"Fuck, babe...your tits," Liam groaned as he sucked on one puckered nipple until it pebbled. "They've grown massive."

"Twins, remember?" she reminded him, voice breathy as he continued to lap and suck at her.

"Fuck. I hope we have twins again then."

"You're supposed to pull out for a while." Elle sounded a little frantic. She didn't want to fall pregnant against so soon after giving birth to the twins. "I don't want to get knocked up again until those little ones are at least a year old."

"Baby, I haven't tasted you in like, two weeks," he told her as his mouth skimmed lower, nipping at the flesh on her belly. It was back to its former tautness thanks to her quick shifter healing. "I'll try, but I can make no promises."

"Maybe we should wait until – ahhhh!" He lapped at her slit, pulling her folds into his mouth before licking up between them. "Fuck! Maybe I can just...just suck you off and then-"

"Fuck no!" Liam turned her around and moved her quickly to the bed. "Your blowjobs could go down as epic in the Dirty Deeds Hall of Fame, but there is no way you're denying me your pussy tonight. I'll pull out, babe. Promise."

She just nodded her head and moaned, not honestly caring what he did once he was inside her so long as he got her there. He wasn't the only one missing sex, but she had been too busy with two newborns to actually really start feeling the pang of her usually riotous libido.

Now that the two little ones were just settling in for a snooze and Elle was all healed up, her whole body ached to be touched by Liam. Once her connection with Jeremiah had broken and the bond grew stronger with a real second chance mating pull, sex with him had only gotten better. He had even brought on her labor when he thrust her into an explosive orgasm right before giving birth, three weeks early.

The babies had been fine. A healthy weight and length, and they hadn't needed to stay at the pack clinic even for one night. Her strong babies who could seem to only sleep for two hours at a stretch before crying to be fed or changed.

With his mouth on her pussy and his hot breath teasing her slit, she cried out, thankful that the babies were far enough away not to hear and be woken up by her lusty moans and deep grunts and groans Liam gave her when they fucked.

She was also thankful for things like baby monitors and breast pumps. Feeding two babies was not fun when they both got hungry at the same time. So, Liam and Elle switched on and off. One baby would get milk directly from the source, while the other was fed by Liam from the stored-up breast milk Elle seemed to be pumping out every hour, on the hour. And it was a *lot* of breast milk.

Liam flicked at her clit with his tongue and groaned as she mewled and became tight around the two fingers he had shoved up her pussy and was using to rub up against her g-spot.

"Fuck, that's good," she sighed out and felt as he sucked at her clit before using his tongue to flick hard and fast at her, sending her spiraling to the edge.

He added more suction and smiled against her while slowly stroking her as she cried out her release in quivering little convulsions.

"How is it *my* pussy tastes better and better each time I devour it?" he asked as he started moving up her body to her nipples – the same ones that were still very sensitive from the constant assault of tiny little baby lips and breast pumps.

"Good luck?" Elle answered as his tongue stroked against her with hard little nips to her stony tipped tits.

"The best of luck, baby. And I'm ready to get lucky right now."

They both froze for a moment as a tiny little cry went out over the baby monitor. Their hearts raced and Liam's dick twitched with the need to be in her, and they both sighed in relief when the little one went back to sleep and they were able to resume.

"Close fucking call," Liam said as he lined up his cock to her moist heat and pushed inside. "Oh fuck, babe. I missed this. Being inside you. Fucking you."

"It's only been two weeks."

"Two weeks of hell," he corrected.

"I'm glad to hear my blowjobs are your definition of hell," she said, sounding amused and slightly irritated. "I'll have to withhold sucking you off since you think so lowly of my skills in that department."

"Fuck...I didn't mean it like that, baby," he said on a swift retreat from her pussy. "I meant that it's nothing compared to my cock being inside you and coming quarts when your tight little cunt squeezes me when you come."

"An orgasm is an orgasm," she said as he thrust inside her with a swivel of his hips. "Are you saying that there is a hierarchy to them?"

"Yes, baby. For me there is, at least," he told her, slamming into her as she cried out. "Most intense orgasms are when I'm fucking you raw and tight. Second is if you made me wear some wretched rubber while I fuck you. Which will never happen, by the way. The day I wear a condom when I'm in you is the day I cut my junk off and feed it to that pack of dogs that's been hanging out on the eastern border. The third is a blowjob. Granted, yours are the best and very close to being right up there with sex with a condom. Well, fuck it. They *are* better than sex with a condom. At least all of me can feel you when your lips wrap tight around my cock."

"Shit...stop talking about condoms," Elle said as she felt the tight coil of her building orgasm tense in her stomach. "Keep the dirty. I like it when you do."

"Oh yeah, I can do that," he told her and continued to fuck her hard and tell her how fucking wet and sweet and tight her pussy was until she was moaning out her release. It honestly didn't take long at all. Abstinence on her part made her needy and ready to explode around him in seconds.

"Get over on your stomach," he told her. "I wanna see that ass in the air for me."

She turned over and stretched out, her knees at a 90-degree angle to the bed and her chest pushed down onto the mattress.

"Fuck...even your ass is a little bigger," he told her and kneaded the flesh in his hands. "Daddy likes."

"Fuck! My ass is bigger? How?" She turned her head back to see if she now had something akin to J. Lo booty, and he smacked a cheek before kneaded the pink of it.

"It's fucking perfect, babe – just like you," he told her, every fucking word Gospel in his mind. "Now stop squirming and let me get back in you. I've got more orgasms to give and I'm feeling particularly generous tonight."

He lined himself up again and pushed through her dripping lips until his balls were kissing her pretty pink pearl. "Fuck...so wet, angel." He could hear the slick sounds of their sex as his hips met with her ass again and again in a tempo that only sped up the longer he fucked her.

"Can't...help it," Elle breathed out in gasping, ragged pants. "I'm...s-so fucking close, Liam!"

He gave her a good pounding as she tightened around him in thick, hot pulses.

"Yeah, babe. That's it. Fucking come for me." He swiveled his hips again and felt the first of the squeezing, sucking flutters of her sex around him.

"Liam!" she cried out, coming around him as he worked her slowly, drawing out her pleasure.

"Yeah, baby. I'm gonna keep you crying out my name until you're liquid in my hands and I'm coming on your tight little body."

He made her cry out his name several more times before he was ready to come, pulling out as his cock pumped strips of white on her ass while he groaned her name.

"Fuck...Elle, baby...yeah." His dick jumped and balls contracted, emptying out as she kept her ass nice and high for him.

She collapsed onto the bed, heavy breathing slowing until she was sure she was going to fall asleep at any moment. Liam lay next to her, coming slowly down from probably one of the most intense orgasms he'd ever experienced.

"Liam, get me something and wipe me off," Elle requested, eyes shut. "I don't have any other clean sheets after Arsen decided to spit up all over two separate sets yesterday."

"Hmm...just like Daddy," Liam said on a mumble. "Messing up bed sheets already and he's only two weeks old. My boy."

"Are you going to continue to call yourself Daddy all the time?"

"Until he learns to say it? Hell yeah," Liam said as vehemently as he could. "That's gonna be his first word. Don't worry. We can keep Mama as a close second."

"You're horrible," she told him. "I was the one that had morning sickness and leg cramps and backaches and went through hours of labor. I should at least get the first word."

"Can't help it, babe," he told her. "Dada's easier for babies to say."

"Un-fucking-fair if you ask me. Mommy gets no respect."

"Yeah, but Mommy gets multiple orgasms. How many was that? Five? Six?"

"I'm not telling Daddy until he gets me a towel and wipes off his slowly drying jizz from my ass."

"I bet it was six. At least I'm gonna tell myself it was six."

"It was none if you don't help a girl out."

"Fine," Liam grunted and got up from the bed, sauntering over to the bathroom and grabbing a clean towel and wetting it with warm water.

"Better?" he asked when he was done and had gotten rid of the towel in the overflowing laundry basket. It seemed that laundry was never-ending when you had twins to take care of.

"Much," she told him and curled into his body as he lay down on the bed. "Wake me if the place catches fire only. You've wiped me out."

"Tough luck, babe," Liam said. "The little pooping, puking mini-me's are set to wake up in a half an hour."

"Fuck."

Epilogue

"Unca Cay-wup!" a two-year-old Arsen squealed from across the back yard before motoring toward the man who had caught his attention.

Elle smiled as she watched Arsen's little legs pump clumsily over the ground only to trip and be caught by his favorite uncle. Caleb.

"Almost ate it, little guy," the female next to Caleb said on a giggle. It had taken a year or so, but Caleb had found his second chance mate in a small town in central Kansas.

Caleb swung the child up into his arms where he rested his chubby little bum in the crook of his elbow while Caleb walked toward the grill behind Liam and Elle's house. It was early July and most everyone in the pack was celebrating Independence Day the American way. Burgers, buns, and a light show later on that evening.

Elle was bouncing a 6-month old on her knee. Serena was off playing with Colleen's first-born, Nicole, while Arsen thought he was much too grown up to play with the little kids. Already.

"How's the weaning going?" Caleb's mate, Jillian, asked when she came up to Elle and sat down on the bench next to her.

"Slow," Elle admitted, looking pointedly at the baby on her knee. "Knox really is a fan of drinking his milk straight from the source. He's gonna be worse than Serena was." It had taken Serena until she was 8 months old before she was drinking only from the bottle. "He won't even look at a bottle. Well, unless he gives it this completely repugnant look like the stupid thing's done something to offend him. I'm so chafed my nipples are about to fall off in protest." She grimaced dramatically.

Caleb scrunched his face up slightly and shook his head to ward away the vision of falling nipples he had in his head.

Nipples just plain popping off a body. Gross. So not going there.

"Angel, I'm almost done with the burgers and dogs," Liam said as he stood by a monstrous grill they had bought the previous summer for cookouts. "Get the kids over here so they can eat first and then we can feed ourselves. I'm motherfu – uhm, flippin' starving."

Liam had a hard time not cussing when he was otherwise distracted or irritable. And keeping the little ones away from the hot grill while trying not to singe something was a daunting task. *You try it.*

"Wanna go to Auntie Jill?" asked Elle of Knox, who was looking up at his mother with his father's piercing blue-grey eyes.

"Come over here, little man," Jill said as she stretched her arms out to the baby. "Got something shiny you can play with."

The shiny thing turned out to be a keyring that was large enough to baby-friendly, but not something that could easily be ruined either.

"Did I miss the food? I'm starving for Chr-" Blake started to say as he walked up to the group.

"Language!" Liam barked out with a flip of his hair. "How can you forget when you have a child?"

Blake shrugged. "Was just with the enforcers," he excused. "They cuss like a bunch of sailors. You know that."

"Well, tamp it down for now," Liam urged. "Little ears and Arsen is like a dang mockingbird. Anything he hears, he repeats at full-volume and at least three hundred times before he gets bored with it. Just got him to stop saying the 'C' word last week. And that's not even that bad."

"What's the 'C' word?" Caleb asked quietly.

"Ends with a 'P'," Elle told him.

"Gotcha." Caleb nodded. Yeah, "crap" wasn't that bad, but it wasn't that great either. And at least it wasn't the word "cunt".

"So, what's the verdict on the food?" Blake asked, not to be deterred. "A man's gotta eat, and I think I just lost ten pounds in water weight training with those pri- uhm, I mean, persons."

"Cool it, Daddio," Colleen said, coming up from behind Blake to kiss him on the cheek. She had the two little girls at her side, both wearing almost identical sundresses. If one of the tots hadn't had Colleen's fiery red mane of hair, they might have almost been identical. Serena had gotten her father's blackish-blue locks and cobalt eyes. "You can swear all you want when the kids go to sleep. I know you need to release some of that aggravation somehow. Punch a bag, go to the basement and cuss up a storm, just keep a lid on the bad words until little ears aren't listening."

"We're getting the kids fed first," Elle told Blake after he looked over at the grill longingly while listening to Colleen's spouting off at him.

"Thank God they're still little," Blake muttered. "If Arsen's going to grow as tall as his father, that kid'll eat you out of house and home before long." His gaze flickered over to Elle. "Good luck with that by the way."

Elle went off to find Arsen who had wiggled out of Caleb's arms at some point, while Colleen got the girls situated at the picnic table, napkins and Wet Ones at the ready. Barbecue was always messy, though the girls were a little neater than Arsen who wore as much food as he ate.

Once all the kids were settled and quietly munching on hot dogs and tiny bites of hamburger, Elle went off to breastfeed Knox in the house, leaving the others to wait for Trace and Helena. They were just coming back from out of town and should have been home an hour ago. Their little one was probably being cranky. One-year-old Damon was the exception to every baby rule. He hated sleeping in the car, loved noise to go to bed to, and preferred staying awake at night over sleeping. Trace swore the kid must've been part vampire.

The parents began to eat food and Liam placed a cheeseburger off to the side for Elle for when she got back from feeding Knox. He made himself two cheeseburgers and made sure everyone was fed before starting on his first.

They were halfway through eating when Jillian stopped, looking away from her plate of food.

"Overcooked?" Liam asked anxiously. He prided himself on his newly found grilling skills and took into account everyone's preferred temperature for their beef. Since they were wolves, almost all of them liked their burgers rare to medium rare.

"No, it's good," Jillian assured him, looking at Caleb. "I've...my stomach's been bothering me some a bit lately."

"Babe, just tell them." Caleb said quietly as he nodded at her with a smile, gesturing the people around them.

She looked back at him, practically whispering, "Not yet. Elle's not here."

"You knocked up?" Blake asked loudly, taking a huge bite of his burger before chewing and effectively stealing Jillian's thunder.

Caleb and Jillian blinked back at him before she nodded her head slightly.

"Yeah, we're going to have a baby," Caleb said, his face flushed with pride.

"Congrats!" Colleen said, grinning like a lunatic at the news.

"I hope iz anuvah boy," Arsen said before spearing a piece of hot dog with a baby fork and jamming the food into his mouth.

"No! Girl! We need anodder girl," Serena said, her high voice squeaking near the end.

The kids went on about what sex the baby would be while the grown-ups congratulated the expectant couple and hugs were given, mostly between the females.

"What's going on? What did I miss?"

Knox was passed out in Elle's arms, comatose from being fresh off the tit, as always.

"Auntie Jill's knocked up!" Serena piped up before going back to her food.

Elle's eyes narrowed.

"Who taught her that phrase?" Her eyes immediately went to the fun, bad uncle. Blake. She was sure her children would be cussing up a storm by the time they were 8.

"Guilty," he admitted with a smile. The bastard didn't look guilty at all.

Elle took the time to admonish him for a minute before congratulating Caleb and Jillian, putting a sleepy Knox in his carrier and walking over to Liam to get her food. She knew he would always save her some. He always did.

There were a number of grills that had been pulled over to the area between the Packhouse and Liam and Elle's home, and many other families were getting down to their dinner. It was relatively quiet for a while as people finished eating and were slowly starting to clean up.

Once they were all done, some of the females set up some games for the kids and mayhem ensued. Arts and crafts for the little ones and sack races and other sports for some of the older kids. They would play until the smaller ones took a nap and would be woken up just before fireworks lit the sky.

"You've done this twice, Elle," Jillian said as they watched the kids play from afar. "On a scale of one to Armageddon, how screwed am I?"

"The twins were difficult," Elle admitted. "When one woke up and cried, they always roused the other. Knox is easier. Serena and Arsen just sleep through his nightly feedings and changings. Thank God they're deep sleepers. You seen Doc D'Amato yet?"

Jill nodded happily. "Yesterday, just to confirm it. Only one baby she can see in there. Thank God. I don't know how you did it with two."

"Liam helped, as did Colleen," Elle said. "At least until her little monster came and was eating up all my time with my best friend. Then she decided to bring the little munchkin over and we shared the load between us."

"I'm afraid I'm going to trip and drop the baby," Jillian admitted. "I mean, we're shifters so we don't get hurt easily, but it's still scary as hell to think of him or her being dropped on their head."

"I always thought I would trip up the stairs when mine were first born. I think every new mom goes through that," Elle said. "That and thinking they don't need to be 'on it' when changing a baby boy's diaper. With the number of times Arsen's 'baptized' me with pee, I should start taking up a collection plate and call myself a minister."

"You having any more?" Jillian asked. "You got three, but you aiming on adding to the family again someday?"

"Don't know yet," Elle said, looking over at Liam who was laughing and making silly faces at Knox. The baby was wide awake again and blowing saliva bubbles, completely riveted by his own salivary gland's prowess. "Haven't had that discussion yet on whether we want more. I know Serena wants a little sister though. I heard her at Colleen's talking to Nicole about having a baby sister. I'm pretty sure she just wants a real live 'doll' to dress up in pink sparkly dresses, though. It may be just a phase."

"She won't like it so much when she's dressing up her baby sister and that baby sister decides to drop a load in her diaper." Jillian snickered a little and laughed.

Many of the toddlers got tired about an hour before the fireworks were set to start and thick blankets and soft pillows were placed on the ground so they could nap until the grand finale commenced. The grown-ups kept the older kids away from the small ones with a movie being shown in the Packhouse's basement while the teens decided to head off in another direction and play pranks on some of the less fortunate adults. They were smart enough to leave the Alpha and his entourage alone.

They all made it back to the clearing about 15 minutes before the show was set to start and took seats on the grass or laid back on blankets to look up into the stars. A comfortable, mumbling hum spread throughout the crowd until the first of the fireworks lit the sky and effectively shut the crowd up.

Liam came up and sat behind Elle, his legs spread and bringing her back into his arms. Knox was looking up sleepily at the vibrant colors on display with a thumb tucked into his mouth.

"Want another one?" Liam mumbled into Elle's ear in between loud explosions of fireworks being rocketed into the sky and going off one by one.

"Another kid?" she asked.

"Yeah, another kid," he answered, amused. "We make some pretty great ones, if I do say so myself, so I was wondering if you wanted to have another."

Elle just smiled, thinking back to her conversation with Jillian.

"I think we do, too," she told him and nuzzled her head deeper into his neck. "And I'd love to have more kids with you."

"Kids? As in plural?" Liam asked.

"Hon, we had twins once," she reminded him. "It could always happen again."

Liam groaned. "They were twice the trouble, though I love them to death."

"Hey, you asked," she told him. "I can't predict if you're going to get another twosome or not."

Liam was quiet for a while as he watched the fireworks display overhead. Elle felt it when he moved his head in a slow, firm nod.

"Okay, let's do it," he said finally. "Let's have another one, even if your ovaries decide to give us another set of mouths to feed."

He went to stand, but Elle jerked him back.

"The fireworks aren't over," she told him. "You think you're going to convince Arsen and Serena to go to bed when there's still bright colors and loud noises in the sky? Not to mention sparkly ones? Have you not *met* our children?"

"Okay," he said and settled back again, relaxed. "But as soon as we get those three into bed, we're going to start trying again. Real hard, baby. Real mother-flippin' hard."

Bonus Chapter 1

The wind on the high plains was heavy as Caleb's medium-sized sedan swerved through torrents of rain and the occasional pelt of wayward hail. His gaze flickered from the south side of highway to the north. The scenes were as different as night and day and threw him for a loop as he saw something completely out of the blue. A funnel cloud. It looked like it was moving fast, and Caleb swore a blue streak as he urged his car forward to beat the inclement weather. Growing up in the northeast, he had never experienced a tornado. Well, it was a year of firsts, but this one beat all the rest.

"Move, car, fucking move!" he gritted out, his foot to the floor over the gas pedal. The mangy car protested weakly and he wished he had thought to trade in the hunk of junk before he had made his way west in search of his fabled second chance mate. The pang he felt whenever he thought of Sheila had lessened over the months since her death, though it never truly went away. Every time he thought of it, he found it hurt less and less until it was only a gently tug in his solar plexus, just a hint of a reminder of what could have been.

The car sputtered and a puff of smoke drifted up and away from the hood before Caleb slammed his fists on the steering wheel, cursing. "Motherfucker!"

He eased over to the side of the straight road and put the car into a reluctant park. His eyes flickered over to the north again, taking in the scene. The funnel cloud had widened, hit the ground, and was now tearing up dried vegetation and debris. His keen eyesight could see the top of a silo tear apart and scatter, and he muttered a few well-chosen words to God.

"You couldn't at least fucking have me breakdown near an auto repair shop?" he asked the roof of his vehicle. It didn't answer back and Caleb opened the door before unlatching the front hood and taking in the damage.

He had no clue what was wrong with the vehicle – didn't even know where to begin to look – and stood there feeling utterly at a loss as to what to do. He wasn't sure how far he was from the nearest town, but he had seen a sign a while ago that said he was fifty miles outside of Pratt, Kansas. The problem was that he didn't know if that had been ten or forty miles ago. He had been too eager to beat the storm the weather forecasters had been going on and on about on the radio.

He kept the hood open before glancing north again, the funnel cloud slightly nearer, if his eyes told true. Closer and...turning his way.

Shit.

Caleb could hear the far-off whinny of a horse to his south, hooves beating hard on the ground as a voice called out a "hyah!' and whistled. Well, at least there were people around, which meant that there had to be shelter from the storm. Shelter and help.

Completely out of his element, Caleb followed the noises of hooves until a cloud of dust upon the horizon lifted into the air like the dust devils he had seen in Arizona and New Mexico. He had been in awe of them, though they had been a bit scary. The cloud to the north, inching ever closer, was fucking terrifying.

He broke into a jog before it became a full-on sprint, the wind picking up at his back and hurrying him to move forward. Some debris flew and a small branch hit his back, causing him to wince at the sting.

"Fucking nature," he grumbled breathlessly as he ran up to and over a whitewashed fence like a hurdler in the Summer Olympics. The wood shuddered from the wind and the telltale creaking of the it made him sure the storm was working its way toward him.

Caleb had stopped at many different packs on his search for a mate and was on his way to one outside of Pratt just before the storm hit and his car decided to take a dump on him. It was a smaller but docile community, full of farmers and blue-collar men and women, real downhome folk there ever was. He could do much worse finding a second chance mate amongst the hard-working people of Penalosa Pack.

As he had made his way across country, each stop was a dead end, his hopes being dashed before his very eyes until he almost wanted to give up. Every time, though, he would get a call from Liam or Elle and their encouraging words would spur him on further until he had made it to the west coast in Washington.

After that, he traveled south through Oregon and California and turned east to trek the southwest states, stopping by known and lesser-known packs alike, and always being welcomed with open arms and a sympathetic ear. It was both heartening and depressing. Each pack, each visit, took a little something out of him until he was sure he would never find this fabled female that was made for him.

A nearby whinny drew him out of his thoughts, and a gelding with a white star on his face and a luxurious chocolatey coat galloped past him before rearing back and almost taking Caleb out with his front hooves. It had been startled by a wayward piece of fence as it flew past them both, heading in a southeasterly direction.

"Hyah!"

The voice was female and close by, and Caleb looked over from his position to see a young woman with dirty blond hair tied back in a messy ponytail. There were smudges of dirt on her face, probably from wrangling the horses, and a determined air surrounding her. It was etched on her face as well.

And what a lovely face it was.

"You!" The woman looked over at him, startled. "What are you doing here?"

"Car." Caleb breathed out heavily. "Broke down. Looking for shelter."

She studied him, doing a circuit over him as if to tell if he was friend or foe. His panic-stricken face and foreign accent must have spoken to her of his status as a visitor to the state, and she nodded her head before her chin jutted upward and she breathed out a sigh.

"Come with me," she told him before turning heel and walking off into the distance.

Caleb ran up to catch up to her, dirt and dust clogging his nose and throat. He coughed a bit and covered his face with his flimsy t-shirt, trying to stem the particles from entering his nasal passages and mouth.

"Name's Caleb," he told her, voice muffled. "Not from around here if you couldn't tell."

The snort she gave told him that she knew all too well he was an outsider. And the woman had a slight mid-western accent from what he could tell, though she hadn't spoken much yet.

"Jillian," she returned. "You're on my parents' farm and trespassing. Since it seems you did so to get away from the storm, I'll turn the other cheek. This time."

She covered her mouth with a soiled bandana and picked up speed, the wind hollering and whooping through scattered copses of trees and brush.

"We got a storm cellar about half a mile from here," she told him.

"Can you run? That twister is making its way swiftly."

Caleb nodded. "Yeah. I can do that."

They started at a slow jog, the air behind them flowing faster, Jillian's ponytail whipping around and stinging her face. It seemed to take forever to move that half mile, but there was soon an old outbuilding that looked worse for wear and a slanted storm cellar at the base of it.

"Used to be part of our old house before an EF5 tornado came and blew it away a few summers ago," she told him, pulling the handle up so they could climb inside.

They both skinned down the steps quickly, Jillian waiting at the bottom to close the doors behind them and secure it with a heavy chain and several pieces of thick wood.

"You can never be too careful," she explained as she placed a third piece of sturdy wood between the handles. "The wind from a tornado can wreak havoc even on the strongest of chains. Had to replace the doors once because I'd only chained them. Near got sucked up into the sky."

Caleb coughed and swore he saw dirt fly out of his mouth. The roar of the wind assaulted his ears as the dust from the loose soil clogged every hole in his face. He looked around, hoping to see a box of tissues or some paper towels he could blow his nose into. All he could smell was the earthy scent of soil. He found a paper towel in one corner on a small beat-up side table and cleared his nose with it.

There were candles and some small cabinets in the cellar, all of them packed with necessities like nonperishable foods and flashlights. Some of the doors were open and he wondered if the scent he was smelling was a scented candle. It was quite lovely. Like fresh apples being baked into a pie.

Jillian lit a few candles and blew out the long-stemmed match before tossing it to the ground.

"We'll save the flashlights for later if need be," she told him, coughing into her hand.

Caleb passed her a towel and she blew her nose into it, using the remainder of the fabric to wipe the grime from her face.

"Do...do you smell that?" she asked, scenting the air.

"That apple scent? Yes," he replied.

"No...not apple. Cedar. Cedar and pine."

Caleb blew his nose again, clearing more of the blockage away. When he sniffed again, he stilled and looked at her.

She smelled of wolf. Wolf and baking apples.

"I only smell apple pie," he said before lifting his nose into the air again. He moved closer to her, leaning in when he was close enough. "Are you wearing perfume?"

She laughed, a musical sound if there ever was one. Something perked in his gut. A sudden hyper-awareness that he couldn't identify.

"I don't even use scented bodywash," she told him. "Too many insects that like to get too close if you smell too flowery. But that scent...cedar with a hint of pine? It's coming from you."

Caleb sniffed his shirt. It smelled like Tide as always, nothing of the great outdoors about it.

"I don't smell anything on me," he confessed, though he took another large whiff of himself. He hadn't even used cologne that morning when leaving his hotel room. He had run out in San Diego and couldn't be bothered to buy more. "But I can smell you're a she-wolf. Are you part of the local pack?"

"Yes. I am," she said.

"Ah, I was heading for a visit to your land. Good to know I was on the right path." His nose still felt clogged and he wondered if there was some bottled water he could use to wash off his face and clean out his nostrils with. Having inhibited senses really irritated him. He relied on his keen senses as a wolf on strange land more than ever. "Do you have any water? I'd like to wash the grime off my face."

She smiled at him.

"Afraid of a little dirt, pretty boy?"

Pretty?

"I'm not some pampered prick with a dick, sweetheart," he told her. "But I'd like to be able to use all my senses on foreign lands."

She handed him a bottle of off-brand water and took one for herself. Caleb used some to wet another paper towel and run it over his face before turning his head upside down and using the water bottle as a makeshift neti pot. He inhaled a bit and choked, causing Jillian to snicker.

"Good idea, though it's not the most comfortable feeling." She mimicked him and breathed a sigh of relief when she felt she could finally smell the air again. Cedar and pine. The fragrance was stronger than ever.

After she blew out the excess water she looked over at him. He was standing, staring at her like he had never seen her before. She blew her nose into the towel, never taking her eyes off him. The look he gave her was strange yet somehow familiar. "You," he whispered under his breath.

"Me?"

"You're my mate," he told her, taking a step forward.

"I...well."

That couldn't be. Her mate was gone, far away from here...just *gone*.

"Impossible," she told him, though something perked up inside her. *Could it be?* "My true mate rejected me a long time ago."

"As did mine," he replied, taking another step forward. "I've been searching for my second chance."

"You were...mated before?" Something in her tone spoke of jealousy, and his lips twitched at her reaction.

"No. We never mated. She...she didn't want me."

"What? Why?"

"She was a greedy, egotistical female who wanted another. A friend and my Alpha," he explained. He hadn't realized he'd gotten so close to her and was only inches away from touching her for the first time. His hand reached out to pluck at a blond lock, though he fell just short of making contact.

"Mine was...he didn't want me either." Jillian looked down, but not before Caleb saw the shame she felt ripple across her face. "He preferred a human female, one he got pregnant."

"Fuck."

She nodded.

"My words exactly." Her tone was half-wry, half-hurt. She had come to terms with her loss. Sort of.

There was a long pause as they both breathed in the other. It was calming, soothing. It was bordering on awkward-as-fuck before Caleb spoke.

"He was stupid, your mate," he told her. "You are exquisite."

Her eyes opened wide and flashed up at him in surprise.

"I look horrible," she disagreed. "There's more dirt on me than on the ground outside and I smell of manure and livestock. I-"

"You are as pretty as a picture and smell like heaven," he finished, finally closing the last few inches of distance to pluck at her hair.

Her breath caught and lip wobbled. It felt like ages since someone had paid her a compliment. The nicest thing she had heard recently was praise when she helped foal a calf just this past spring. There was little time for niceties and kind words when tending to animals and a farm, and that particular birth had been quite difficult. It started out as a breach.

Caleb caught a tear just as it slipped past the rim of her lower lid.

"Will you reject me too?" she asked. Her eyelids fluttered and Caleb's thick brows darkened in response.

"Never."

A weight she didn't know she had carried lifted from her shoulders on a sigh. Her eyes closed briefly, leaning into his large hand.

"Thank you." She sniffled as his hand cupped her cheek gently.

It may not have been the most ideal of meetings, but Caleb was grateful for it just the same.

And the next day, having marked and mated, they left Kansas for New York state.

Bonus Chapter 2

The applause died down slowly as Elle stepped off the stage at the Norfolk Tavern. The last set of the night had been a success, though her throat was feeling worse for wear after a third encore. Fortunately, she had thought ahead and put out all the stops by singing *Elastic Heart* by Sia. They had slowed the tempo down and turned it into more of a ballad, but it somehow worked.

And the crowd had eaten it up.

Piano nights had somehow morphed into the most popular time to visit the tavern, and a moderate cover charge was now collected at the door. They'd had to start taking reservations after Elle came back from her "maternity leave" after having the twins, Serena and Arsen. Though she had recuperated quicker than a human, she felt it would have been too telling if she had come back too soon, and instead took the usual few months away from performing at Norfolk Tavern. She wasn't ashamed of her inner beast, but she didn't know how the crowd would take it if they knew she wasn't all human either. And Norfolk was blossoming under her name. It was now a popular place to take a date or go out for a celebration. The extra money went into refurbishing some of the older parts of the building and they had gotten new signage put up just a few months before.

"You killed it out there, angel," Liam told her, folding her into his arms as soon as she left the stage. As always, she melted like butter in his embrace.

"Thanks," she croaked.

Liam laughed and pulled out a mug he had prepared for her while she was onstage. Piping hot tea with honey to soothe her throat. She sipped it and closed her eyes, humming at the calming sweetness.

"Good?"

"Mmm...very."

"Hey Elle, I got someone here that wants to speak with you," Dave called out when he came up to her and Liam, toting a tall female with winged glasses and a smart suit. She was dressed in red and black, from her black-rimmed glasses to the red spiky heels on her feet. She smiled softly, but it looked too practiced. The woman was all business underneath.

"Hi. I'm Elle Stark." She thrust her hand out to the woman who shook it briefly before introducing herself.

"Margaret Attleboro," the woman returned in a husky alto. "Pleased to make your acquaintance."

"What can I do for you, Ms. Attleboro?"

"Please, call me Meg," the woman told her, a genuine smile leaking through her professional persona just a touch. "And I was wondering if there was some sort of backstage space we could talk in. Privately."

Dave nodded and headed back to one of the refurbished rooms that they used as a dressing room for the performers. Well – only *one* performer, unless you counted Dave's piano accompaniment.

Dave left them there and Meg took a seat before Liam and Elle sat on the Chesterfield couch across from her.

"I'm not one for small talk, so I'll cut to the chase, Ms. Stark," Meg prattled off quickly.

"*Mrs.* Stark," Elle corrected, glancing in her periphery to Liam and moving her left hand a bit. It set the plum blossom ring that Liam had given her ages ago off to sparkle and Meg's eyes flickered down.

"Mrs. Stark," the older woman amended. "That's such an unusual wedding ring. It's quite lovely. My apologies on my faux pas. You...well, you just seem too young to be married."

"I'm twenty. Almost twenty-one," Elle obliged. "What can I do for you?"

The woman cleared her throat and crossed her legs. Liam relaxed a little, his hand moving over to cup Elle's right in his and running a thumb over her knuckles.

"Dave has spoken highly of you," Meg told her. "He happens to be a distant cousin of mine whom I'm visiting and he asked me to watch you perform." She paused. "I must admit, I didn't expect much from a small-town singer such as yourself, but I was impressed. You're like a young Ellie Goulding with a smattering of Rachel Platten. It's appealing. Do you ever write your own songs?"

The question startled Elle. She was purely a cover singer. She didn't have the proper inspiration or desire to write her own songs.

"No. I never thought to write my own stuff," she said honestly, her eyes wide. "I like singing, but I'm not really writer material. I put my own spin on certain songs, but that's where my creativity ends."

"No matter," the woman shrugged off. "We could always hire writers for you."

Liam sat up quickly at her words.

"Ms. Attleboro-" Liam sounded almost pained.

"Meg."

"Yes, Meg," he hurried through. "What exactly are you proposing? Why would my m-wife need songwriters to sing here at the tavern?"

The older woman's eyes widened as if startled the couple before her hadn't put two and two together.

"Why, I'm proposing that Mrs. Stark sign a record deal with my label. We're based in Los Angeles. It's an up-and-coming new label by the name of TKO Records. We've already signed several big names and are looking to expand to signing on newer, less-known artists."

"No." Liam looked over at Elle, startled she had made her decision with such ease. He had known she loved to perform from the moment he had first heard her singing in the shower, but if he had been pressed for an answer, he wouldn't have been able to decide whether the big time was what she yearned for.

"Mrs. Stark-" Meg began.

"Meg, with all due respect, I don't want to sign with a record label. I don't want to be away from my family," Elle stated. "I sing for fun in my free time. That's it. I have twins and a...husband at home to care for. On Fridays and some other nights, I sing here. That's all I want. Nothing more, nothing less. I'm happy where I am. No amount of fame of money could make up for the time lost with my family."

"Are...are you sure, Elle?" The woman seemed bewildered by the flat-out rejection.

"I appreciate it – more than you know, but I couldn't be away from my children and husband for significant amounts of time," Elle explained. "There was a time not too long ago I would have taken for granted my family and the bond we share, but when...well when we were estranged, it made me realize how much I would miss them if I couldn't see them with regularity. I love my life now and don't want it to change even in the slightest bit. I want more children and to expand my growing family. My friends are all having babies and I want to be there to see that. Even if you told me I wouldn't have to be away for more than a week or two at a time it would still be a hard pass. I'm sorry."

The woman sighed and shook her head.

"I hope you don't regret your decision in the end, Elle."

Elle smiled over at Liam who looked almost as proud of her as he did when Arsen and Serena were born.

"I could never regret this decision."

***

"Angel, as much as I appreciate what you did in there, can I ask why?" Liam questioned on their way home that night. He was driving Elle's brand-new hybrid vehicle and the ride was as silent as advertised. Even the radio was off in the aftermath of the startling offer.

"I told her why," Elle answered. "I was away from my family for months and I felt horrible. I wouldn't wish it on anyone. I want to see every step of our children's growth whether it's their first steps or the first projectile vomiting incident."

"Jesus." Liam looked a little green at that prospect. Their twins were still in their milky spit-up phase. He wasn't looking forward to the 24-hour bouts of stomach flu that toddlers got.

Elle laughed at Liam's squeamishness. From dirty diapers filled with poo to spit-up, Liam seemed less than thrilled about most of the unsavory aspects of childrearing.

"Still, I wouldn't miss even the tiniest milestone," she told him, the cool breeze from the open window drying the sheen of sweat from her face and neck. It felt heavenly after the hot lights of the stage. It was her least favorite part of performing. She felt sometimes that she might melt under their steady glare.

"Well, I appreciate your coming to a decision so quickly." Liam placed a large hand on her knee before stroking it with his thumb. "If it took you took long to make a decision I might have had a cardiac episode. I wouldn't have liked you being so far from home for too long."

Elle looked over at him and smiled.

"Don't be silly," she told him with a laugh. "If I had said yes, I planned on kidnapping you and the kids to bring with me. There's no way I could be without them and you for that long."

Liam looked over at her, surprised. "Then why didn't you say yes if you were planning to bring us with you if you agreed?"

"Liam. If I had somehow become famous and made it big, what do you think would happen? Paparazzi, for one. They would find out I was a wolf, find out where I lived, and we'd have all sorts of strangers encroaching on pack grounds. Not exactly ideal for the security of the pack."

Liam nodded. He hadn't thought that far ahead, but was glad his little mate did. That would have been a disaster of epic proportions. A security snafu.

"Besides," Elle continued. "What if there was a tour? Being away from Plumbrook for that long would kill me. And I couldn't take you and the kids on tour. You, for obvious reasons. What's a pack without its Alpha? And who would take care of the kids while I was onstage? It's a bad idea all around. And one I'm honestly not interested in even thinking about."

"Let me ask you this, then." Liam looked over, then back to the road. "If you didn't have me and the kids, would you have taken Ms. Attleboro up on her offer?"

Elle thought about that and decided quickly that, no, she wouldn't have taken her up on the offer.

"I would not have taken the offer." Her tone was firm, though Liam thought she might have been a little too vehement.

"And why not?"

Elle shrugged.

"I like singing for the fun of it and once a week, maybe twice in a pinch, but I couldn't make it my livelihood. I don't have it in me."

And that seemed to be the end of that as far as Elle was concerned. Nothing Liam threw at her, no scenario, could get her to change her mind. Not that he minded, but he was puzzled all the same. Even a small amount of celebrity could be addicting and heady. He would know.

When they finally reached home, Elle quickly went upstairs to wash off her layer of makeup. Without it onstage, she looked washed out. She put on the minimum required to look decent, but that was by far still too much for her. Besides, wearing makeup when you had two babies throwing strained peas and applesauce was a pointless endeavor. It would be like wearing your underwear on the outside of your jeans.

"Are you ready?" Liam asked, his cobalt eyes sparkling merrily.

"Absolutely," she told him and made sure the baby monitors were all on before heading downstairs to give them to Colleen and Blake. They were watching TV on low, Blake rubbing Colleen's protruding stomach with soft caresses.

"Some woman from LA wanted to sign Elle to a record deal," Liam told them in soft tones.

"What?" Colleen had never moved so fast into a sitting position since becoming pregnant with her little girl.

"Jesus, Col," Liam griped. "The kids are asleep. Inside voice, please."

"Shit, shit, shit! Sorry!"

"What did you say?" Blake asked, looking over at Elle.

"I said no, of course," she told him, holding back a scoff.

"Oh." Blake looked back at the TV, seemingly uninterested.

"Oh?" Colleen gave him some serious side eye. "Our little Elle gets a bona fide offer from a recording studio and all you have to say is *oh?*"

"What do you want?" Blake shrugged. "She said no, so it's a moot point. But good on ya, kid." He winked at Elle before turning his eyes back to the television.

"You're a stranger to me sometimes, Blake," Colleen muttered, crossing her arms over her large belly.

"Good," he said. "It'll be like losing your virginity all over again later tonight."

Colleen rolled her eyes before putting a hand out to Elle to grab the baby monitors.

"Just for that you get dirty diaper duty tonight," Colleen told Blake. "It'll take me a month to get up the stairs. By the time the dookie fairy gets her fat ass there, Arsen will have leaked through onto the sheets. That kid has some serious toilet moments coming in his teen years." She looked at Elle and Liam, her brow drawn up. "Good luck with that by the way."

"Jesus," Liam muttered. "You ready?"

"Yup," Elle replied with a grin.

The two of them walked out the back of their home and toward the tree line. The cool night hair ruffled their hair as they stepped behind a set of trees to the north of the underground cells. It was their favorite place to shift with a nice low branch for Elle to place her clothing on for after their shift.

It had become tradition after the twins were born that they shifted every Friday evening together. It let their wolves commune with nature and each other. The adrenaline from Elle's performance wreaked havoc on her nerves, and there was nothing as relaxing as letting her true nature come forth. They swam, they mated. During the winter time their jaunts weren't as playful, but sometimes they hunted together, Liam always feeling the need to catch the largest buck he could for them to dine on. They shared his kill and came back stuffed to the gills with fresh venison.

"Ready?" Liam asked as he stripped out of his boxers, the last bit of his clothing to go.

"Ready.

She looked back at him. He was her second and truest chance at happiness. Through every hardship, ever faltering step, she never once regretted meeting the man that showed her true love and unending happiness existed.

She hoped their Friday night shifts never came to an end.

R.K. Knightly

Contact Info

To contact the author, please email rkknightlybooks@gmail.com

Facebook page: https://www.facebook.com/RKKnightlyBooks/

Wattpad: https://www.wattpad.com/user/HereLiesSnoops

Inkitt: https://www.inkitt.com/RKKnightly

Patreon: https://www.patreon.com/RKKnightlybooks

Acknowledgements

A hearty thank you goes out to my hubby who had to deal with my irritable ass and the fact that I ignored him anytime I was "in the zone" with one of my books. I probably agreed to a lot of things I will regret later on, but thank you for being patient when I ignored whatever idea or suggestion you tried to float past me while in my own little world of the supernatural.

To all my amazing readers on Wattpad, Inkitt, Dreame, and Patreon, thank you for your encouragement and kind words, and especially thank you to my subscribers on Patreon for believing in me and putting a few bucks in my pocket to help me get this far.

Thanks to Beth and Sara for editing help on my works. Lord knows self-publishing is difficult and I couldn't have done this without you!

Tori gets big props for helping with my cover. Smooches!

And finally, thank you Mrs. Michaels, my second-grade teacher. I should have listened to you years ago. P.S. - I got better at drawing at some point and now my stick figures have boobs. Love you!

About the Author

R.K. Knightly is a pen name for a civil servant based in the San Francisco-Bay area. Born in New Jersey, she moved to California in 2007 with her husband, a San Francisco native.

First interested in poetry from a young age, she wrote her first short story in second grade. It was a little mystery/thriller she drew the pictures for. Her teacher, Mrs. Michaels, told her mother that she should think about writing as a career, though she should probably look into hiring an illustrator for the art work. Ms. Knightly took journalism classes throughout high school and creative writing courses in college.

A lover of all genres of books from autobiographies to sci-fi, Ms. Knightly started writing erotic romance in early 2018. After a few months and two books, she came up with an idea for an erotic supernatural romance which has become popular on the Dreame app. Now she splits her time between the two genres, though her most popular works on Dreame are her supernatural novels.

In her spare time outside of writing, Ms. Knightly spends times with her fabulous extended family, including her 5 fur-babies and "cat lady" husband.

To purchase her works from Dreame, please see:

https://www.dreame.com/search/?kw=r.k.+knightly

Works:

The Claimed Series:

The Claiming (Lulu.com)

Back From Beyond (paperback=Amazon and ebook=Dreame)

Say My Name (Amazon e-book and paperback)

Bait and Switch (Coming Soon)

West of Destiny (Work in Progress)

The Triad Series:

There's no Going Home (Dreame e-book)

There's No Going Back

There's No Going Forward

Odd Woman Out (Work In Progress)

The Conquest Series:

Impulse (Amazon=paperback and Dreame=e-book)

Redemption (Amazon=paperback and Dreame=e-book)

Provocation (Amazon in e-book and paperback)

Impulsive Ever After (Amazon in e-book and paperback)

The Blood Bond Series:

Once Bitten, Twice Shy (Dreame)

Of Blood & Consequence (Work In Progress)

The Second Chance Series:

Bitter Consequences (Dreame)

The Hunter's Daughter (Work In Progress)

The Sovereign Series:

Fighting Kane (Dreame=e-book Amazon=paperback)

Conquering Kolton (Coming Soon on Amazon in e-book and paperback)

Championing Kade (Coming Soon on Amazon in e-book and paperback)

Louisa's Lamentations (Coming Soon on Amazon in e-book and paperback)

Love is War Series:

Collateral Damage (Amazon in e-book and paperback)

The Savage Series:

Savage Melody (Coming soon to Amazon, e-book and paperback)

Savage Beat (Coming soon to Amazon, e-book and paperback)

Savage Elegy (Work In Progress)

Standalones:

Beneath the Surface (Dreame)

The Fallback (Amazon in e-book and paperback)

For Ms. Knightly's Patreon page where future work is always being updated regularly, go to: https://www.patreon.com/RKKnightlybooks

For free samples (usually the first 5 chapters) of some of her works, please go to her Wattpad page at:
https://www.wattpad.com/user/HereLiesSnoops
or Inkitt at: https://www.inkitt.com/RKKnightly

Made in the USA
Monee, IL
23 November 2022